To Melc
Hope you
and thanks for the support

[signature]

War of the Wizards
THE BEGINNING

by
James Fuller

Bloomington, IN Milton Keynes, UK

AuthorHouse™
1663 Liberty Drive, Suite 200
Bloomington, IN 47403
www.authorhouse.com
Phone: 1-800-839-8640

AuthorHouse™ *UK Ltd.*
500 Avebury Boulevard
Central Milton Keynes, MK9 2BE
www.authorhouse.co.uk
Phone: 08001974150

First published by AuthorHouse 6/12/2007

ISBN: 978-1-4343-1153-5 (sc)

Printed in the United States of America
Bloomington, Indiana

This book is printed on acid-free paper.

<u>Special Thanks To</u>
My beautiful wife who has helped me with this entire book from page
one. She has inspired me and encouraged me and put up with me.
To my family and close friends for supporting me, Adam you
have no idea how much you I appreciate your help with this.
To all my friends on Opendiary.com, for all your
help, support, thoughts and strength.
This book is for all of you.

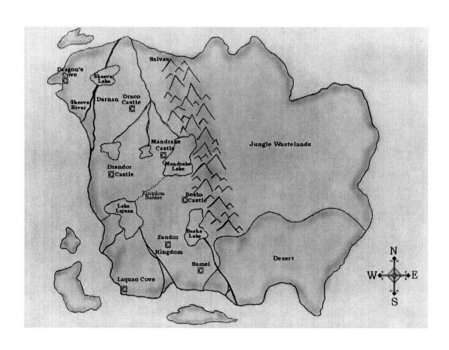

Chapter 1

"You all have been selected for your unique talents." The man in black shouted for all those to hear him as he paced the length of hundreds that were dead silent and kneeling before him. "You all will have a part in history this night." He roared, but was the only one, for the large crowd was there against their will by shackles and gags. "Do not fear my gifted friends; I shall never forget you and yours gifts that you will give." The man in black teased with a twisted smile. "You are all aiding in a great cause… my destiny!" He hissed throwing his tattooed arms up high in the air with such authority that the sky answered to his call and lighting exploded everywhere, thunder shaking the very earth for miles. He began chanting in a forgotten language and with each word the crowd wailed in such an agony that it could have awakened the dead from their eternal slumber, as their very essence was extracted from the unwilling bodies and flowed into the man in black who stood there laughing up at the heavens as he grew stronger with each soul that surged into him.

~   ~   ~

Meath woke in a cold sweat; his long brown hair was matted to his head and he was breathing deeply, his heart pounded hard in his broad chest. After a few moments his green eyes cleared from the sleep and dizziness to refocus upon his small castle room window. The sun still wouldn't rise for an hour.

"I've got to stop having these nightmares." He groaned, running his hands through his thick shaggy hair. He knew there was no point trying to sleep again, he would only have the same nightmares and he knew better then to be late for another one of Ursa's lessons. Ursa was like a father to Meath, he had come across Meath abandoned in the woods as a baby and had taken him in as his own and given him a life no orphan could have dreamed of.

After a few moments of catching his breath, Meath crawled out of bed making sure to step on the bear skinned rug, and not the damp, cold, stone floor. He had killed the bear on his seventeenth year as a test of his bravery and a stupid bet with his friends, it had almost cost him his life. With a wave of his hand and but a single thought the candles in his room came flickering to life. The flames flickered and swayed in the room's slight breeze, which made the shadows dance across the bare stonewalls. Meath glance around his room as if expecting to find something or someone there. He looked left to right starting at his large wooden door moving across his desk and washbowl, past his large brass mirror and oak dresser to his window. Satisfied with finding nothing he walked over to his mirror to have a look at himself. His hand touched the scar on his left shoulder where the bear had left a reminder. Even though Meath was only nineteen his build and size along with his facial features made him looked several years older, which had always helped him and his friends when they had snuck out to the tavern in the summer to get drunk off wine and ale when they were far too young.

His muscles were young but firmly toned, powerful from all his intense training as a soldier he had finished only several months ago, and all the hard manual labour Ursa had made him do while growing up. Ursa had called "character building", though Meath was sure it was just chores to keep him out of the way. It was those years in the army that Meath had made many of his friends, they had all been brought there as boys and after a few hard years of training and a handful of battles, they left as warriors. Many of his friends were stationed in the castle as guards, or in the army that stayed near the kingdom to stop any of the barbarian raiding parties from the east in the jungle wastelands. When Meath had become a full-fledged soldier at eighteen, he returned to Drako Castle to receive his new training as a wizard under the study of Master Ursa.

Not just anyone could become a wizard, they had to be born with the gift. When a child with the gift was born, their eyes were pure white with no pupils, and after a few months they would turn normal and their gifts would be locked away until their bodies had grown and their minds developed enough to handle them. For most it took till their seventeenth or eighteenth year before their minds could begin to control their gifts. In some cases children could access them in times of need or distress but normally died in the process or shortly after, for the gift could do great damage to both body and mind if one did not know how to control it

It took great control to use the gift and overuse would drain the body and mind of strength sometimes taking days to regain it. Most people feared magic and anything that they didn't understand, so they would kill their children or abandon them somewhere when they discovered they had been born with the gift, Meath had been one of those children whom had been abandoned. In Zandor, the neighbouring kingdom, anyone with the gift was put to death. In Zandor they believed the gift to be the work of the Keeper, but in Draco Kingdom they were finding that the powers of those with the gift could be used for the greater good for everyone. For the last ten years the gifted had been accepted by most of the people in Draco Kingdom. Their ability to heal wounds, sicknesses and their rare gifts of the elements were a great aid in the wars and battles they had with the savages in the wasteland and other foes. Though it was slow in process because of parents to ashamed to admit their child was born with the gift for fear of what others might think or say, there were now a few places throughout Draco Kingdom that were trying to train those with the gift. Though it seemed few were ever born with the gift, or they were too scared to come forth and admit that they were gifted for fear of being judged and ridiculed and even hunted down in rare cases. It was rumoured that there were secret cults that found others with the gift and trained them to use their powers in such ways that only the gods should know how to do, and save them from a world of hiding what should be treasured as the great gift it was.

After looking over himself and washing his face, Meath grabbed his, dark brown leather robe and threw it on. He felt the weight and warmth of the robes embrace him as they slid down the length of his body. Though he would rather be in his buckskin pants and vest then his new wizard's robe, he knew that after his day's studies and training, he could go back to his regular clothes. Next he grabbed his belt, which had to be put on just right for all the pouches and pockets of herbs and potions to be at a ready hand. Ursa was always sure to check, making sure he had it on properly. Meath finished dressing and felt the grip of hunger in his gut. He took one last look out his window and saw the first few rays of the sun coming over the tops of the mountains. He knew the cooks would just be getting up and it would be awhile before they had something to eat, but he wasn't going to wait. He would go now and see what he could stumble upon for breakfast. Before closing his thick wooden door, he waved his hand again and the candles flickered out.

As he made his way through the castle's long, wide hallways he noticed a lot more activity going on then normal. For this hour of the morning there were normally only a few guards and a handful of servants about, but now the stone hallways were full of servants running everywhere and looked to be in a serious rush. As he walked through the halls side stepping through people, he couldn't help but glance at every wall hanging he passed by. They were colourful drapes and paintings of lands far away and of beasts that only the bravest of men went seeking. Ursa had told him stories as a child of each picture and had explained what they were and where they were found to the best of his knowledge. Ursa's stories were always long and full of detail and when he told them he seemed to bring them to life, as though you were really there, no matter how many times you heard them. Before Meath knew it, he was down the stairs and coming around the corner to the kitchen. He could hear Maxwell, the head chef, barking out orders to his kitchen staff. The sound of pots being clanged around and people yelling the names of food they needed to get prepared for the morning. It was a little strange for the kitchen to be this active in the morning he thought to himself. The kitchen was one of the largest room's in the castle, for it had to be to feed the vast amount of people that lived there. On the far wall were huge granite ovens that baked and cooked the massive amounts of bread and meat. There were large wooden tables and shelves all around the giant room, which housed many pots and other cook wear that was needed. Beside the great ovens was the slaughter room; five butchers worked in the small room cutting and preparing the different types of meat for the cooks and the cold cellars.

"Maxwell what the hell is going on in here, what's the rush?" Meath interrupted while he moved out of the way of several passing servants. The big fat cook turned around to face him, his face was covered in flour mixed in with other food he had been dealing with and he looked a little frustrated and exhausted.

"Meath what are you doing up this early? You're never up this early are you sick?" He asked as he barked orders off to people in the room, and he watched them long enough to see that they were off to do as he had told.

"I couldn't sleep very well again. Now answer my question what's going on?" Meath yelled again trying to drown out the many sounds around him and the voices of so many; it was hard to believe that anyone could understand anyone else in there.

Maxwell almost burst out laughing. "You mean to tell me you haven't heard? Well it doesn't surprise me I guess since you never pay any attention to what people are saying anyways. The king's daughter, Princess Nicolette, is returning by mid-morning, and the king is having a feast. We've been up all night preparing for her arrival, and if we fall behind the king will have my neck in a rope, so I really must leave you now and see to some things." He ran his thick hand through his blond, greasy hair, smiled a tired smile and then hurried away into the thick mass of people and food, barking orders as he went.

Meath knew the king wouldn't harm Maxwell in any way. The two had been friends for a great number of years. The King was as kind hearted of a person as Meath had ever known. He had even let Ursa bring Meath into the castle and be schooled and trained in things normally only nobles or wealthy merchants could put their children through.

Meath's mind drifted back to what Maxwell had said, the princess was coming back to Draco Castle today. He wondered how he could have possibly missed that, this was huge, he smiled at the thought of the princess, his old childhood friend whom he hadn't seen in several months.

"You make a better pillar then a doorway Meath!" One of Maxwell's kitchen staff grumbled at him, slightly annoyed at the towering boy in his way.

Meath snapped back to reality and apologized to the man, and without getting in any one else's way managed to score a chunk of freshly bake bread and some dried, spicy deer meat, along with a small jug of honey milk. A fine breakfast indeed, he thought with a small smile. He got out of there as fast as he could, before someone thought he looked like a good candidate for helping with something as he so often did.

Meath started back to his room to eat. Now that the castle was beaming with more activity, he didn't want to get in the way. When he had reached his room and closed the door it was silent enough that he could hear himself think again. He pondered the news he just heard and couldn't believe he hadn't heard it sooner. He thought back to the last week and tried to recall anything or anyone that would have clued him into it. He had been so busy lately with his training that he guessed he must have missed all the talk and commotion.

"So the princess is coming back." Meath said to himself as he ate. The last time he saw Princess Nicolette was at the last spring renewal festival when all the lords, ladies, merchants, and wealthy families came to Draco Castle to celebrate the beginning of a new year with a week-long festival of dancing, eating, games, drinking, gambling and best of all, the warriors challenge. Soldiers, warriors and champions from across the land came to test their strength, bravery, skills and honour in gruelling challenges, and then finally one on one combat with dull blunted swords to pick the year's finest warrior.

Even then Meath hadn't spent as much time as he'd have liked with Nicolette, he only got to see her a couple times each year now, since her mother died three years past. Now when she came down, she spent most of her time with her father. He understood that and it wasn't like they didn't spend time together, but it wasn't the same as before, and he couldn't expect it to be anymore. They had both grown up so much through the last few years and had done and seen so much that was so different. They weren't kids anymore, things were different between them, there were more thoughts and feelings now then there ever was before. Meath gulped down the last of the bread and meat and went to his window. The sun was now just about half way out from behind the lush, dark green mountaintops and it was almost time for him to be in the library with Ursa for his lessons. Just as he got up and grabbed the last of the things he would need, there was a knock at his door.

"Come in." Meath called out as Ursa walked in, his long white hair was as it always was, straight down his back and held together with a black string. Not a hair seemed to be out of place. His white robe seemed to shine like the sun in the dim room. Though the man was nearing his seventieth year, he still managed to get around better then most half his age and he looked like he was only entering his fiftieth year. Ursa was also one of the most powerful wizards that lived in Draco Kingdom, which was rumoured to be why he was still so agile and full of energy, but even his powers were limited. There were only a few wizards in Draco Kingdom that could match Ursa's skills and a small handful that were rumoured to be able to out do him, though it had never been proven.

"Ah I see you are already up, good, good then. So I take it you've finally heard the news yes?" Ursa said in a tone that sounded as if he was excited, as he cleared the distance from the door to Meath in a few long strides of his long, bony legs.

"Ya I heard that Princess Nicolette is returning." Meath said as he yawned and stretched his arms trying not to tip the old man off that he was actually a little excited himself to see her.

"Have you been taking that tea I gave you to help you sleep?" Ursa said, already knowing the answer. "No matter, lose sleep if that's what you want, but I'll accept no blunders in your studies because of it, but that's not the point." He stammered almost to fast for Meath to understand. "The princess isn't just coming back, she is coming back to be married to

Prince Berrit in several weeks. All the royal families from Zandor will be here soon too, for the wedding." Ursa said again almost too fast for Meath to comprehend.

Meath could feel the blood in his face drain out and his stomach turn, he knew she was well past the age that most were married and it really shouldn't come as a surprise but it did.

"Meath!" Ursa said snapping Meath out of his thoughts. "Are you ok?" You look like you've just seen a spirit." Ursa chuckled.

"No I'm fine." Meath lied, trying to compose himself.

"She is a princess Meath and can only marry a prince. Your childhood puppy love cannot continue my boy. I tried to tell you it would never work, back when I first noticed this problem accruing." Ursa reminded him. "You should have known better by now." Ursa told him compassionately.

"I know… I just thought that… I don't know." Meath rambled still lost in the moment.

"Thought somehow it would work?" Ursa finished for him with a sigh. "Meath its time to wake up from that dream, besides there are plenty of servant and farm girls around that even you should be able to find someone to put up with you. I mean your not that ugly and irritating." Ursa teased getting a smirk from him.

Meath sighed deeply. "Ya you're right, I guess its time to grow up and stop living in the past." Meath replied.

"Of course I am right!" Ursa said. "Now for the reason I am here. I need your help preparing for her highnesses arrival. So study is cancelled for the day, now hurry up there is plenty to do." Ursa informed him with a gesture to the door.

~ ~ ~

"Your highness, it is but a few more miles to Draco City, I sent a rider to tell them of our arrival and he has returned with good news, they are ready for us, and your room and a warm bath has been made ready for when you get there." The large bearded soldier said as he rode up beside her carriage.

"Thank you Rift, it will be good to be home again I haven't seen it in many years." The princess replied as she pulled the hood of her deep blue traveling cloak off, letting her long brown hair breathe in the fresh morning air.

"It has been awhile since I have seen my homeland, as well your highness. It will be good to be back, I wonder how much has changed since the last time we were there." Rift said while thinking of something he would enjoy doing while they were back as a grin formed on his face. "It will be good to see your father and everyone again." The Captain said cheerfully.

Nicolette smiled. "Yes it will be good to see the old bear again." She replied with a laugh, remembering calling her father that when she was a little girl and him going along with it and chasing her around her room roaring at her.

Ever since she could remember Rift had been there for her, watching out for her and protecting her when she needed it. The scar across his chin she barley even noticed anymore. When she was a child, she remembered she use to call him scar face and run from him trying to hide, because he scared her. But now she had grown a liking for the man and found his rough features calming, although he was a fierce warrior who had killed many, she knew the man inside; he was more of a gentlemen then he ever let on.

He was oath bound to her, till death. He had been her mother's, Queen Lavira's champion, before she had died. On her deathbed she had made the captain swear a blood oath that he would protect Nicolette from any harm till his last breath. After her mother's death from a strange sickness, when Nicolette was on her fourteenth year, her father sent her away to be raised in Dragon's Cove where her Aunt Jewel and her husband Lord Marcus lived on the coast of Draco Kingdom in the west. Her father knew he could not raise her the way she should be raised as a lady without her mother, for King Borrack didn't have it in him to take another wife. Only a woman could raise a girl into a woman, and he had too much to deal with, with wars and his Kingdoms affairs to give his daughter the time she needed.

It was a two week ride with a group this big, a single rider with little sleep could make it in four days time, but the risk of killing a few horse's was great. But with a personal royal escort of five hundred of Dragon Cove's finest and battle-hardened soldiers, the trip was slow going.

As they traveled along the road to the castle Nicolette felt the over-whelming joy of being back in her homeland. In Dragon's Cove you could see for miles, for the land had few hills and even fewer trees, the terrain was made of long grassy fields and rocks, and the air was salty and dry from the sea. Once they had crossed the mighty Sheeva, every step from there brought them into a thick, dense jungle where the eyes couldn't begin to grasp all the colors and hues that were around them and the air was sweet and fresh even though it was fairly humid. As she looked out the window of her carriage, into the deep growth of the forest, she watched some monkeys playing in the trees, some of them watched the large group that paced by, being sure to keep there distance and out of harms way. Nicolette envied the monkeys, for they lived in peace and freedom and could do as they wished living not for responsibility. She sighed at the thought of what had brought her back home after all these years, for soon she was to be wed to Prince Berrit of Zandor. A man she had only ever met a few times in her life as a child. Though, he was a handsome man, she remembered he lacked everything else she had hoped for in the man she was to marry. He reminded her of a snake, one that was willing to do anything to better himself, no matter what the cost. He was also Zandorian, which made him bull headed and ruthless. She had pleaded with her father to find another suitor but he had insisted that it be him, for with their marriage the two Kingdoms could finally work together to rid themselves of the barbarian tribes that threatened both lands, and come to an agreement on those with the gift and finally end their kingdoms never ending feud. The fate of her soon to be land and people counted on this marriage, being the only pure blood of the royal line of her father King Borrack, and her mother Queen Lavira, there was no one else.

After Nicolette was born, her mother was left barren, and could no longer conceive child, and her father; being madly in love with his queen, never took another to his bed to gain another heir. Even when her mother had died, Borrack never took another wife or a mistress to his bed.

"I can't wait until we're finally done this long boring trip." Tami said with a very irritated tone as she took her eyes from one of the side windows.

"I just wish father were here, he always knows how to make the trip seem shorter with all his stories." Her younger sister Avril replied.

Tami ignored her and looked over to Nicolette. "What's a matter with you today? You've hardly said anything since we broke camp this morning." She said in that same flat annoyed tone she always used when she wasn't pleased, which was most of the time.

Nicolette turned her attention from the window for the first time in hours. "I just have a lot on my mind, I'm sorry I didn't mean to be rude."

"I bet you can't wait to see Prince Berrit, I hear he is the most handsome man in Zandor, and he is fearless and nothing scares him." Avril chatted to Nicolette with wide eyes of excitement for her. "I can't wait till I get married I hope I am as lucky as you." Avril said still wide-eyed with childish excitement.

Tami laughed. "No man will ever want to marry you, you're too ugly and annoying."

"Will too. You're the one that will never get married you're too mean." Avril spat back well she stuck out her tongue at her older sister.

Nicolette just turned back to the window while the two sisters, that she had spent a great deal of her life with argued back and forth as always. Normally she would try and stop them but right now she just couldn't bring herself to care, all she could think about was what her life with her new husband was going to be like. Maybe it wouldn't be all that bad, maybe Prince Berrit would be all that she had hope for in a man. She had found that once, why couldn't she find it again? She wondered if Meath was even still in Draco Kingdom, it had been a while since they had last seen one another and even then it had been awkward and different between them, almost like they had grown apart but yet hadn't. Last she had heard he had just finished his training as a soldier and would begin his training as a wizard. She was sure he would have found someone by now, he was nearing his twentieth year, a fully trained soldier and a training wizard in a castle. She hoped he had, someone nice that would give him everything he needed and deserved.

"Hey you still in there?" Tami said waving her hand in front of Nicolette's face getting her attention.

"Make ready your highness; we are almost in Draco city, and it looks like all the people in the city have come to welcome your home coming." Rift said as he rode past her towards the front of her carriage to see to no one getting in their way or delaying them, and to bark final orders at his men, who now held their banner up high, flapping in the warm breeze, marching in perfect formation as they had learned to do.

Nicolette looked out her window to see the gathering of people that came to welcome her back with cheers and whistles. Though they hadn't even reached the actual city limits, to her surprise there were more people gathered here then she would ever have expected. As she rode past them she threw out copper coins mixed in with the occasional silver or gold coins and rare spices to those fast enough to grab them. Nicolette had to wonder if they actually had come out to see her arrive or to see what handouts might be given. She didn't mind all that much either way, she knew the folks on the outer limits were but poor families and farmers. The thought that she had just helped them, even as little as a copper coin, made her smile.

As the soldiers, wagons and carriages made their way through the now crowded streets in the city towards the castle, she couldn't help but notice how much of the city had changed in the last several months since she had last been there for the spring renewal festival. Buildings seemed newer and bigger than before. She could not believe how different things now looked in a short time, and how many more people now seemed to be living in the city. Before long all she could hear was the people chanting her name and asking the creator to show her favour and many years of happiness and to bare many healthy children. As she neared the castle walls she remembered when she was a little girl, when her father would come home from war or a trip, she and her friend's would stand on the wall above the gates and watch him ride in with his troops. Now others were on the walls watching her arrive. She could see the small children up there pointing her way and waving, she almost expected to see him up there, but knew he wasn't, though she had to stop herself from looking.

Before long, they were inside the walls of the castle and only a few moments away from the enormous front doors of the grand feasting hall, where her father, his advisors, lords and ladies and people of high favour to the kingdom waited for her. There seemed to be many more then she remembered here as well. The driver pulled up as close as he dared so not to spit up dust towards the king and his guests. Rift helped her out of the carriage and on to solid ground. Nicolette made her way towards her fathers open arms and wide smile.

Since Ursa was the king's closest friend and advisor, he was summoned to be there for the arrival of the princess, to weave spells of luck and to ward off any danger that might lurk about. And since Meath was his apprentice, he too stood at the doors of the feasting hall waiting to see his old friend and the future queen of Draco Kingdom. Though a lot of the royal families had yet to arrive, the courtyard was full of people readying food and water for the mass of men and their horse's.

~ ~ ~

Meath watched as the carriage bearing the princess' royal colours of bright blue and gold pulled up to where they all stood. He watched as a familiar man, that he knew to be Captain Rift, the princess' champion, get down off his horse and open the carriage door, providing his hand to help her down. Meath's eyes grew wider as he saw the tall, slender, womanly figure step down to the ground and started towards them.

"If you keep staring at the princess like that my boy, you're going to find your head on the chopping block." Ursa whispered without even looking at Meath. Meath shook his head and tried to regain his posture, but he could not help but stare, this was not the girl that he had once stole a full basket of her favourite candy apples from Maxwell for. Nor was it the girl he had shared his first kiss with back when they were both not more then ten winters old, but the most beautiful creature he had ever laid his eye's on. Since the last time he had seen her only seven months before, she had grown into a woman. Even at only seventeen winters old she had the poise and grace of a woman twice her age.

"My darling daughter you are looking more like your mother every time I see you. How was your trip? I heard you had trouble with that cursed river again, you are not hurt are you?" King Borrack asked as he embraced his daughter and held her for a long moment, his eyes even tearing up a bit.

"The trip was lovely father I almost forgot how beautiful this country side was, and how fresh the air tastes." The princess replied, through the long hug, her eyes glanced over to where Meath stood. Their eyes met quickly, but she glanced away before anyone noticed.

"Where are Lady Jewel and Lord Marcus and Mathu?" Borrack asked when he figured he had hugged his daughter long enough, though he did notice Jewel and Marcus had sent their lovely yet annoying daughters along. Though they seemed to be busier with barking orders at their servants as to which of their things should be brought up to their rooms first then anything else.

"They could not make it, for Lord Marcus has come down with the fever and was not well enough to travel." The princess said in a tone of sadness. Everyone knew few who came down with the fever ever recovered, and those that did were never the same. "But they send their love and respects, and even some of their fine brandy you like so much father." Nicolette added with a smile.

"That is such a pity, I was so looking forward to seeing them both again, I do hope he will be ok." Borrack said. "Well let us not talk of such things now, no daughter of mine is going to look and smell like that while she's staying in my castle. Take your maidens up to your room, there is a bath and fresh clothing waiting for you. I will have a servant bring your things up to your room, and then when you are ready we will feast until we burst. I just might sample some of that brandy you've brought along." With that said the king walked back into the massive hall where the feast was to be held, on his way he barking out orders to servants to make sure that everyone of his new guests had there things brought to there rightful places, where drinks, food and a bath were waiting for them all.

Chapter 2

The feast began by midday and a hardy amount of food and treats were piled high on every table in the massive hall. Servants ran this way and that to keep each table fully stocked and clean while everyone ate and drank enjoying themselves. The centre table ran half the length of the room and was square in the middle, while other smaller tables were set up parallel with the grand table off to the sides. The main table itself could seat over three hundred guests, the hall itself could hold six times that many comfortably. The feasting hall was the largest room in the castle and was full of royalty, lords, ladies, captains, generals, rich merchants and the best entertainers in the land.

The huge room's walls were decorated with all Draco Kingdoms castles flags, banners and of beautiful tapestry art work which showed pictures of all the kings and lords that Draco Kingdom had ever had. Along the bottom of the walls were swords, shields, suits of armour, and gold and silver acquirements that the kings had won from the many battles with the barbarians and other wars that the kingdom had known in its time. King Borrack's most prized token was hung above his picture; the sword and battle helm of Azazel, the old barbarian leader that the king himself had slain a few years ago on the battle field in single combat.

The people from the city and small communities around Draco all gathered outside the feasting hall doors in the courtyard and overflowed into the streets, having their own celebration for the princess's return. They all knew that once those inside had had there fill of the meal, all that was left came out for them, which was always more then even they would be able to finish. Barrels of wine and beer and a few other ales were tapped and placed everywhere the eye could see so that none would go thirsty throughout the long night in the hall. Bards from all over had come to sing their tales of lust and love, past battles and the loss of great leaders before their time, and got paid handsomely to do so throughout the night with tips from drunken patrons.

At one end of the great table sat King Borrack, to his right his royal champion Halpas, Princess Nicolette, Rift, Master Ursa, Lord Dagon and Lady Angelina of Mandrake Castle with their two sons Ethan and Leonard along with Mandrakes champion Jarroth. To the kings left sat Lord Tundal, Lady Tora of Drandor and their daughter and son, Salvira and Thoron with their champion Raven and then the two sisters from Dragon's Cove, then many more rich families, generals and merchants that lived in or around the city sat on either side the rest of the way down the grand table and to the tables on the sides.

"This is a fine turn out, and its all for you my daughter!" King Borrack roared as he swayed on his seat, trying not to appear too drunk, though everyone knew he was well past that stage. "I am glad to have you home again, you have become a beautiful woman and shall make a fine wife." He slurred.

"I completely and fully agree... I think?" Lord Dagon slurred, as he too seemed to be having a hard time keeping his balance in his chair and keep a steady tone in his voice, his two sons were no better off.

"I haven't had this much fun or ale since I was married." Lord Tundal hollered as he slapped Raven's back and made him spill his drink all over himself.

Raven stood, up doing well to hide his own drunkenness in his form, "You my good Lord Tundal, have spilled my drink, and what man would I be if I did not challenge you after such an act." Raven bellowed out while steadying himself on the back of his own chair.

The group at that end of the table went quiet and watched while the rest of the party went on having no idea of what was happening.

"Well Raven my good man I being a man of... of... of honour shall accept your challenge." Tundal stammered out to him standing up.

"Oh dear not this again, Tundal you can't be serious, not tonight." His wife Tora begged him, while looking for support from the others.

"I am sorry my wife I must defend my... my... well you know that word I am thinking of." Tundal replied meeting Raven's gaze.

"King Borrack will you not stop this madness?" Tora begged giving him a half annoyed and half pleading look.

"I am sorry my lady but I can not, this is between these two drunken fools." The King said with a chuckle. And Tora just sighed and started talking to Lady Angelina, trying hard to ignore her drunken husband.

Lord Dagon stood, " Well lets have it then you two, though Raven my good man I have known this man my whole life he's going to have his drink drank and pissed out before you even get passed the foam in your cup!" Dagon roared for all to hear and laughs sprang up from all around them cheering the two men on.

"Well Raven let us get this over with." Tundal said with a wink too his good friend who by now couldn't hide his own smile and chuckle about it all.

"May the bestest man win." Raven winked back and slammed his beer to his lips and drank for all he was worth. But he knew he had already lost when he heard Tundal cup hit the table and everyone cheered, but he finished his brew just the same.

The two laughed and clapped hands, more to keep each other up right then anything else as the ale went straight to their heads.

"Father… I do not feel so good!" Thoron moaned as he fell to the floor and vomited all over himself and a lot more on the floor around him.

"That's what happens, my boy when you drink too much!" Tundal cheered as he watched his wife Tora and his daughter Salvira carry the drunken child away to clean him off as a servant ran over to clean the boys mess from the floor, before anyone else saw it, or slipped.

No one else seemed to notice the mess; they were all having too good of a time and Lord Tundal's boy had not been the first to vomit nor would he be the last this night.

Then one of the bards came up to them and started to play his harp and sing an old war tale that King Borrack and Halpas and a few others at the table had fought in against the barbarian's old leader Azazel. They all went quiet and listened to the grand tale of how Borrack killed the heartless beast in single combat and turned the tide of the war with a single blow of his sword.

"If I would have known all it would take to shut them up was a bard to sing that song, I would have had it happen an hour ago." Lady Angelina remarked to Nicolette, and the other ladies around the table, and they all shared a laugh.

Now that the men had quieted down at this end of the table while the bard sang the tale, the ladies began their talk and gossip about this and that and others affairs.

"Master Ursa, wasn't your apprentice Meath going to be here?" Nico-lette asked the wizard, ignoring her father and the others drunken behaviour. "It has been a while since we last saw each other, I figured he would be here so that we might catch up on our lives."

"Yes, that is a little strange, he seemed happy to hear of your return this morning. Well I am sure he is around somewhere. Making a fool out of himself no doubt, or trying to impress a lady. He is at that age that he should be trying to find a nice young lady to settle down with himself, though I pity the poor girl that does decide to settle down with him." The wizard said with a chuckle and a glance around the room trying to spot Meath for her, but gave up shortly after, shaking his head to the young Princess with a look that said he could not see the boy.

"Well I think I will go get some fresh air and see if I can find him, he can't be far off." She replied as she stood up and made her way through the crowd of people that were dancing and singing all around. She knew no one would notice her being gone for sometime. No one except Ursa even looked to watch her as she left.

~   ~   ~

Meath took another long hard swallow of the dark brew in his cup, and knew this would be his last cup of the night for he had already drank more than his fill and was feeling its affect well enough to know if he had any-more he wouldn't get up the next morning. He looked down at the small engraving on the large branch of his favourite childhood climbing tree. He sighed, Ursa was right; even as a child Meath knew it was just dream and could never happen, but now he couldn't help but feel the sting of what would never be. He wondered if he would ever find someone else whom he would care so much about or someone that could make him smile when he was down and sulking. He knew he had passed up many opportunities to get to know other girls while he had been growing up and couldn't help but feel foolish now for trying to hold on to some lost hope and dream. He knew once the Princess and Prince Berrit were married they would live in Draco Castle and he would forever have to see them together.

Meath thought about leaving and going back to the army again some-where far where he could forget her and all of this, but he knew Ursa or the king would never allow it. No, Meath knew he had to stay and finish his training and accept his fate as Draco Castle's future war wizard. He would take Ursa's place one day when Ursa finally grew too old or died. Though Meath could hardly believe Ursa would ever die, the man never seemed to age or slow down. He finished off the last of the ale in his cup and dropped it to the ground, and then he slowly made his way down the tree, slow enough to accommodate the effects of the ale.

~　~　~

Nicolette walked through the less used halls of the castle so as not to be seen by as many people who might want to stop and congratulate her. She had a funny feeling she knew where he might be this night, she had already checked his room and the kitchen knowing he used to go there and talk with Maxwell. That left only one more place, the royal garden where as children they had spent many of their fun filled days growing up and playing games. Luckily everyone was in the hall or to busy to pay her much notice while she made her way through the castle to the north west end where the garden was located.

She walked out into the garden and under the clear night sky. She looked around as so many memories flooded back to her. She walked down one of the well-kept paths towards the west end corner where as children had claimed it as theirs.

~　~　~

"I thought I might find you out here." A soft, calming, voice said from behind him, he turned to look and his hand fell short of the branch he had intended to grab and he fell the last few feet to the ground with a hard thud and a groan. Meath lifted his head to see who had caused him to fall, he heard a familiar laugh and knew right away who it was.

"I thought after all these years you would have figured out how to finally climb down from there." The Princess giggled.

"Well it helps when people don't sneak up on you while you're doing it." Meath groaned, as he stood up and patted himself off. When he looked up at her, their eyes locked. In those short moments that they shared, it seemed that all the time they had spent apart faded away as if there hadn't been a day gone by that they had not talked or seen one another.

"You look as lovely as ever your highness." Meath managed to spit out, kicking himself for not thinking of anything better to say, but still their eyes did not drift apart.

"You too have grown into quite a handsome man since I last remember. And you know you don't have to call me by my title, you of all people should know that by now Meath." She replied sounding almost hurt that he would call her that. "So why are you out here and not at the feast? I was hoping we would be able to catch up and talk." She asked but already knew the answer.

"I… I just could not bear to see you yet, knowing that it would not be like it was." Meath replied while fighting the urge to run over to her and be near her.

"You know there hasn't been a day gone by that I did not think about you." She said as they closed the gap between them and embraced in a long hug.

"Nor I." Meath whispered just loud enough for her to hear.

They pulled away to arms length and gazed into each other's already moistened eyes, for what seemed like hours they just stared into each other knowing and feeling everything the other one wanted to say all this time. Slowly their lips drifted together and entangled in a passionate kiss that not even all the bards in the world could come to describe in a lifetime of writing and singing.

Meath hadn't realized what had just happened when he heard an angry voice rushing towards them at pace.

"Get off of her you foul flea infested dog!" Rift bellowed as he ran towards them with his dagger drawn and ready. "How dare you take advantage of the princess like that?" He barked as he pulled her away and put a good distance between the two.

"No, Rift it's not what you think…" Nicolette said in a panic so he would not hurt Meath, but Meath stood his ground and did not falter a step in fear or worry.

"Your highness I have been around long enough to know what that was! And I made a promise to your Mother to keep you away from dogs like that one." The Captain said in a tone that made the hairs on Meath neck stand on end, but still he did not move an inch but just stood there staring at Nicolette. "Besides, your father sent me out to find you, he wants a word with you." And with that Rift took her hand and led her back towards the party. Nicolette looked over her shoulder and met Meath's eyes once more mouthing sorry, before she was out of sight.

~   ~   ~

Meath stood there for some time before finally returning to his room but not before he made a few stops to refill his mead cup along the way, which he drained just as fast as he filled, trying hard to drown the confusion, hurt, sadness and yet happy feelings that now consumed his mind and heart. He laid on his bed, his thoughts assaulting him no matter how hard he tried to stop them so he could find rest this night.

"I have to see her again!" He whispered to the air. "I have to know what we are going to do about this. This cant be how this is going to end, it just can't." Though he knew there was no way they could make it work, he held on to the thought anyways, until he finally fell fast asleep.

~　　~　　~

For the next few days they were both kept very busy preparing for the grand wedding that was soon to take place, they did not get another chance to be alone or even talk to one another without someone being within hearing range. They only shared brief moments of eye contact when they were near enough of each other. Their eyes spoke more then any words could at that moment. Rift also seemed to be keeping a close eye on the both of them as to stop any further contact such as the night before. Several times Rift even passed by Meath and glared at him reminding him of his place.

Meath spent a lot more time on his studies for those days trying hard to ignore his frustrations. Ursa was more then willing to spend the extra hours each day with him, teaching him several new potions and even a few new techniques with the elemental part of his gift. That and the late nights he spent in the warrior's den helping train new soldiers. He had volunteered his time to help teach them in hand-to-hand and weapons combat. Not really for them but for himself. It helped him take his frustrations out physically. But practice was over for the night and now Meath sat alone in his room starring at the flames of his candles. It was the last night before the arrival of the Royal families from Zandor. The last few days he hadn't even seen her, the last he heard they were having problems with her wedding dress and so she was stuck in her room with a handful of seamstress's. Meath fought hard to get a grip on his emotions and what was happening. He knew there was nothing he could do to stop what was going to come, and even if there were they'd never get away with it, it would only make matters worse. He knew he had to let this go… let her go.

He clenched his fists hard and glared angrily at the flames as if they had done him this harsh wrong. The flames grew brighter and more intense every second until they had almost reached the roof, then he slammed his fist against his bed frame, the candles burst and hot wax sprayed everywhere but none came his way. After only moments in the dark Meath conjured a flame on the palm of his hand. Though he could feel the fierce heat that came off the flame, it did not burn him for it was part of him. A wizards fire would not burn that which yields it, though the other elements still could do the caster harm. As he stared into the flame it began to grow, and form into an almost liquid ball, which soon was larger then his head. The fire went from a natural yellowy orange, too a deep red with an almost clear white layer on the outside. Meath knew he shouldn't add his emotions into his castings but he couldn't help it. With a swift throw the blazing ball shot out his window and into the night sky, where it dispersed after a few hundred feet. He sat there staring off into the dark for almost an hour, until finally there was a light knock at his door, which shook him out of his meditation.

He lit the one remaining candle that had survived his wrath, while his door creaked open and a slender figure dressed in a black cloak slipped in and quickly shut the door behind, being sure to check that no one had seen or followed them. Though with the light of one candle was not enough to see well, he knew who had come into his room and his heart felt as if it would stop. She turned to him and pulled off the hood of her cloak and her brown hair streamed down her face, and her light brown eyes glistened in the weak light as she looked at him.

"I had to see you again; I couldn't stay away any longer." Nicolette whispered as she made her way to where he sat. Meath could tell she had been crying, for even in the dim light he could see her eyes were red and puffy.

"If we are caught like this again, we might not be as lucky as last time, this is treason, and it will be my head and your honour." Meath whispered back as he put his arms around her as she rested her head on his shoulder. He really didn't care, he wanted her more then anything he had ever dreamed, and death would only be a sweet release to living life without her.

"Then my life they would also have to take for I do not think I can do this Meath." She whimpered as she wept pressing herself harder into him. "I do not want to marry him Meath, but there is nothing I can do, the fate of my kingdom depends on it. I don't want this kind of responsibility I just want to be normal." She wept even harder.

They held each other in silence for a long time neither needing to speak a word, for both could tell what the other was thinking and both knew they could do nothing to change the outcome. Before either one knew it they were asleep tightly in each other's arms.

~   ~   ~

They both woke with a jump and in fear as the door flung open to Meath's room. The tall, powerful figure of Ursa stood there looming down at them not with anger in his eyes like they feared they would find, but they were filled with concern and knowing what would have happened if any other had found them like this.

"Foolish children do you not know what will happen if anyone finds you like this? This can not be Meath!" Ursa stated as he paced the room in a rush and more frustrated then Meath had ever seen him before. "It is time for you to get back to your room your highness before anyone notices you're missing, like a very conclusion jumping champion of yours, who would very gladly skin alive my dim witted apprentice here." Ursa said calming himself a little.

"You will not tell anyone about this, will you master Ursa?" Nicolette asked as she straightened her clothes afraid of what he would say.

"Your secret is safe with me, but I warn you now do not let this happen again, if it had been any other who had come through that door you would not be so lucky. If anyone finds out about this its treason for us all." He replied as if annoyed that she needed to ask. He hurried her towards the door and watched for a moment to make sure it was safe for her to leave. Once she was gone and he had closed the door, he turned to Meath with a deep scowl.

"What are you trying to do, get yourself killed? You fool. You can't just have the king's daughter come and spend the night in your bed, what were you thinking? Have you totally lost your mind? You half witted moron, I can't believe you would do such a foolish thing." Ursa blared as quietly as he could, but with enough effort to show his disapproval and frustration.

"Nothing even happened we just..." Meath tried to get out before he was cut off as he too straightened his clothes.

"That's not the point fool, the point is she is a princess and you are not a prince, she is betrothed to another, do you know what would be happening to you right now if it had been anyone else that came through that door? You would be dead you stupid boy, but not before they tortured you for many days and what good would that do you? Not to mention destroying the princess's reputation along with the chance to finally unite Zandor and Draco. Not to mention destroying our great kings royal bloodline. Who would want to marry our fair princess if she was not pure? Did you not stop to think that what you were doing will affect more then just your little world? No, what your doing will effect us all, your little heart break is the least of any of this." Ursa stated, in an irritated voice from having to explain what Meath should already have known.

Meath glanced towards his window and bit his lip for he knew better then to argue with the wizard, and he knew Ursa was right. Then Meath noticed it was still quite dark out and asked. "How did you know she was here?"

"If you must know I saw it in a vision last night and decided I had better make sure it was true or not. And to my surprise it was, I thought you were smarter then that my boy. Now enough of this talk, we do not need any by passers to hear of the treason that has just taken place here." Ursa said as he completely calmed himself. "The prince along with the other royals from Zandor will be here by mid day, and the king has asked me to prepare a grand show for the wedding that will take many days to see too and I require your assistance, since you are my only students who knows how to conjure fire without burning someone. Plus you know how those Zandorians are when it comes to the gift; we cannot afford any mistakes. Now get dressed we have lots to do before the day is done." Ursa barked trying to hold his disapproval out of the tone in his voice and yet there almost seemed to be softness there as well.

~　~　~

The trumpets sounded as the large group from Zandor made their way through the city towards the castle. Many in the city rushed off to greet their new allies while others muttered curses and threats under their breath. The two kingdoms had only been linked in the common goal to rid both countries of the barbarians, but more often than not they were at war. It was well known that not everyone on either side was welcoming this alliance, but both sides knew if they were to defeat the savages, they had to join forces in the long term.

Once again the castle was in a fluster to make room for the thousand men and women that came from the south for the wedding. The group flooded into the courtyard and they all made way for the royal carriages so they could get as close to their welcome committee as possible. Since those from the south did not yet approve of those with the gift, Ursa and Meath were not asked to be there. So King Borrack, Nicolette, Tundal, Dagon, their wives and children and the daughters from Dragon's Cove, only the richest merchants and their families a few dozen servants awaited the Royal family from Zandor, though many more were there at a distance or watching from the castle walls and many windows.

The commotion and talking stopped as King Dante and his beautiful Queen Glenelle were helped from their well made and well decorated carriage.

"How did your trip fare?" King Borrack asked after everyone had climbed out and were making their way towards him and the others.

"It would have gone a lot smoother if you kept your roads up and didn't let them get riddled with pot holes and fallen trees." Prince Berrit answered in a tone that showed his disappointment as he looked down at his dusty traveling clothes, his cheeks flustered with anger. His little brother Kayrel shook his head with agreement.

"Mind your tongue Berrit or I'll..." His mother Queen Glenelle snapped as she smiled and greeted the others with all smiles.

"The trip was long and tiring, but I forgot how beautiful the landscape was. Makes me wish I would have taken over this country when I might have had a chance." King Dante joked as the two kings embraced and gave each other a pat on the back. Though the two kings had never truly gotten along, they did their best to put on a good show for those around. "And this must be my soon to be daughter in law." Dante said as he took Nicolette's hand in his and kissed the top of it smiling up at her with approval. "She will make you a fine wife, son. There is none more beautiful then this little flower you see here before you." He boasted with pride, as he looked back to his son. Who was still patting off his traveling clothes of all the dust, he seemed to be more worried about that than looking up to see the women he was to marry. When he was done his eyes met hers and he was transfixed by what he saw, a malicious grin formed on his face, but no one seemed to notice.

When Nicolette saw the look he gave her, it sent a shiver up her spine and she felt like running, but she stood her ground as the young prince who was not much older then her walked up to her holding out a fine gold necklace that had a rather large pendant full of diamonds and rubies. It must of cost more then most common folk could make in a lifetime.

"But a small gift for my future bride, there will be many more where that came from after we've wed my sweet." Berrit said in a tone that made Nicolette's guts twist and turn in disgust as he leaned in and kissed her palm his tongue flicked her wrist so fast no one noticed, except Nicolette. She almost cried out but instead thanked him and allowed him to put it around her neck. His touch sent more shivers down her spine; it was what she might have envisioned death's touch to feel like, but she hid it well and only Berrit seemed to notice, only extending his grin all the wider.

For several minutes everyone made small talk about t
their families and land were doing, how one another were
the hordes of Barbarians and how excited they all were al
ding.

"Well I am sure after your long trip you all would enjo, a oath and
some refreshments, a good feast and an even better sleep. Tomorrow we
shall start on the new treaty and finally wedding plans that will please everyone." King Borrack declared while he greeted the rest of his new guests
and ordered servants to go and help with everyone's things.

"Must we do that so soon?" Berrit moaned for no better reason then
to hear his own voice and to stir the waters a little.

His father looked at him shaking his head, hoping he would not cause
a scene about it but knew his son better then that.

"I do not know if you know this, boy, but your wedding is but a few
days off and there will be no wedding if we do not work out a suitable
agreement for all of us. And everyone knows how stubborn Zandorians can
be." Borrack replied hoping to end it there with the last laugh.

"What did you just say to me?" Berrit yelled taking a step forward and
going into a defensive posture.

"There is no need for this, nor rude words meant to cut." Queen
Glenelle looked to King Borrack as she said the last words wanting to add
some cutting words her self but held her tongue. "We are all here to make
peace, not continue this feud." Dante's wife said stepping in the middle of
everything hoping that it wouldn't break into a fight.

"Yes you are right my lady. I am sorry for my words, Young Prince
Berrit." Borrack said trying to sound pleasant. "That is truly no way for a
King to act when welcoming new friends to his home and I do hope you
can find it in your heart to forgive my prudence."

"My son accepts your apology, and once we are through getting refreshed and rested we shall all feast and drink, for I am sure no other
kingdom anywhere could throw a feast like our new dear friend King Borrack." King Dante replied back staring his son down who looked as if he
was going to try to argue some more.

"Then I shall see you all in a few hours time." King Borrack said as he
gestured his servants to help with the other things.

~   ~   ~

They all gathered into the massive, elaborate library and found their
appointed seats, while several servants brought in drinks and food. For

king a new treaty that everyone agreed on could take many hours, even days. And days it did. Only those with a say in how the country was governed in both kingdoms were allowed to be at the meeting, along with two scribes, who wrote franticly trying to keep up with everything they agreed on and discussed. They all sat around a large wooden table in the centre of the library, King Borrack, Ursa, Lord Dagon and Lord Tundal sat on one end well King Dante his advisor Kabreil, Prince Berrit, the younger Prince Kayrel, Lord Andras of Besha, Lord Zefer of Samel and Lord Bartan of Laquao sat at the other end. Though the princess was to have a part in ruling Draco, she did not need to be present for the making of the treaty.

"The killing of those with the gift must stop and that is final." King Borrack said angrily, as if his nerves were wearing thin. This matter had been the only thing they could not come to an agreement on and it was now late into the third night of this never ending battle. "They are people, just like the rest of us and should not be treated as if they were the plague itself."

"I told you I will not allow those demons into my land, they're nothing but trouble, and you should ban them all from your land as well. They will be the death of you, of us all. They're unnatural and evil I tell you." Dante yelled as he pounded his fist on the oak table, and the others from his kingdom roared their agreement. "They are the Keepers spawn; no good could come out of them."

"Lord Andras, did you not seek Master Ursa's help when your son Kain was sick? And you, Lord Bartan did you not do the same when your wife Nisheena suffered from that viper bite? Even though you hate him and his kind, he did not deny you his help, though he could have. He helped you for no price other then knowing he was helping save a life." Lord Dagon howled. "You did not seem to hate those with the gift then!" Andras and Bartan both went silent and looked away from his glaring eyes; they could not deny the claim.

"Not all with the gift mean to do harm with it." Ursa finally said, though knowing those from the other kingdom didn't want to hear or listen to anything he had to say seeing how this discussion was about people like him. When it had all began they had even had the nerve to demand that Ursa not be present to this topic. "Those with the gift could be a great help to your kingdom, not only with those who are ill but with the many battles against our enemies." Ursa stated, though he knew it wouldn't help.

"But there is no way for us to know which one's are good or not, so it is better just to keep them from our land. We've had too many problems

with those beasts, attacking the innocent and killing them without mercy.
" Lord Zefer put in as he looked around the room at everyone. Then the arguing started all over again.

"That and our physicians do just as good of job as any demon." Zefer's son yelled.

"Well if you didn't call them beast and put them to death every time one was seen, I'm sure they're would be far fewer problems. People tend to react differently when there not being hunted down like a dog." Lord Dagon barked again. "Of course there is going to be a handful that will still be resentful for the life time of fear and torment that you and even some of us have given them. But in time hopefully that will stop when they learn they have nothing to fear."

"If your physicians did half as good of job as you say they do then why is the death of wounded and sick so great in your kingdom?" Tundal remarked slyly with a raised brow.

"Silence!" King Borrack yelled over the voices of everyone, and they all went silent. "When I am gone, my daughter and your son, will inherit my kingdom, and I'll be damned, if I am going to let you change the laws that protect those with the gift that I have worked so hard to lay out over the last few decades. It is late and we all need sleep to clear our heads and rethink this so we can come to an agreement. We will continue this tomorrow morning."

Everyone growled silent remarks as they got up to leave towards their rooms, until it was just Borrack, Ursa and Dagon that were left in the library.

"Why are they so stupid?" Dagon said to himself as he shook his head in disgust, draining off the rest of his wine as he got up and left to his room.

"Your Highness, tonight I sensed a great evil from someone that was here." Ursa whispered to the king. "I suggest we watch those Zandoreans better while they are here."

"I too sensed something I did not like tonight, my dear friend. But then again when I am around those people I always do. But we too need our sleep if we are to keep this bunch from killing one another." Borrack replied with a yawn and a gesture towards the hallway that went to his room.

"I shall see to it that no leave's their rooms unnoticed tonight your majesty." Ursa said as he walked the king to his room and set up a ward on his door so that none could enter without him knowing. Then instead of going to bed, he went for a walk to help himself think of what he had learned and heard this night in hopes that tomorrow's discussions would go a little better.

~ ~ ~

It was a warm night with a cool, sweet, smelling breeze as Nicolette sat alone in the royal garden by their tree, she wished he'd show up and have found away to make things better, but she knew there was none. She knew it was better that he didn't show, this was something that couldn't be. She would have to learn to love another and forget what they had. She knew it would be better for both of them to never see one another again. At that thought tears formed in her eyes, she couldn't bear not to see him again. Nicolette sighed as she picked a blue rose from the bush beside the bench; it smelt so sweet, it tickled her nose.

She took one last look at the tree and got up, slowly making her way back to the castle to find her bed, when she heard voices coming from behind a large group of fruit trees, not far from the path. She thought it a little odd for anyone to be out this late in the royal garden and went to see whom it was. As she walked silently up to a large apple tree that over looked where the people stood, she peered out and saw three dark figures standing together, all hooded in black.

~ ~ ~

"Once I am married to that wench of a princess we can finally rid ourselves of Borrack and Master Ursa, and then, I will find away to dispose of my new darling wife. She will be of no use to us when I am the new king of Draco kingdom." A voice, which was not Prince Berrit, said with a sinister chuckle behind it.

"We will have to keep a close eye on that wizard Ursa. He is powerful enough to cause us trouble when he catches on, he is no fool. It might be best if we make him disappear sooner then planned." The soft voice of a woman said tipped with venom.

"We shall dispose of him soon enough my love, he and the other's here with the gift shall make fine treats and soon none shall stand in our way for what we were destined to achieve." The first voice said again with such authority that it seemed to quake the ground itself.

"As long as we keep to the plan, we shall all have as we want." The second man said with a voice that Nicolette recognized but could not place a face too. She stumbled back as fear coursed through her veins like fire with what she had just heard. Just as she was about to turn, a hand went over her mouth she went stiff and almost fainted.

"It is I, your highness." The old wizard whispered as he turned her around to face him, he then slowly led her away from where they stood.

"Ursa we must warn my father, there are…" The wizard cut her off.

"Yes I know my child, there is great evil at work here tonight. I too heard what you did and we must tell the king at once and we must be wary on those we trust." He whispered searching the area for any sign that anyone had caught on to them. "Stay by me and do as I say."

The two silently made their way through the castle's many hallways and chambers to avoid the midnight patrols and anyone else that was about at this hour. When they reached the kings cambers, they burst through the doors of the great room to warn the king. Once they were in the room, Ursa lit the candles and king Borrack awoke in a rage.

"What the hell is going on here?" He muttered as he rubbed the sleep from his eyes seeing who had barged into his room.

"Your majesty, there are those who plot against you in the castle this night." Ursa gasped as he made his way to where the king was getting out of his bed.

"Are you sure? Who are they?" The king replied as pulled on his blue robe.

"We do not know father, but they said they were going to kill you and then me, it sounded like prince Berrit but it was not his voice." Nicolette cried as she tried to make sense of what she had heard and was saying.

"There are three that plot your death maybe more but I haven't figured out who they are." Ursa told him. Just then Halpas entered the room with his sword drawn and breathing hard.

"What is going on in here? Is everything alright your majesty?" Halpas said through long hard breaths as if he had been running a long way, though his room was not far down the hallway.

"Halpas, I am glad to see you. There seem to be traitors among us that plot at mine and my daughter's death. Search the castle for anyone out of their rooms and bring me prince Berrit and the rest of those Zandorian bastards so we can get to the bottom of this once and for all. Alert all the guards as well, I want this castle locked down tight until this is solved, I will take no chances." The king ordered.

"Yes I know." Said Halpas as a flash of metal cleared the room and imbedded itself deep in the king's throat, the tip peering out the back of his neck. His eyes went wide with pain and betrayal as his hands grabbed the dagger in his neck and thick dark blood drained over the top of his fingers. He fell to the ground gurgling for breath that he could not find.

Ursa flung his hand out towards the traitor and a great line of fire flew from his hands with a hiss and hit Halpas square in the chest, he burst into flames and was dead before his corpse hit the ground.

"Father!" Nicolette screamed as she ran to his aid, but knew there was nothing she could do to save him. "Ursa help him please!" She cried cradling her father's head.

"I had not anticipated this." A man said as he walked into the room, he was dressed all in black and had the cold look of death himself. His skin was golden brown tanned and his eyes looked like pieces of coal.

"You foul demon." Ursa yelled as he cast a massive ball of energy toward the man but it hit an invisible wall around him and faded into nothing more than sparks, Ursa's eyes went wide.

"It will take more then that to be rid of me, great wizard." The man laughed as he waved his hand and a wave of power sent Ursa flying back into a statue of the dead queen Lavira that the king had in his room.

"Who are you and why are you doing this?" Nicolette burst out as she cried over her father's dead, limp body, staring up at the dark man with fear and hate.

"What's the matter princess don't you recognize your soon to be husband?" As the man spoke the words, his features changed into Prince Berrit. Both Nicolette and Ursa gasped at what they had just witnessed. "I had other plans for you wizard, but I guess you killing the king, Halpas and the princess will have to do as my story." The false prince said with a sly grin.

"No one will ever believe you." Ursa barked as he stood to his feet and tried to think of something he could do to get the princess to safety.

"Just watch!" The man said with a tone of pure evil as he closed the distance to where the princess sat. Ursa cast a great wind that the man had not been expecting, he flew back into the wall beside the king's bed and crashed through the bedside table and to the floor with the wind knocked out of his lungs.

"Run you highness we must get out of here!" Ursa yelled, while casting the spell again which only pushed the dark man harder against the wall and floor, they ran out of the room and down the hall. Moment's later three guards rushed into the king's room ready for a fight.

"What is going on in here?" One of the young soldier's said as they entered the room and saw the body of their king and what was left of Halpas lying on the floor.

"That cursed wizard Ursa has killed the king and kidnapped the princess." Prince Berrit bellowed as he tried to get up. "Halpas and I tried to stop him but he used his evil against us." The Prince howled as he caught his breath and got to his feet.

"What are you talking about? Ursa would do no such thing and what are you doing in the king's room?" Before the soldier could finish a bolt of light cut through him and his companions killing them instantly.

"What is going on in here?" Yelled another soldier that got to the room with a small army of men behind him a minute later.

"Ursa has gone mad he and he tried to frame me by bringing me here and killing the king." Berrit tried again, needing this to work before his plans simply dissolved.

"What?" They all asked not sure what to make of this.

"Hurry you fools! He has kidnapped my future wife and your future Queen!" He yelled at them, which seemed to get them on the move.

"Sound the alarm, Master Ursa has killed the king and taken the princess." One of the soldiers screamed to the men who had finally come running from all the noise. Once they had heard the news they fled to spread the word and stop them from escaping.

The false prince knew word of mouth would spread and sooner or later it would be worded right for all to believe.

~   ~   ~

"What are we to do now?" Nicolette asked as she tried to calm her breathing and stop the tears that flooded down her cheeks.

"We must get to Meath at once, he will not be safe for long. They will go to him to get to me, so we must get to him first, and then get out of here." Ursa whispered as he made sure the next hallway was clear for them to go through.

"Where will we go, what will we do?" She asked as if it mattered, for anywhere would be better then here. Her entire life had just taken a plunge and she was trying to come to grips with what had just happened.

"I do not know yet your highness, but I promise you I will keep you safe and figure this out, but first we need to get Meath, get out of here and get somewhere safe." Ursa said as they scurried down the hall, towards Meath's room. As they turned the corner, there stood four guards that were searching for them.

"Why would you do this Ursa? How could you? Maybe those Zandorians are right about those with the gift. You will not escape us wizard."

The closest one said, they ran towards them spear ready to strike, Ursa had no choice but to kill the guards, he released the gift and the men's ribs cracked and splintered under their armour as the arc of power hit them sending all four of them to the ground twitching and convulsing.

It had taken longer then Ursa had wanted it to, to reach Meath's room, but to avoid being caught and the death of more confused men they had to be careful, as it was he had to use his powers more then once along the way to fool or kill the guards, for now most of the castle had heard the lies that the false prince had told and were looking for them everywhere. There would be a great reward for the ones that brought him down. When they entered Meath's room he was sitting on his floor meditating how Ursa had taught him.

"There's no time for that now boy, you must get your things, we must leave at once!" Ursa said in a tone of great rush and urgency as he paced by him leaving Nicolette to watch the door.

"What in the nine hell's going on?" Meath asked confused as his meditation was broken, his vision still slightly blurred.

"There is no time to explain that now, the king has been murdered and we must get out of here now or we will surely join him." Ursa blared out as he grabbed some of Meath's things and threw them to him. Meath put them on still not quite sure of what the commotion was about but was not about to argue. When he was dressed and they had made sure it was safe, the three ran down towards the kitchen, being sure to stay out of sight of all the guards that searched high and low for them. Ursa did not want to kill any that he did not have to, for they were just men following orders and they did not know the truth nor would they listen to it.

When they finally reached the kitchen, which had yet to be searched, it was still dark and empty. Ursa made enough fire in his hand so they could see where they were going, but not enough to give themselves away to any people that might happen to come that way next. From here, they could go out the side door of the kitchen to the stable yard, and steal some horse's to make their escape. There was no way they could get far enough fast enough on foot. Though Nicolette had stop crying, Ursa could tell she was having a hard time fighting her emotions and staying focused at what had to be done. Meath, still not sure of what was all happening followed beside Nicolette trying to comfort her as best he could without speaking; he knew the wizard would explain when they had time and right now all hell was breaking loose, he knew he had to trust Ursa.

"What in blazes is going on?" Came the voice of Maxwell from behind them, they turned to see him standing there with a giant meat clever in his hand. Once he had seen who it was he put the weapon on one of the near by tables. "Meath, Ursa what in hell is going on?" The chef asked in a voice that showed his disapproval that there were people in his kitchen this late. Then his eyes widened when he realized who was with them. "I am so sorry your highness, I did not know you were here, I meant no disrespect." The fat chef added as he bowed his head up and down.

"Maxwell we need to get out of the castle now." Meath said just loud enough for the man to hear and realize something was wrong in his tone.

"Why, what is going on?" He replied with a look of surprise reaching for the weapon again.

"There is no time for that now." Ursa cut in. "Just know what you will later hear is not how things really happened. Now are there any horse's nearby that are ready to go?"

"What are you talking about?" He started but stopped short, for Ursa's look was enough. "Well yes of course, the evening patrol horses are being fed out back as we speak." Maxwell said while looking around as if something was going to jump out at him at any moment.

"Good." Ursa said flat out. "I would suggest you go back to your bed Master Maxwell, and pretend none of this happened, for your own safety." Ursa called back to him the three ran to the door leaving Maxwell standing there scratching his head in confusion. Not being one to doubt Ursa, Maxwell was fast on his way back to his bed.

They ran through the stable yard without being seen and found the horses that Maxwell had said would be there, as they mounted the beast's, soldiers on the wall caught sight of them.

"There they are!" One of them yelled.   "Stop them."

They kicked their horses and galloped off towards the gates at full speed, a large group of men from both kingdoms stood their ground waiting to stop them. No one had started closing the gates from up top yet.

"We may have to kill some of them to get out." Ursa yelled over the noise of the galloping horses to Meath, his hand started to glow with fire. Even from the distance Meath could see the eyes of the warriors, widen with fear as the ball of flames bellowed out and hit the centre of their cluster. The men scattered and dove out of the way screaming in terror. Others lay on the ground rolling back and forth trying to put the flames out, but wizard's fire was not extinguished that easily. As they rode past,

Meath could smell the burnt flesh of those whom had moments ago been standing in their way, ready to cut them down to stop them.

As they rode down the dimly lit road through the city as fast as they could, Nicolette couldn't help but look back at her home and think of what had just happened. She knew they would chase them, but it would take awhile to saddle up a team to follow, and for the confusion to get straightened out.

~   ~   ~

When the three of them had made it many miles from the city, they were forced to slow their pace, for the horses were gleaming with sweat and needed to be rested.

"So would someone mind telling me why we are running for our lives from our home?" Meath finally asked, now that a spare moment had come and things seemed to have calmed, looking around at both of Ursa and the princess for some sort of answer.

Ursa walked over to him and began explaining what he and the princess had witnessed in the garden to what had unfolded in the kings room until they made it to Meath's room.

Nicolette sat on her horse staring off into the trees, as her mind didn't seem to want to work at all. She just stared off into the night sky, her mind blank.

"You mean to tell me the man from my dreams prince Berrit?" Meath uttered in bewilderment as he shook his head in disbelief.

"No I'm guessing the prince is dead and has been for a long time. As for your dreams, I would not jump to such conclusions. But we don't have to time to figure this out yet." Ursa said as he watched the road behind them. "It won't be long until they pick up our trail and find us."

"Where will we go, what will we do?" Nicolette asked again coming back into the conversation as she fought back the tears that consumed her as her mind began to come back to her a little.

"We will go to your uncle Marcus; he is the only one that has not been ill informed of the true murder of the king. And we should be able to make it there before the rumours do if we make haste." The wizard replied with a sigh of remorse for the girl. She had been through more tragedy the last few moments then in all her life. He knew it was far from over, he did not know what help Lord Marcus would be, but it was the only place he could think of that they could go for help.

"We must stop and take care of the band of soldiers that will be coming for us." Ursa said as he dismounted his black and white spotted mare, and started looking through the saddlebags for supplies that they might need and discarding what they did not so they could lighten the load on the horses. "We won't make it far with an army of Draco's and Zandors finest looking for us." He continued.

"What are we going to do to stop them? We can't just kill them all, some of them are our friends! We need to tell them what's going on, then we will have help." Meath exclaimed as he too searched for things his horse carried that might be of use.

"We will do as we have too. They are men led by deception and lies and want their future queen back, along with whatever bounty they were promised to bring us down. They will not be interested in hearing our side of the story." Ursa replied as he put his head in his hands. He had already used a great deal of his powers to escape and feared he would not have enough to finish the task to get them to safety this night. "And I am sure a lot of those coming for us will not be our soldiers but those from Zandor."

"Once we show them that she is alright and you weren't trying to kidnap her they will listen." Meath said as if trying to convince himself more then the others while he took a swallow of water from the skin he had found on his horse.

"I think he's right, they will listen if I tell them." Nicolette finally cut in as Meath handed her the water and nodded his head in agreement.

"Maybe your right your highness, but we need to be ready for it if they don't." Ursa said wishing it would be that easy, as he pulled a fine jewelled sword from its hiding place in the saddle and handed it to Meath, who held it in his hands for a moment, getting the feel for the blade. It was heavier then he was use to but it would have to do if things went bad.

~   ~   ~

As they waited on the path for the advancing search party, Meath counted each man that came into view. There were thirty men, most were Zandorean soldiers that were armed to the teeth, in full body armour, swords, spears and a few bows. He saw Keithen, who was his friend and fellow apprentice wizard. He rode at the side of the party and stared straight ahead at Ursa and Meath as they rode closer, the band stopped a hundred feet ahead of them.

"It is ok princess, you will be safe soon. If you surrender now, you will be granted a quick death wizard. If you resist, you will suffer slow for the traitors you are." The captain yelled as he and his men dismounted from their horses and drew their weapons. Bowstrings were pulled back and notched.

"You don't understand, things are not as they seem, they did not kill my father, Prince Berrit did." Nicolette screamed back trying to find the right words to convince them, but it all seemed to come out too fast to make any sense.

"It is a trick, they have used their powers on the princess to control her mind, we must stop them before they do anymore harm to her." Keithen yelled to the warriors as his horse shifted uneasily from the noise of the yelling men. He smiled to himself feeling good about having the power to command people, even though he did not know if even the strongest with the gift could control someone's mind. But that didn't even matter, they would believe him no matter what he said, his grin widened as he grew drunk from the power he was realizing.

"What's it going to be wizards? You cannot kill us all with your powers, even you are not that strong." The captain yelled back, in a tone that showed he was not afraid, and yet not so sure of his claim.

"I've all ready told them all you can do and how you would do it Ursa, and everyone knows Meath is not much of a threat with his gift, not compared to me that is. Just give up and you will die by my hand instead of one of these true haters of those with the gift." Keithen yelled to them feeling cocky behind this wall of armed men.

Meath tightened his grip on the sword. He now knew what Ursa had said was true, they would never believe their story. Confrontation seemed to be a forgone conclusion, for these men didn't care for the truth, they were already pumped and ready for battle.

"I am ashamed I ever taught you a thing Keithen, you are a sorry excuse for an apprentice and will never be a wizard because you are weak of mind and spirit." Ursa yelled back knowing that they would have to kill the young man if it came to blows, but he had already made his peace with that thought.

"Why aren't you listening to me? You are being fooled! Ursa is helping me, he is not the monster." Nicolette tried to reason with them once more but they paid her little mind now.

"You had your chance traitors, prepare yourselves. Men, let's not allow king Borrack's name go in vain." The man shouted as he pulled his full-faced helm down over his head.

"Do not do this captain; we do not need to shed blood this night, just listen to us please!" Ursa said trying one last attempt to stop what he knew he could not, it was too late and the captain had already given the order to attack.

Ursa raised both his arms high in the air and bolts of light flashed from his fingertips with a deafening crackle and tore through the chests of the closest men, they fell to the earth looking down at the large gaping holes that now allowed their guts to spill from their charred bodies.

Without thinking Meath let loose a blast of fire that engulfed three soldiers as they ran towards him, they did not die quickly but rolled around on the ground as their skin blistered and melted from their faces. He met another of the warriors with a thrust of his sword, it ripped through the man's chest plate like butter and protruded out his back, while an enemy's sword just missed Meath's arm. Meath put his boot to the dying mans chest and tore the blade out to meet another, with a quick slash to the throat, his blood sprayed across Meath's face. The lust of battle had over taken him now and death was all he could smell as his training came back to him in full. Meath turned just in time to see another soldier swinging his sword at him, their swords met with a loud clang as Meath discharged his gift and a bolt of light sent the remains of the man flying back into the dirt, smouldering.

The five bowmen had a hard time aiming with all the fighting but finally an opportunity came and all five fired at Ursa hoping to bring the great wizard down fast while he seemed to be distracted.

Ursa waved his hand and a gust of wind shifted the arrows off course and into two of the on-coming soldiers.

Ursa fell to his knees as he felt his powers began weakening when his hands hit the ground a wall of fire tore from the earth a few feet in front of him and five more men went down screaming from the brutal inferno they had stepped into.

Meath moved just in time to miss the blast that shot from the earth, but just as he did a man that he did not see before thrust his spear into his thigh and he fell with a cry. As he stared up at the large warrior that stood above him with his spear held high, ready to take his life, he watched the mans eyes go wide and a trickle of blood steam from his mouth as he fell to the ground quivering. Meath looked up and there was Nicolette standing with a short sword held tight in her shaking hands.

"They are too strong, retreat!" The last of the men ran to their horses and galloped off into the mist as fast as they could. Keithen had given the order and fled long before the rest did, he hadn't even tried to help.

"We must not stay here, they will send more after us and we might not be so lucky next time, not until we have time to regain our strength." Ursa said as he finally got to his feet. He looked over to where Nicolette and Meath were and saw the princess cradling him in her arms crying.

"I don't know what happened he just passed out." Nicolette cried as she held him tighter, ignoring the blood that was staining her blue cloak, already stained with much blood from this night.

"He is not use to using that much power at once, he will be fine in a few hours, now tie off his wound and help me put him on his horse, we must go now!" Ursa said as helped her put Meath on his horse and they rode off down the dark misty road leaving the dead and dying men behind them.

Chapter 3

"What do you mean they got away?" Prince Berrit yelled, slamming his fist into the table his, face flaring into a bright red.

"Relax son, they won't get far, that wizard can't stop all the troops we send after them." Dante said trying to calm his son down. "And we all know no one hunts those with the gift better then Zandorians!" Dante finished with a snarl.

"This doesn't make sense, why would Ursa do something like this? He couldn't have, there must be something missing from the picture." Lord Dagon questioned as he looked around the room as if expecting an answer, but he knew he wouldn't find any.

"If that bastard so much as harms one hair on her body, I will see him starved, beaten, skinned and left for the buzzards." Berrit hollered at all those in the room while he paced back and forth from one end of the table to the other.

"You said his apprentice was with him?" Dante asked the young wizard that had survived the slaughter of the first group that had left in search of the kidnapped princess.

"Yes, Meath is not nearly as strong as Master Ursa in the arts of his gift by any means, but he was trained as a soldier, and wields a sword with ease." Keithen replied with a stutter. He had never been in a room with so many power figures, and he could hardly control his nerves.

"Yes I remember Meath well, he was trained in Drandor and made top ranks in almost everything he did, he even gave my champion Raven a good work out in battle practice. He is an exceptional fighter and he wields the gift as well which makes him a very dangerous person." Lord Tundal said to the crowd of royals while he rubbed his chin trying to grasp all that he had heard this night.

"I still do not understand why they would do something like this, what reasons would they have for kidnapping the princess?" Dagon said again still looking for an answer. "There must be some mistake... There has to be! Ursa and King Berrit were good friends, he would never have done this on his own mind, ever!" Dagon said more to himself then the others.

Berrit turn to face Dagon with a snarl. "Oh believe me my good Lord Dagon" Berrit hissed. "It was Ursa. That demon came into my room, put some sort of spell on me and the princess that made us go to the king's room with him! We couldn't even talk or scream for help, believe me I tried and I am sure so did the princess!" He bellowed as he stormed around the room recounting his horrifying experience to everyone yet again, being sure to keep it exactly the same as before, for any mishaps could ruin everything. "Then after he killed the king and told me he was going to frame me for the death of the king and princess. That's when Halpas tried to intervened." He stopped at the table and downed a cup of wine before continuing while everyone sat silently waiting to hear the tale in full yet again. "Then more guards showed up and he killed them too, then grabbed the princess and ran off with her, leaving me alone in the room in hopes his plan worked." He said the last part with sadness as he sat down.

"We will find her my son, just stay calm." Dante said while patting his sons back, trying to comfort him as much as he could.

"It still doesn't make any sense at all." Tundal replied.

"You doubt me?" Berrit screamed across the table. "Who else could have blasted those men like that? I sure as hell don't have the gift!"

"There are many witnesses that say they saw Ursa and Meath killing our own men to get out of the castle with the princess." Dagon said, though everyone could tell it pained him to do so.

"I did catch that little whelp trying to make a move on her highness the night of our arrival at the feast, in the garden." Rift finally said, he had been summoned to the library council for briefing; he was to lead the next group of soldiers that were to go looking for them.

"WHAT!? Why did you not tell us when it happened? I would have had his head of the block and the vultures would have pecked his skull clean by now." The prince screamed at Rift as he glared at the captain with such a look that even he flinched back a step.

"I am sorry your majesty I only thought it..." Rift tried to say but was interrupted as prince Berrit threw his wine cup at him.

"You only thought what? Now the princess is in the clutches of those demons and who knows what they will do to her!" The prince yelled again his face looked like it couldn't go any redder then it already was. "Whatever happens to her will be on your hands captain! What kind of champion are you anyway? The princess would be in safer hands with the keeper himself then yours." Berrit muttered knowing full well the words would cut the captain down hard.

"Son calm yourself, we will get her back, and you will still be married, they would not be foolish enough to harm her." His father reassured him. "She is their only leverage, now go captain Rift and bring her highness back to where she belongs, take as many men as you need. Bring the bastards that did this back alive… if you can." King Dante barked.

"Yes sir." Rift said through a smile as he turned and marched down the hall, Berrit's words continually running over in his head.

"I knew we should never have trusted those beasts. They should all have been killed long ago." Lord Bartan muttered as he folded his arms and glared off at nothing.

"We cannot judge all those with the gift on the actions of two." Tundal barked back as he stood up from his chair. "And we still don't know what the motives are or why they are doing this. They could very well have a perfectly good reason."

"When will you people ever learn, they are the work of the Keeper and can never be trusted." Lord Zefer replied as he crossed his arms and spat.

"It has been a long night, there is nothing further we can do, so let us return to our beds and try to get what sleep we can this night." King Dante said as he pushed his chair back and got up with a stretch.

"Yes I suppose your right." Tundal said while he turned and made his way out of the library. Soon all of the others followed and went back to their rooms.

~ ~ ~

"I do not trust that prince Berrit. Ursa would never do this." Dagon whispered to Tundal as they both knelt down in front of the giant statue of the Creator in the castles church.

"I do not believe he would either, but one can never know for sure." Tundal whispered back with a sigh.

"You do not believe that little whelp, do you?" Dagon said in shock trying to keep his voice low.

"I did not say I believed him, but what if he's telling the truth, maybe Master Ursa has been planning this for a long time, some say he can see the future." Tundal replied well looking around to see if anyone was listening.

"What does this gain him? He is now a wanted man. If he wanted gold, he could have just as easily robbed the treasury." The Lord of Mandrake said trying to keep his voice down.

"I do not know dear friend, but let us keep our ears and eyes open, if one of those Zandoreans are behind this I will personally slit their throat and piss down it." Tundal said as he rose off his knees and patted his friend on the back in reassurance.

~　~　~

Nicolette poured more water onto the piece of cloth that she had torn off from her nightdress and was using it to help take Meath's fever down. Ursa had told her to watch him through the night and to make sure every hour she forced a fowl smelling mixture down his throat that would help his mind and wound recover faster.

They had stopped riding and had gone off the main trail hours ago to avoid being seen by another group of soldiers the false prince had sent after them. Even though they were a few hundred feet from the road she could still hear the warriors as they rode past looking for them. Every time she heard another group pass by, her grip tightened on the dragger Ursa had found for her on one of the horses. Ursa had taken the time to cover their tracks well enough for the night that even the greatest trackers would have a hard time finding their trail, and with the last of his powers that he would risk using, he healed Meath's leg as best he could. Now he too rested for the night. She could tell that the old wizard was drained of strength and energy. He sat with his legs folded and his back straight against a huge trunk of a tree, his hands were on his lap and he did not move. She couldn't even tell if he was still breathing, even when the insects of the night crawled over him in search for food he did not stir. Nicolette could not help but feel so alone and afraid, for if they were found now they were surely doomed.

Though she was not experienced in the arts of battle and the gift, she knew if they were found this night, they would not have the strength to defeat another attack. She shuddered at the thought of what would happen to Meath and the great wizard if they were caught. She held Meath's hand tighter and ran her fingers through his thick brown hair, which was still matted with dried blood from the battle. Nicolette wished he would wake up and talk to her, so she wouldn't feel so lonely. With everything that had happened she just needed someone to talk with so she could keep her mind from thinking about her fathers' terrible death and betrayal.

~ ~ ~

Meath woke with a jolt and jumped to his feet, searching for his sword or any weapon that might be in reach. Then he saw Nicolette sitting where he had just been lying, she was looking up at him with a smile. He fell to his knees, the pain in his leg finally hitting him although it was no match for the pain in his head. His skull was pounding so hard it made his vision blur and his stomach turn so violently, he turned and retched on the ground.

"It's alright, we are safe Meath." Nicolette whispered as she went to help him back to where he had slept only moments before.

"My head is killing me, what happened?" He mumbled as he rubbed his eyes trying to clear his vision.

"You blacked out from using too much of your gift, Ursa said." She explained while helping him steady himself. "I have never seen anyone with the gift use it like you two did back there." She said with a shiver as she remembered the screams of the men who had been burned alive. "Is that what war is like?"

"So that's what happened, I have never had that happen before." Meath said as he rubbed his temples. "I have never killed with my powers before." He said as he stared off into the dark growth of the jungle, as flashes of what he had done came back to him as well as some of the faces he had known personally.

"You did what you had to, they would have done worse to you." Nicolette said trying to ease his mind.

"If only they would have listened to us." Meath whispered as he shook his head and looked over to where Ursa was sitting. "How long have I been out?" Meath asked her, still wincing at the pain coursing through his head.

"Most of the night, the sun should be rising soon." She replied. "But you should rest more, and drink this." She held out a cup of one of Ursa's remedies. "Ursa told me when you wake to get you to drink this."

"I'll be fine I just need this pounding in my head to go away." Meath said as he breathed deeply and put his head in his hands trying to centre himself

"That's what the drink is for, you stubborn fool." The voice of the one who had made the drink said. Both their eyes went straight to where the wizard sat. He was looking at Meath and shaking his head. "I am surprised we are not dead, with you two talking so loud, I'm sure the enemy could have easily found us." Ursa said as he stood up and stretched. He was still feeling a little drained and weak but knew they had better get moving now that Meath had regained consciousness. If they ran into another group anytime soon they would be forced to run.

"Now drink up boy, we have to get moving. We will have to stay off the main roads and not let anyone see us, for surely the rumours have travelled faster then we have this night." Ursa said as he went to where he had tied the horses.

Meath took the mixture and held it for a few moments, looking at it with a sour look on his face, and then he put the cup to his lips and drank the green liquid as fast as he could.

"Damn it! That is worse then the stuff you gave me to help me sleep." Meath said as he coughed and tried not to gag the bitter tasting potion back up. "You think you would try and make your potions taste a little better after all these years."

"Why? I never tire of seeing that look on people's faces." Ursa said with a smile and a chuckle while he patted his horse's neck and talked to it softly.

"You are a cruel old man you know that." Meath said as he stood up and noticed the pain in his head was subsiding already. Now he could feel the intense burning from the wound in his leg.

"How are you feeling, Master Ursa?" Nicolette asked as she went to the horses with the blankets they had used during the night.

"I am fine your highness, and call me Ursa, I only make people I don't like call me by my title." He said with a wink as he handed her one of the water skins.

"You also can call me by my name and not my title." She said after she took a large gulp of the stale water and smiled wearily.

"I will try to do that my dear." Ursa said with a nod of approval. "Meath, what is taking you so long? Get a move on it, we have no time to dilly daedal." Ursa snapped jokingly not even looking back at him while Meath was slowly limping his way over to them.

"Well my bloody leg hurts, and my body feels like it has been beaten half to death." Meath bellowed back as he stumbled and fell, Nicolette went to his aid and helped him to his feet again, letting him use her for support.

"Well of course, it will hurt for awhile, that's what you get for stepping in front of a spear. But it is just stiff, you know how wounds work when they have been healed with the gift, or have you not been listening when I try and teach you? If you don't like my healing job I guess you're going to have to learn to do it yourself then." Ursa grunted back to him while he mounted his horse and looked down at the two. He couldn't help but smile as he saw the affection the two had for one another. As children he had watched them when they were together and knew those feelings would only grow stronger, though it could never happen between the two, Ursa always wished it could for them.

With the help from Nicolette, Meath managed to get to his horse without falling again. Before getting on his horse, he gave his sore leg a final stretch. He knew it might be a long time before he would have another chance. Once they had all mounted up, they rode out of the forest in silence onto the road that they had abandoned earlier. Though the horses had not been fed, they still seemed eager to ride. They all knew the horses would not last the day of hard riding that was ahead of them if they were not watered and fed soon. They would have to stop at one of the small towns on the way, and hope they could get in without being recognized. The closest town was Darnan thirty miles to the west along the main road to Dragon's Cove. The news of the princess's kidnapping would have reached there by now, but Ursa knew some of the people well enough that if they were discreet, they could tend to the horses and make it through without any problems.

As the three rode swiftly down the road, Meath noticed that they had not passed any travellers since they had left their camp. He knew that more then likely the guards had set up roadblocks along the roads and were checking anybody who travelled on it. They would search everyone and everything, even if they had to break it to do so.

Meath looked over at Nicolette and saw she was looking back at him. He couldn't help but admire how strong she had been through all of this. For Meath and Ursa this was a lot easier, they had been trained for things like this, prepare for battle, fear and betrayal. Nicolette wasn't. She was a princess and should have never been put through anything like this.

"I am sorry about your father." Meath finally said wondering if he should have just kept his mouth shut.

"Thank you... I just can't believe he's gone and that this is all happening... it all feels like a bad dream that I cant wake up from." She replied while starring down at her horse.

"I am sorry. I didn't mean to bring it up and make you sad, I just…" Meath stammered out before getting cut off.

"Its ok Meath, I know you didn't mean anything by it… It's something I am going to have to get use to I guess." She said as she looked back up at him and smiled a weak smile.

"I am sorry I could not stop your father's death." Ursa said in a tone of great sadness. It was his job to help protect the king and he had failed.

"It wasn't your fault, no one could have known Halpas was a traitor, not even you." Nicolette remarked as Meath and her rode up closer to him. That was all she said for a long time, Ursa just stared straight ahead watching the road. Nicolette and Meath rode in silence and did not say anything else for a long time until Meath could no longer handle it.

"We have to stop and take a break, my leg is killing me and the horse's need what little water we can give them from the skins or they're not going to make it the rest of the way." Meath finally said. The last hour he had been in extreme pain, but he did not want to slow their pace. Now he could take it no longer, and the horses did need the water.

"Yes I guess it is time we rest the horses and stretch our legs a little. We will be in Darnan soon and we will need all our wits about us." Ursa said as he stopped his horse and dismounted.

"I think it would be a good idea if we changed our clothes while we are here, we are not exactly dressed like common folks, and stand out like a lame horse." Meath added as he dismounted. He held on to his horse for support as he slowly worked the kink out of his leg.

"Yes did you not think I already thought about that?" Ursa said slyly as he pulled out one of the dark grey blankets that were in his saddlebag and handed it to Nicolette. "Cut a hole in the middle and put it on, no one will believe we are poor folks if they see that fine silk night dress you are wearing." Ursa said while he pulled out another blanket from Meath's saddlebag for himself.

"What about me?" Meath asked as he walked over to them, his leg was starting to feel a little better now and he wasn't limping as badly.

"What about you? You were lucky enough to be in your room when all hell broke loose back there and besides, you always look like a beggar." Ursa said as he finally cracked a smile. Nicolette tried to hide a small giggle while she pulled the dirty blanket over her head. "But you might want to hide that sword under your cloak, it might give us away." Ursa said to Meath.

"Ya I know, the jewels on this thing are worth more then the horses." Meath added ignoring Ursa's comment as he tucked it under his grey cloak so the handle would not be seen.

"So how do I look?" Nicolette asked them as she tried to conceal her hair in her new travelling garb.

"Hmm it needs something." Ursa remarked as he bent down to the ground and grabbed a hand full of dirt and rubbed it on her face, and then he stood back and took a look. "There, almost perfect." He said as he did the same to himself and finished making sure his white robes were not visible.

"So I wonder where everyone is. We haven't run across anyone yet? No guards, no travelers, no one." Meath remarked while he looked around expecting to see someone.

"Yes I know, that is a little odd, but no matter. There will be a road-block just before we get to Darnan. We cannot afford to be recognised, we have neither the strength nor the power to take out a roadblock and get away with it. So that means we need a plan to get in." Ursa announced as he looked at their surroundings and was already conjuring up with a plan in his head.

~ ~ ~

"They were here, all three of them sir." The tracker said over his shoulder to Rift while he traced his hands over the footprints on the ground.

"How long ago damn it!" Rift yelled while looking down at the man from his horse.

"They must have left just after dawn I would say. From the looks of their tracks they are going to Darnan, probably to get new horses and supplies, though it would seem foolish, they must know the news would have reached there by now and that getting in would be near impossible." The man said while mounting his horse and waiting for new orders.

"Oh believe me, nothing is impossible for Ursa. He is a very well connected and a cunning man. But why would they bring her there? It doesn't make any sense, where are they going?" Rift said out loud to himself while he pondered what to do. "Shahariel, you come with me. I might need you to find their tracks again and we will make it much faster just the two of us. The rest of you follow as fast as you can." Rift ordered as he kicked his horse and it sprang in to a run, Shahariel following in a hurry as the other fifty warriors tried to keep up. With their armour and weapons they couldn't keep the same pace.

~ ~ ~

As Meath neared the group of men, fear gripped at his gut and he couldn't help but wish Ursa was with them, but he was already waiting on the other side of the roadblock in the town somewhere. It had looked so simple watching Ursa go through, the guards didn't seem to pay the wizard much notice, they weren't looking for a simple looking old man dressed as a beggar by himself. Ursa had played the part so perfectly, the hump back, the limp, even begging the guards for a few coins, which they had given him for him to go away. Meath shook his head. He had to concentrate and had to play his part just as convincingly, if not more so. They were looking for the princess and she was with him, walking beside him, they had let the horses go a few miles before they had got to the town. The horses were too noticeable as royal guard horses and would have given them away in a heartbeat.

He looked over to Nicolette and could tell she was just as scared as he was. He knew as well as she did that if this didn't go right, they would never see each other again. He gave her a reassuring grin that everything was going to be fine, though he didn't quite believe it yet himself. He took one last look at her as they came to a halt in front of a large, clean-shaven soldier.

"Remove your hoods.' The soldier commanded as he stood in front of them with his hand on the hilt of his sword.

"What is the meaning of this?" Meath asked in a raspy, irritated beggars voice as best as he could, all the while hoping it wasn't too much or not enough.

"I said remove your hood or I will remove it for you." The man said again this time with a fiercer tone behind his words as he stepped closer.

"Alright relax my good man, no need to get physical." Meath said as he pulled his hood off his head so the man could see his full face. The man glared at him for a moment then looked over to Nicolette who still hadn't taken her hood off.

"I said take off your hood! This is the last time I ask." The man yelled as he took a step over to Nicolette. She slowly pulled her hood down and let her red hair fall down her back. The soldier stared at her for a moment and then turned and walked back to Meath.

"I am sorry for the delay but we are looking for two wizard assassins and a girl that they kidnapped. I can see that you are not them so carry on." He said as he stepped out of the way and waived the other men out of the way so they could pass. As Meath and Nicolette made their way through the mass of men that formed the roadblock, the man that had stopped them yelled. "Hey wait, stop."

Meath's heart jumped into his throat, they had almost made it. Meath stopped and turned to face the man, his hand moved to the sword that was hidden under his cloak as he could feel fear grip him again.

"You look like you might be a man of sport, if you see two men, one older one younger and a woman with long brown hair, there is a reward of five thousand gold pieces for the capture of these men and the safe return of the girl." The man said as he caught up with Meath.

"Really, that much? I will have to keep that in mind and if I see them I will be sure to come inform you." Meath said with a nod as he turned and continued walking into the town as the soldier ran off back to his post.

"That was too close." Meath said after they were out of hearing range.

"I can't believe that really worked." Nicolette replied as she pulled her hood back on and stood closer to Meath so they could talk easier. She felt safe by him she always, had even as children.

"I have to say, the red hair was a good idea." Meath said while he looked at her and smiled.

"Of course it was, I thought of it." Came the voice of Ursa who was now walking behind them with his head down. "Follow me at a distance and make sure no one see us together." With that he turned down a side road between two buildings, all the while keeping up his begging for every person he passed.

Meath had a hard time following the old wizard, he looked so much like all the other beggars, he even had the walk of one. More then once Meath and Nicolette lost sight of him and each time after only a few moments he would appear behind them again.

"We are almost there, keep your eyes open and do not lose sight of me again." Ursa huffed as he looked up at Meath and shook his head.

Meath could only imagine the words that went with that look, it was the same look Ursa always gave him when he had done something to annoy the wizard. Meath chuckled to himself; he had always known that nothing Ursa said was meant to hurt, but to teach him.

"What's so funny?" Nicolette asked as they followed Ursa down another back alley between two larger buildings that looked to be houses of rich merchants.

"Oh what? Sorry, I was just thinking of what Ursa would have said to me if he could've back there." He replied to her. As their eyes met he could not help but want to stare into them forever. Her eyes were an alluring brown and gold and the longer you looked the longer you wanted to stay.

"Stop you fools, over here." Ursa beckoned as he flung one arm into the air to get their attention.

"Meath!" Nicolette whispered as she waived her hand in front of his face and he jerked his head back as he came back to reality.

"What, what is it?" He stammered as he looked around looking for danger, then back at her after finding none.

"Ursa is waiting for us over there." She said with a knowing smile and they started towards the gateway of a large, well-kept house that Ursa stood by with his arms crossed.

"What did I tell you Meath? I told you to keep your eyes open and watch me, you are too easily distracted boy!" Ursa barked as he waved the doorman over to open the gate.

"What do you want? We do not give to beggars, go bother someone else." The short, skinny, black haired man said as he came towards the gate.

"We are not regular beggars." Ursa said as he lifted his hood off and look up at the man.

"Oh my, Master Ursa I am so sorry for my insolence, I did not know it was you or else I would never have…" The man stammered out but was cut short.

"Yes, no need for that Adhar, just open the gate and bring us to Master Saktas." Ursa urged the man.

"Yes, right away Master Ursa." Adhar said as he opened the large metal gates and ushered them in while he ran out and made sure no one was watching.

As they followed Adhar down the flawless hedged path to the main doors of the mansion, Nicolette couldn't help but gasp at what she saw. Every bush and tree in the yard were cut and shaped perfectly like animals, some she did not even recognize. Though the yard was not as large as the royal garden, everything was perfectly placed to make the most of it.

"Padiel, come and see to Master Ursa and his guests things, put them in the nicest guest rooms we have, and make sure there's a bath waiting for them." Adhar yelled to the stable boy that was standing near the front doors flirting with one of the maids.

Adhar lead them up the stone stairs and through the large wooden doors, the intense smell of roses filled their noses.

"Wait here, I will go and fined the Master and tell him of your arrival, I am sure he will be very pleased to know you are here." Adhar said as he bowed his way out of the room.

Meath and Nicolette sat down on one of the davenports while Ursa stood pacing the room as they waited for Saktas to arrive.

"So who is this guy anyways?" Meath asked as he looked around the grand room full of expensive paintings and statues stretching his sore leg.

"He is an old friend that may be able to help us." Ursa replied while he examined one of the paintings on the wall.

"I recall my father talking about Master Saktas before, he is a well respected merchant in Draco. When my mother died it was Saktas who found the great sculptor, Zomen to make the statues of my mother." Nicolette said as she got up and started wondering around the room looking at all the different art.

"Yes that would be me." A rough, husky voice said as a man came through the doublewide doorway that Adhar had disappeared through. All three of them turned to see the tall, well built older man that stood before them, dressed in only the finest clothes.

"Ursa my old friend, it is good to see you." Saktas said as he cleared the gap between them and shook Ursa's hand in a way that neither Meath nor Nicolette had ever seen.

"This is not a social call Saktas, but a matter of great urgency." Ursa responded.

"I assumed as much old friend. I hear it is because of you that all those soldiers are in town. They say you killed King Borrack and kidnapped his daughter." Saktas laughed in a tone of knowing better then to believe what he had been told. "And I guess this young lady over here is Princess Nicolette?" He said as he looked over at her. She took her hood off so he could see her face. "Nice touch getting her passed the guards with that red hair, what did you use? The ruby berry?" Saktas said with a wide smile on his face knowing the trick well.

"It is true that the king has been murdered, but not by my hand. There is a great evil in Draco and I fear the worst kind of outcome." Ursa said as he starred into Saktas eyes making the man shiver.

"I see, let us not talk of such things here, let us go to where we can talk in private, but first you three can bathe and then we will eat, and you can tell me all about what's going on." Saktas said in a voice of realization that things were a lot worse then he had first thought.

~ ~ ~

"Captain Rift what brings you here?" The soldier asked while walking over to greet him and his companion with a salute.

"Where are they?" Rift yelled as he jumped down off his horse and threw the reins to another man.

"They have not come by this way sir, or we would have surely seen them." The man replied.

"What? You idiot they are here in Darnan, how could you not have spotted them? They couldn't have made it over the walls, that means they came through the roadblock." Rift screamed as he threw the man to the ground and kicked him in the gut.

"I don't understand sir we have not seen anyone that looks like them and no one in a group of three." The man begged as he crawled out of Rifts way.

"Well of course their not going to look like themselves, I know their here somewhere, we followed their tracks and they lead us here." Rift roared as he walked past the man and shouted orders to the other men that now gathered to see what the commotion was.

"What's going on here?" The commanding officer barked as he rode from the town to the gather of men that had formed.

"The assassins are here in Darnan you bloody fool, you were given one easy task and you could not even do it." Rift bellowed as he marched up to him.

"How do you know this for sure?" The officer asked, still not sure of what to make of the situation, but knowing full well of Rift's reputation and not wanting to have the man on his bad side.

"Because we followed them here by their tracks you moron!" Shahariel said as he too left his horse and came up behind Rift.

"Search the entire town and the towns outskirts. Leave nothing untouched, search every home and every street, every ally, and every man, woman and child. They are here somewhere and we will not let them go any further." Rift yelled so all the men could hear him. "We stop them here, ten thousand gold and a jump in rank to whoever brings them to me!"

~　～　~

After they had all bathed and had a new change of clothes brought to them, they met in Saktas's private meeting courts. They all ate their fill of meat, cheese and fruit, and Ursa explained to Saktas what had happened back in Draco castle and how they had managed to escape, making it to Darnan.

"My word, I have to say you three have been through an awful lot since last night." Saktas said as he got up from his chair and walked over to the stone fireplace, emptying his pipe in the fire. "I am sorry to hear that your father is dead, Princess. He was a great man and a damned good friend." He said as he bowed his head and placed his hands on the mantel.

"Thank you." It was all Nicolette could say, even though it had only been a day, it felt like ages since it had happened.

"So how can I help you Ursa?" Saktas asked as he turned around to face them. "Name it and if it is within my powers I shall see it done."

"We need an army so we can march in there and kill that bastard, Prince Berrit, or whoever the hell he is." Meath roared as he stood up, the pain in his leg had subsided a while ago and he could feel his gift coursing through him again.

"We need you too go to Draco and let Lord Tundal and Lord Dagon the truth of this matter." Ursa said, ignoring Meath's outburst.

"That's it? You do not want me to kill this man, this fake Prince Berrit?" Saktas said, confused as he walked back to his seat and sat down again, poring himself a mug of wine.

"No Saktas. He is strong with the gift. He is like no other I have ever encountered, just tell the Lords of Draco Kingdom the truth, but make sure they do not give themselves away about knowing this information. They must play along with this bastard until he can be stopped. I fear if we just confront him we will have a lot of dead men on our hands." Ursa said.

"But if we just kill him it will all be over and done with, wont it?" Saktas replied still not knowing why killing the false prince would not work better. "He cannot read minds that's impossible, so I say I just go there tell the Lords the truth, then we kill him as soon as we get the chance."

"I fear it will not be that easy my friend, this man does not seem to be a fool and there is still another that we have not identified, nor what part they play in this, or if there are more of them. We must root them all out before we act." Ursa said as he finished his meal and filled his mug with cold fresh water. He did not want to drink, he needed all his wits about him.

"Master Saktas, Master Saktas there are a large group of guards at the gates demanding to be let in." Adhar said as he ran into the room unexpectedly.

"What? What do they want?" Saktas asked as he stood up and went to the servant.

"They are here to search the place. They know Ursa and the others are here in the town." Adhar blurted out while trying to catch his breath. "They have orders to search everything."

"I see, well take Ursa and his friends to the escape tunnel I will go and deal with the guards." Saktas said as he patted Adhar on the back and turned to Ursa. "Well it seems my old friend that our visit has been cut short, as always. I will go to Draco and do as you ask, just promise me you will keep the princess safe until this is all settled. We don't need those damn Zandoreans ruling our country."

"I will my friend and thank you for everything." Ursa said as they shook hands again then started to follow Adhar down the hall.

~ ~ ~

"What do you want? Those you seek for are not here in my home. I would not harbour criminals. Who do you think I am?" Saktas snapped at the soldiers who now infested his yard, they had not waited for the gate to be opened, they simply broke it down and started their search as ordered.

"We have orders to search everywhere, Master Saktas." The soldier said as he ordered his men into the house.

"I can not believe this. Your brutes better not break anything that you cannot replace or afford." Saktas stated as he crossed his arms in anger, hoping his friends had made it to the tunnel by now.

After a few minutes one of the guards ran out carrying the princess's bloody, ripped nightdress and behind him followed most of the other soldiers that had entered his house.

"What is this Lord Saktas? Looks to me you have lied to us." The soldier said as he drew his sword and pointed it at his throat. "You two, arrest him, the rest of you continue to search the house and around the area. They may still be in there hiding." He said while he mounted up on his horse and Saktas was restrained and forced to follow him.

~ ~ ~

"Captain Rift, this man knows where the princess is. We found her night dress in his house and other signs that they were here" the soldier announced as he rode up to where Rift and the tracker sat eating and threw Saktas to the ground in front of them.

Rift jumped to his feet knocking the small table that was in front of him over as he ran to Saktas, heaving the man to his feet.

"Where are they?" Rift blared out as he shook the man like a rag. "Where!? I demand that you tell me, you are a traitor to the throne."

"I don't know what you're talking about." Saktas bellowed back as he tried to stand his ground as best he could through the violent shaking.

"Don't play dumb with me you fool, tell me what it is I want to know and I will spare your life." Rift yelled as he punched him in his midsection and let him drop to the ground.

"I told you I don't know what you are talking about." Saktas coughed and spit as he stared at the ground.

"Fine if that is how you want it, bring me a rope. You will die a traitor's death, you rat." Rift snarled as he kicked Saktas in the face and knocked him back to the ground while all the men around him cheered.

"What are you all standing around for? They are in the town now find them and bring them to me." Rift ordered to all the soldiers, while he was brought a long rope and a horse.

"Well? Will you not spare your own life and tell me where they are? Or would you rather…" Rift stopped his sentence and looked at the rope and back at Saktas with an evil grin.

"Death does not scare me and neither do you." Saktas spit at him knowing his fate was already sealed.

"You will regret that you foolish bastard!" Rift hissed.

"I regret nothing." Saktas answered standing to his feet with pride as he awaited his own death.

Chapter 4

Adhar lead the way with a torch through the cold damp, escape tunnel that Saktas had dug for escaping a barbarian attack or other enemies he might have encountered through his years. Ursa, Meath and Nicolette followed closely behind trying to stay as close to the light of the torches as possible for the tunnel had an eerie feeling to it. As they hurried through Meath had to give credit, it was well built with strong wooded beams and completely encased in good quality wooden boards. It must have cost a fortune to build and even more to keep those many workers that built it quiet.

Nicolette held on tightly to Meath's hand. She never did like the dark, or the things that might dwell in it. Every now and then he would look back at her and smile to assure her everything was fine. It upped her spirits a little more every time he did, she was glad he was with her and knew he would not leave her side.

"Meath!" Nicolette cried as she tightened her grip on his hand and pulled him to a stop.

"What is it?" He asked as he turned to look at her, then he saw and realized what the problem was. A large black spider was crawling on her shoulder.

"Hold still, its ok. This will only take a second." He assured her as he pulled out his dagger and flicked it to the ground. She exhaled and hugged him hard.

"Thank you, you've always been good at saving me from those creepy things." She said as she shivered at the thought of the creepy crawling arachnid.

"Will you two hurry up, we do not have all night." Ursa yelled back at them. They had stopped a few feet in front of them to see what the hold up was, and now waited impatiently.

Meath and Nicolette ran to catch up and tried not to slow them down again. Most of the way everyone was rather silent, the tunnel seemed to go on forever. They had been walking for two hours when Meath finally broke the silence again.

"How much further till were out of this foul smelling place?" he asked.

"Another mile or so." Was all Adhar said as he kept walking, his demeanour was as though the tunnel was no different then being outside.

Finally they came to a dead end, and Adhar pulled on a cord and a rope ladder fell from a hole in the roof.

"Well, this is it my friends." Adhar said a little excited, but with a hint of sadness for his task in their journey was over.

"Thank you, Adhar. I will not forget this, and tell Saktas I owe him one." Ursa said as he embraced the man with a good hug.

"You will be a half mile to the north from the road. There will be a small path that will take you most of the way and Saktas wanted me to give you this." Adhar said as he handed Ursa a large pouch of gold and silver coins and a pack full of dried meat, bread and cheese. Ursa took it and smiled. Saktas had always helped him out when he needed it, and now he needed it more then ever before. Adhar held the ladder while Ursa climbed up to the top and Meath closed the distance between them.

"Thank you for your help." Meath said, not sure what to say to the man he only met a few hours before, he seemed a little odd.

"Anything to help you on you way." Then he paused for a moment as he fiddled with something under his cloak. "My Master wanted you to have this, it was for his son, but when his son dead, he didn't have the heart to get rid of it. He always knew it would come in handy one day." With that said Adhar handed Meath an oddly shaped sword that felt a lot lighter then any sword Meath had ever held before.

"Give him my thanks." Meath said as he shook the man's hand and started his climb up, glad to be almost out of the damp, dingy tunnel.

"And for you your highness, my Master wanted you to have this. He found it on one of his adventures not to long ago." Adhar said as he handed her a small hand held crossbow, with a pouch full of small bolts for it. "The bolts are tips with a rare poison, so be careful."

"Thank you. I don't know what to say." Nicolette said as she leaned in and gave the man a small kiss on the cheek, which seemed to brighten him up. He held the ladder for her as she made her way up.

The opening at the top came out of a large old stump that lay in the middle of the dense jungle. They all filled their lungs with the fresh night air and were happy to be above ground again.

"I didn't know how much longer I could have taken that moldy smell." Meath coughed as he took in another deep breath.

"Here, everyone eat this. It will help you keep your strength up. We will not be stopping to rest tonight, we must keep going and get as far away as we can." Ursa urged as he handed out some dried smoked meat. They all ate quickly knowing Ursa wanted to get moving as soon as they could.

Meath pulled his new sword out of its sheath and looked at it. It was the most beautiful sword he had ever laid eyes on. The blade curved slightly upwards and was only sharp on one side. It was the same thickness and width the whole way down the blade. It was made from a metal Meath had never seen before. The hilt was dragon's wings, the head of the great beast rested on the beginning of the blade, the body and tail wrapped itself ever so perfectly around the handle. The handle was big enough to place both your hands on but it was light enough that you could swing with one easily. Never in Meath's life had he ever seen a better weapon, nor did he think he would ever hold one that matched this one. It felt so right in his hands as he swung it this way and that getting the feel for it. Meath knew that to craft such a sword must have taken years and only the finest materials and most talented blacksmith could have forged such apiece. And only the deepest of pockets to afford such a weapon.

"You will have time to play with your new toy later." Ursa said as he got up from the stump. He took Meath's old, jewelled sword from him and started to pry the gems out with his dagger and with the help of his gift a little to melt the gold holding them.

Meath put the sword back into its sheath, which he also had to admired for even it was perfectly made with black tanned leather with silver stitching that formed strange markings and symbols down both sides. He couldn't make out what they said for it was in a different language and the dim moonlight high above wasn't bright enough to study it much further.

Once Ursa was done getting all the jewels that he could get out he started to lead the way down the path. Meath and Nicolette followed behind as close as they could; the jungle was a bad place to be alone at night. You never knew what might be stalking in the dark or what snake you might stir while walking by. The path was grown in and hadn't been used in a long time, a few times they had to stop and find where the path continued.

Nicolette found Meath's hand again and their fingers entangled comfortably. She felt safe when she held his hand and she loved the way it made her feel, even in the deep jungle in the dead of night, when death could find them at any angle, she felt somewhat safe.

It was not long before they had reached the road and Ursa stopped them once again to catch their breaths. They had traveled fast through the woods so as not to run into any beast that might be lurking about and might try to make a meal out of the small party.

"We will rest for a few moments, but then we must get moving again. We will stay close to the woods encase we need to hide in a hurry. We will trust no one, and try not to be seen. Anyone traveling will surely be looking for us." He said as he pulled off his water skin and took a drink and then handed it around.

"It sure is humid out tonight." Meath moaned as he wiped the sweat from his brow and fought away the bugs that were buzzing around him.

They traveled long into the night and more then once had to hide from passing patrols and travelers that looked for them or would give them away for the reward that followed. Meath could tell that Nicolette was beginning to tire; she held onto his arm for support and was having a hard time keeping up. He knew she was not accustomed to all this traveling on foot for long hours on hard terrain like he was, but they had no choice but to keep moving. Even Meath was beginning to stumble around a little for it had been awhile since he had traveled this hard. Not since his days in the army.

"We will stop here so the princess can catch her breath." Ursa called back as he turned around and realized he was a fair distance ahead of them.

"I'm ok, I can keep going." Nicolette said but her voice and heavy breathing gave her away.

"We will stop anyways. I am not as young as I used to be and I need to rest my weary bones." Ursa said with a smile and a wink to Meath so she would not feel as bad.

"It's been awhile since I got this good of a work out." Meath yawned as he stretched his limbs. Meath couldn't believe how well Ursa could do this and not seem too tired at all, but he knew better then to question the wizard. He knew Ursa was always full of surprises and might be using a spell or potion to keep him going.

They did not rest long before all three of them stopped and went dead silent, straining their ears.

"Quickly, get into the trees, someone is coming!" Ursa whispered. The three ran into the over growth and sat in silence as they peered out on to the road to see who was happening by.

~   ~   ~

"Do you really think what everyone is saying is true?" A familiar voice that Meath thought he recognized said.

"Of course not you dolt, Meath would never have part in killing the king and taking the princess. Do you even listen to yourself when you talk?" Said another voice that Meath knew as one of his friends from the army.

"But why else would it all have happened, people just don't make up stories like that, and Meath always did have a thing for the princess, you remember? He always used to talk about her." Said the first voice again and now Meath knew for sure that it was who he thought it was.

"How could you ever think something like that of our friend?" Zehava growled as he slapped Dahak across the head, catching his friend off guard. "Smarten up Dahak. We know Meath better then probably anyone and I say something fishy is going on here with this whole thing. The story and facts don't add up or even make sense for that matter. No, something is wrong with it all."

"Ouch. Why do you always do that? It hurts ya know." Whined Dahak, who was now rubbing his head from the light blow he had just received.

"Good, that's the point and if you didn't want me to slap you think you would learn not to say such dumb things all the time." Zehava laughed as he looked over at his friend who was still complaining.

"It's ok they're friends of mine, they will help us." Meath whispered to Ursa as he climbed out from his hiding place and back onto the road.

"Stop you fool, it could be a trap!" Ursa called as he tried to grab him but missed.

"Holy shit!" Zehava yelled as he pulled back on the reins and stopped the horses just in front of Meath.

"Please don't kill us Meath, we are your friends, remember?" Dahak whimpered as he hid behind his arms and slowly peered out to see what might be coming his way.

"I'm not going to hurt you Dahak, how did you ever make it in the army with a girly scream like that?" Meath laughed as Zehava jumped down from the wagon and clasped his arm.

Zehava patted him on the back for a moment then pulled back. "Meath, are you a sight for sore eyes. Please tell me what their saying isn't true, you had no part in the king's death did you?" He asked almost afraid to hear the answer.

"Of course not Zehava!" Meath said, as he looked his friend in the eyes to assure him.

"Well we had better go and join them." Ursa groaned as he looked over to Nicolette and shook his head with a small chuckle.

"It's a trap get down." Dahak yelled again as he bailed off the side of the wagon and took cover behind the horses.

Zehava looked over to his friend and shook his head. "Will you relax, you are worse than my little sister, ya chicken shit."

Dahak slowly made his way around to where they stood and was still a little uneasy, but tried not to appear so by standing straighter.

"Sorry about that Meath, but with what everyone's been saying it just starts to make you believe it, ya know." He said with his head down, not wanting to look his friend in the eyes.

"So what the hell is going on?" Zehava finally said not being able to hold it in any longer. "In the last two days the whole country has gone ballistic and everyone is looking for you three."

"It's a long story, one better told when we are not all standing here in plain sight for someone to find us." Ursa said urgently as he scanned the road and woods.

"Oh of course, climb in the back, there's plenty of room, and no one will check back there cause we're part of the army." Zehava replied as he jumped back up to where he was sitting and waited for everyone to be seated so they could start moving again.

Once everyone was seated and ready Meath and Ursa told them what had really happened. By the time the story was done Nicolette was fast asleep on one of the wooden crates of arrows, she was using Meath's leg for a pillow and one of the tarps for a blanket.

"Well that all makes a little better sense from the rest of the rumours." Dahak said once the story was told, still feeling a little dumb for how he had acted earlier.

"It all sounds so unreal I can't believe what's happening, what the hell's going to happen with everything now?" Zehava asked, still shaking his head in disbelief at what he had just heard.

Ursa sighed. "I wish I knew, all I know is our best chance is to get to Dragon's Cove before the news travels that far and hope that Saktas tells the other lords of what's really happening."

Dahak slapped Zehava shoulder. "You had better tell him."

Zehava sighed and looked back at Ursa. "I hate to say this but Saktas won't be making it to tell the lords."

"Why the devil not, what happened?" Ursa said as he stared at the young man waiting to hear what he had to say.

"Well we just came from Darnan after dropping off some supplies, they found your old clothes when they searched his house. They hung him in the court yard for everyone to see that he was a traitor." Zehava managed to finish saying. Ursa sat back, closed his eyes and went silent. "He is still hanging in the main square as an example for what happens to traitors." Zehava finished, though wishing he had bitten his tongue on the last part.

Everyone sat there for a long moment not sure of what to say or do.

"Is he going to be ok?" Dahak asked waving his hand in front of the wizards face.

They rode in silence for a while, no one was sure what to say, for the news of his friend seemed to hit the old wizard hard.

"So what have you guy's been up to since I last saw you?" Meath asked trying to change the subject and lighten the mood a little.

"Not a hell of a lot now that I think of it, just moving supplies for the army, we're taking this down to the river cause there has been a large amount of barbarian attacks down there, and they are going to try and go in and end the threat before it gets to out of hand." Zehava answered.

"So Meath you're a wizard now, you should show us something." Dahak asked with wide eyes his head bobbing up and down like a child being asked if he wanted candy.

"Ya I've only ever heard stories of what people with the gift can do I've never seen it first hand." Zehava piped in excited to see as well.

Meath looked over at Ursa who still had his eyes closed and didn't say anything. "Ok, I guess there's no harm in that." Meath held out his hand and a small orb formed in the middle and slowly grew into a ball of flames. His two friends just sat there starring into it with their mouths hanging as far down as they could go.

"What are you doing you darn fool!" Ursa snapped, and the ball of fire that rested in Meath's hand crackled out and disappeared with a loud bang, which was loud enough to wake Nicolette. "I told you not to waste your powers, and what do I find you doing? Showing off in front of your friends like some cheap jester. By the Gods, do you not realize what kind of mess we are in? We can not afford to waste any strength or advantage we've got!" Ursa barked in frustration and anger.

"He didn't mean anything by it Master Ursa." Dahak said trying to help, but the wizards just turned his attention to him and glared at him angrily, until he turned back around and sat in silence.

"I hate to interfere but we're coming up to the next town." Zehava said hoping not to anger Ursa anymore with the news.

"Good, can you get us in without getting caught?" Ursa asked while he slid back behind a box and waited for an answer.

Zehava just smiled. "Of course we can, they won't look in here, I know everyone."

"Once we're in, take us somewhere that no one will be around, we cannot be seen." Ursa said as he covered his head with a tarp. Meath and Nicolette were already hiding under a tarp on the floor.

~ ~ ~

Zehava pulled the wagon up to one of the less used stables; he was still a little shaky from getting passed the guards. He motioned for Dahak to check the area and to come back when it was safe for them to get out.

Dahak returned moments later. "It's clear, everyone is either asleep or at the tavern getting drunk."

Zehava opened the back and helped them out. "I'll go ask the stable master if you guys can stay in the hay loft for the night."

Before he could go far Ursa stopped him "No we will just hide while in there, no one can know we are around." Ursa stopped and grabbed two gold coins and gave them to Zehava. "Tell him you two will be bringing some ladies around tonight and would like some privacy till morning." Ursa said with a wink.

Zehava smiled and nodded his agreement and ran off to see to it. Meath helped Dahak tend to the horses and got their feed ready while Nicolette stretched and walked around in the barn to get her legs from being so stiff. Soon Zehava was back with the ok that the stable master would let them have their privacy in the top loft with no questions as long as they kept it down.

"We must leave as soon as we can in the morning the sooner the better." Ursa told the two soldiers, who he knew would be sleeping in the barracks so no one would think anything odd.

"No problem Ursa, we will be here just before the sun comes up, but we had better go check into our sleeping courtiers, if were not there someone might come looking for us." Zehava said as he and Dahak started off into the centre of the town.

When the two were out of sight Ursa turned to Meath. "Are you sure they can be trusted? That Dahak seems like the type that might talk if the pressure was on him."

Meath looked hurt that he would say such a thing. "I wouldn't have climbed out and stopped them back there if they couldn't be. We all trained together and fought together, they are as trust worthy as you'll find." Ursa just nodded his head as he walked into the barn and found the ladder that led to the loft.

"We had better get some sleep; tomorrow will come fast and trouble may come faster." Ursa yawned as he held the ladder for Nicolette and Meath.

~ ~ ~

Ursa woke early the next morning, the sun had just started to break through the darkness from behind the mountains and the mist was just starting to lift from the ground. The air smelled so sweet from the light rainfall they had had during the night. He got up and walked over to the window in the far corner of the loft and looked out at the small town. Only a few people were up and out feeding their livestock this early. He sighed, he hoped going to Dragon's Cove was the right answer and hoped that once they were there with the help of Lord Marcus, they would find away to over come the false wizard prince and all this treachery. He had already lost two of his good friends; he didn't want to have to jeopardize anyone else's life. Though he feared many more lives would be lost before this was over and that many more problems lay ahead.

Meath woke to the smell of ruby berry; he opened his eyes to see that Nicolette had closed the gap sometime during the night and now was asleep right beside him. Though she had washed most of the dye out of her hair the fragrance was still there. He smiled, even in sleep she was beautiful. Meath slowly got up and moved off the stack of hay they had used for beds, making sure not to wake her. He looked over to the window and saw Ursa looking at him with a half smile half grin on his face and didn't know what to make of it. It was a look he had never seen before. A look a father would give to his son after doing something remarkable and proud.

"What is that look for?" Meath asked as he stretched and walked over to him. Ursa just turned around and looked back out at the town and breathed in deeply.

"Answer me, what was that look for?" Meath asked again a little more eagerly this time. But he knew the wizard was only going to toy with him.

"Ever wonder why things happen the way they do and why?" Ursa asked without taking his eyes from the window.

Meath shook his head; he hated it when the wizard used riddles. "Well of course I do but what does that have to do with my question?"

"Everything and yet nothing." Was all Ursa said.

"You know you really need to start just saying things in english and not in riddles all the time." Meath argued in defeat.

"One day you will understand my boy, that I just did answer your question in english." Ursa laughed as he started towards the trap door to the loft, just as he reached it there was a light knock from the bottom and Ursa removed the lock and open it. Dahak peered in for a moment then said. "Ok we're ready to go."

"Make sure you bring the wagon around as close as you can so we can get out of here with out anyone seeing us." Ursa reminded him.

"Will do sir… I mean Master Ursa." Dahak answered and hurried down the ladder to see to the task.

Meath woke Nicolette and helped her down from the stack of hay and then helped her pick out the small pieces left behind in her hair.

"Its time to go, you can sleep more on the way." Meath said as she smiled at him sleepily. She had almost forgot they were running for their lives. She had been dreaming of her and Meath's childhood when they lived carefree and would play in the garden for hour's everyday.

~ ~ ~

It was not long till the group was making fast time down the road towards the army encampment by the river, it wasn't more then half a days ride till they would be at the river crossing. Though none of them knew yet how they were going to make across without being seen. There was only one way across that was safe and even that wasn't always a guarantee not to mention they had to pass right through an army encampment to use it.

But Ursa didn't care if he had to light the place a blaze they would make it across one-way or another.

Meath stared out the back of the wagon and watched as they past by all the trees and noticed they were slowly becoming less dense and the different species the closer they got to the Sheeva river. Even the wild life started to change instead of monkeys he started to notice squirrels and other small, hardwood creatures.

Dahak reached into one of the leather bags on the side of the wagon and pulled out a half of loaf of bread and a block of cheese, hr cut it up and handed it out to everyone.

"It's not a lot but it will have to do for now until we get somewhere that we can get more supplies. Maybe we can get some in the Sheeva rivers encampment. Though I highly doubt that, I am guessing we are gonna try and be through there as fast as we can like we did the last small town." He said as he hungrily tore into his meal. They all ate slowly for now that they didn't have to hurry it was nice to actually taste the food.

"So how do we plan on crossing the Sheeva River anyways and get through without being killed?" Zehava asked while he drank from his water skin.

"We? Once you get us to the camp you will do as you were ordered to do and deliver these supplies. We will find a way to sneak across on our own." Ursa said sternly.

"What do you mean? We can't come? You need us!" Zehava argued.

"We could use their help ya know Ursa, the more of us there is the better our odds if we run into trouble again." Meath added in a matter of fact tone.

"The more of us there are the harder it will be to hide and not be noticed." Ursa replied calmly to Meath as if he should have known that was coming.

"Ya I think Master Ursa is right… uh… we should just let them out a bit before we get there and do our job Zehava." Dahak said shyly expecting another slap from his friend.

"No way! I am sick of this delivery boy shit, and I sure ain't gonna let my friends go off into this kind of danger without my help." Zehava barked back, growing tired of this. "This is much more important then what we are doing now."

Ursa looked squarely into his eyes sternly "You will do as you're told understand?"

"No, I will not back down, this is just as much as my kingdom and my problem as it is yours!" Zehava fumed angrily at Ursa. "This is my princess and my future as much as it is anyone's and fate brought us together for a reason and I'll be damned if I will be treated like a kid. You're going to need all the help you can get on this."

"He's right Ursa, he has a right to help save his kingdom, that is what he was trained for." Meath put in, stopping Ursa from saying something.

"Holy shit, what in the nine hells going on up there?" Zehava yelled as the others came up front to have a look at what he was seeing. They were still a few miles away from the camp but the sky was full of black smoke and it was coming from where the camp was located.

"It must be under another attack." Dahak cried as he drew his sword and looked around expecting something to jump out at him.

"We must get there as soon as we can." Zehava yelled as he slapped the reins down hard on the horses and they sprang into a full galloped.

Nicolette gripped her small crossed bow in one hand and her dagger in the other as she felt fear start to grip her again. So this was what it was like to rush into the heat of battle she thought.

Meath noticed Nicolette's hard grip on her weapons and tried to ease her mind with a small smile, but knew that would not help, the closer they got to the camp the more intense the smell of smoke and death became.

They stopped the wagon just out side of the encampment walls, the gate had been burnt down from constant flaming arrow and torch attacks. There was a horde of half charred half butchered bodies all around where the front gates use to be of both the defenders and the savages. Though they could tell the savages had lost a lot of warriors weakening the gates to get through. Nicolette gasped in horror when she climbed out and saw the sight, it made her stomach cringe as she fought back the urge to vomit but couldn't hold it for long.

"It looks like we're too late." Dahak coughed for the smoke and smell of burnt flesh was overwhelming and made everyone's lungs burn and eyes water.

They all walked in to the camp with weapons drawn and ready to fight, but the place was a barren wasteland now. The only thing that moved was the smoke as it slowly drifted up into the sky being wisped away by the light breeze. Even the ravens and other scavenger birds hadn't even shown up yet, the battle had just ended moments before. Once they had gotten to the centre of the camp they knew for sure it was too late, the battle was long over and it didn't look like there were any survivors; at least none that had stuck around.

"Meath, Zehava you go check out the north side see if anyone's alive and try to help if you can, and try to find out what happened here. The rest will come with me to the south to do the same." Ursa sighed as he tried not to look at the slaughtered bodies. "Meet back here in ten minutes, and if you find anyone alive that can't be helped, you know what to do." Everyone knew what had happened, the barbarians had attacked while the fort was weak and low on supplies and it looked like they had attacked in full numbers, not just a small party.

~ ~ ~

Meath and Zehava walked through the burnt rubbish to one of the far sides of the camp and found nothing but bodies of many. When they reached the barn they both stopped and had to turn their heads from the sight before them. All the children and women of the camp were nailed to the walls of the buildings and had had their body whipped and burned and left for the crows the bodies that lied on the ground were the husbands and fathers that had been forced to watch before they too were brutally killed.

"This is maddening!" Zehava screamed as he fell to the ground and vomited from the smell and sight, his head had gone dizzy and his legs weak for even in the battles he had seen never in his life had he seen something like this.

"Who could do such a thing?" Was all Meath could say. Though he knew Barbarian tactics were less then human, they knew well the art of pain. They continued down the barren, blood soaked road being careful not to step on the chunks and pieces of flesh that scattered the ground. They followed the red road that lead to the other far end, there was no one left alive and they both knew it. But they kept going in hopes of find one of those bastards that had done this or one person that had been able to hide.

Once they had gotten to the end of the road they saw something that made them even more sick to their stomachs where the cooking fire's were now had people tied to the spits and were roasting over the fires and from the twisted expressions left on the bodies they knew they had been alive when they had been place over the flames.

"I can't believe this, why... how could they have broken through? There were almost three hundred men at this camp." Zehava cried as he tried to take in what he was seeing.

"I have no idea, my friend, but we had better get back, maybe the others found someone and know more." Meath said trying to take the sight in himself. Never in his whole life had he every seen such massacre and gore such as this.

They started their way back when all of a sudden Zehava fell to his knees and his hand went to his neck.

"What is it?" Meath asked when turned around and got closer to see if his friend was all right.

"Run." Was all Zehava could say before he fell to the ground in a heap. Then Meath saw the small wooden dart sticking out of his neck.

"Damn it!" Was all he managed before another dart hissed out and caught him in the shoulder, and he too fell to a heap and into blackness.

Chapter 5

Meath woke with his face to a cold dirt floor and his hands bound tightly behind his back. He shifted to his side and sat up, the drug was still flowing through his veins and it made him sway a little. So many thoughts assaulted him and swirled in his mind.

"Nicolette!" Meath moaned barely loud enough for him to hear.

Meath's eyes began to focus and he saw Zehava was laying a few feet away. Meath looked around his new surroundings for the first time. They were in a small, bared cell that was in a larger wooden building with many other cells like theirs. Everything they had had been taken off of them, only their clothes remained.

"Zehava wake up!" Meath urged as he crawled to his friend on his knees, trying hard to keep his balance as he gave him a shove. Zehava moaned and started to come around a little.

"What the hell is going on, where are we?" He groaned as he too slowly sat up and shook his head to try and clear it from the drug.

"I don't know, we must have been caught by the barbarians is my guess." Meath whispered, he did not know who might be in the dark room with them and he didn't want too. Meath closed his eyes and concentrated hard on summoning his gift and burnt through the leather straps that held his hands, and then quickly untied his friend while keeping an eye out in case anyone was coming.

"What's the plan?" Zehava asked as he rubbed his wrists and worked the blood back into his hands.

Meath stood up; the cell roof was just high enough for him to stand under. He went over to the bamboo bars and looked around, there seemed to be many cells just like theirs but he could not make out if anyone was in them are not.

"So let's do this, use your powers and let's bust out of here." Zehava said as he stood beside him. Meath grabbed the bars in his hands and closed his eyes, the wood started to smoke as he burnt them from under his hands. Then he pulled and with a small snap the two bars broke.

"Man I wish I could do that! Think of all the fun we could have had back when we were younger." Zehava said in awe as he worked his way through the gap that was just big enough to squeeze through. Meath went next scanning the area with every step.

"Ok now, let's try and find something we can use as a weapon." Meath said, but Zehava was way ahead of him and had already found a long bamboo pole, which wasn't being used for anything.

"Already found mine." He said as he swung it in the air a few times to gain a feel for it.

Meath looked around found a large branch that would work well enough for a club. "Well it's not a sword, but it will work now to get out of here." Meath said with a sigh.

"I wouldn't try to escape if I were you." A voice said from one the cells in the far corner, both Meath and Zehava swung around in shock that someone else was there. They walked over to the cell and looked in.

"And why not, I'd rather die out there then in here." Zehava said well he peered in at the ragged figure.

"You won't make it. They won't kill you if you stay here, you'll just be put to work, and if you're a good worker you will be treated well enough. Sometimes they even let me out to run around a bit." The man explained almost excited at the thought of is short escapes. They could tell he had been a prisoner for a long time by the scars all across his chest, back, and down his arms.

"I'm not going to be no one's slave." Zehava said to him, disgusted that someone could just give up on freedom so easily.

"We will free you and we all can leave here, we stand a better chance as three." Meath said as he grabbed the man's bars.

"No don't do that!" He screeched. "I've have tried to escape before and this is what happens." He whimpered as he held out one of his hands, missing three fingers on it. "You will never make it out, no one ever does."

"You don't really want to stay here do you? We can make it if we try." Meath asked again, not sure why the man would not at least a chance at freedom.

"You will see." Was all he said as he crawled back into the far corner of his cell and started rocking back and forth, off in his own world.

"He's nuts, he's lost it." Zehava chuckled under his breath to Meath. "Forget him man, he wouldn't do us any good out there anyways."

Meath looked at his friend and shook his head. "No, you're right, he's been broken. No matter, we will get out of here, there ain't no way I am going to end up like that."

They both went over to the doors of the building and peered out the small cracks in the wood. There were four guards that stood twenty feet away with spears and axes. Beyond the guards was what looked to be a small village, Meath counted everyone he saw, women and children included. The barbarians trained their women and children to fight along side with them so their numbers were much greater in times of war.

"I counted twenty six." He whispered.

"This might prove harder than we thought." Zehava whispered back.

"If we stay together and kill fast I think we can make it, we'll run for those trees over there and from there we just run for our lives and stay together until we find a place to lay low for a while." Meath said as he pointed to the forested area not far from them.

"Ok my friend, it's now or never I guess." Zehava replied with a crazed look on his face showing he was ready for a fight.

Meath kicked the doors open, called his gift and a flash of light collided with the first two guards at the entrance. They crumbled to the ground, spewing blood from the gaping wounds created and calling for help in their native tongue with their last breaths. The other two guards hooted and hollered as they ran towards them, weapons held high and ready to strike. Zehava ducked under the swing of one of the guards and smashed his pole into the back of his legs, dropping the man to his knees. Reflexes based purely on instinct, Zehava reversed direction and connected with the man's skull, not enough to kill the man but enough to slow him down. Another came around the corner, Zehava caught the man in the neck with a mighty blow that sent the man fumbling back until he tripped over a log and collapsed, his windpipe crushed.

Meath was still engaged with the first guard, which was taking way too long for his liking. He could tell the man had many seasons of fighting behind him, but the moment came when Meath saw an opening and took it with a great swing, Meath's club exploded into the man's face, shattering his jaw and cheek bones. With the guard out cold, he quickly gathered his thoughts and moved on.

The two started running towards the tree line but stopped short as they made it around one of the huts. There in front of them stood three dozen barbarians with bows and arrows knocked and pointed straight at them. Beyond them was at least six dozen more, training with swords and axes that they had stolen from the dead soldiers back at the river encampment. For a few moments there was only silence as the barbarians almost seemed worried.

"This isn't good!" Zehava said as he gripped the bamboo pole hard in his hands, not sure of his next move.

"No, I think this would be where we give up." Meath said back to him as they both lowered their weapons slowly, hoping not to startle the bowmen. One of the barbarians walked out from the group yelling at them in a language neither Meath nor Zehava could understand.

"You think they're going to kill us now?" Zehava asked as he followed the man's finger and went to his knees.

"I think they would have done that already if they were." Meath said through a gulp as he too went to his knees.

The man that had walked towards them now screamed at them face to face while he picked up Meath's club and raised it high and the air, chanting. In one mighty swing it all went black…

~ ~ ~

"I couldn't find them anywhere." Dahak said as he walked up closer to the wagon, kicking a small rock on the ground in frustration.

"We know they were ambushed over on the far corner of the encampment." Ursa sighed pacing back and forth in front of the wagon.

"How do you know that for sure?" Dahak asked scratching his head thinking that if they had figured that out, they should have come and found him.

"We found their tracks and followed them to where they ended." Nicolette sobbed; she couldn't believe what had happened when Ursa had told her. She felt so alone now that he wasn't there to protect her.

Ursa walked up to her and put a comforting arm around her. "It is alright my child, we will get them back."

"What? Ok who took them?" Dahak cried as he ran his hand through his short brown hair pacing around in a circle, his eyes raced back and forth from Ursa to Nicolette.

"There must have been some barbarian scouts left here to see if reinforcements would come and when they did how many there would be. Where their tracks ended this is all we found." Ursa said as he held out a small wooden dart, with barbarian markings on it.

"Well what are we doing here we have to go after them, lets find their trail and find them!" Dahak shouted as he looked at the wizard and started to think of what might be happening to his friends.

"Calm yourself, we will go and find them but we had to wait until you got back." Ursa scuffed as he shook his head at him. "You do know what this means right Dahak?" Ursa asked unnervingly.

Dahak stood there a moment not sure of what he meant. "No, what?"

"It means we are going to where they took Meath and Zehava, which is also the same band that took out this camp, which means we are going against an enemy far greater by number and strength than us." Ursa said with a wink.

"Hey… hey…" Dahak stammered for a moment. "Zehava and Meath are my best friends and have saved my ass more times than I can count. I know they would come to help me if it was the other way around." Dahak said surprisingly calm. "So if hordes and hordes of barbarians are what we find and have to go through to save them… then so be it!" He finished with more then a little fear in his tone but still he stood tall and committed.

Nicolette just stood there not sure of what to do are say. Her heart ached at the thought of what those savages would do to him, she had seen the things they did to the people here, the pictures still flashed through her head. The urge to fall to her knees and cry was all she wanted to do, but she had to be strong… for Meath and Zehava.

"We cannot stay here for much longer; troops will be arriving any-time now to see what's going on. We will pick up their trail if we can, but they are very good at hiding their tracks." Ursa said as he started to search through the wagon for useful things.

"Well I saw a food market that's not too badly damaged over there, I will go and find what I can that will not spoil so we have more food." Dahak replied as he ran behind a still burning building.

"What if he's already dead?" Nicolette asked Ursa not wanting to know the answer, as tears again welled up in her eyes.

"My child, if they were planning on killing them, we would have found their bodies and not this dart." He said trying to ease her fears, though he wasn't so sure he believed his own words.

Nicolette slowed her breathing a little before she mustered up the cour-age to ask. "Then what will they do to them?"

"I do not know for sure." Ursa lied, he knew they would become slaves and if they did not break or submit to their new masters orders they would be killed and eaten or much, much worse. But he did not want to worry the girl anymore then she already was. He just hoped Meath had the sense not to use his powers, and could hold out until they could find them. Or else they would be as dead as the men and women of this camp.

~   ~   ~

Meath woke again but this time he was not on a floor like he expected, he was suspended above the ground by his hands, which were tied to a large wooden beam in the centre of a large round hut. He looked around, looking for Zehava, but there seemed to be no one in the room with him. The room was almost totally empty other then a large wooden table in one corner which was covered with deer hide, and a fire pit a dozen feet from where Meath hung. There was a small hole in the centre of the roof that allowed fresh air in and smoke to travel out. He looked down to the ground which he hung above by a few feet, there was a white powder in a five foot circle all around him with weird symbols and crafted pieces of wood and clay that were made into odd shapes and symbols. Some looked like small people, as others looked like strange beasts.

"Well I'm not going to hang around here all day." Meath said to himself as he tried to burn the leather that was holding him to the roof. A sharp pain coursed through his entire body, it felt like fire flowing through his veins, and his screams could have awakened the dead. The pain lasted a few moments after he stopped trying to burn the ropes. He almost blacked out from the searing intensity of it and it left him disoriented and convulsing.

"You will find your powers are no good to you now, wizard. That circle guarantees it." A man said so very calmly as he walked into the hut. The man was tall and slender and was wearing a brown leather loincloth with a large white tiger skin draped over his back. The tiger's head rested on the man's head while the front paws were pinned together across his chest leaving the back claws to scrape the floor as he came closer.

"What the hell is going on, where is my friend?" Meath yelled, but he was too weak to sound very threatening.

"Your friend is of no concern to you now, believe me you should be much more concerned about yourself. As for your other question, you have the gift, and I want it!" The man said with a hiss and an evil glare.

"What? You're crazy, that's impossible." Meath laughed, knowing full well that it was an insane suggestion. That was one of the first things Ursa had taught him, that one's gift could never be transferred to another.

The man looked him in the eyes with a deadly sure smile. "Oh I assure you it can be done, and you will soon know how, of course you will never be able to try it, for after I am done you will not survive the ordeal." Meath stared at the man he truly seemed to believe what he said and Meath was starting to believe him too.

"Who the hell are you anyways, you maniac?" Meath questioned, trying to keep his cool and not give the fact that he was truly terrified away.

The man paced the room not sure whether he should answer the question or not. "Who am I? I am one who should not be taken lightly."

"What? Are you afraid to tell me your name? You're pathetic!" Meath spat down at him, but it did not seem to faze the man, he just smiled and kept pacing.

"'I'm pathetic', says the one hanging from the roof, unable to do anything." He laughed as he walked over just out side of the white circle.

Meath knew it would not do much good but he did it anyways, he threw his legs up and tried to kick the man in the face, but the man just side stepped and laughed a mocking laugh, as he watched Meath swing back and forth. It was a big mistake, the leather straps had tightened from the effort and hurt his wrists even more.

"What is in a name anyways? I guess it really doesn't matter if you know, you won't live long with that information. So if you must know it is Kinor." He said as he walked over to the table and pulled a large knife and small bowl out from under the blanket. He came back over to Meath and smiled as he slammed a fist into Meath's abdomen, knocking the wind from his lungs. Then he grabbed a hold of Meath's leg and cut deeply into the back of his calf. The blood soaked through Meath's pants and started to drip to the ground and into the small bowl Kinor had placed.

Meath's arms were starting to burn and the feeling of helplessness was beginning to consume him. His thoughts raced as he tried to think of something he could do to get down, if he could only get free he could show this Kinor what damage he could do.

"You bastard! When I get down from here you're going to pay for this." Meath yelled as he tried to kick him again but to no avail.

"Well I hate to leave since things are just getting good, but I have to prepare for the ceremony that will be taking place tomorrow night, you have until then to hang there and try to get away." The man laughed as he picked up the bowl of blood and left the small hut without so much as a glance over his shoulder.

Meath hung there from the beam, his mind raced at what to do, but as long as he was in this circle there was nothing. As the hours went past and the sunlight faded away, his thoughts brought him to Nicolette. He wondered if she was ok. He knew Ursa wouldn't let any harm come to her, but the ache in his heart from not knowing grew by the minute. He wondered where they were and if they were going to try to save them, or if they thought he and Zehava were dead, and just continued across the river to Dragon's Cove. He shook his head. He couldn't lose hope, for hope was all he had now. The cut on his leg kept bleeding for many hours, until it healed over to a scab. But he had lost a lot of blood and now the wooden floor below him was stained with it.

~   ~   ~

Zehava sat in the cell beside the one him and Meath had escaped from earlier and wondered where they had taken his companion. He groaned as his stomach grumbled from hunger, wondering if they were even going to feed him. It had just gotten dark outside and Zehava wondered if Meath was even still alive.

"I told you, you two would never make it." The man in the far cell said as he moved over closer to him.

Zehava sighed. "Yes well I guess you were right, do you know where they would have taken my friend?"

"He has the gift; they will have brought him to the ceremonial hut, for purification." The old man said as he swatted at some flies that were buzzing around him.

"Purification? What the hell are they going to do to him?" Zehava asked as he got as close to the man as he could so not to miss a word.

"Kinor will take his essence and grow more powerful. He has never been able to prefect it but he is sure it will work this time." The man told him as he caught one of the flies and ate it.

"What that's nuts, that's impossible, what will happen to Meath once it done?" Zehava barked, as he feared for his friend.

"The ceremony will surely kill him, it always does." He laughed as if Zehava should have already known that.

"Shit! Meath what have we gotten are selves into." Zehava muttered to himself wishing Meath were there to help think of something to get them out of this mess.

"Don't worry, you will not be killed if you do not anger them again and try to escape. The only thing I can tell you is do as they want and things will go easier for you. I tried to stay strong when I was first caught but it did me no good." The man told him with a serious tone while nodding his head up and down.

Zehava sat back against the bars of his cell and put his head between his knees and asked. "When will this ceremony take place?"

"It takes a day to prepare for so tomorrow night sometime." The man replied with no compassion.

Just then the doors to the building opened a few feet and a girl walked in with a large pot and two clay bowls. She walked past Zehava's cell.

"Ah supper time, thank you Shania." The man said as he took the bowl full of stew and started to pour it down his throat, not even caring that is was still very hot. Then she walked over to Zehava's cell and knelt down and looked in at him. He crawled over to the bars, he didn't cared if the food tasted bad, he would eat anything right about now. But she did not pour him a bowl, she only stared at him smiling, like a child would to a new pet.

"Don't I get any food?" Zehava asked, more begging then anything as he looked over at the pot of stew. It smelt so good it made his mouth water and stomach growl.

"When I am ready to give it to you, you may have it." She told him with an accent that wasn't as barbarian as he would have guessed. She continued to smile at him. Zehava was taken back by the fact she could speak his language but he guessed with all the slaves they have caught they would have picked up on it.

"So what do I have to do to get some of that food?" He asked her as the thought of just grabbing the pot was in his mind. It was close enough he could grab it and spill as much as he could onto his floor before she could stop him, but he held off on the urge. He knew she was going to toy with him and make him beg for it, she was a savage and he was the enemy.

"I haven't figured that out yet." She paused and thought of something then asked. "What is your name?"

"My name, what does that matter?" He replied not sure where this was going.

She sat down on her knees and it looked as if she planned to stay a while. "Cause I want to know the name of my new slave."

"What! I am no ones slave!" Zehava growled angrily at the suggestion.

Her smile grew and she laughed a little. "Yes you are, my father just gave you to me. You're a very interesting slave too, and cute. I hope your good cause I would hate to have to have my father whip you."

Zehava's eyes widened a little as a new level of fear coursed through him. He had only heard stories of what the savages did to their slaves and after seeing what they had done to the man in the other cell, he knew the stories were true.

"So tell me your name." She asked again, still with a polite girlish tone. Zehava figured he had better tell her so not to anger her, for at the moment she seemed to like him.

He sighed as he submitted. "My name is Zehava."

"I like that name, sounds strong and warrior like. I guess I won't change it, I was going to call you Tork, but Zehava is good." She giggled. Zehava guessed she had to be about fifteen or so and was surprised at how different from the rest of the barbarian women he had seen and heard of.

"One more question and I'll give you a little food. What's it like where you came from?" She asked as she crossed her legs and leaned in ready to hear what he had to say. The whole time she didn't take her eyes off his, he began to think he might be a little more than just a work slave.

"Well we don't have slaves for one thing." He stated as his eyes stared hungrily at the food.

"That's not what I wanted to know, but I'll give you a half a spoonful for effort, you'll get more if you tell me what I want to hear." She teased as she put some stew in his bowl and handed it to him. He gulped it down greedily, it was better then he had first expected, and helped take the sting out of his gut. He knew if there was any chance of him escaping he needed to have his strength up, so he decided he would have to play along with her game.

Zehava sighed as he told her what Draco looked like and explained to her what it was like there. He never knew he would feel like this talking about his home, but knowing if he didn't he would starve seemed to take the joy out of it and made him feel like a true slave.

"It sounds so wonderful there I wish I could go there one day." Shania said as she filled his bowl with stew.

Zehava's mind raced as he thought he might have found his ticket, if he played his cards right he might have a chance. "Well I would be glad to take you there one day maybe; it would be great to have someone to share it with." He hoped he hadn't over done it, but she just giggled again and looked at him all the harder.

"Do you find me pretty?" She asked him as she tilted her head slightly. With the moonlight that shone through the cracks in the jailhouse he got a better look at her. She had bright red hair that shone in the moonlight like fire and emerald green eyes that seemed to pierce right into his soul, and a slender figure that was very well toned. Even if she hadn't been beautiful he would have told her what she wanted to hear, but he had to admit she did have a strange appealing look to her.

"I do, you are very pretty." He whispered just loud enough for her to hear, he could tell she was blushing.

"Do you want to kiss me?" She asked after only a moment of silence. She edged a little closer to the cell, moving the pot so she could be as close as possible.

Zehava couldn't believe what was happening, he had the strangest feeling that he wanted to kiss her, and he didn't know if it was simply to get a chance at regaining his freedom or for the chance to kiss her. "I do." He said as he leaned in closer, their lips touched and parted just slightly, she put her hands through the bars and pulled his head closer.

"What the hell is going on in here?" A large, red bearded man screamed furiously, he was now standing at the entrance with a vicious looking whip in his one hand and a fierce look on his face.

"Father! I was just playing with my new slave." Shania said with a scared tone in her voice as she backed away and grabbed the pot of stew and got up. He didn't seem interested in what she said as he just glared straight at Zehava with a burning hatred.

"Go home now Shania, I have to break in the new slave and show him his place in his new world." He yelled at her in their native tongue, but didn't take his eyes off Zehava.

"No father, he doesn't need to be broken in, he will do as I ask him too." She cried trying to spare Zehava the beating her father would surely give him.

"I said go home!" He yelled at her again as he slapped her hard and she fell to the ground, dropping the pot of stew. She looked back at Zehava with tears in her eyes as she stood up and ran out of the building whimpering.

The man stared long and hard at Zehava, with an icy, dark glare. It seemed like forever before the man moved towards him. Zehava could feel a lump well up in his throat as the man let the slack from the whip hit the dirt floor.

"Well slave, looks like I came in just at the right time." He said in a cold tone that made Zehava's heart want to stop. Zehava could smell that the man had been drinking. "Thought you could take advantage of my daughter did ya? I will teach you for such shit." He slurred through his teeth as he opened Zehava's cell, and cocked the whip back.

Zehava flinched as the first blow caught him across the leg and tore through his leather pants into his flesh. He knew he was in for one hell of a beating, and there was nothing he could do but take it. He doubted with the distance between them that he could reach the man in time to do anything but get even more of a beating. The man didn't say another word as he whipped Zehava, he just kept whipping him as hard as he could. Time seemed to stop, the only sound was the crack of the whip, each time it found Zehava and licked another part of his tender flesh and slashed it open. Never in his whole life could he remember being in so much pain and being so afraid. All he could do was curl up on the floor and hide his head while the man whipped his back and legs in rage.

Zehava didn't notice when the man had stopped hitting him, his body had become numb and cold. He laid there in a puddle of his own blood and tears, and stared blankly at the flies that buzzed around and fed on it. What seemed like hours passed before he had the strength and courage to move, afraid that the man might still be watching him, although he had left long ago. Zehava dragged himself into the far corner of his cell and curled into a tight ball and whimpered himself to sleep.

He woke with a moan as something soft and wet touched one of his fresh wounds. Tears welled up in his eyes, as he feared to look at who was there with him.

"Its ok, I'm not going to hurt you." The familiar voice of Shania whispered to him, while she stroked his blood soaked hair back and cleaned his wounds on his back and legs. "I can't believe he did this to you, I never thought he was going to stop." She whispered to him as she helped him sit up and start to remove his tattered shirt. Zehava moaned in pain as the shirt dragged across his flesh and re-opened the wounds on his back.

"I am sorry it hurts, but I must clean them or they will fester and get infected." She said so soft and gently that Zehava figured it must be what an angel would sound like when you die. He almost wished he hadn't woke up.

"I did not scream." He said as his head began to spin again and he fought to stay conscious.

"I know." She whispered back, knowing full well that warriors pride themselves on never screaming or begging for mercy when at the hands of an enemy no matter the pain they are put through.

It seemed like it took her forever to clean all his wounds, but once she was done she applied a sweet smelling paste to them which made them tingle and took a little of the sting out of them by numbing them all together. She laid him back down and rested his head in her lap as she fed him more stew to help him get his strength back. As she helped him eat she hummed a soft melody that in itself helped relax him, the song seemed to help ease the pain.

Between mouthfuls he asked her, which took more strength then he ever though mere words ever could. "Why are you helping me like this?"

"I don't know." She paused. "I have never met anyone like you before, and since I first saw you tonight I've had this strange feeling coursing through me." She stayed silent for a while. "When I first saw you and looked into your eyes I saw something I've never seen before. Something that feels so wonderful and fulfilling, it just makes me want to be around to help you." She stopped getting caught up in what was racing through her mind.

"I must get out of here." He groaned as he tried to sit up, but couldn't his head fell back into her lap.

She went silent for a long time as she caressed his head with her soft touch. Zehava looked up at her and saw tears streaming down her face. "Would you take me with you?" She asked as she looked down at him. Zehava could tell she was serious and in her eyes he could see something but didn't know what it was. It could have been concern for his well being or fear for what her father might do to her if he caught her here with him again, he didn't know, he didn't care.

"Yes." Was the only word he could muster at the time. Her eyes gleamed, and her beautiful smile returned as she slowly got up and covered him with a blanket she had brought. She kissed his forehead lightly and climbed out of his cell, closing the door behind her.

"I can't leave without my friend." He moaned as he rolled over to look at her. All she did was nod her head and then scurry out the door and off into the darkness, leaving Zehava alone again.

~ ~ ~

Meath had tried to sleep but couldn't, his arms hurt so much and his stomach would not let up while the cut in his leg throbbed. He had no idea what was going to happen to him and that alone frightened him, what if what the mad man had said was true? Of course it didn't matter, he knew he was dead either way. He had prayed to the Creator to make sure Nicolette stayed safe, he had prayed for her before he prayed for Zehava or even himself. He wondered if he would ever see her again. He had not tried to use his gift again since the first time, he never wanted to feel that kind of pain again and he knew trying would not help. Meath wondered if Ursa knew that such a circle existed that could block one's powers. He looked up at the small hole in the very top centre of the hut and seen it was still quite dark out. He never had felt so helpless in his whole life then he did at that moment. Meath looked up at the hole in the roof again and saw someone looking down at him. He thought it might be Death coming to take him away.

"Who's there?" Meath whispered, wondering what trouble he was in now.

"Shhh." The figure whispered back as it climbed in through the hole and on to the beam and sat down above him.

"Who are you?" Meath asked. As the slender figure came closer, he could see it was a young barbarian girl.

"My name is Shania. You aren't as cute as the other one." She giggled softly.

"What other one? You mean Zehava, you've seen him, is he alright?" Meath asked almost to fast for her to understand.

"Yes, I kissed him, but then my father caught us and beat him, he is not well." She said back as tears began to well up in her eyes.

Meath was not sure what to make of the first part, but he understood what "beat him" meant.

"What is going to happen to him?" Meath asked not sure what else to ask, he didn't know what was going on.

"For one who has a worse fate, you sure ask a lot of question about your friend. Nothing bad will happen to him again... I won't let my father do that to him again, that's why I am going to free him." She said well she laid down on the large beam and stared down at Meath.

Now Meath was really confused to what the hell was going on. What the hell did Zehava do to this girl, it must have been one hell of a kiss he thought to himself.

"When are you going to free him?" Meath questioned.

"Tomorrow night, he says he will not leave without you, but I do not know how I can save you too." She sighed while she tried to think of a way.

"What? You can't just leave me here, un-tie me and take me to him and we can all leave tonight!" Meath pleaded as he swayed in the air.

She giggled again. "You look so funny hanging from there like that. He is too weak to travel tonight, he needs time to rest. I will save him to-morrow night like I had planned. Well everyone is waiting to see if Kinor's ceremony works, that's when I can slip him out of here."

"Un-tie me please, you can't leave me here." Meath begged knowing this was his one chance and he didn't want it to slip away.

"Sorry can't do it, I need you to stay here so tomorrow night I can get him out. I can only save one of you, not both. I have already thought about it and there is no way." Shania whispered to him as she sat back up apologizing and started to climb back up through the hole.

"No wait come back, please don't leave me here." Meath yelled after her, but it was too late she was already long gone.

Meath hung awake for the rest of the night wondering if there could have been anything he said that would have changed the outcome of his encounter with the savage girl. He figured she had already made up her mind before she had come to see him. At least Zehava would get out, Meath thought as he pondered his own fate. Still nothing came to mind, he was doomed, but if was going down he was going to do it well.

The sun had been up for a few hours when Kinor came into the hut, with a small bag of items that he was going to use for the ceremony Meath guessed.

"Ah, I see you are still awake, didn't sleep well last night?" He asked with a mocking laugh.

Meath ignored him as he watched him walk over to the large table and pull the blanket off to reveal what was underneath. There were small and large knifes, some curved some as small and as thin as they possible could be without breaking when stabbed into human flesh. Beside them were eight metal symbols attached to long metal rods, Meath knew what those were for. The man then started to pull from his bag small pouches of herbs and powders and placed them on the table. Once he was done he called out in the savage tongue to someone out side. A large man carried in a big metal pot full of red-hot coals. Meath's heart began to pound hard in his chest as Kinor placed one of the metal symbols into the coals and sprinkling one of the pouches of herbs on the fire.

"And what the hell do you plan on doing with that?" Meath barked already knowing the answer.

"Every two hours you will receive one of the Dark Ones symbols, one on each of the bottoms of your feet, another on each of your palms, two on your chest, one on the small of your back and the final will be on your forehead at midnight." The man said in a sickening tone as if he was going to enjoy doing it. Meath closed his eyes and begged for the Creator to help him out of this somehow.

"Would you like to know the rest of what will happen to you?" The man asked eager to tell Meath, knowing full well it would torment him.

Before Meath could even reply Kinor started to tell him. "First I will drink a cup of your cold blood, which I got from you last night, then a cup of your warm fresh blood. Then I will begin to burn the Dark Ones symbols into your flesh and in-between each symbol I will chant and pray to the Dark Lord until each symbol is burned into your body. Then I will cut out your tongue, your eyes, your heart and most of your brain using your own blade." As he said that he pulled out from behind him Meath's sword. "Then I shall turn them into a paste and eat them while I chant the chant of the Dark One. Afterwards, I shall receive your powers and knowledge to help strengthen my own."

Meath stared in horror at the mad man, he could not believe what he had just heard.

"Well, there are a few other small details to what will happen but those are less amusing aspects of it." Kinor chuckled as he called in his native tongue again and the large man that had carried the pot of coals came in again and ran over to Meath and grabbed his legs and held them tightly. Kinor pulled the symbol from the coals and walked over to Meath, and seared it into the bottom on his right foot. Meath held back the urge to scream and cry out for he didn't want Kinor to have the satisfaction.

"There that wasn't so bad now was it? You didn't even scream, I like that, nice and quite." Kinor said as he walked back to the table and replaced the symbol where it had first been.

"I'm going to kill you, you bastard." Meath growled as his foot pulsed in agony and tears ran down the side of his face. His stomach cringed at the smell of his burnt flesh.

"Now, now there, you know as well as I do there is nothing you can do to me." He said, his tone shifting to a less pleasant demeanour. Meath just spat at him, hitting his leg. Kinor wiped it off and motioned for the man still holding Meath's legs. His fist connected hard with Meath's ribs and a loud crack echoed off the walls around him.

"Do that again and I will show you true pain boy." He hissed as he stared angrily at him. "Leave us now, but do not go far. I may need you again." He told the large man.

Kinor then took a larger pouch off the table and poured black sand around in a circle a little smaller then the white one around Meath. Once he was done he drew the symbols that he was burning into Meath in the sand and placed a very strange statue in the front of the circle closest to Meath, then sat down in the centre of the circle and started to chant an odd melody.

Meath assumed the statue was of the Dark One, but he didn't understand what everything else was for, nor did he want to. While Kinor chanted, Meath prayed to the Creator. The chant grew louder and more intense with every moment, then it would slow again and start all over. Time dragged on forever while Kinor chanted and Meath hung there helpless. When the chant finally stopped, Kinor got up and got another symbol off the table and placed it in the coals, sprinkling another herb over the glowing embers.

"Maybe you'll scream this time." He said with a sinister laugh as the man that held Meath came back in and grabbed a hold of his legs again. Once again, Meath was branded with another symbol of the Dark One, but he did not scream.

"Very well done, but you will break before this is over and even if you don't, it will not change the outcome." He said as he sat back down in his black circle and began to chant again.

It was the same routine each time Meath was branded with a new symbol, and each time Meath didn't scream and Kinor would compliment him and go back to chanting. Meath didn't know what would get him first; the agony of the burns or the mad mans droning chants.

Meath was beginning to see that nothing mattered anymore. The outcome would be the same. He was going to die by the hands of this lunatic; the only thing that brought him comfort was knowing Zehava would be freed, that they both would not die here.

The increasing pain from the brandings blurred Meath's thoughts, exhaustion was slowly over powering his senses. As Kinor's chants became more intense and alive, so did the pain in Meath's body. It felt almost like his soul was being tortured along with the body with each chant and tone from Kinors melody. Meath shuttered at the thought that maybe the

Keeper was here helping this savage shaman. He pushed the thought from his mind and tried to centre himself off somewhere else where the pain could not find him.

It grew late into the afternoon and the sunlight was beginning to fade. Meath only had three symbols to go until that part of the ceremony was over. But this time it was slightly different. Kinor stopped chanting and heated up the next symbol, but before he burned it in to Meath's chest, he carved an X in the centre of his chest where the next burn would go. It was the same for the following symbol and the chant changed to more of a mad howling.

Meath wondered if Zehava was free yet or if the savage girl would wait until midnight to free him. Meath had just less than two hours to live and for the last two burnings he thought of nothing but Nicolette and how he would never get to see her beautiful smile again. He remembered the last time he had seen her at the wagon, she was so terrified and disgusted by what these savages had done. He was glad she would never see what they had done to him here. He just wished he could tell her how much he cared for her one last time.

Meath had become so weak from hunger and the burns he could barely move, but it didn't matter anymore he knew he would not get away when they took him down to finish the ceremony, he was as good as dead and he was almost ready to except it, he was almost ready to embrace it.

Chapter 6

Zehava sat in his cell waiting for Shania to return for him, she had only stayed for a short while when she fed them lunch, for her father had been watching her by the door. She had attached a note to the bottom of Zehava's bowl, which read.

"*Be ready to leave just before midnight.*"

Zehava was still very weak and extremely sore, he hoped he would be able to do what had to be done to get out. Every part of him ached with pain from the wounds, but the paste that Shania had applied the night before really seemed to be helping. He tried to stand but the pain shoot through him like daggers and he fell to his knees, fighting back tears again.

"I had better not do that again. Better to save my strength until it's time." He moaned to himself, as doubt started to consume him. He knew it would take everything he had to be able to move, he hoped she didn't expect him to run the whole way. He shook the thought away. He would do whatever it was he had to do to get away; he had to for Meath and Shania's sake, as well as his own.

He wondered how Shania was going to get Meath out of the ceremonial hut without being caught. From what it sounded like he would be heavily guarded. It didn't really matter as long as she could and the three of them could escape, if they couldn't he was sure they would not surrender. This time he and Meath would die fighting.

It had just begun to get dark when the man from the other cell was brought back; they had taken him before Zehava had awakened. He thought it was strange that they had left him there and not made him work today, but after the beating he had received last night, he guessed they didn't want him to die before they had at least gotten some work out of him. He knew if he was going to be ready tonight he had better get as much sleep as possible. It didn't take long for him to fall fast asleep in his condition.

~ ~ ~

Zehava woke a few hours later with the sound of the door to his cell being opened. He rolled over slowly so he didn't reopen his wounds to see Shania standing there with a leather bag full of supplies. In her hands were also all of his things that the barbarians had taken from him when they had first been caught.

"You got my things back, thank you." He groaned as he gripped his sword in his hands, it felt good to the touch. The metal handle was cold on his hand but soon warmed under it. He slowly stood and Shania helped him steady himself as he strapped on his sword belt. She carried his other things, the sword itself was almost too much extra weight, but he felt better knowing it was there again.

"So how do we get Meath out of the ceremonial hut?" Zehava asked while he looked at her as she helped him out of his cell, for he was not very steady on his feet. Then he noticed that she didn't have any of Meath's things and was wearing a disappointed look on her face.

"What's going on here, why don't you have any of Meath's things?" He barked weakly at her, trying not to waste what little strength he had.

She looked at him with tears in her eyes. "I can only get you out of here. Your friend is the distraction we need to leave without any problems."

"What! You plan on letting him die? How could you? I told you I'm not leaving without my friend!" Zehava said angrily as he pushed her away and pulled his sword out and started for the door. He collapsed a ways away from it. The pain from moving so fast had torn some of his wounds open again and had almost made him black out, but he fought it back and forced himself up again, his anger helping to fuel him.

"You will never save him, all the warriors are waiting outside and around the hut he is in." She begged him as she ran to his aid and tried to help him up again.

Zehava turned to her and glared. "I will not leave my friend here to die. He wouldn't leave me, no matter the risk."

"Once again you try to escape, this time with her, you'll get her killed too. Don't drag her down with you." The man from the cell yelled as he shook the bars of his cell. "She is a good one not like the others, do not take her away from me… I need her." He yelled out loud but only Shania and Zehava heard him.

"Silence, I can make my own choices." She yelled back at him icily and he shrank back down into the far corner whimpering.

"Where is he being held?" Zehava asked coldly.

"It may be too late already, you'll never save him. Let's just leave, you and me, we have a chance he doesn't." She begged again while trying to grab his hand in hers, but Zehava pulled it away and almost fell again. "You don't understand, we'll all die if we try and save him."

"Where is he?" Zehava yelled again not wanting to hear anything else.

She walked him over to the doors and pointed across the village to a small hut where everyone in the village now gathered around, it was the same hut that Meath and he had made it around before they were caught again.

"How many are there in your village?" He asked, not that it mattered. He knew it would take a miracle to save his friend, but he had to try.

"There are seventy-two, there were many more but after the battle at the river we lost well over half our army. You can't even stand on your own how do you plan on beating all of them?" She cried to him in a saddened tone, knowing if he attempted what he planned, he would be lost.

He didn't say another word but opened the doors to the jailhouse and started to walk out towards the crowd with his sword in hand. It took every ounce of strength to keep up right as he fumbled over to them. The night air helped clear his head a little, but started to tighten his muscles almost right away. As he neared the group he thought to himself, what he should yell before he ran to his death.

"Prepare to die you savage bastards!" Zehava coughed as loud as he could, while he steadied himself with his sword pointed in the dirt. The wounds that had re opened now dripped blood onto the ground and stung fiercely, he hoped they would not toy with him and just kill him fast. He also hoped he could take at least one or more of the monsters down with him before he met his maker.

The group, which waited out side of hut, turned and watched as Zehava stood there with his sword in his hand. They all started to howl in laughter, one man stepped out and challenged him with just a small dagger while he mocked Zehava's pathetic attempt to threaten them. The group howled louder while yelling taunts, some even threw small rocks at him trying to knock him down. But Zehava stood his ground. He wanted to die well, not on his back helpless.

Zehava lifted his sword, held it tightly in his shaking hands and took a step forward as two massive balls of flame flew from behind the large group of savages and hit their cluster with a huge explosion that sent a great deal of them flying through the air, some in flames and some already dead. The explosion blew many others face down into the hard ground, while the bodies of the ones that had been hit fell burning onto their comrades, injuring and killing even more. The blast caused Zehava to fall back and hit the ground hard. The man that had challenged him ran towards him with his dagger held high. Zehava looked up just to see the man fall dead with two arrows sticking out his back. He looked over to where the crowd of barbarians had been and swore he saw Dahak in the midst of them swing his sword franticly, killing as many as he could before they realized what was happening or could get up off the ground. Then he felt a hand on his shoulder as he turned to see Shania pulling him away from the battle.

~   ~   ~

Ursa held up his hands and arcs of light struck another large group of savages that were frantically searching the scene, still wondering what was going on, they didn't seem to know if this was part of the ceremony or not, their screams were deafening. Nicolette stood beside him with a dagger in one hand and her small crossbow in the other. She fired into the crowd of barbarians that were running this way and that trying to find out where the attack was coming from. It was not hard to hit a target and the poison on the arrows didn't take long to slow and kill. Ursa summoned another great ball of flame as a small group of archers formed by a mud hut notched their arrows to fire at them. He released his flame before they could aim their bows, it impacted the small group sending pieces of them every which way and killing them all.

Dahak ran this way and that slashing everything that moved, he was covered in blood and wanted nothing but more. He had never been so afraid in his life and yet so full of life, but he didn't care, he wanted his friends back. He turned just in time to see two savages come at him with spears levelled, he threw his sword as hard as he could and it landed with a thud in one of the barbarians chests, then he side stepped another thrust and caught the man with his dagger in the back, he pulled the bloody knife out with a twist, gore poured freely from the fresh wound as the man tried to crawl away, but Dahak finished the savage quickly by slashing his throat. He quickly picked up the fallen man's spear and threw it at another barbarian coming his way, but missed. The man ran towards him with his axe in hand and a savage war cry. Dahak closed his eyes realizing his time had finally come; he was actually surprised he had lasted this long in the battle he decided he would die in with a smile. A few seconds passed and nothing happened, he opened his eyes when he heard a thud and felt something hit his leg. The man laid dead a few feet in front of him with one of Nicolette's arrows in his back, his axe had just grazed Dahak's leg and hadn't even made it through his pants. He didn't waste any time retrieving his sword, prying it quickly out of the gurgling mans chest and began fighting again. By now the enemy was a lot more organized and he was beginning to tire and realized he was taking his fair share of cuts and gashes from the battle.

~ ~ ~

"What the hell is going on out there?" Kinor bellowed as he was holding the last red hot symbol in his hand about to burn it into Meath's fore head, which hung down from lack of strength Meath had lost all hope of stopping the ceremony and no longer fought against them.

"Go check and see what the commotion is all about." He yelled to the large man that had helped him through out the ceremony. Meath was barely conscious and hadn't even heard the attack that was happening outside, he could only hear Kinor's deep frantic breathing and twisted chant.

The man returned seconds later. "The camp is being attacked!"

Kinor turned around and barked "What? By who?"

"There is a wizard and a girl. I did not see anyone else but there must be an army out there for the camp is in ruins and there are bodies everywhere." He huffed as he grabbed a knife from the table and stood by the door waiting to be told what he should do.

"Damn it I am almost done. Well, well looks like those people you were with are trying to save you." He laughed as he lifted the symbol up again, but stopped as he heard a thud and a twang and a piercing pain shot through one of his shoulders, which caused him to drop the branding rod. He turned around and there was Nicolette trying to re-load her cross bow. His helper lay dead on the floor with her dagger in his chest.

"You little bitch." He yelled as he cleared the room and slapped her before she could reload. He hit her so hard that she spun around and crashed to the ground.

"Don't think this is over, we will meet up again boy." Kinor yelled as he pulled out the arrow and threw it to the floor as he ran out the door.

Meath hung from the beam forcing himself not to black out while he looked down at Nicolette's form on the ground. He wished he could get to her and help her. He started to wonder if she was even there? He wondered if he was already dead and this is what you saw in the after life.

"Meath." She said weakly as she pulled herself off the ground and looked up at him. "What have they done to you?" She cried out as she ran to him. He tried to lift his head but he couldn't, he had no strength left. He just stared down at the floor and the white circle that had held him there. She stared up at him in horror as she saw all of the burn marks, cuts and blood covering his limp body.

Nicolette grabbed his sword off the table and cut through the leather ropes that had hung him from the roof for the last day and a half. He fell to the earth with a crash, and laid there, out cold. Nicolette lifted his head and cradled him as she cried, thinking he was dead.

Ursa and Dahak soon ran into the hut and saw Nicolette cradling Meath's limp body. Ursa saw the white sand circle that she was laying in and cursed under his breath.

"We are too late." Dahak cried, also thinking Meath was already lost.

Ursa ran over to Meath, but made sure not to go inside of the circle and felt for a pulse. "No, he is still alive, just very weak. We have to leave here, we can't hold them off much longer."

Just then a young barbarian girl ran into the room and Dahak put the tip of his sword to her throat and stopped her in her tracks.

"Please don't kill me. I am here to help." She whimpered as she looked at them franticly.

"What? Why the hell would you help us, we're the enemy?" Dahak barked confused, looking back at Ursa to see if he should kill her.

"Your other friend is outside waiting for you, we brought horses." Was all she said as a reply, fearing for her life. Dahak looked out the door and saw Zehava swaying like a branch in the wind on a horse waiting for them.

"She's not lying, Zehava is out there." He said to Ursa and Nicolette with a smile.

"Good, grab Meath and get him on a horse, let's get away from here as swiftly as we can, we have got what we came here for, there is no need to over stay our welcome." Ursa said as he helped Dahak carry Meath out to the horses. They had only been in the camp for a few minutes and already it looked as if a mass battle had taken place, some of the huts had already caught a blaze and a great deal of barbarian bodies scattered the large opening in the camp, the smell of battle was thick in the air as was the smell of death. Dahak used one of the fallen savage's blackened bodies as a step to help him throw Meath on to the horse, while Ursa continued to wreak havoc on the enemy to keep them at bay.

The young savage girl was already mounted behind Zehava and he looked just as bloodied and beaten as Meath did. He had no shirt on and Dahak could see the whip marks and cursed under his breath.

"Follow me." The savage girl yelled to them when they were all mounted up. They did without question, Dahak rode along with Meath so he could keep him on the horse, and Nicolette rode behind Ursa and held on to him for dear life.

As they followed Shania down the small path that was just big enough for a horse, two barbarians rode hard after them and made easy time catching up with less weight on their horses.

"We have trouble behind us." Dahak yelled to Ursa as he held on franticly to Meath's bouncing limp body.

Ursa turned and looked back, he was already weak from using a great deal of his powers to kill so many and he did not want to waste anymore then he had to. He still had to try and heal the two. He flung his hand back towards the on coming warriors and a strong gust of wind collided with them and sent them flying off their horses to the ground hard.

~ ~ ~

"We finally lost them." Dahak bellowed tiredly as he came back from searching the area.

They had ridden the horses almost to death before they found a spot they could camp for the night that would be safe and well hidden. Now the small party sat around watching Ursa work what healing he could do on the two that were so close to death's icy grip.

"What the hell were they doing to him?" Nicolette cried as she sat there starring down at Meath, hoping he would be all right.

"Kinor was trying to take his gift." The savage girl said while she sat on the other side of Nicolette beside Zehava.

Ursa sat between the two young men, holding their hands in his. He concentrated every ounce of strength and power he could into the task at hand and was not paying any mind to what was going on around him. The cuts and burns on both the two men's bodies slowly began to heal and the scars too began to fade away in front of everyone's eyes. Ursa's body began to shake uncontrollably as he focused even harder. The wounds began to heal slower then they had at first as his powers began to weaken. Before all the wounds had been healed Ursa had blacked out from the effort, his mind could no longer take the strain.

"What happened to him? He's not done healing them." Shania yelled as the few wounds that were left on Zehava's backstopped closing up.

"He used everything he had to help them." Nicolette whispered as she stared down at the one remaining burn on Meath's chest just above his heart, everything else had healed but that one.

"But he's not done." She whined as she started searching through the leather bag she had with her, pulled out a clay container and started applying a white paste on Zehava's few remaining wounds.

"Is he going to be alright?" Dahak asked Nicolette as he knelt down beside her and looked at the three sleeping bodies.

She sighed. "I hope so, Ursa just needs rest, then he will finish healing them in the morning before we leave."

Dahak retrieved the blankets that they had brought with them from the wagon and covered the three figures that now lay in the middle of their camp. He prayed they would have no problems tonight, everyone was tired and the strongest of their group were unconscious. They would be sitting ducks.

"So who are you anyways and why do you speak our tongue and why the hell did you help us?" Dahak asked the young girl that had not left Zehava's side since they had met. He picked at the dried blood that covered him. He hadn't even realized that many of his own wounds were serious and should be healed as well. It didn't take Nicolette long to realize it too as she helped him clean and wrap the deepest wounds.

Shania didn't take her eyes from Zehava's form. "My name is Shania and I can speak your tongue because I learned it from the slaves my people had taken in battle. As for why I helped you, I did not do it for you." She paused. "I did it for him."

Nicolette and Dahak were a little taken, but chose not say anything.

"Well we thank you for your help." Nicolette said, wondered if she should. "It must have been hard for you to help us with what we were forced to do to your people"

Shania started to cry for a few moments then calmed herself enough to reply. "They are only half my people, my mother was of your race, she was a slave, my father took her to his bed and has hated me every since I was born, I am a half breed and was not a son." She stopped and just stared at Zehava.

Dahak stood there silently not sure of what to do are say. "Well I had better go and stand watch." He said after the last of his injuries were treated as best they could be for what they had and he slowly backed up and went off into the night.

"I am sorry to hear that." Nicolette said to her, then started searching through a bag and found a loaf of stale dusty bread and a few apples that Dahak had found in the ruined encampment by the river. She handed Shania some and it took her a few moments but she finally took it.

"What do you have to be sorry for? You were not conceived by rape and hated and beaten because you're not of pure blood." She snapped as she bit into the apple still not taking her eyes off of Zehava.

Nicolette knew she had better change the topic, she didn't fully trust their new companion and didn't want to anger or sadden her anymore then she already was in fear of what the outcome might be.

"What happened to Zehava?" She asked, after she finished her apple and lifted Meath's head a little to pour some water into his dry mouth. He coughed and spit most of it back up but some had gotten down. Then she handed it to Shania and she did the same for Zehava.

Shania sat quietly for a while before she answered. "My father caught us kissing and beat him for it, I thought he was going to kill him." After she had said that she leaned down and kissed Zehava's brow and wiped the sweat from it with her shirt.

Nicolette was surprised that the girl had taken so fast to Zehava and was willing to give up so much for him so soon. Nicolette had so many things she wanted to ask, but figured she had better wait until morning, they had all had a long day and night. Both of them fell asleep beside the two battered men holding their hands through out the night, while Ursa was still in between the two out cold.

~   ~   ~

Dahak watched from a distance and knew it was all up to him to be the look out and make sure all was safe. Though he soon realized that if they were attacked in the night they would all likely be killed. He stood with his back against a large tree staring off into the night, as thoughts of the battle flooded back to him. He couldn't believe it had all happened, he couldn't believe that he had survived, that any of them had. It was all so much so intense, so alive and so fulfilling. As he remembered everything, his adrenaline began pumping into his system again, helping him stay alert and awake.

Chapter 7

"Sir, another rider just came in from the East with news that another town was massacred." A young soldier huffed as he came into the library swiftly.

"Another one? That makes fourteen." Lord Dagon bellowed while running his hands through his hair in frustration.

King Dante paced the length of the library with an angry look on his face. After the first three towns had been sacked, all the lords had been called for a meeting, even the eldest of sons. Through the last two days riders kept coming with bad news of another town, village or army encampment that had been ran sacked and pillaged by savages. They had all been in the library for hours this morning trying to come up with something that might make sense to all the resent attacks and find some sort of pattern so they could determine where to set up a counter attack.

"The attacks don't seem to be patterned or of anywhere of major importance, they looked to be random attacks so far Sir's." The young soldier reported knowing full well that was what was on all their minds.

"Those savages are up to something, they had never attacked like this before." Dante said thinking out loud as he rubbed his chin almost forgetting anyone else was in the room with him. "They are using tactics not common for their race."

"But how...? And where did they learn such tactics?" Lord Zefer stammered to everyone in the room.

Tundal slammed his fists into the table and burst out. "We must do something! We cannot just stand by and have our country fall to the hands of those bastards."

"But what? We can't stop what we can't find. Once we know where they are we can kill them, but they seem to be moving their camps every few days and they're not in large groups, they only group up when they're going to attack." Dagon sputtered. Everyone was stressed to their limits already and it was slowly getting worse as tensions grew.

"We need to send all our armies further out and in larger group's to root these bastards out and finally put an end to this once and for all." Dagon's oldest son Ethan commanded.

"We cannot divide our army until we know what we are up against. If our forces are run thin when the time comes we may not have enough men to stop them, and whatever they might be planning." Prince Berrit said as he put his head into his hands and ran them back through his hair. Since there had been no one else and he was going to be the new king of Draco, the lords had granted him the right to help rule Draco. The country needed a ruler now more than ever and he and his father, King Dante were all they had.

"Who's to say they are up to anything other then the usual raids and pillaging?" Lord Andras asked coldly as if he could not believe that mere savages could be so intelligent. "They have made attacks similar to these before. They're mindless savages and they've just gotten lucky in attacking our weakest points. They have yet to take anything of great value."

"Of no great value? I should cut out your tongue. Hundreds of my country men have been slaughtered." Dagon growled angrily. "So don't you go and tell me we have lost nothing of value."

"Most of them have been poor farmers and peasants." Lord Bartan's son Edroth said carelessly.

Ethan jumped from his seat yelling. "Well maybe here we value a man's life beyond that of the size of his wealth."

Dagon grabbed his son's arm and pulled him back down to his seat but gave him an approving wink.

"If only Borrack were still alive, he would know what to do." Dagon muttered as he leaned back in his chair and crossed his arms.

"Well he's not! Stop thinking of things that you know will not help, he's dead and we are not, but we might join him if we don't stop this out burst of barbarians soon." Berrit hissed as he glared across the room at him.

"Stop it! Fighting amongst ourselves is not going to solve this problem or make it go away, we must work together on this." Dante yelled as he spun around and stared at everyone. "My son has the right to rule until the princess returns and they wed and make it official, you all agreed and signed the document. The rest of us are going to have to leave and go back to Zandor to make sure this hasn't happened to our kingdom, if those savages are attacking here and have not yet started it there, they will soon.

Zandor is weakened with myself and the rest of the lords being away. We will leave in two days, but until then we will help with the problem here as best we can."

"Once we have found where they are gathering you can send a large force out to stop them, you have the strongest and most battle hardened warriors from your kingdom here at Draco Castle. I have already sent my best scouts out to help search for them and I will leave them here until they are no longer needed." Lord Bartan said looking almost concerned.

"I too have sent out my best to help in the search for these murderous bastards." Zefer also replied.

Tundal sighed. "We thank you all greatly for your help and advice, but I ask you again; leave half the men you came here with so we can start to send out bigger patrols to unearth these groups so that we might rid ourselves of this headache, and be at ease in finding our beloved Princess and your future daughter in law."

"I have already told you, I will leave only a hundred, that's the best I can do, we still need to make it back to Zandor and with war breaking out, the roads will not be safe travel. I will not jeopardize my family." Dante said as he stopped pacing and turned his attention to the crowd sitting at the table. He had been racking his brain at how he could help more, but didn't know how. Until he knew what was going on back in Zandor he could spare no more men.

"You have a massive army of a few thousand strong camped out side of the city, six hundred that you've already dispatched to help root the barbarians out and a hundred more that are in groups looking for the princess. I think you will be safe enough, there can't be that many savages out there." Lord Andras muttered with a curse, he was tired and they had been here all day and still hadn't come up with anything other then what would have been done considered obvious at the start of the morning.

"I believe they're doing this to make us consider there are more of them, just to scare us into making the wrong choices so they might stand a chance." Zefer's son Zeke finally put in, he had been holding back, hoping he wasn't going to sound like a foolish child.

"I fear the worst, I sense something very wrong with what's happening. I have sensed it since the king was killed." Tundal moaned rubbing at his temples.

"We will get her back, they will find her. Rift is out there, he will bring her back. If not him, one of the groups of men we sent will get her back." Dante said, though now was beginning to wonder if she was even still alive. Nothing like this had ever happened before, a king assassinated and the only heir kidnapped, leaving the country in turmoil. Though they had tried to keep the princess's disappearance from spreading to the city and town folk of the country, they were sure it would leak out sooner or later if it hadn't already.

"We all want the princess to be returned safely and she will be, but that is not the matter at hand." Berrit cut in, knowing if he did not stop this talk it would go on long into the evening. There was nothing they could do about her kidnapping that wasn't already being done. "How many soldiers are in the whole kingdom?" Berrit finally asked.

"There are a thousand that are battle hardened, and fourteen hundred that are not in Drandor that can be ready to ride as soon as I give the order." Tundal answered, knowing full well it would take at least a week for a rider to get there and deliver the order.

"Mandrake has eight hundred battle hardened and a thousand not, which will also be ready as soon as the word is given." Dagon said as he watched everyone around the table wondering where this was going and hoping Berrit had an idea.

"And what about Dragon's Cove, does anyone know?" Berrit asked the lords, but it was not them who answered him.

"I was there last summer to train, last I heard they had nine hundred hardened and four hundred not." Ethan replied. "But I don't know now, most of them have come here with the princess."

"That means eight hundred are left in Dragon's Cove, with an army like that we will not be stopped, we will stop these savages, there can't be that many savages in the whole world." Berrit roared hoping to lift their spirits a little.

"If they continue to attack like this there will be no one in the kingdom left other then soldiers and what good does having an army do if we can not find the enemy? They have already killed hundreds of people in the last two days." Dagon barked.

"This just doesn't make sense, why are they going after small towns that don't have anything to do with food or supplies? The only places they have hit so far that matter to food and supplies are the army camp by the Sheeva River and the smallest camp that guards the boarder to the wastelands." Lord Bartan said.

"It would be easier to come up with something if this was our own land but its not, you Lord Tundal and Lord Dagon should have better knowl-edge of why they are attacking what they are." Bartan's son Edroth said in a bitter tone, he did not care if Draco fell or not, it was not his problem, he just wanted to go back home and finally get a taste of war and battle, but he did not want to do it here. He wanted to be remembered as a war hero in his own kingdom.

"We are doing everything we can you little whelp, do you not think if we knew we would be doing something." Dagon snapped at the fifteen-year-old child as he pushed his chair back. From the first day he had met Edroth he hadn't liked him. He would grow be a cruel and heartless Lord.

"How dare you speak to my son that way, I have killed greater men for less." Bartan barked back with his hand on his sword ready to get up and defend his son's honour.

"Ha! I'm sure you have oh great Lord Bartan I am so very sorry." Dagon hissed in defiance fed up with this all.

"Stop it, damn it! We have a very big problem at hand and we need to work together to put an end to it." Dante yelled with an icy glare that put all three back in their seats. "Edroth, this was King Borrack's land. Only he would know it best, Lord Tundal and Dagon are doing the best they can with the little knowledge of this part of their kingdom. It would be the same if Samel was attacked and you had to try and figure out why. It would not be so easy when it is not your land to know."

"If Ursa was here he'd know what to do and how to stop those bastards." Dagon whispered hoping no one heard him.

"What did you just say?" Berrit snapped. "What if Ursa was here? It is because of that demon that your king is dead and your princess and my wife to be are gone. How dare you bring up his name in my presence!"

"Son control yourself, it was a simple mistake, I should hope. Ursa was the only other man that would know how to stop these savages." Dante said seeing that Dagon was not going to defend what he had said and that he was the only one that had a chance of calming his son's rage and he did not want things to progress into anything more violent.

"We do not need those gifted devils, we have stopped thousands of barbarians with no gifted demons and we will do it again." Berrit barked as he sat back down and tried to contain his growing anger.

"Where are your gifted friends now? When they are needed?" Bartan taunted looking at the Dagon and Tundal.

"There are two in Dragon's Cove, three in Drandor, and only one in Mandrake, the rest live on their own. Those that we know their locations have already been summoned to Draco. Alas it will take at least a week for them all to get here, and only Ursa knows the whereabouts of the other great wizards that have helped us in the past." Tundal replied wishing King Borrack was still alive.

"We do not need their help, and why do they hide, afraid that someone will learn the truth of their work for the Dark One?" Berrit hissed.

Dante turned to his angry son. "You need all the help right now you can get son, even though I do not agree with those with the gift either, they may be of use in this fight."

"How could you say such a thing?" All the lords from Zandor asked in shock, for their king had never once said anything of the sort about those with the gift before.

"I stand by my word that I will never let those with the gift live in my kingdom, but I also stand by my word that I will not let a dead man's one wish be ignored. Borrack saw something in those with the gift and though I do not agree, those with the gift will always be safe in Draco." Dante said in a tone that rang through the room.

No one could believe what they had just heard; never had anyone from Zandor ever said such a thing.

"And I have made sure my son knows this as well, though he too is from Zandor, he will not kill or order anyone with the gift to be killed unless they have,, by Draco's laws, done something to deserve it. Borrack and I never had seen much eye to eye, but I will respect his one wish." Dante finished, standing proud. He himself never thought he would ever stick up for those demons or say the words he did now, but if it had been his one wish he knew he would have wanted it done and that was worth honouring.

Lord Dagon and Tundal and Ethan all stood and saluted King Dante, with smiles on their faces. While Berrit tried to smile, everyone could tell he had not willingly agreed to what his father had said. The other lords from Zandor just looked back and forth from one another in disgust.

"How many of these gifted will be arriving?" Berrit asked, still trying to hold back his anger.

"There are twenty two of them that we know of but we told the messengers to tell them if they know of more to bring them as well, though singly their powers do not match Ursa's, together they are a force to be reckoned with." Tundal answered as he sat back down.

"Fine. Have them come and see me at once when they arrive, and I will put them to use." Berrit grunted crossing his arms in announce.

Before anything else could be said, a rider burst through the doors. He looked to be half dead with hunger. "Sirs, I have just come from Mandrake!" He coughed as he put his hand on one of the many bookshelves to steady himself. "A large group of barbarians gather a few miles away from the castle, they look like they are going to try and take Mandrake." He huffed urgently as he tried to stay on his feet.

"What!" Dagon yelled as he jumped to his feet and ran to the man and helped steady him.

"Yes my lord, before I left there was over three thousand gathered ten miles north east of the castle and more just seem to keep coming." He bellowed as he swayed.

"They can't truly think they can take Mandrake do they?" Lord Andras asked with a laugh.

"I have to get back to my castle, and make sure they do not. Mandrake is weakened right now for the moat is dried up and being cleaned and repaired and one of the side walls is under repairs from a catapult accident." Dagon barked as he sent the man to get food and rest.

"Take a thousand men of your choice, with you and your men back to your castle, you should be able to wipe them out with ease." Berrit said as he got up and went over to the man, who seemed to be having a hard time grasping what he had just heard.

"What? Only one thousand? Give him at least two thousand so that he can butcher those heathens." Tundal yelled as he went over to his friend. "Then afterwards he can wipe out every one of those bastards from Mandrake to Drandor, then my forces will join and will march to Dragon's cove and back to here and kill every last one of those monsters before they can gather and do anymore damage."

Berrit turned to Tundal. "We cannot have our whole army spilt up, what happens if they try and take Draco? We will need to have men to stop them. Until we know what they are up to we must not make such rash decisions."

"I leave at once, that many will do, thank you. I trust my family is welcome here until I have things there under control." Dagon asked.

"You need not to ask, they shall remain here until all is well, now go and save your people, send us swift word of your victory and many savages heads." Berrit replied, shaking Dagon's hand and wishing him a fast horse and a swift, bloody sword.

"May the Creator grant him many kills." Andras said well he grabbed an apple from the bowl of fruit on the table and wiped it off on his shirt.

"I pray he gets there in time. If Mandrake falls we will have a severe problem on hand." Tundal muttered.

"Stop this talk of problems, we will prevail. We have fought these savages for eighty years and more they have never taken one of yours, or our castles." Berrit barked trying again to break the depression.

"Lord Tundal, I would suggest that you too should return to your castle and make sure nothing happens." Dante said as he finally sat down.

"My castle is safe enough. I left only the best in charge, I will not leave my best friends and fallen King's castle alone while a Zandorean rules." Tundal said, though not meaning to say it out loud.

"You need to learn to trust my son, Tundal. We are not enemies anymore, we are here to work together, I just hope you can learn to see that." Dante said in a saddened tone.

"I will not let my new kingdom fall, I will fight the same as I would if it was Zandor, and you must believe me." Berrit explained a little hurt by what Tundal had said.

"I am sorry but I think I will be of better use here until we have things figured out, I am the only one left here that knows about this countryside and what might help." Tundal replied, trying to cover up his last statement.

"It is up to you, I welcome your help my friend." Berrit said as he walked back to his seat with a glare.

Everyone bantered ideas back and forth for the rest of the day and well into the late afternoon hours, only taking one break to be with their family and to eat dinner with them, then it was back to the library to see if they could figure more out and come up with a better solution.

~ ~ ~

The sight of the massacre still loomed in Rifts mind as he and Shahariel rode down the road towards Dragon's Cove. They had lost the princess's tracks after the burnt down encampment and had crossed the river hoping to pick them up again. There had already been soldiers there that were cleaning up the mess and burning the bodies. It would take months to repair the damages done. Rift had waited there until his men had caught up and then ordered them to stay behind and help. They had only been slowing him down anyways. He had been trying to work things out in his mind as to why Ursa would do such a thing, but he could not come to a realistic conclusion. He hoped when he found the wizard that he didn't have to kill him. Ursa had helped him a few times when he had been sick or injured in battle and had been a dear friend to his beloved late queen and king, but Rift would kill him just the same if he had too, along with little urchin Meath, too. Rift knew it would take everything he had to take the two wizards down, for they had the gift and he did not, he would have to find away to get the jump on them, or get them in their sleep. Even an arrow to the heart. First he had to find them, he hoped the princess had not been harmed and was still alive. He had to believe she was, or the thought of failing his vow would haunt him for the rest of his days.

"You sure seem to be stuck in your thoughts today." The tracker said as he rode closer.

"I can't get my mind around why they would have taken her. It just doesn't make any sense." Rift replied looking at the man hoping he may have come up with something.

"I wish I had an answer for you, but I do not. Perhaps if I knew them better I might, but I have only heard stories about Ursa." Shahariel told him honestly. "Are you sure none of their bodies were back at that camp?"

"I checked every one of the bodies, none were them." Rift grunted he did not want to think of what happened back there. He had seen worse but still the sight of slaughter did not please him, he had never liked killing, he had only done it because he was good at it.

"Are you sure Dragon's Cove is where they would be headed?" The tracker asked.

Rift truly had no idea where they were headed, only that Dragon's Cove seemed to be the place, for no one yet knew of the kings death and princess's kidnapping. He was sure the news would reach there before he did, but not by far. "It is the only place that I can think of that they would go."

"But how do you know for sure, I mean if I was them I wouldn't go there, what's there for them? If they go there they must know they will get caught. Not even Ursa could stop from being arrested or killed there, he's not that powerful." The tracker bellowed out.

"My senses tell me to go to dragon's Cove and they have never steered me wrong." Was all Rift could say, he just hoped he was right. It had been tearing his insides apart that he had not yet been able to save the princess. If she was hurt, he would never be able to forgive himself. He whispered a silent prayer to Queen Lavira asking for her forgiveness and that he would bring Nicolette home safe.

"Well ok then, I just hope we don't run into any of those barbarians out here." The tracker said as he looked around. "They sure did a number back there on that camp, of course there are hundreds of their tracks around these parts it hard to determine which ones are your Princess's."

"They do not show pity or mercy to anyone, they are heartless beast." Rift said with a sigh. He had seen many battles against them, and many people killed because of them, his father and brother being two of them.

"So, why are you out looking for the Princess and not anyone else?" Shahariel finally asked.

"I am oath bound to her, I am her protector." Rift said, surprised that the man did not already know and why he wouldn't have asked already.

"Ya well if the princess is missing, shouldn't there be more out looking for her other than just us?" Shahariel said, he had been wondering this for a few days now, of course he had also not been one to pay attention to all the talking, he was in it for the money and that was it.

"There are more out there looking, but they are searching further into the jungle and on other roads." Rift replied, he had wondered why more men had not been sent out himself, but knew that there had to be lots out there, they had just not come across anyone else yet.

"Well I just though with a princess missing there would be more to it then this, but I guess nothing like this has ever happened before." The tracker said with a yawn. They had been traveling with little sleep for days now and it was beginning to take its toll on him.

"We will make camp once we get to that rock pile up the road." Rift said for he too needed to sleep. He needed his strength so when he found her he would have all his wits about to save her.

The land had already began to flatten out and the trees had thinned a lot since they had crossed the river. If the princess were out there, it wouldn't be hard to find her here. It would also be harder to get the jump on them with this little cover. But he would find a way when the time came, he always did.

~ ~ ~

They made camp just as the sun began to set and the first few stars began to shimmer in the darkening sky. They made a small fire and cooked a rabbit that Shahariel had caught earlier that day. Rift had not let him light a fire before, a fire gave away your camp at night, but they had found a spot by the rock pile that the fire couldn't be seen very easily and Rift himself wanted a hot meal tonight.

"So do you think we will really find her?" Shahariel questioned. The rabbit hissed over the fire as the juices dripped onto the hot coals.

"I will not stop until I do." Rift barked back, irritated that the man would say such a thing knowing his mood.

"I'm sorry I didn't mean anything by it, just trying to make conversation." The tracker said as he turned the rabbit so it wouldn't burn.

Rift got up and checked the horses and made sure they were tied up well enough for the night. While he was there he patted his horse's neck and whispered to it. "We will get her back, won't we my friend."

The princess had given him the black stallion four years ago. She had purchased it in the city from a horse breeder that only came by every few years, she had never told him how much it cost but he knew that she would have paid handsomely for it; not many horses were as strong and fast as this one. The horse gently nuzzled its head into Rifts shoulder as he scratched behind its ears.

"If you don't get over here soon I'm going to eat all this with out you." Shahariel chuckled over to Rift while he came back and sat down on a rock by the fire.

"Well give me piece of that, and I'll tell you how bad a cook you are." Rift laughed, it had been the first time he had laughed in awhile.

"So the man does know how to laugh, who would have thought." Shahariel smiled as he cut off a huge chunk and handed it to him.

Both men ate greedily until there was nothing left and then shared a loaf of hard bread and a few berries they had found along the way.

"We will take turns on watch tonight. After what happened back there at the river camp we should not let our guard down." Rift said as he wiped his mouth from the juices from the meat and crumbs from the bread. They had not been taking watch the last few nights before they had come across the slaughtered encampment, but he figured now would be a good time to start again.

"Ya, I was thinking the same thing, I guess I'll go first." Shahariel said with a sigh.

"Wake me in three hours." Rift told him as he got under his blanket and rested his head on his pack.

"I will don't worr…" Then all was silent.

"What forget how to talk?" Rift asked, he turned around just in time to see the tracker fall into the fire with a spear in his back.

Within seconds Rift jumped out of his bedroll and had his sword in hand. He looked into the dark and he slowly made his way closer to a pile of rocks so he would have cover from the attack and could see where it was coming from. He heard the sound of something slipping off a rock and looked up just in time to see a dark figure dive at him from above. He was slammed into the ground hard when the man hit him. Rift pushed the body off, the man had impaled himself right onto Rifts awaiting sword. Another spear hit the rock he was standing beside with a spark, Rift side stepped the next one and threw his dagger blindly into the darkness in the direction in spear had come, when he heard the scream knew it had found its target, though doubted it was a fatal hit.

Rift ran to his horse and cut it free, leaping onto its back while another dark figure ran at him from the side and jabbed a spear at him. Rift moved just in time and caught the man across the chest with his sword. He kicked his horse hard in the ribs and it sprang off in full gallop. Two figures stood in the horse's path, but the horse did not stop and knocked both men down hard as it stormed off into the night. Rift held on tight for he couldn't see more then a few feet in front of him and with no saddle, he prayed the horse could find its way along the road.

Chapter 8

"Meath, you cannot stop what is going to happen, soon I will be a god!" The man in black taunted.

Meath stood there in the sheer darkness. All he could see was the man that had been haunting his dreams for several months. They both stood only feet away from one another, but there was no ground, nothing, just darkness.

"Where are we? What the hell is going on?" Meath yelled, but yet his voice didn't seem to go any further then the man in front of him.

The man laughed. "You really are a fool you know, you have no idea what is going to happen, there is nothing you can do, I cannot be stopped."

"Who are you, why are you doing this?" Meath cried trying to get closer to him, but his legs did not seem to work.

"Why? Why you ask? Because it's my destiny, it's my right, it is why I was born." The man laughed back at him as if the question didn't need to be asked.

"I will stop you." Meath barked and tried to swing a punch at him but his arms didn't seem to work either.

"It's too late, you've already been marked." The man said with a wide grin.

"Marked? What do you mean I have been marked?" Meath asked confused still trying to move.

"You can't stop fate foolish boy." He laughed again with a laugh that sent a cold feeling over Meath's entire body. "We will meet again soon and next time I will get you." Then the man started to fade back into the blanket of darkness, his last words echoing over and over. "I will get you…"

~ ~ ~

Meath woke covered in sweat, his heart racing, he looked up to see Nicolette sitting over top of him.

"What the hell happened?" He cried as he tried to sit up but pain surged through and him his eyes went wide as he fell back down.

"Its ok Meath, we got you out of there, you're safe now." Nicolette whispered to him softly, trying to calm him down.

Then it started to come back to him, flashes went through his mind as he remembered being caught and hung from the beam in the small hut, and the ceremony that was being done to him.

"Where is Zehava?" Meath asked in a weak voice.

"I am right here my friend." Zehava coughed from beside him. Meath looked to the direction of his friend's voice. Zehava lay only feet away from him and didn't look much better then Meath felt.

"You two gave us quite the scare." Ursa said as he walked over to them. "You are very lucky to still be alive."

"How the hell did you get us out of there?" Meath muttered still trying to calm his heart and mind down.

"Very luckily and very fast." Ursa said as he handed Nicolette a wooden cup with another one of his foul tasting potions.

Nicolette helped raise Meath's head as he drank it down not even bothering to fight it, he knew it would help and right now taste was the last thing on his mind.

"I am sorry Meath, I did not get to you and stop what that crazy bastard did to you." Zehava moaned as he sat up wincing from the pain of the already healed whip wounds, he had already been up for an hour. The potion Ursa had given him to help numb the pain and aches in his body was beginning to help.

"There is no need for apologies, you both were in need of help, and you Zehava are lucky we showed up when we did you crazy half wit. What in the nine hells did you think you were going to do? You could barely stand let alone fight off a group that big and save your friend. That was the most senseless act I have ever seen." Ursa barked at him with a shake of his head. "But I will give you this, you are a loyal and brave half wit."

Zehava chuckled softly, "Well if I would have known you were going to show up I would have stayed where I was."

"The last thing I remember was that guy, I think Kinor was what he called himself, he was trying to take my gift and he only had to burn the last symbol into my head and then kill me and eat parts of me, he was walking over to me with it in his hand and then all goes blank." Meath coughed as he tried to recall what happened, after that his mind was a mess.

"Why didn't you just blast him with your gift?" Zehava asked looking over at him.

"I couldn't, he did something to my powers, all I remember was this white circle of sand around me it seemed to block me from using my gift somehow. When I did try it sent a pain through me like nothing I have ever felt before, and I sure as hell wasn't going to try it again." Meath answered trying to sit up again, but Nicolette pushed him back down and gave him a look that prompted him to stay put.

"Yes I know, I saw it when we got you out of there. The white sand that you saw is very rare, and can only be found in a few places in the world. It has a power all of its own and when the right spell is used, it can block even the greatest of wizard's gift from being used." Ursa replied with a grave look on his face. "Wizards, sorcerers, mages and witches pay a kings ransom for that sand."

"Well how is it made?" Zehava asked.

Ursa paused for a moment contemplating how to explain it. "Well no one really knows, there are a few legends but who is to say which one is real or not."

"Why didn't you ever tell me of such sand? That's something I think I should have been told." Meath barked softly trying not to move.

"Yes well I would have one day, but it wasn't important at the time, you had other things to learn." Ursa said bluntly.

"What the hell was he doing to me anyways? He thought what he was doing was going to give him my gift." Meath moaned as he looked into Ursa's eyes, he wanted to know the truth if this was possible.

Ursa stood up and looked down at him. "You know as well as I do that it's not possible my boy. The man was crazy, and was just wasting his time torturing you."

"Well whatever he was doing it sure wasn't very fun." Meath coughed again. He looked at his hands and saw that the burns were gone, even the scars could not be seen. "Well at least those burns are gone."

Nicolette looked up at Ursa, wondering if he was going to tell him or if she should. He gave her a nod knowing it might be best if she did. She sighed and looked back down at Meath.

"They're not all gone." She whispered as she pulled the blanket down to his stomach revealing the one burn on the left side of his chest that still remained.

Meath couldn't see it well but he felt around with his hand and traced its pattern with his finger. "Why is this still here?" He asked.

"It wouldn't go away. Ursa tried everything it just wouldn't heal." Nicolette explained looking down at him as her eyes welled up with tears. She couldn't imagine the pain the burns must have caused Meath or anything else they had done to him in that hut.

"It is one of the eight symbols of the Dark One. It means slave to his will and greed." Ursa remarked while looking at him with a deep concerned look.

"What the hell does that mean?' Zehava asked before Meath had a chance to while he looked from his friend to Ursa for an answer.

Ursa started to pace back and forth. "I do not know yet, it could mean nothing, but the fact that it will not heal could mean many things. But let us not worry about this yet, we have more important things to worry about then a witless shamans torture tactics."

"I had another dream, but this one was different. He spoke to me this time." Meath finally said, deciding that now would be a good time to tell Ursa and that maybe it would help him figure out what the burn meant.

Ursa spun around and walked over to him. "What did he say?"

Meath thought back for a second. "He said that we could not stop him, that we could not stop fate, and that I have been marked."

Ursa began to pace again. "Did he say anything else?"

"Not that I remember, what does all this mean?" Meath replied as he forced himself to sit up, Nicolette helped him and did not try to push him down this time.

"I wish I knew, I really do." Was all Ursa said as he lost himself in his thoughts while he paced.

Meath knew Ursa would tell him when he figured it out so he turned his attention to Zehava. "What happened to you?" He asked.

"Well let's see after we tried to escape I woke up next to our last cell and then I met a very strange girl who seemed to like me a lot as her new slave." He chuckled, shaking his head at the thought. "Then her father caught us talking and he damn near whipped the skin off of me." Zehava flinched at the thought of the whip again, the wounds still felt fresh even though they had been healed. Ursa had told him that it would feel like that for a few days until the mind convinced the body they were truly gone.

Meath thought for a moment. "Talking eh? That's not what a strange savage girl told me. She told me her father caught you kissing her, she also told me she couldn't save me and that I was the distraction for you two to escape."

Zehava looked into Meath's eyes. "I would never have left you there." He said in a more serious tone then Meath had ever heard him use.

"I know my friend, I know." Meath assured him not blaming him for anything.

"I can't believe she was going to leave you there, I told her I wouldn't go without you." Zehava growled as he shook his head.

"She never told me that!" Nicolette said angrily as she helped Meath take a drink of fresh water, they had been lucky enough to camp near a creek.

"Speaking of which, where is Dahak?" Meath asked after taking a large gulp of the cold water, which helped take the bitter taste out of his mouth.

"Him and that savage girl went out hunting before either of you woke up." Nicolette said still angry about what she had just heard.

"What, she's here with us?" Meath and Zehava asked at the same time.

"Yes, she helped us escape once we had found you two. If it wasn't for her we might never have gotten out of there alive, we still had to find Zehava but she had already put him on a horse and found us. Though now that I know she was going to leave you I will have to talk to her about that." Nicolette said with a tone at the end that Meath had never heard from her before and thought it funny that she was getting so riled up about something that turned out fine anyways.

"The last thing I remember is standing out there in front of all those barbarians, holding my sword and wondering how I was going to kill them all." Zehava laughed as he took the water attempted a drink, but ended up wearing more then he could swallow. "I must have been delirious from loss of blood and too much pain."

Ursa still paced back and forth a few feet in front of them, not paying any attention to them or their current conversation, as he pondered what Meath had said he had heard in his dream and what the burn mark might mean. He could not think of anything good, and he feared the worse outcome from it. Nothing that had to do with the Dark One was ever good and with all that had happened and that was happening he knew it would only get worse before it got better.

"We're back. Hey, they're awake." Dahak said as he walked back into camp with a rabbit and a duck in hand. Shania walked just a little behind him with three rabbits.

"We got food for the day, and lots of it." Dahak said as he plopped down pulling out his dagger and began gutting the rabbits. Shania dropped her kills down by him and ran to Zehava's side.

"You're up! How are you feeling?" She asked worried as she stared hard into his eyes, finding his hand with hers and held it to her face like a child would a wounded animal.

Zehava laid there for a moment not knowing what to do or say. "I am alright, a little sore still but Ursa tells me that will past in a day or two." Now in the day light he could see her perfectly, she was very beautiful even more then he had first thought. She was wearing a single strap deer hide top that showed off her well toned stomach and figure and a short deer hide skirt, which made for easy moving and flexibility without ripping or catching on anything.

"I am glad you are ok, so when you are better we can go see the place you told me you would take me?" She asked looking into his eyes with a big smile.

Zehava looked at Meath and Nicolette for help but found none. Both of them were looking at him just as confused. "Umm not right away, no." Zehava managed to say." We are kind of in the middle of something of dire importance." Was all he could think of to say, he did not know how much she already knew of what was going on, hell he didn't even know what was going on himself anymore.

"But you promised." She whined as she crossed her arms and pouted girlishly.

"I can't believe you were going to leave me there!" Meath barked weakly at her as he turned to her, but she could tell he wasn't angry with her.

She looked at him with a half smile. "I'm sorry, I really did want to help you too, but there was no way I could have gotten you out. Your friend must really like you, he was going to try and save you regardless of the fact that he was half dead and there were so many."

"You could have untied me when you came and talked to me. We could have found a way out then." Meath replied remembering the feeling of hopelessness after she had left the hut.

"Things all worked out in the end you should be happy, better then dead." Was all Shania said, then she turned her attention back to Zehava.

"You let all this happen to him? When you could have freed him earlier?" Nicolette shouted angrily at her.

Shania looked back up at Nicolette and didn't say anything, just sat there, frozen.

"I can't believe this, you knew what they were going to do to him and you didn't help him when you had the chance and could have gotten him out of there!" Nicolette stormed angrily about to stand up, but Meath caught her arm and coxed her back down.

"Hey you had better get over here and clean your kills, I'm not doing it for you." Dahak yelled over to Shania, trying to break up what might have turned into a very messy problem.

Shania kissed Zehava's palm and went to work on helping with the game they had caught, very happy to have a reason to get away from Nicolette's angry glare.

"After we eat we must get moving. We still have a few days hard travel before we get to Dragon's Cove, and travel is going to be slow with these two hurt so badly." Ursa said as he stopped pacing and sat down. He started putting some branches in a pile, with a wave of his hand they began to burn and dispersed a light smoke. He had been well aware of the feud going on around him and thought it was now time to put an end to it before it became more then just words.

"Ok, well once I am done this I will go find some poles to start making litters to drag these two on." Dahak replied, not looking up from his task.

"Smart thinking, so he does know a thing or two." Ursa joked at him, with a wink. He grabbed the rabbit that was ready to go and placed it on a stick over the fire to roast.

"I will come with you, until you are done what it is you have to do, and then me and Zehava will leave and go do what he promised me for saving him." Shania said in a tone that she was coming and that was that as she finished cleaning the last of her rabbits. Dahak looked over to her wondering how she had done it so fast.

"You are more then welcome my child, but know that the road we travel will be long and hard and could be very dangerous." Ursa said, looking her in the eyes to see her reaction. He knew she would be a big help for she was raised by barbarians but didn't seem to share their blood lust. She seemed to be very smart and bush savvy, which would be a useful skill over the next few days until they reached their destination.

Shania brought him the ducks. "I am used to that, I'll be ok. Besides, you might need me again." She smirked. Ursa just nodded and continued to cook their dinner.

They cooked all the meat on the fire so they would not have to stop and cook it later, for at night it would be dangerous to have a fire. They made sure only to eat half of the food, so they had more for later that evening. Dahak and Shania built two litters that they strapped onto the back of two of the horses and used all the blankets between the two so that Meath and Zehava were as comfortable as they could get. Being dragged behind a horse and on a bumpy road was not a very smooth ride. But they had no other choice. They had made the litters easy to attach and detach, so if they needed to they could do so and hide them in case they ran across an army patrol that was looking for them or any other trouble. Ursa figured if they ran across anyone, they could pass as towns folk from the army encampment and they were a larger group, he didn't think they would have any problems.

They traveled slowly down the road. Nicolette decided to walk beside Meath while the others rode on the horses. She was so glad he was back with her and safe, she had never felt so alone without him, not even when her mother had died. She did not sleep well the night before, she kept having nightmares of what was being done to him. She couldn't believe after all that he was still alive. She looked down at him, he looked a lot better then he did when she had found him hanging from the beam in the hut. Nicolette only wished she could have killed that man, that Kinor, for what he had done. She guessed the poison from her arrows would have gotten to him minutes after he ran out. She could feel the anger flare up in her at the thought of the barbarian shaman, the rage knowing if she had another chance she would put a dagger deep in his chest. Though the thought of killing him filled her with glee, the fact that she would actually be happy she killed someone frightened her. She wondered if that was how everyone felt after battle or if it was just her.

"I was so scared I would never see you again." She whispered to Meath as he laid there flinching from each bump in the road that jolted him this way and that.

"I thought I was a goner, all I could think about was you, and how I would never see you smile again." He replied with a weak smile. Her eyes brightened and a small smile formed across her lips.

"Princess, pull up your hood, we are coming up to a group of people and we don't need another to recognize you." Ursa said as he looked back at them and gave Meath and Zehava a glance to be ready for trouble. They both moved their hands to their swords that were concealed under the blankets. Even though both of them doubted they would be of much use in a battle, there was still an intimidation factor with numbers.

Ursa rode up to Shania. "My child, stay close to me and go along with what I say." He told her.

"Why? What do you mean?" She asked with a puzzled look.

"Well these people may not take kindly to you, for your kind has killed and destroyed their homes." Ursa replied, keeping his focused on the group ahead as they neared.

"I didn't do anything, I did not do these things, my people did but I did not." She argued annoyed that the wizard would finger her out like that.

"Yes my child but they may not see it that way, just go along with anything I say and we will make it past them with no problems." He remarked hoping she would understand and not take offence to anything he might have to say. Shania just nodded unsurely still not sure of what he meant.

They neared the large group of people that must have survived the attack back at the encampment or possibly another near town. Most had nothing but the clothes on their backs while others carried precious things they had grabbed before they fled. Things they did not want to leave for the savages to take or destroy. Some walked beside horses or mules while their wife's or children rode on the beast's back. Others walked beside friends or loved ones, helping them walk struggle along the road, to tired or wounded to do it alone. Others lay on litters like the one's Meath and Zehava were on, that were dragged by horses or people.

As they came closer to the group of people, they began to glare at Shania, some cursed under their breath as they passed, as others gripped weapons they had brought with them.

Ursa knew they had better pass these people quickly before someone got the courage to attack the savage girl or recognized them for whom they were. He kicked his horse softly to speed it up a little, hoping the increase of speed would not be too hard on Meath and Zehava. They had almost made it passed the group when Ursa noticed a mother and father crying over a young boy on a litter with an arm missing. Even from the distance, Ursa could tell the wound was beginning to fester badly and knew the boy would not make it more then a few days if he wasn't helped. Ursa cursed himself and stopped his horse. Shania did the same, looking back at him wondering why they had stopped.

"Why'd we stop?" Nicolette asked as she walked to Ursa who had already gotten off his horse and was rummaging through his things in the saddlebags.

Once he had found what he had been looking for, he turned to explain, "That boy will not make it more then three days if he does not get help, and I can help him. I can't bring myself to just leave him to die." Ursa said, and by the time he was done talking, Shania was off her horse and had come over to them.

"What's going on? We can't stop, we are almost past them and I now see what you meant, they don't seem to like me." She said while looking back at the group watching the cold stares they were giving her.

"I will only be a few moments, there is something I must do." Ursa replied as he went over to the family.

"What are you doing?" The mother asked as he neared them.

"I am going to help your son, that wound is infected and he will die if it doesn't get treated." Ursa told her as he began mixing some herbs and colored liquids together.

The father looked down at him then up at Shania who was walking over to see if she could help. "What the hell are you doing with one of them?" The man yelled as he pushed Ursa aside and stood in front of his son and wife with a rusted old sword in his hand. "We don't need your help! This is a savage trick or something, you're going to poison him." The man roared at Ursa.

"I would do no such thing." Ursa barked back. "And as for her she is my slave, and will do no harm if she knows what is good for her, and believe me she knows what's good for her." Shania looked at Ursa in shock with a hurt look on her face as she was about to protest, but Ursa stopped her before she could. "Now slave, get me some clean rags from my horse and bring them to me before I whip you for being slow and forgetting them as it is."

The man stared down at Ursa for a moment longer still not sure whether to believe him. His wife took hold of his arm and whispered to him. "Let him help our son, he is right, he won't last more then a few days and I cannot bear to lose another child."

The man had a tear in his eye as he nodded his head to her, then stood aside. "Do what you can for him, but I will be watching you and if I see anything that shows foul intent I will kill you." He growled, though most of his anger had already subsided.

"I mean your son no harm, now will you please hold him down, this is going to sting him a little." Ursa told the man as he took the severed limb and squeezed it hard, pushing the puss out to prevent further infection. The child screamed in pain, and kicked, trying to pull away but Ursa did not stop. He knew it was the only way to save his life. Already a large crowd began to stop and watch what was going on, wondering what the strangers were doing.

"Where are my rags you filthy little bitch?" Ursa yelled over his shoulder at Shania, hoping the poor girl knew he didn't mean any of it.

She ran over to him and handed him the rags with a sour look on her face, showing she was not pleased with this. Ursa took the rags and used one of them to soak up the blood and yellow ooze, which now dripped from the infected stump. Then he flattened another on his knee and dumped half the mixture he had made onto it and smeared it around. He placed it onto the stump of the boy's arm and tied it on tightly the child moaned a little at the sting it caused.

"This should keep it from getting worse, in about six hours clean the wound again and use the rest of this, and do what you saw me do again." Ursa told the couple as he stood up.

"Thank you! Thank you!" The women cried as she held her boy tightly and looked up at Ursa, tears steaming down her face.

The man stared down at his son for a while before walking over to Ursa who was now at his horse packing his things. "I am sorry for the way I reacted before."

Ursa turned to him and said. "I understand, I am just glad I could help." Then the man held out his hand and shook Ursa's wildly.

"I will not forget this, if one day you need anything, I will do what I can." The man told him. "We will be at Dragon's Cove, we are moving there where it's safer. If you need us, that is where you will find us." He said as he ran off to be with his family.

"Let go of me!" Shania screamed as she tried to pull her arms free of the two men that now had hold of her and were pushing her to the ground.

"What is the meaning of this?" Ursa commanded as he ran over to them, Dahak was right behind him while Nicolette stayed with Meath and Zehava who were trying to see what was happening.

"Its savages like this one that destroyed our homes and killed our friends and families." One of them barked as he wrenched on Shania's arm.

"You will let go of her at once!" Ursa commanded in a deep violent voice.

"Not until we have our vengeance on this little bitch." The other yelled. By now the group of people had gathered around and cheered their agreement with their weapons held high.

"This savage girl had nothing to do with your tragedy she has been my slave since she was but a baby." Ursa beckoned. "And if you do not unhand her I will have my men remove you from her very unpleasantly." Ursa said while looking at Dahak and giving him a look that he should step in. Dahak drew his sword and held it tightly, trying not to show he was worried about the situation.

Both men stopped pulling at her and just held her as they turned their attention to Ursa and Dahak.

"You would attack your own kind to save a savage?" One of them asked with a menacing stare.

"To protect my property that I paid for, yes I would. Now let her go unless you want to join your dead comrades, I will not say it again!" Ursa warned them as Dahak took a step forward.

Both men released Shania and took a step back. She ran and hid behind Ursa as they began to back up towards their horses.

The crowd was disgruntled and started yelling taunts and curses towards them and then began to throw rocks and dirt in disgust, while jeering their weapons and poles in the air.

"Get on your horses, now!" Ursa yelled as he ran to his and mounted up as fast as he could, yelling back to Nicolette to jump on one of the litters as they kicked their horses and bolted out of the mob of people as fast as they dared in hopes not to cause Meath and Zehava too much pain.

They rode hard only till they had made it around the next bend in the road and knew the mob was not following. Zehava and Meath laid in absolute agony, holding on for dear life, while Nicolette hung on tightly to the sides of the litter, trying not to put all her weight on Meath's already sore body.

"I am sorry about that, you two." Ursa said back to them when the horses had slowed down to their regular pace.

Meath and Zehava both moaned their disapproval, but knew it might have been the only way they could have gotten out of there in one piece.

"I can't believe you said those things to me!" Shania protested as she crossed her arms and looked away from Ursa with a pout.

"I am sorry about that, my child, but I warned you that that might happen." Ursa sighed.

"I know… But I didn't think it was going to be like that, those things really hurt." She grumbled more to herself then him.

"I thought we were really in for it back there." Dahak cut in while looking back down the road to make sure no one was coming after them.

"Hey what's that over there?" Shania asked as she pointed over to a large pile of rocks where a flock of birds were gathered.

"Some dead animal that was moved off the road I'd bet." Dahak answered as he looked over to where she was pointing.

"No I think it's something else, it doesn't look right. Let's go take a look." Shania said as she rode her horse over to it.

"We don't have time for this, we must keep traveling." Ursa called to her.

"Hey its some guy, he's got one of the other tribe's spears in him and two other bodies of men from another tribe like mine." She called back to them as they turned their horses around and rode over to have a look.

"Oh no!" Nicolette cried as she ran over to the half charred body that laid face down in the dirt. "That's Rift's saddle bag and things."

Shania flipped over the body so Nicolette could have a look at it. "So is that your friend?" She asked.

"No its not, it's someone else. But why would he have Rifts things?" Nicolette asked, not expecting an answer.

"He must have killed your friend and stole his stuff, it happens all the time." Shania said walking back to her horse. "Then a tribe found him and killed him."

"I do not think that is how it is." Ursa said as he looked at Nicolette, who was looking at him now holding back tears. "I believe this man may have been traveling with Rift, there are the other mans things over there. It looks like they were ambushed and Rift got away, Princess. But we should not stay here for long, that mob will see us again soon and may not let us leave so easily next time" Ursa said as he turned his horse back to the road as gently as he could, trying not to hit the large rocks with the litter that were scattered every where. He was hoping that the princess would trust his words and not think about what might have happened to Rift, although it seemed more likely she would believe the latter.

"How do you know he got away?" Nicolette cried, following in behind them, walking beside Meath again.

"Because his body is not here, your highness." Ursa replied hoping he was right. "Besides you and I both know Captain Rift, and know well that he would not be taken down so easily."

"Who is this Rift guy anyways?" Zehava asked her once they had started down the road again.

Nicolette stared down at the ground as she walked. "He is my champion."

"Oh ok, well what would he be doing out here?" He questioned painfully while trying to move into a more comfortable position to absorb the bumps a little less painfully.

"He must be looking for me, but how he knew where to look I don't know." She answered, looking at the ground hoping he was ok.

Then Ursa cut in. "I have known Captain Rift for a long time your highness, he is a smart and cunning man. It is his job to know how to find you, he looks to be going to Dragon's Cove. Maybe we will see him there."

They traveled the rest of the day and only ran across a few smaller bands of people making their way to the city. None seem to take much notice to Shania or the others. By nightfall they had stopped and found a secluded spot to make camp that they would not be disturbed by other travelers that passed by. Ursa set up wards all around their camp and Dahak and Shania took turns keeping watch throughout the night.

Chapter 9

Dagon, his champion Jarroth along with the thousand men he was allowed to take and his original three hundred, traveled long and hard down the road to Mandrake, they only stopped late at night to sleep a few hours then were back traveling long before the sun came up again. It was hard traveling but the soldiers were use to it and not a man complained. The first town they had passed they had only stopped for a mere hour to replenish food and water for both the men and their horses. Lord Dagon spared no expense in buying every horse, mule and ass the town's folk would sell, often spending twenty gold coins for a single horse and saddle, which one could normally buy two horses for the price. Dagon didn't even hesitate, in handing over the money. Even after buying forty more horse's from the town's folk still almost half his army marched on foot.

They had been traveling for four days and still had another two, maybe three days hard travel to go until they reached Mandrake. Dagon just prayed he would not be too late to save his people and castle. He hoped Mandrake could hold the barbarians off till he arrived with help. The second town they passed along the way had been one of the towns that had already been massacred. Not a soul stirred, it was a barren wasteland of ruined buildings and butchered corpses. The town was now over run with vultures, ravens and other scavenging beasts looking to score a meal off the already decaying bodies.

Dagon and his men had not stopped at the town but rode straight through, there was nothing they could do except keep riding in hopes they would not find Mandrake in the same condition.

"My lord there seems to be an abandoned wagon up ahead." A soldier reported as he rode from the front to give him the news.

"Well get it out of the way, we do not have time to slow down and help anyone." Dagon demanded already angry that they were not making better time. He really had wished the devastated town they had just passed hadn't been sacked. When he had last ridden through the town on the way to Draco Castle for the princess's wedding, he had noticed that the town had thrice the horses in it then the town they had first purchased horses from. He had been counting on saddling up another hundred or more of his men.

"Everyone seems to be gone, there's no one around with the wagon, it's just sitting there." The soldier replied, a little nervous that he would make his lord all the angrier with the details.

"Get it out of the way damn it! We do not have time for delays!" Dagon yelled at the man, wondering why he still sat there. "They must have just left it behind and ran for their lives knowing they would be slaughtered if they stayed."

"Yes sir, right away, sorry my lord." The man said as he rode off to the front of the army to deliver the orders.

A group of men pushed the wagon and slowly moved it off the road, when a horn sounded off in the trees not far from the where they stood.

"What the devil was that?" Jarroth asked and looked at Dagon as worry poured down his face.

"Shit, it's a trap! Everyone arm yourselves!" Dagon screamed as he drew his sword and searched the grounds with his eyes wondering where the attack would come from.

Arrows flew from the tree line as dozens of barbarians came out of nowhere, with bows notched, loaded and ready to fire a second assault into Dagon's army. No one was prepared for this, men fell like deadwood off of their horses from the spray of arrows that flooded the sky about them, while others got thrown off their startled and wounded mounts, crashing hard into the ground and trampled by the terrified horses. Men ran this way and that trying to find a hiding spot before they were cut down by the mass of streaming arrows.

"Make two lines on either side of the road! Shields together men hurry!" Dagon screamed to his men as he ran from his horse with his shield and sword in hand to stand in the lines that were forming. They faced both sides of the road so one another could stop the steady flow of arrows from hitting the line watching their backs.

"What are we going to do my lord?" Yelled Jarroth, who stood beside him waiting for more orders.

"We attack them before we are slaughtered." Dagon said as he ducked his head behind his shield from the next assault of arrows.

"Just give the order my lord and we will follow." The captain yelled to him from a few men down and everyone cheered their agreement.

"ATTACK!" Dagon cried as he lifted his sword in the air and charged into the trees, hoping to get to the attackers before they restrung another deadly battering of arrows.

Dagon and his men met the charge of savage's head on with full force and cut down the large ambush party. The battle did not take more then a few minutes and only with the loss of a few dozen more men. The barbarians that had survived ran into the dense jungle with ease and disappeared into the mass of trees and overgrowth without a trace. Dagon's men wanted to follow them to avenge their comrade's deaths, but he ordered them not too for he knew that's what the enemy wanted.

"Captain, bring me a fast report of the dead and wounded." Dagon yelled to him as he finished off the last wounded barbarian that was holding his guts with his hands, trying to keep them inside, while screaming in his native tongue at him.

The captain ran off to do as he was told, while the rest of the men helped their wounded comrades and tried to find all the run-away horses. In the few minutes the attack had lasted, so many lives had been taken.

"Sir it was not your fault that we were ambushed." Jarroth said to Dagon as they walked back down from the trees and on to the road knowing he was blaming himself for this.

"I should have seen it sooner, when that soldier told me there was a wagon." Dagon muttered cursing himself for not being able to save the men who had just been murdered. He still could not believe the barbarians were using such strategic attack methods.

"There was no way of knowing sir, not even you could have known what was about to happen." Jarroth assured him.

"Maybe your right, old friend, we cannot let this slow us. We must get to Mandrake. This was just to slow us down, those heathen bastards. I will not rest till I kill them all!" Dagon growled when he had reached his horse, it had gone to war before and was use to the heat of battle and did not scare easily.

"My lord there is a hundred and twenty one dead and eighty four wounded." The captain reported to him when he returned, breathing hard from running around gathering the numbers.

"Put the dead in a pile and burn them. We cannot spare the time to return them to their homes. As for the wounded, the ones who can still fight, patch them up as best we can and put them on horses. The ones that can not, send twenty good men with them back to Draco." Dagon replied, as he could not believe they had lost that many men in such a short time.

"Yes my lord." The captain said as he ran off again to see to the new orders.

"Not in many years have I seen an ambush do so much damage that fast." Jarroth muttered to Dagon who was wiping his sword clean of blood on his horse blanket.

"Neither have I, normally it was our side doing that much damage." Dagon put in grimly.

Dagon sheathed his sword and grabbed the nearest man who was dragging a body to the burning pile. "Tell the others at the end of the army that those who still have horses ride ahead and meet me in the front." The man ran to a horse and took off with haste to see it be done.

"What are you planning on doing my lord?" Jarroth asked as he returned with his horse. Battle hardened as well, his mare had only ventured a few hundred feet away.

"We need to get to Mandrake, we will take those who have horses and ride south, and when the others are done here they can catch up later." Dagon replied as he mounted his horse yelling the orders to the men he passed as they pulled the bodies of men and horses to the pile that was already set ablaze and sending the smell of seared human flesh into the air around them.

~ ~ ~

When the army of those with horses was assembled at the front, they continued to ride hard onwards. What once was an army of thirteen hundred strong was now less then nine hundred. Over two hundred men had stayed behind looking for their horses and cleaning up. Dagon was truly beginning to wonder if he would make it on time and have enough help left to stop the savages that threatened his home.

~ ~ ~

"The barbarians are marching towards the castle, sir Furlac." A guard yelled as he ran into the grand hall where Furlac, the advisor of Mandrake and Lazay, Mandrake's wizard along with most of the castles generals and captains all sat strategizing their defences, weaknesses and how they might use both somehow to their advantage. The barbarian army had come out of nowhere in the last week and everyday it swelled even larger as more tribes joined the masses.

"How soon will they be upon us?" Furlac asked, frustrated and not really wanting to know the answer. They could have a week before the barbarians attacked and still not be ready.

"Within the hour I'm afraid." The man stammered, scared out of his wits and not hiding it well.

"What was the last count of their army?" Lazay asked also not wanting to hear it.

The man thought about it for a second before answering. "Over six thousand, I believe it was, master Lazay."

"May the creator have mercy on our souls." The head General of the Mandrake's Army mumbled as he put his head in his hands and began to pray to the Creator. Many of the others began to pray or curse under their breath as well.

"We are all going to be slaughtered!" One of the captains cried as he stood and began to pace franticly, racking his brain for any hope at all in making a stand escaping.

Furlac stood from his seat with a worried look on his face, knowing he had to lift their sprits or there was no way they could win. "We will not be slaughtered. We have held this castle for over a hundred years from these monsters, we will do it for another hundred. We must not lose heart before the battle has even begun, damn it! Now we all know what we must do, let us get to it so we may send these bastards to the Keeper below. Let us make our Lord Dagon proud in his stead. We will not lose his castle!" He yelled triumphantly, stirring everyone's inner strength and pride as they all roared with him.

Everyone rushed from the hall to their posts to set up final preparations for the siege at hand. No one had ever seen an army of savages this large before, nor did they ever have to defend the castle when it was this weak. The west wall was still under repairs and was nowhere near ready for an attack. Though the moat had been filled already, Furlac still feared what was to come of the night. Of course they would had to begin their attack just before dusk. Tonight was going to be long and bloody. Only the Creator could save them now.

"I wish Lord Dagon was here, he would know what to do better then me." Furlac muttered to Lazay while he stared at his withered old hands, knowing he was not the young, strong, brave soldier he was so many years ago.

"As you said my friend, do not lose heart before the battle has even begun, we will not lose our castle this night!" Lazay said as they both walked down one of the hallways to the battlements to see the oncoming barbarian horde.

As they made their way there, men passed by running weapons to all the men who had not already been armed, and running buckets of water to the draw bridges and anywhere else that might be at risk of a fiery assault. Other men stood in groups that they had trained together in and wished each other luck and courage and many kills.

Once they had reached the battlements, they saw the enemy army at large. Through the darkening sky, they could see all the torches of those who marched before them. It was an eerie sight seeing thousands of small lights slowly make their way towards them. It was like a bad dream that they could not wake up from.

"Tonight is going to be a long night." Furlac sighed as he looked at Lazay, hoping the man could say something that would lift his own spirits.

"I pray my powers can hold out through the night. Tomorrow will be easier to hold them off in the light while I rest and regain my strength." Lazay said as he truly wondered if he would be able to make it through the night. He had never used his gift to the point of having nothing left, but he knew tonight he was going to find out what it was like. How now he wished he would have kept his apprentice for another year of final training, before sending him off on his own to find a town or city in which to make a name for himself. Even a new apprentice would have been helpful now, but he wanted to have sometime to himself to hone his own gift before taking in another.

"As do I my friend, as do I. But I must go and see that everything that can be done is being done, I wish you well and kill as many of those savages as you can." Furlac said as he hugged his friend, taking one last look at him as he walked away back into the castle, wondering if it might be the last time he would ever see him.

Lazay stood there, still watching the mass of men march on the castle. He could not remember ever being so scared in his life. He began walking the length of the battlements, yelling words of encouragement to the archers, rock throwers and tar pourers on the wall. They did not seem to hear a word, they only stared at the death that marched their way. They had used most of the tar on the repairs to the wall but still had enough to do some damage to the enemy when they tried to scale the walls and swim the moat. The five catapults were placed by the walls, aimed in the direction of he on-coming masses. It was a shame they had not been able to collect more boulders for them, but with the barbarian army out there they had not had much luck in finding more without losing men. The boulders they did have were now being smothered with tar and flammable oils to be set ablaze before they were launched off into the enemy.

All the city folk that had not run off elsewhere trying to escape certain death had been brought into the castle days before and now every man had a weapon and was going to fight. The wall around the city they had decided not to try and defend, for it would scatter and thin out their forces too much. The city was now an empty place where only the stray cats and rats inhabited. Everyone had only been allowed to bring into the castle what they could carry. The city would likely be looted clean within a few days. The women and children who could not fight were put into large guest rooms where the city entertainers did their best to help them forget what was happening outside and entertain the children so they did not get scared.

The black smiths and woodcrafters of the city had been working day and night for almost week making spears, arrows, swords and amour for everyone, with little or no sleep, but resources inside the castle were running dry and now they used what little metal and wood they had left to make arrows.

Lazay made it to the end of one side of the battlements and watched for a moment as men raced to fill every arrow quiver as full as they could and still leaving good size piles of arrows beside the quiver. Mandrake had three hundred trained archers and another two hundred city folk, which stood beside them with bows in hand. All of them were on that wall ready for the oncoming battle. Every bow in the city and castle had been gathered and had a man to it. With an army of almost two thousand trained soldiers and twelve hundred farmers and men from the city, they could hold the castle. At least Lazay hoped they could. He wished more of the city people would have stayed, they could have doubled their army, but he did not blame them. If he could have, he too would have ran. He didn't know what was worse; the thought of losing or the wait to find out.

~   ~   ~

"Fire!" One of the soldiers manning the catapults yelled as five flaming boulders sailed through the air and crashed into the mass of enemies that now were only a few hundred feet from the castle wall and still swarming their way through the city to the open fields in front of the castle walls. The screams of the wounded and dying men from the catapult boulders could not be heard over the taunts and cheers of the enemy, as they charged onward, not slowing their assault.

Arrows were being shot at will into the swarm of men and women that charged towards the castle walls, but in the dark it was hard to pick a target that could be hit. The barbarians had large wooden shields held above their heads to stop the attack of arrows.

"Save your arrows men, only fire when you know you have a sure hit!" A captain yelled to his men as he walked the battlements, making sure that everyone was doing their part and being sure that for every archer they lost another man took his bow and his place.

The savages had attacked both drawbridges and the weak wall, which had divided the archers thinly between the two walls. Buckets of water could not be filled and dumped fast enough on the wooden draw bridges and now they were almost burnt through. Once the doors had already fallen, it was going to be hell to keep them out, but on the other side of the doors waited twenty four hundred swords, axes and spears, thirsting for the blood of their attackers.

The attack had only gone on for two hours but yet seemed like days, the barbarians had wasted no time in sending flaming arrows over the walls to keep the castle busy trying to put out all the small fires. That and they had taken haste to making sure those door came down, the doors had been the target of hundreds of blazing arrows and spears, thick with a flammable sap from a certain kind of tree deep in the jungle.

They had only lost a hundred men on the walls to arrow attacks from the barbarians. The savages had concentrated their attack on the two doors hoping to bring them down as fast as possible so their masses could swarm in and over take the castle.

The catapults had run out of boulders within the first hour of the battle and now sat in the courtyard while men scrambled to fill the large bowls with whatever might kill a man. The catapults had done the most damage so far, by laying close to a thousand barbarians to waste in the fiery rain of terror, but now they were almost useless. The archers on the wall had wasted more arrows then men they had killed and the enemy had not tried to scale the walls, for they knew what awaited them if they did.

Lazay stood on the wall looking down at the mass of men as he summoned another two enormous balls of fire on either hand and threw them down with tremendous force. The flaming balls hissed down into the crowd and exploded sending charred men this way and that. He was trying to spare his powers so he could have enough to use all night, but already he was beginning to weaken and the battle had only just begun. He made sure he picked his targets well, and went for large groups, and if he could spot out the enemy's generals or captains, he went for them. But barbarians all looked the same and targeting their leaders was harder then he could have imagined.

"They are breaking through the doors!" Shouted an archer as he aimed for a barbarian that had moved his shield and now taunted those inside by pissing towards the castle. Six arrows found the man's chest as he died in his own waste.

Lazay went to his knees and closed his eyes while he put his hands on the warm stone floor. He concentrated as best he could with all the noise going on around. He flung his arms into the air and a large wall of flames burst from the ground almost as long as the castle wall and five feet thick, right in the middle of the enemy's army. The screams could be heard throughout the castle as a few hundred men died horribly by the huge blaze that only burned for a few seconds. The quick blast held those on the other side back from advancing closer for a few minutes while they watched their comrades burn to death, wondering if they would find the same fate if they continued forward. Lazay knew he was almost drained, he could not keep this up. The last aggression had taken a lot out of him. He pulled himself off the ground, a man helped steady him and bring him inside one of the small rooms on the corner of the battlement where he was safe.

"That was amazing!" The man said as he helped sit Lazay on a chair.

"I can't keep this up, my powers are almost spent." Lazay told the man as he swayed in his seat and sipped some cold water.

"You, what are you doing? Get out there and fire some arrows and kill something." One of the captains yelled as he walked by and the man ran off to do as he was told. It was a lost cause, they would never be able to hold them throughout the night and Lazay knew that. If there were another wizard at the castle, they would be able to do so much more damage. But he was all they had and he could only do so much for so long. "If we can only hold on a few more hours till morning, we might stand a chance." He muttered to himself, knowing full well that even if they did hold out until morning, night would come again and they were doomed.

"Stand ready men, and kill fast." A general yelled as the north doors collapsed into the moat with a hiss as the flame died out. The barbarians were already in the water, swimming towards the breeched opening and wasting no time. The tar pourers began the assault of dumping the boiling black muck down onto the approaching enemy. The tar was not a large help, it was hard to pick targets, but the ones it had found screamed and bellowed as they kicked and grabbed at others in the water pulling them down with them to their watery graves.

The enemy archers now fired at will over the walls and through the doors into the men that stood inside waiting for them, wave after wave rained down upon them, men fell dead or wounded everywhere. They had not been expecting this now and had little time to react. The barbarians climbed out of the moat and through the doors into the castle. The archers on the walls did their best to kill as many of the swimming savages as they could while their shields were down, but slowly began to thin even more as the enemy archers picked them off the walls.

"Stop their archer's, damn it! Fire! Fire!" A general screamed as he too let loose an arrow into the enemy archers that continually launched arrows over the walls into the heart of Mandrakes tired, weakening army. They had all thought the enemy had used most of the arrows to take down the doors, they now realized how wrong they had been. They also realized they weren't just fighting stupid brute force savages, theses warriors knew what they were doing and were doing it well. They were using tactics like none of them had ever seen before.

"The other door has just fallen!" Someone yelled from the crowd of soldiers.

"Shit! Hold them off damn it, don't let them through." Yelled another general that was now running towards the other door in hopes to help hold off the intruders.

The arrows that continued to fall from the sky into the centre of the army were truly beginning to take their toll. There seemed to be more bodies that lay on the ground then on their feet fighting. The men still standing tried to hold off the hundreds of savages that now entered the castle ready to kill.

"We can't hold them off sir!" A young soldier screamed as he fought furiously at oncoming barbarians and was already covered in blood head to toe and tiring fast.

"Yes we can damn it we have no other choice." The general yelled back, as he charged forward swinging madly, taking limbs and heads off as he went. Within a moment, an arrow found him and struck him in the neck, dropping him dead to the ground with the many others from the spray of arrows.

Lazay stumbled out of the room and looked down at what was happening and cursed. He ran to the edge of the wall and yelled to all the men still on the wall. "Pour the rest of the tar into the moat!" No one knew what he was going to do but they did not hesitate to do as their wizard told them at a time like this.

He concentrated everything he had left into what he was about to do, when his eyes opened flames began to grow from the moat and burn anyone and anything that was in it. He held onto the edge of the wall as he gave every last ounce of power he had into this last attempt to hold them off and kill as many as he could. His body began to shake and sweat poured down his face in steady streams. The flames grew hotter and hotter with every moment. Even after he had succumbed to the exhaustion and passed out, his wizards fire still burned and would for a while.

"Quickly men, kill the bastards before more can make their way in!" A captain yelled as he and his men charged into the group of savages that swarmed them at the openings. Barbarians were cut down like grass as the soldiers killed with everything they had. This might be their last chance to save their lives and none wasted any time in dispatching the enemy.

Both openings in the wall were being guarded by the wall of flames that still burned on the surface of the moat. The tar and bodies of the dead continued to fuel the flames, thought it was slowly beginning to die down, as the wizards fire had no more power being pumped into it from Lazay.

"Lazay has bought us some time, bring him somewhere safe to rest." One of the captains ordered to a few men that were still killing the wounded enemies that were scattered all around. They had killed every last barbarian that was inside their walls and now hurried to block up the doors with wagons, bodies, barrels and anything else that would help hold the enemy off for any amount of time. The archers on the wall did their best to keep the enemy archers from firing over the wall, but arrows still soared over and found targets in the courtyard. By now most men had their shields over their heads as they did what they had been ordered to do.

"Pile their dead by the catapults, and bring me the remaining tar and oils." A general yelled to some men that were catching their breaths.

"What are you planning on doing?" Furlac asked him as even he now was armoured up and going to do his part in the fighting. They needed every man they could get, even if they were old and weak.

"We may not have boulders but we have bodies to send over the walls at those bastards." He bellowed back with a twisted exhausted smile as he ordered more men to start dragging more bodies over. "Collect every arrow that can be fired again and get them to the archers on the walls!"

"General, the fire is beginning to die down more." A man on the battlements yelled down to him.

"How much longer do we have?" He yelled back to the man.

"Maybe five minutes sir, but the moat is steaming hot and may be to hot for them to swim across." The man yelled back.

"Good, do your best to keep them from getting across." The general yelled as he turned his attention to other matters.

By now the pile of bodies were well stocked by the five catapults and every last drop of tar and oil was being heated and dumped onto the corpses.

"The moat will not stay hot for long with the steady flow of water coming into it from the lake." Furlac said to the general as he helped pull arrows that could be re-fired from the bodies that were being loaded into the large buckets of the catapults. Each one could hold about five bodies.

"Sir the doors have been blocked as best they can be, what else needs to be done?" Reported a group of soldiers that ran over to them and waiting for new orders.

"Tell the archers to save their arrows for those that swim across the moat and for our unprotected areas, and tell every fourth archer to come down into the court yard. I want two groups of them watching each door, when those monsters break through again I want them to run straight into a wall of arrows." He said to them and watched them start to run off. He called back to them and they stopped to hear him. "Tell them to find swords, axes or spears for when they run out of arrows." He left it at that, the others understood and continued to run off. He looked around the courtyard. It was in ruins and all the men were half dead with exhaustion and wounds.

"Sir the catapults are ready to fire." A soldier reported before an arrow found his back and sent him to the ground, coughing up blood and gasping for air.

"Fire at will and keep firing until there is nothing left to fire, and someone help this man." Was all he said, the enemy arrows had stopped plummeting into the courtyard after a few more moments. Bodies after bodies were shot over the walls into the enemy. They were not as affective as the boulders had been, but still did more damage then anything else they had tried.

"Sir they are swimming across the moat again!" One of the archers yelled as he fired down at the intruders that swam helplessly to the other side.

The archers were already in place at both doors, with bows ready and arrows notched, each archer had fifteen arrows, after that they would charge in with swords.

"Get your spears and swords ready men! Hold them out as long as you can!" He yelled as he and Furlac ran over to the doors, stabbing through the holes at the savages.

The wagons and barrels that had been used to block the doors did not last long against the enemy's axes and swords that hacked through them. Soon there were gaps big enough for men to start climbing through and even with the best efforts of the soldiers inside, they could not keep them out for long.

The soldiers blocking the holes were fast to move aside as streaks of arrows were flying into the mass of barbarians climbing through. Each archer held their shots until they had a kill, being sure to make their arrows last, while other soldiers slashed and stabbed from the sides into those that arrows did not find. Soon the arrows were depleted and archers and soldiers were fighting side by side, trying desperately to keep the invading monsters out. Both doors were holding and the barbarians were being hacked down as fast as they were coming in, only for the fact that they had to climb over their dead or dying comrades before they could ready themselves to attack and the defenders of Mandrake wasted no time in exploiting this to their best advantage.

"Sir Barbarians have scaled the walls on the east side!" Someone yelled from the battlements as savages began charging towards the archers on the wall cutting the unsuspecting men down.

"Shit! Retreat to inside the castle!" Furlac cried as he began hacking his way to the castle doors, every man that had heard him did the same.

The battlements and courtyard were now streaming full of barbarians that killed all those too slow to get inside the doors before they were closed and locked. None of the archers had made it off the wall before they were butchered and thrown over the sides either into the moat or onto the courtyard ground.

"We can't just leave them out there to be slaughtered." Soldiers yelled at Furlac and the only general that had made it in before the doors had been locked.

The general slapped one of the men hard across the face. "They are already dead you fool, and if you open those doors so are we. Don't let those men out there die in vain. They fought and died so we could get in here and hold a little longer."

Now in the feasting hall of the castle stood what was left of Mandrakes army, four hundred men were all that was left, most too tired to stand straight or wounded and bleeding and wouldn't make it much longer anyways.

"These doors will not hold them out forever, and it won't take them long to find the other doors into the castle, we make a stand in the upper hallways where the women and children are being kept." Furlac yelled to everyone making his way through the crowd and to the staircase to lead the way.

"Me and the wounded will stay here and make a stand, and hold them off as long as we can, kill as many as you can men… and die well my friends!" The general yelled to his men as he saluted to those who stayed behind while the others who weren't wounded too badly followed Furlac up the stairs.

"Sir I just want you to know that it was an honour to serve under your command." One of the wound men said as he limped over to him and saluted as best he could. As all the others stood and did the same, the general stood there looking at what was left of his army and his friends. They were all good men and had fought better then anyone could have ever asked for, and over the years he had gotten to know most of them well enough to call friends and now as they stood there about to make their final stand he couldn't stop the tears that now steamed down his blood stained face.

"Never has there ever been a group of braver men and never could a general be more proud of the men who served under him." The general roared in respects to the men that were about to die by his side.

The doors behind him were already being chopped down and through the holes everyone could see the hundreds of barbarians that were about to come through and take their lives.

"I never could have picked a better group to die by my side!" The general yelled to them over the screams of savages at the doors. "And I am proud to die by your sides, I will see you all in the after life as we dine in the great halls of the Creator, now let's send as many of these bastards to the Dark One as we can!" He screamed as he turned around when the doors fell and the hall swarmed full of barbarian warriors that lusted for blood.

~ ~ ~

Furlac order men to grab anything from chairs to tables in the hallways and rooms that they passed by on their way to where the women and children were being kept. Fear coursed through his veins like never before.

He knew they would not be able to hold off the enemy for much longer, and so did every man that was still alive.

"Block up both sides of the hallway with whatever you can find." He told everyone once they had reached their destination. He had just over two hundred men left with him now. He ordered men into the rooms with the women and children to get who ever was willing to fight.

"Sir what are we to do once the barbarians get here?" One of the men asked as he had just finished blocking up one side of the hall as best as he and the others could.

"We kill as many of them as we can." Was all Furlac could say, he couldn't believe this was how it was going to end, that they had failed and had nothing left to do but wait for the enemy to cut them down.

"Sir almost all the women will stand and fight with us." Another man said as he came out of one of the rooms.

"Good, make sure everyone has a weapon." Furlac ordered even though he knew they didn't have enough to arm everyone.

"Yes sir!" The man said as he ran off to divide the weapons between everyone that now gathered in the large hallway prepared to fight to the death, which was assured.

Furlac walked over to a group of soldiers that he knew personally and knew would see to the task he was about to ask them. "I need four of you in each room with the women and children."

They all looked at him confused at why they were being sent into the rooms when they should be out here fighting with the others.

"When the time comes do not let..." Furlac choked as he finished. "Do not let them take the children and women, spare them the fate they awaits them when we fall."

All the men there closed their eyes and knew what he meant for them to do. They were to be the mercy killers, so the women and children didn't have to suffer the barbarian's wrath of rape, torture and cruel beatings.

"If you do not have the stomach or heart I will find others who do." Furlac told them, but none of the men said no and made their way to the rooms not looking back at the others.

Those in the hallway hadn't heard what was said to the group that now entered the rooms, but knew by the look of Furlac's face what he had asked them to do. All understood it was better this way.

Now in the hallway stood a weak army, of two hundred battered men and scared witless women, and less then half were armed. The ones that had been lucky held bloody swords, daggers or broken arrow shafts while others had taken some of the instruments that were in the rooms that were used to maintain the fire places or anything that could be used as a club or would do damage.

Furlac turned to them as he stood in the front of the hallway await-ing certain death, he could not help but shed tears over all that had and were about to die. All he could hear was the whimpers and cries of those who stood ready to fight in the hallway as they prayed to the Creator for strength and courage, and the faint taunts and footsteps of the barbarians that searched the castle for them.

When the barbarians had found them, they stood on the other side of the pathetic barriers that had been placed at either end screaming and laughing at the group of terrified people. Then once enough of them had gathered they began their way through the tables and chairs and other things that blocked their path as the slaughter began.

Furlac swung as fast as he could and took down as many as he could that came his way but it was a never-ending battle, for everyone that he killed five more showed up. He looked over to see one of his men take a blow to the legs and fall screaming in pain to the ground as another man took his place from behind him and continued the pointless defence. Be-fore Furlac could swing again, a savage blade slashed across his mid section, spilling his insides onto the already blood soaked floor. He fell to his knees his eyes bulged wide as he slumped against the wall while savages passed by him paying him no mind for he would not last much longer and could fight no more. All he could hear was the screams and cries of those being annihilated and butchered. A single tear streamed down his face before death found him.

The castle echoed of the cries of the scared and dying, it had only taken a few minutes and the carpets were drenched in thick blood and gore. The few that were left had surrendered and were given no mercy, but one after the other so the ones that were still alive had to watch have their throats slit from ear to ear or their wrists cut to die slowly.

When the barbarians broke through the rooms where the children and few women were being kept, the rooms were a bloody mess of freshly slain bodies and each of the four men sat there in the middle of the room on their knees waiting for death. They were not killed as they had hoped for, they were tied to post in the courtyard like dogs. The savages wanted them to live with knowing the deed they had done.

Chapter 10

Ursa had paid an innkeeper six gold coins to get them a room in the already bursting inn. Six gold coins were more then enough to get almost anyone a room anywhere, and the skinny innkeeper had changed his mind very quickly about who was going to be allowed a room once he was flashed the gold. He smiled wide and he told them to wait a moment while he ran off to kick someone out of a room and was back within a few minutes with a servant girl whom lead the way to their room.

Meath and Zehava had done their best to climb the stairs without help, but they were both very stiff and sore, although they were recovering faster than everyone had expected. Ursa had made them get out of the litters and start walking part of the way to help stretch their muscles, and at night they had to drink another potion that helped ease the muscles and body, which both of them voiced complaints about the taste everytime.

The six had no troubles getting into the city of Dragon's Cove, they had just trailed in with some other town's folk and looked more like refugees. They had dressed Shania up a few days before so she wouldn't be noticed as a savage, they didn't want to have any more problems with angry mobs. She didn't fight the idea for long before she submitted to making herself look like a common farmer.

Once they were all settled in the room Nicolette finally asked the question she had been wondering since they had decided to get a room in the first place. "Why don't we just go to the castle?"

"Well I don't know about the others, but I would rather keep my head on my shoulders." Ursa replied as he stretched his old bones and wondered when their meal the innkeeper had promised would arrive. His belly ached and he could hear everyone else's bellies groan and rumble with hunger too.

"Why would you lose your heads?" Shania asked, confused. No one had told her much about what was going on yet, only that they were running for their lives and needed to get to Dragon's Cove.

"I guess we should let her in on everything." Zehava said as he rested on one of the beds in the room while Meath occupied the other. Everyone looked back and too one another, wondering who was going to start.

"We can get into the castle without being seen, I lived here a good part of my life, and I know how to get in and out without being caught." Nicolette said before anyone else had a chance to say anything.

Ursa closed his mouth, he was about to begin telling Shania what she had just gotten herself into but now turned his attention to what Nicolette had just said. "Well why didn't you say that before child?"

"Well no one asked, and I thought we would just go and tell them what had happened. They will believe us, the have too." She said while getting up off the end of the bed that Meath was on.

"Well, this changes things. I guess we don't need a room after all, can you get us in there tonight, and to Lord Marcus and Lady Jewel?" Ursa asked, already knowing the answer as he packed up the few things he had taken out of his bag to begin making a potion for Meath and Zehava.

"Of course I can." Nicolette said with a smile as she picked up her things and was glad to be going to the castle and back to her aunt Jewel.

"Does this mean we have to move again?" Meath moaned as he put his head into the pillow and closed his eyes, dreading the thought. He just wanted to sleep in a soft warm bed again without having to worry about being killed or caught by anyone.

"Yes it does, now get up and let's go, the sooner we get in and tell them what's going on, the sooner you can rest." Ursa barked, as there was a knock at the door. When he opened it, there was the servant girl that had shown them to the room, standing there with a large tray of freshly cooked fish, chicken, stew, bread and cheese.

"Well there is always time to eat first." Ursa smiled as he thanked the girl for the food, gave her a silver coin and watched her run down the hallway.

"Thank the Creator, I'm starving." Zehava gasped as he pulled himself into a sitting position on the bed, he was glad that they didn't have to go anywhere just yet.

As they ate Ursa filled Shania in on what was going on, everyone else just ate in silence letting the old wizard tell the story. She sat there on one of the wooden chairs in the room, the story did not seem to faze her at all.

It was like she had known from the beginning what was going on and was not worried at all.

"And that my child is how we got to here and now." Ursa finished while he used a chunk of bread to soak up the last bit of stew in his bowl and pushed it into his mouth.

"I guess you guys are lucky I decided to help. You would never have made it out of that camp without me." Shania boasted with pride to everyone, feeling important to the group after hearing what they had gone through and that she had helped in a big way.

"And we all thank you a great deal. Now let us get going. The sooner we get in the sooner we can try and get this all figured out and stop the false prince from what ever he is trying to do." Ursa commanded as he dusted off the crumbs from his cloak and grabbed his traveling bag, handing it to Dahak.

"Why do I have to carry everything all the time?" Dahak complained as he put the bag on his shoulders along with Meath's, Zehava's and his own.

"Because I am old and your two friends are too weak to do it on their own." Ursa told him with a wink and an all-knowing smile.

"Ya well it's not my fault they got hurt, they always get hurt." Dahak moaned while he tried to balance the weight of the packs.

"You'd think a big strong man like yourself would have no problems with those little bags." Shania teased him as she followed Ursa and the others out the door.

~   ~   ~

It was a fairly long walk to the castle still from where they were in the city, it took even longer with the two recovering from injuries. They had split into to two groups Ursa, Nicolette and Meath were in the first that stayed a ways ahead of the others so not to look so suspicious and be recognized, even though the city was now full of strange people from other towns and villages, they didn't want to look to out of place. The others followed at a safe distance behind, making sure to look as if they were searching for a place to sleep and eat.

"It's over here, follow me." Nicolette whispered as they neared the castle wall finally. She found an oddly shaped stone in the wall and began walking away from it into one of the outside gardens that didn't receive as much attention as they needed. Ursa and Meath followed making sure that the others saw where they were going and waived to them to catch up.

"Where are we going?" Dahak asked once they had caught up to the others and realized they had gone a good distance away from the castle walls now.

No one answered him, the only one that knew was Nicolette and she just kept walking as silently as she could through the garden, which was now dense with over grown fruit trees. The path they were following was well in need of a year's worth of trimming.

Nicolette stopped in front of an old dirty gazebo that looked like it hadn't been used in at least half a century. Behind the gazebo was a small, murky pond that was inhabited by small reptiles and swamp bugs.

"This place sure is creepy." Meath said as he looked around, wondering if something was going to come out of the small pool.

"So how are we going to get into the castle from way over here?" Shania asked while she walked over to see what Nicolette was doing.

Nicolette pushed a tiny stone underneath the small bench that was built into the side. There was a soft click and the floor of the gazebo in the centre began to lift and shift to one side with a soft rumble and there in front of them was a set of stone stairs that led down into a dark tunnel.

"Damn, there are secret tunnels everywhere!" Meath said as he walked over and looked down. It didn't look any nicer then the one they had used to escape in Darnan.

Nicolette grabbed one of the torches that were hidden behind the steps, it was a torch she had used one of the times she wanted to leave the castle when she lived there. She held it towards Ursa who sparked it to life as he waved his hand over top of it.

"I don't want to go down there." Shania whispered as she slowly backed away from the opening, with terror in her eyes.

"What's a matter?" Zehava asked her grabbing her hand and stopping her.

"Maybe she's afraid of the dark." Dahak laughed as he wobbled over to the stairs and looked down and whistled.

Shania began to tremble and tears welled up in her eyes and she clung on to Zehava, as if she got any closer to that opening she would be sucked into the darkness forever.

"I don't like the dark, or small places!" She cried hiding behind Zehava.

Everyone stood there not sure what to say or do. It was the only way into the castle without chancing death.

"Its alright, my child. There is nothing to worry about, it will be fine." Ursa comforted her, wondering why she was so afraid. It was in his experiences that barbarian women were afraid of nothing, just like the men but he supposed everyone had their fears.

"It's the only way I know, and it's not that far. It will only take a few minutes." Nicolette assured her as she pulled out another torch and lit it with the other, handing it to Zehava.

"We can't stand around here all night." Meath urged them, not sympathizing with Shania. He was still uneasy about her.

Nicolette lead the way down the stairs with Meath right behind her, Shania held on to Zehava's hand as if the Dark One himself was in that tunnel. With a third a third torch, which Dahak carried in the back, there was more then enough light to see everything clearly, yet Shania was still terrified.

"So is there a secret tunnel in Draco?" Meath asked. As children Nicolette and him had always wished there was and had always tried to find one.

"Of course there is, there are a few of them." Ursa said as he rested a comforting hand on Shania's shoulder, which made her jump slightly.

"Really? Why didn't you ever tell me before?" Meath barked back at him. "I asked you all the time as a kid and you just ignored me."

"Because then it wouldn't have been a secret, now would it?" Ursa laughed at him.

"I can't believe it after all these years that I have looked for one and you knew there was and you didn't tell me." Meath said shaking his head in disbelief.

"Well if I would have told you, you would have told everyone in the city I am sure, it wasn't like you didn't have a big mouth." Ursa replied with a grin.

Meath just shook his head, for now he didn't really care, they all had a lot more dire things to worry about.

"We're at the end." Nicolette whispered back to everyone as she placed her torch on the wall and pulled a metal lever. There was another click and the wooden wall in front of them slid to the side, making an opening just big enough for a person to fit through.

On the other side of the opening, there was very little light and everyone wondered where they were now. The smell of fresh raw meat was thick in the air and the room they stepped into was cold enough to see your breath.

"Where are we?" Meath asked, knowing that was the question on everyone's mind.

"We're in the meat cellar, right under the kitchen." Nicolette explained while she felt her way to the stairs and began climbing them as the others slowly followed.

She opened the large doors slowly, hoping no one was in the kitchen this late. The princess peered through the crack of the door and found no one in sight. She quickly opened the door the rest of the way and crept over to the side doors making sure the hallway was clear and waived everyone closer.

"Lord Marcus's room is down this hallway and up those stairs. They moved his room closer to the kitchen so Jewel could get him anything he wanted, since he doesn't want too many people helping him. He hates knowing he is sick and fights tooth and nail with almost anyone that tries to help him." She whispered and they quickly made their way down the hall to the stairs.

Just as they made it half way up the stairs, a patrol of guards came around the corner from the top and saw them.

"Stop right there, intruders!" One of them yelled down at them drawing his sword.

Everyone froze. They didn't know whether to run or to fight or what. They just stood there on the stairs, staring up at the four guards that were now making their way slowly towards them with swords and spears in hand.

"It's the princess and Ursa!" One of the others shouted as they got closer, fear glazed their eyes at the realization that there was a wizard and his apprentice, not just thieves like they had first thought.

"Don't try anything funny, wizard. You will not stand a chance." Another one said to them while tightening his grip on his sword and licking his lips, trying to steady his hands.

"We need to see my aunt and uncle right now!" Nicolette cried to them, they stopped and looked at one another for an explanation.

"It's ok your highness, you are safe now. Come up here quickly so they don't hurt you." The first guard said to her.

"No, you don't understand, they're not going to hurt me. You've got it all wrong." Nicolette cried again, hoping they would listen but knew it might turn out as it had when they escaped Draco. She didn't want more men to die because of the lies that had been told.

"Everything will be alright princess, just give me your hand and come up here where it's safe." The guard said with his hand stretched out trying not to get to close in case the other intruders tried something.

"Look you half wit, you have no idea what's going on, now get out of our way before I end your pathetic life." Ursa finally commanded, hoping that it would scare the men into fleeing.

"I don't think so wizard." A voice from behind them barked up at them. They turned to see who it was and saw Rift coming up the stairs from behind them with an arrow locked tightly in his bow and pointed straight at Ursa's heart. "Don't try anything wizard, not even you are fast enough to stop this arrow."

"Rift, don't!" Nicolette yelled as she ran down to him, but Meath grabbed her arm as she passed him stopping her.

"Let go of her you filthy, little whelp or you will taste steal." Rift hissed at him, but did not take the arrow or his eyes off Ursa.

"Its ok Meath, let me go, he won't hurt me." Nicolette whispered to him, Meath nodded and let go and she walked down to Rift and stood in front of the arrow.

Rift eased the arrow forward and grabbed her arm pulling her down and behind him and pulled the bow back again so it was ready. "Now arrest them!" He yelled.

"No Rift, you don't understand! They did not kidnap me, they're not the enemy." Nicolette cried to him trying to get past him.

The guards started down the stairs towards them and Meath, Zehava and Dahak drew their swords, well Shania pulled out two twin daggers from inside her cloak.

"We mean no harm to anyone, just listen to us." Ursa said while waving his hand at Meath and the others to put their weapons down.

"What is the meaning of all this?" Lady Jewel cried as she came out of her room and stood at the top of the stairs with her arms on her hips, wondering what all the noise was about.

"It's alright my lady, we have things under control. It's Ursa and his band of traitors." One of the guards told her.

"Oh my Nicolette dear child, are you alright?" Jewel cried as ran down the stairs part way and stopped behind the guards.

"Jewel, tell them to put their weapons down. We are not here to cause problems, we are here for help. What you were told is not how things happened." Ursa begged her, hoping that all the years they had known one another would save them from a fight.

Lady Jewel stood their not sure what to do, everyone looked to her waiting for her to speak. She looked into Ursa's eyes long and hard before she spoke. "Put your weapons away, all of you. I believe them."

"But my lady, they killed King Borrack." One of the men yelled in protest.

"I do not believe so, and if they did, they would not have come here. Now I said put your swords away and leave us. I will call you if I need you." She commanded with anger, Jewel was still not too sure if she was doing the right thing, but her heart told her she was.

The four guards looked at one another as they made their way up the stairs and passed lady Jewel. Rift remained at the bottom of the stairs with his bow ready and the princess behind him.

"Rift, I said lower your weapon and leave us." Jewel said to him sternly.

"I mean no disrespect lady, but I will not leave. It is my duty to protect the princess and I am still not sure if what you are doing is wise." He replied, his eyes still rigidly fixed on Ursa and the others.

"Fine, I understand your concern. You may stay, but put the bow down before someone is hurt." She ordered him softly before speaking to the others. "So what brings you here? What is going on if what we have been told is not true?" Jewel asked, looking to Ursa for answers.

"I do not think it wise to talk of these things here in the stairwell." Ursa said, while the others sheathed their swords and Rift lowered his bow uneasily.

"I understand, follow me then." Jewel said and everyone walked up the stairs and followed her to a large room that was full of seats and a grand fireplace and table. The guards that had met them at the top of the stairs waited just down the hall and watched them as they passed, making sure that they were close if they were needed. There were more of them now, all with bows and arrows at ready.

They all found a seat and Jewel ordered a servant that passed by to bring food and drinks. Ursa began to tell the story once again, of the false prince Berrit and everything that had happened to them.

Rift sat there watching them with his hand on the hilt of his sword, still not sure whether this was a trick or not. He sat next to the princess and allowed no one to sit to her other side.

When Ursa was finished, lady Jewel sat there in complete shock and disbelief and didn't say anything while she absorbed the news she had heard.

"You would not lie to me would you Ursa? We have known each other a long time, and up until I heard the news a few days ago, I would have never doubted you, ever." Jewel said firmly.

"My lady, you know I would never lie to you, if it were in my powers I would have stopped him when I had the chance. But like I said, he is far more powerful then I, and anyone one I have ever encountered. We had nowhere else to go. We had to leave Draco, and fast. The only place I could think of was to here." Ursa replied to her gravely.

"Well I understand and I am glad you came here, but you know you could have done things differently and not break into my castle and cause a ruckus." She said to him and the others with a half smile. "I just wish my husband was well and could help figure this out, I am not too good with these matters." Jewel said as she fought back tears. "Since you are here Ursa is there anything you can do for him?" She asked changing the subject.

"I do not know my dear, the fever can almost never be stopped, but if you take me too him, I will do what I can." Ursa told her with a bow of his head. Lord Marcus was also one of his dearest friends and he hoped there was something he could do for him, if only to numb the pain.

"I hope you don't mind waiting here for a few moments everyone, I will be back in a while, feel free to eat and drink as much as you like, it looks like you all have had a long hard journey." Jewel said while she and Ursa got up and left down the hall to go see Lord Marcus.

~ ~ ~

Everyone sat silently in the room for a long while, not sure what to say or do. Meath was surprised that lady Jewel had trusted them so quickly, but he guess the friendship between Ursa and her was very strong. Rift just kept staring at them like they were going to jump up and attack at any moment. Finally Nicolette couldn't take it anymore.

"Rift its ok, they're not the enemy, they're friends, they saved my life!" She bellowed at him folding her arms and glaring hard into his eyes.

"I am sorry your highness, it's just everything that has happened and that I was told is hard not to believe." Rift said looking at her and removing his hand from his sword.

"Ya Rift relax, we're all friends here." Dahak said as he reached over and grabbed a piece of cold chicken and began eating.

Rift shot him a glare. "We may not be enemies but we are far from friends."

"Someone sure is grumpy." Shania giggled, the look on Rifts face amused her and she could not hold it in.

"Mind your tongue, savage, or I will cut it out and hang it on my wall as a trophy." Rift barked at her and she stuck it out at him mockingly.

"Rift I think you should leave." Nicolette told him angrily, wishing he would be more understanding.

"Not for anything, your highness." He replied back.

"Then stop being so rude to my friends!" She shot at him. She knew it was his duty to protect her, but sometimes he was too protective and this was one of those times. Even though she understood why he was so cold towards them, all this time he thought they to be the ones that had killed her father and kidnap her.

Rift put his head down. "Yes your highness, I am sorry."

Meath stood up and started to walk around the room, even though he was still sore, he knew that if he continued to sit his muscles would tighten up on him. He went to the balcony to get some fresh air. He looked down into the large courtyard; there were only a few people down there, some tended to horses and the others were guards that talked and drank now that they were off duty. Meath wondered how long it would take for the news of them being here to spread to everyone in the castle. If it were anything like Draco, by morning almost everyone would know.

Zehava came out onto the balcony with him and rested his arms on the edge, looking over to Meath.

"Well now that were here I wonder what is going to happen next." Zehava sighed.

"I don't know, I guess we wait 'til we find a way to stop this crazy man back at Draco. Then after that I guess things will go back to the way they were before all this happened." Meath replied with sadness in his tone as he stared blankly.

Zehava looked at his friend again and understood some of the sadness in his eyes. Once things were back to normal, the princess would have to find another prince to marry and once again, Meath and Nicolette would not be allowed to be together. In the midst of everything happening, there was no one to stop them, but here things would be different. He gave his friend an understanding nod. He himself was beginning to like Shania more and more as the person she was and didn't know what was going to happen with that. He knew people would never accept her as just a person. She would always be a savage or a murderer. He himself didn't understand why he was so attracted to her, she was beautiful but there was something else that just pulled him to her.

Once Lady Jewel returned she apologized for taking so long, and told them that Ursa was going to stay with Marcus for a while to see what he could do for him.

"Now then, Shania your name was? I would like to thank you for helping save these men and I want you to know you are welcome here as long as you would like, and should there be any problems regarding your race, you will come to me and I will see to it that they are dealt with." Jewel said with a bow of her head in thanks. "Now for the rest of you, my servants will show you to your rooms, where there is a bath and fresh clothes waiting for you all. I am sure you are all very tired. Nicolette, you know where your room is, it has not changed since you left. As for you Meath and Zehava, if you would like there will be someone waiting in your room once you are done your baths to give you a massage to help with your muscles and wounds."

"Zehava doesn't need anyone, I will do it for him." Shania cut in with a smile as she jumped out of her seat and ran to him as he came back into the room from the balcony. "And I will stay in his room too." She said matter of fact like.

"Oh, alright then. Well I will send someone to your rooms in the morning to get you for breakfast and we will talk more then. Until then, it might be wise to stay in your rooms and keep a low profile. We will try and keep your presence here quiet as long as we can." Jewel said as she turned and told the servants which rooms to put them in and then went off to be with her husband and Ursa.

~ ~ ~

Meath soaked in the hot tub of water, it felt so good to be clean again, and he forgot how nice baths felt. The hot water helped ease his aching body and the smell of cedar and lemon oils that had been added in the water helped relax him even more. Once the water began to cool off he decided to get out. He dried off and walked out of the small bathroom in his towel. There waiting for him was a young blond servant girl that had a table set out and a basket of massage oils and creams at the ready. She was wearing a thin white see through silk robe and stood there waiting for Meath to lie down on the table.

He stood in the doorway not sure what to do. He had heard stories from other soldiers of what sometimes happened when getting massages, and with what she was wearing and the look in her eyes he knew this was one of those times.

"Don't be afraid I won't bite." The girl said. "Unless you want me too." She added with a giggle.

Meath still stood there, wishing he had put on some clothes before he had come out, but he had forgotten that someone was going to be there.

"I don't think I will have a massage tonight, thanks." Was all he could think to say, hoping it would be enough and she would just leave.

"Nonsense, I heard what happened to you and if anyone needs a massage anytime in their life, you do now." She said as she walked over to him and took his arm, leading him over to the table.

Meath didn't know what to do, he could really use the massage but that's all he wanted. He was too sore and too tired to argue. He laid down on the table as she began to pour warm scented oil on to his back and rub it in softly. Meath moaned as he closed his eyes. She put just enough pressure on to his sore back and shoulder muscles and massaged in such a way that he could almost fall asleep. He couldn't believe how good she was at this, he had only ever had a few massages in his life, but already this was the best and she had only just started. The oils she was using were tingling his muscles, loosening them and numbing them.

"You've got a lot of knots in your back, but I will work them out, I promise." She whispered in a sweet tone as she began using her knuckles and gently pushed and rotated them into the knots.

It seemed like hours had gone past while she slowly moved down to his lower back, climbing onto the table to get a better position about halfway through.

Meath didn't even notice her climbing up, he was so relaxed that someone could hit him and he didn't think he would notice. His eyes opened wide and his heart skipped a beat when he felt his towel being gently pulled off, he didn't know what to do, he knew he should stop it now before things got out of control.

"I think that will be good enough for tonight, thank you." He said as he lifted his head off the table.

"But it's just starting to get good. I promise it will get much better." She purred to him as her hands still slowly went down his back.

"No, I am really tired and should get some sleep, you have done a great job." Meath said as he rolled over, which he quickly realized was a mistake. She now sat on top of his naked body with a smile on her face as her hands began to rub his chest.

Meath grabbed her hands to stop her and she leaned in and pressed her lips to his, parting his lips with her tongue and kissed him deeply. She freed one of her hands and moved it down to his leg and began to rub it gently. Meath pushed her off of him and she fell to the floor. He grabbed his towel and quickly wrapped it around himself as he got off the table.

"What the hell is a matter with you?" She asked as she got up. "I am not good enough for you?"

"I am sorry, but I only wanted a massage." Meath gulped. He had feared this would happen.

She grabbed her things and stormed out of the room insulted, and didn't say anything else, only glared at him. Meath didn't care if she was mad, he sat on the end of his bed, glad she was gone.

"That was awkward." Meath whispered to himself as he laid down and decided it was time for him to get some sleep.

~ ~ ~

Nicolette stood outside her room on the balcony enjoying the fresh air, wishing Meath could sleep in the same room like Zehava and Shania. She wondered what was happening right now with him, she knew what most massages entailed, and shuddered at the thought at what might be happening. She wanted to go see him, but didn't want to know what was happening and knew she would never make it out of her room unnoticed. There were four guards outside her door that would be there all night. She sighed, she wondered what would happen now that they were here. Would find a way to stop the false prince? And then what? Meath and her would have to return to being friends, no one would ever let them be together as they wanted to be.

Nicolette cursed herself for being of royal blood and not just a commoner; she wished they could just run away together and never have to worry about any of this. But she couldn't. She had a country to rule and get back to once the false prince was stopped. And now the country was flooding with barbarians that also had to be dealt with. She wished her father were still alive, he would know what to do. She began to cry, she had almost forgotten about her father's death with everything that had happened and now she had time to grieve. She wished Meath were here, he would have the right words to help calm her, he always did in his own awkward way. She walked back into her room and closed the balcony doors and crawled into bed, crying herself to sleep.

~ ~ ~

Ursa sat by Lord Marcus's bed on one side while lady Jewel was on the other. He had done everything he could for him, but the fever had already gone too far for anything to do much good. All he could do for the man was help ease the pain with medicine and what little magic that would help, and that would only do so much.

"I am sorry my friend, that I cannot do more." Ursa sighed as he handed him the strongest potion he knew and helped him drink it down.

"Ah no worries, you've already done more then the rest of those fools have done for me. I am just glad the rumours aren't true, they had me worried for a while, I almost believed them." Marcus coughed as he laid back down.

Ursa had tried to use his healing powers to help but they didn't seem to have helped at all. He wished there was something he could do for the man.

"Don't look so sad, I'm not dead yet." Marcus said with a weak laugh. "The kingdom is in rough shape right now Ursa, the barbarians are attacking all over the country. And I fear they will try for here since Dragon's Cove is weak with me laying here in this bloody bed." He moaned and cringed at a shot of pain that went through him again and he fought back the pain with his fists gripping the blankets, his knuckles went white.

"We should let him rest, I will go to my chambers and see you in the morning." Ursa said as he got up. Lady Jewel followed him the door and hugged him deeply.

"I thank you for your help, tomorrow we will find away to save Draco and free your name of treason." She told him and watched him saunter down the hallway before returning to Marcus's bedside for the night.

~ ~ ~

In the morning everyone met in the same room they had gone to talk the night before. The table was filled with more food then twenty people could eat at one time. Everyone made small talk until they had eaten his or her fill. Once the table was cleared, Uvael, Dragon's Cove's advisor and Antiel and Lepha, the two wizards that lived in the castle all showed up for the meeting.

Meath, Zehava, Dahak and Shania were told they could leave if they wanted to and that if the others came up with anything they would be informed. But Nicolette, since she was now Queen of Draco, was asked to stay and learn a few things about ruling and strategies.

The others left with no complaints, this was not for them to learn, nor did they want to. They all went down to the garden to enjoy the morning air and warm sun that now shone brightly in the blue sky.

"So I wonder how we are going to beat this evil wizard." Dahak said as he lay down on the grass and looked up at the sky.

"Why don't you just send an assassin to kill him in his sleep?" Shania asked, not understanding why this was such a hard task.

"He's too smart for that, it wouldn't work. He would sense something wrong before anyone could get close enough to do it." Zehava told her and looked at Meath to see if he was right. He didn't know much about the gift, only what people had told him.

"Yes those with the gift as strong as his would know something was wrong." Meath assured him, Zehava smiled glad, he had gotten it right.

"Why not poison him then? That always works." She asked again.

"Ya that should work, shouldn't it?" Dahak said looking at Meath.

"It might, but first someone that's still there that could do that needs to know the truth, which might be a lot harder then you think. Send anyone new into the castle and they will be being watched for sure." Meath told them, not really wanting to talk about this. He stared up at the blue sky, thinking of Nicolette.

"Well what are we gonna do while the others are talking?" Zehava asked, not wanting to just sit around all day. He felt rather well today and his muscles weren't hurting enough to slow him from doing much.

"Well lets go fishing or hunting, that's always fun." Dahak replied, he loved fishing and knew his two friends did as well.

"Hey that actually sounds like a good, relaxing idea." Zehava answered looking from Meath to Shania, wondering what they thought.

"You guys go on with out me." Meath sighed as he got up.

"No way, not gonna happen, your coming with us, man. You can't do anything at the moment about you're problem, so you are coming with your friends and going to go fishing like we did before." Zehava ordered him with a stern look.

Meath signed again, he knew Zehava was right and after a few moments submitted to the idea. "Fine, what the heck, it will be fun and relaxing." He smiled.

"Damn rights, let's stop off at the kitchen first and score some ale, can't go fishing without downing a few." Dahak grinned.

"This is just going to make it easier to out fish you Dahak." Zehava laughed.

"Ya ya, it's not really about fishing, it's about having a good time with friends." He replied sourly.

"Sure it is, you're just saying that, that's not what you would say if you figured you would out fish him." Meath joked as they all started to the kitchen to get the ale and some food for the day.

Chapter 11

Nicolette sat bored hour after hour in the room with everyone discussing different plans for disposing of the evil wizard that now had infested Draco. Plan after plan was talked over and faults were found in them all, it seemed almost impossible to stop this enemy without knowing more about him, and what his real plans were, but something had to be done.

"I have an idea." Ursa finally said. He had been silent the last half hour and now spoke. Everyone stopped talking and listened intently. "I am going to try and find the answers we seek, by going to see an old friend."

"And what would this friend know that we don't already?" Dagon Coves advisor asked.

"Maybe nothing, maybe everything. He knows things others do not and is very powerful with the gift of foresight, he may be able to help." Ursa told them.

"Well where he is, and how long will you be gone?" Jewel asked him.

"I will be back in a week, hopefully with the answers we seek." He replied eagerly.

"A week? It may be too late by then!" One of the generals barked.

"Take anything you need and as many men as you want." Lady Jewel told him.

"I thank you my Lady, but I shall go alone for this journey. Do nothing until I get back, we do not need the enemy to know you know." Ursa said, standing and brushing himself off.

"That is foolish, your name still has not been cleared of its charges and the country is filled with barbarians." Antiel said.

"I shall be fine." Ursa said as he looked at everyone and bowed starting out of the room.

"Give the stable master this token and tell him you need the fastest horse he has." Jewel told him throwing his the small coin shaped token.

"I thank you again my lady." He said and was about to leave before Jewel called back to him.

"Ursa if you are not back in a week time we will be forced to act some how." She told him.

"I know." He said as he left.

"Well I guess we will talk of things later, it has been a long day, and we could all use a rest from this, if anyone thinks of anything at all that might help, find me." Jewel said as everyone cleared out of the room.

Nicolette started towards the hallway and went towards Ursa's room. She couldn't believe he was leaving, and wanted to say good-bye and wish him well on his trip. When she reached his room his door was cracked open slightly and when she entered he had his back turned and was searching through some things that he would need.

"I knew you would show up, that's why I left the door open." He told her not even looking back.

"Well I wasn't about to let you leave with out saying good-bye and thanking you for helping me and saving my life." She said and he turned around to face her.

"There is no need to thank me my child." Ursa said as he walked over to the princess and gave her a deep hug. "And as for good-bye, I'll be back before you know it." He said pulling away winking at her with a smile.

"I know but I'll miss you. Are you going to say good-bye to Meath and the others?" She asked him.

"If they were around I would, but they are more then likely off getting themselves into trouble." He chuckled as he threw the rest of his things into his pack.

"Speaking of Meath, I leave you in charge of making sure he stays out of trouble, that boy seems to find problems around ever corner." Ursa laughed.

"I will, I promise, besides he needs a break for once, if I have to I will chain him in his room." Nicolette laughed with him.

"Good idea, but I bet he will do something foolish and hurt himself in there too." Ursa smiled as he picked up his pack and hugged her again. "Tell the others I will be back in a week's time. You will be safe here till I get back."

"I will tell them and thank you again for everything Ursa." Nicolette said as she fought back tears. "And may your journey be swift and safe."

~   ~   ~

Lady Jewel, Nicolette and a few others watched from the towers of the castle as Ursa rode away down through the city. As she watched him disappear Nicolette wondered where Meath was, after him and the others had left this morning she hadn't seen him.

~ ~ ~

"Well that was a great day fishing." Zehava said as they rode back to the castle. Their arrival and identities were not known to many so they had no troubles going through the city to go fishing or coming back.

"Ya I am glad I decided to go after all." Meath replied back a little tipsy from the ale almost forgetting all his worries.

Zehava looked over to Dahak with a huge grin. "I told you I would out fish you." Everyone laughed but Dahak.

"Yes, well like I said, it's about having fun." He grumbled back at him.

"Didn't look like to much fun for you, since you lost all your hooks Dahak." Meath bellowed out in laugher and so did everyone else.

"Ok, ok that's enough picking on him, he's gonna start crying." Zehava cracked.

They rode up to the stables and gave the horses to the stable boy as all four of them stumbled through the courtyard towards the castle.

"Well I am going to go bath and eat something, I'll catch up with you guys later." Dahak said, still a little sour about all the teasing.

"That sounds like a good idea, me thinks." Zehava said, glad Shania hadn't drank that much and could help him walk straight. "Whatcha gonna do Meath?" Zehava slurred.

"I think I'll go for a walk and see if I can't sober up a little." He said as he looked around to see if she was about.

"Ok man, well I will see you later on then." Zehava said as he pointed Shania where to go she helped him along not complaining at all.

~ ~ ~

Meath walked around the outside of the castle checking the garden and making sure to look up at every balcony he passed, hoping to see her. He sat down on one of the benches in the garden for a while watching the different colored fish swim in the large pond. The sky was just beginning to turn a crimson red as the sun slowly sank into the sea. It was a beautiful sight and he wished she were here with him to see it. Of course he knew she had seen it a thousand times before, but never with him. The red and orange colours mixed together so well that it almost seemed magical and he wondered if there was some great power behind it making the sky look like this. Like the Creator himself was blending the colours to his will.

Meath got up after the sun had totally faded away into the sea his head had cleared from the ale. Although his stomach grumbled from hunger, he did not feel like filling it. He wanted to be with Nicolette even though behind these walls nothing could happen between them, just to see her and talk to her would have satisfied him. He knew that he would not see her tonight so he went straight up to his room to sleep off the rest of the buzz.

Meath opened the large oak door to his room and walked over to his grand feathered mattress with its soft cotton sheets and pillows. He sat at the edge of the bed and took off his boots and leather vest and riding pants. He rolled into the bed and covered himself with the light wool blankets. His hand moved instinctively to where she would be if she were sleeping beside him, a light sigh escaped him as a tear creased his eyes. He rolled over to face the bedside table and heard the sound of paper crumbling under the pillow. His eyes shot open as he reached under and found a letter from Nicolette.

~ ~ ~

Meath paced his room unable to sleep after reading the letter, every few minutes he looked out the window, cursing the sun to hurry up and rise. As he paced he thought about the fastest way to get to the far end of the Cove. It had been years since he had been there and his memory of the path was foggy, but he knew he would find his way, nothing was going to stop him from getting there on time. His gut ached from hunger so he ate some of the fruit out on the table in his room that was refreshed everyday. It would fill him until later when he decided to eat a full meal.

With a few hours left until sunrise, and not able to take another pace across the floor, he filled the large tub with cold water and began to boil several large pots on the fireplace. He poured some cedar oil into the water as he climbed in and scrubbed off the smell of fish and ale. When the warm water touched the scar from the burn on his chest it sent pain coursing through his entire body. His fingers traced the design as he wondered why it had not healed like the others but the thought quickly diminished.

Once his bath was done he dressed in a clean pair of dark brown leather pants and instead of putting on his regular light brown leather vest he searched the dressers in the room and found a black, cotton long sleeved shirt. Normally he would never think of wearing such things but he wanted to look his best and surprise her. He looked in the full body mirror placed in the far corner and decided he looked surprisingly good in the shirt. Meath smiled to himself and looked out the window again to see that the sun would be coming up soon. He grabbed his sword and dagger and strapped them on and with one last look in the mirror, ran his hand through his hair and left.

~ ~ ~

He snuck down to the stables and found a horse that would not be too hard to sneak out quietly. He put the reins on the horse but nothing else and led the beast out to the back gates. He was surprised to find no one watching them at the moment. He climbed on to the horses back and took off into the dark towards the Cove.

Meath tied his horse on a branch next to the white mare that was already tied to it. His heart raced at knowing she was already waiting for him, the path he followed was well kept, but still if one was not careful could slip and fall down into the rocky death that waited at the bottom.

The smell of the sea filled Meath's nose, as he got closer to the edge of the Cove, the sound of waves crashing against the rock walls was very soothing. The path forked in font of him one lead west to the end of the Cove where one could look out over the sea at the highest point, the other which he took lead north, down a ways to a small grassy ledge half way down the rock wall which over looked the sea from a different angle where no one could be seen from the main roads.

As the grassy opening came into view, he could see her standing with her back to him looking out into the sea as the first few rays of sun poked their way into the sky. She was wearing a white cloak and the morning breeze played gently with her hair.

Meath stood there at the opening staring at her, not wanting to disturb her just yet. She looked like an angel, no sculptor or painter could ever capture the true beauty she possessed. Finally he couldn't take it anymore, he walked slowly over to her and she turned to see him and a smile formed on her ruby red lips and her eyes glistened with joy.

"I didn't know if you would find the letter or not." She said after a few moments of silence.

Meath stared at her for a moment. Underneath the white cloak she was wearing a shimmering white silk dress that hugged her curves. "I almost didn't, but the fates were with me I guess."

He walked over to her until their bodies were almost touching he looked deep into her eyes. "I love you Nicolette, like I never knew love existed." He whispered to her.

Tears welled in her eyes as she hugged him to her, his arms wrapped around her. "And I you, my true prince."

The words shot through him like ice and his heart raced, he wanted nothing more then to run away with her so they could be together and not have to live with the hurt of being forced apart by bloodlines.

"I give myself to you, my love." She whispered to him as she looked back into his eyes.

Meath was taken back by the words. "But you must be pure for when you are wed to whom ever it is you are to be betrothed." Meath stammered.

"Maybe if I am not pure he will not want me and will cast me away and my family will take my title away and we can finally be together." She said, more seriously then anything he had ever heard her say before.

"Are you sure? I don't want you to ever have regrets." He told her while searching her eyes, but could not find anything but love for him in them.

"If we can't be together, I want to know my one true love was my first." She said as she pulled him closer. Their lips met and parted in a passionate kiss.

Meath held her hard against him and the kiss seem to last for hours, slowly they went to the soft grassy ground, making sure not to break the kiss. He moved his hand down and unclasped his sword belt, which made a small clink as it hit the ground. He moved his hand slowly up her white dress and up her bare thigh, she moaned as he could feel goose bumps across her bare skin. Meath kissed down her neck and untied her cloak while he continued to kiss down to her silk dress strap and slowly slid it down her arm, kissing ever inch of the way.

He felt her hands unbuttoning his shirt and her hands upon his chest. He never dreamed of ever feeling her hands on his skin like this, nothing had ever felt so right to him before. He moved to the other side of her neck and did the same to the other side, feeling her body under him arch, her heartbeat sped up and her breathing deepened. His hand had made it all the way up her thigh as he discovered she was wearing nothing under her dress. He pulled the dress down and exposed her to him completely. He gasped at the sight and brought his head down to her bare chest to taste and tease them with his tongue. Her moans grew louder as he kissed her deeply again.

Meath sat up and undid the straps on his leather pants and freed himself of them. He saw she was blushing girlishly a little and he grinned as he went back to tasting her sweet mouth.

As he parted her legs she winced, as her innocent's was lost. He made sure to be gentle not to hurt her anymore then he had too. But after a while, all either knew was their passion for one another, their bodies were joined as one now and no one could take what they now shared away.

~ ~ ~

Meath watched her in awe as she straightened her dress and lay up against him. Never in his life had he ever been so happy, he never wanted this moment to end, but knew it soon would. The sun had long been up and if they stayed much longer there would be no hope of either making back into the castle without being caught.

"We had best be getting back, my love, before Ursa finds us gone.' Meath said with a chuckle. "We don't need his wrath coming down on us again, or Rift's for that matter, I am sure he still wants my head."

Nicolette was silent for a short time before she replied. She had almost forgotten to tell him. "Ursa isn't at the castle anymore. He has left to seek out an old friend that might be able to help us."

"What! He left?" Meath said surprised by the news. "When!?"

"Mid day yesterday." She told him, hoping he wasn't going to be mad that she hadn't told him sooner.

"And he didn't even say goodbye." Meath said disappointed.

Nicolette cuddled up to him glad to be in his arms. "He did tell me to tell you he said goodbye and for me not to let you get into any trouble." She giggled.

"Well you're not doing a very good job, cause us being here is trouble." He teased as he kissed her again.

"I can't take much more of this." Someone said from the trees and they stepped out into the opening.

Meath jumped to his feet and grabbed his sword as a man he did not know came into view. With a ring Meath's sword was free and at the ready. Nicolette grabbed her cloak and hid behind Meath, staring at the man.

"Who the hell are you? And what are you doing here?" Meath yelled at the man, hoping they had not been followed and caught by spies of the castle.

"Calm down there's no need for a weapon. My name is Daden." The man said coolly as if his name was important. His voice was soft but sturdy and firm.

"What do you want? I should kill you for spying on us." Meath barked again.

Daden laughed. "And you yourself would be killed if anyone knew what you two just did."

"What do you want?" Nicolette asked, still standing behind Meath making sure her clothes were not showing anything she didn't want this man to see.

"Well princess, I am here for Meath." He said bluntly.

Nicolette looked up at Meath and didn't know what to say.

"Like hell I'm going anywhere with you." Meath laughed at the man and cast a glare of challenge.

"Well actually you are coming with me, one way or another." Daden said taking a step forward. "And don't try to use your gift on me, I am far stronger then you." The man lifted his hands as giant trees that were growing near the path crashed into the ground behind him. He didn't move or flinch an inch, like he knew exactly where they would land.

Meath took a few steps back, pushing Nicolette back with him towards the path that lead down to the rocks.

"Where do you think your going?" Another voice said from that path with a smooth flowing accent that neither had ever heard before.

Meath and Nicolette's heads shot back to see a girl standing there blocking their escape.

Fear filled Meath's body as he gripped his sword tighter, he didn't know why these people wanted him, and he didn't want to know.

"Just come with us peacefully and everything will be fine, I promise." Daden said as he walked closer to them, hands outstretched.

"What the hell do you want with me?" Meath ordered, making sure to watch both the strangers.

"That is not to be discussed here, but you will not be hurt I promise you that." The girl behind them said softly.

Meath knew the only way they were going to get away was if he surprised them and acted fast. He grabbed for his dagger as he ran towards the man with his sword ready. Meath got two steps before he was hit in the back by a large controlled burst of wind that sent him face first into the ground. He lifted his head to see the man standing above him.

"Remember Meath, you did this, not us. We didn't want to hurt you." He said as he stabbed a small dart into Meath's arm as he fell to the ground out cold.

The girl walked past Nicolette as she stared at Meath's body, tears streamed down her face. "Leave him alone please!!!" Nicolette cried.

"What do we do with her?" The girl asked with a little worry behind her voice.

"Nothing we were sent to get him." He relied as he lifted Meath up. "I suggest you leave, Princess. There's nothing you can do for him, he's coming with us."

"Why? What did he do? Don't take him from me please!" Nicolette cried, wishing she knew what she could do or say to stop these people from taking him.

"Whatever, no matter. Stay here asking yourself why all you want, we're leaving, grab his things Kara." The man said as he slung Meath over his broad shoulders.

As the girl came forward to grab Meath's sword and belt, Nicolette ran to his sword and picked it up holding it an inch from the girls face.

"Oh please, what are you going to do with that?" The girl laughed openly.

"Let him go or I'll kill you, I swear it." Nicolette screamed as the sword shook in her hands.

Both the strangers laughed loud, Daden almost dropped Meath. "Please Princess, I don't want to hurt you, but I will." The girl said.

Nicolette went to lunge the sword forward into the girl's chest, but her sword was slashed aside and to the ground before she could even blink, Kara's foot was a top Nicolette's blade and Kara had a very slender short curved sword at Nicolette's throat.

"What did I say? Now be a good little princess and stay put and you won't get hurt." Kara whispered to her. "We promise to take good care of your boyfriend here."

"Stop playing around Kara and let's go." Daden yelled back to her, he made his way into the wood in absolute silence.

Kara winked at Nicolette and opened her palm as dust flew into her face causing Nicolette to cough and shield her eyes.

By the time the dust had cleared the two wizards and Meath were long gone. She sat there holding on to Meath's sword, crying for what seemed like hours before she ran back to her horse which was still tied where she left it, she rode back to the castle as fast as the beast would go.

Chapter 12

Meath woke to the sway of the horse he was on, he opened his eyes to see his hands were bound by a weird looking rope which was tied to the saddle. His head shot up and if it wasn't for being tied to the horse he knew he would have fallen off. He felt like he was drunk, everything was disoriented and blurry. He tried to focus on the people in front of him but could not make them out, his horse was tied to the horse in front of him, he wondered where he was being taken and whom these people were. Meath closed his eyes hard trying to clear his mind, when the last thoughts he could remember came back to him, Nicolette, the cove, the strangers. His anger raged as he yanked on the ropes to slow the horse but the beast did not pay him any mind.

The horses stopped and the figure in front of him turned to look back. "Look, he's awake now. We should stop and rest the horses now anyways." The woman said.

"You're right, but make sure we don't let him out of our sight." A man grumbled sounding clearly unhappy.

"I don't think he's going anywhere anytime soon, the drugs we gave him will keep him tame for a few more hours it least." The woman said with no concern in her voice at all.

The man got down from his horse and helped the women down from hers and they came over to him. "If we let you down will you be good?" The man asked Meath mockingly.

Meath didn't understand what was going on, his mind was a mess, all he knew was he didn't know these people and he was sure they knew where Nicolette was, and if he was going to get back to her he had to play along with them. At least until whatever drug they gave him wore off. He tried to talk, but no words came out, so he nodded his head in agreement.

The two strangers helped him down from his horse, his legs felt like jelly as the world spun circles around him. The strangers walked him over to a tree and rested him up against it. Meath knew even if he wanted to there was no way he could escape these people in the state he was in, and first he had to find out where he was.

"You stay here and watch him, I remember a creek being around here somewhere, I will get some water for the horses." The man said as he grabbed a large water skin from his horse and went off into the trees as silently as death.

The women went to her horse, grabbed something from her bag and walked back over to Meath. "Here, drink this. It will help stop the effects of the drug." She whispered to him, making sure her companion was nowhere around.

Meath wasn't sure he should trust her, but he realized if they wanted to hurt him they could easily do so in the state he was in. She pressed the small container of liquid to his mouth and he drank it in a few small sips.

"There. In a few moments things will start to clear up and you'll be able to talk and walk again." She told him as she sat down on a near by log.

She sat there looking at him, and slowly things started to clear up a little, Meath's vision began to focus and mind began to grasp things and clear up. By the time things had cleared enough for him to realize he was in trouble, the man had returned and was watering the horses.

"Why are you doing this to me?" Meath finally managed "What do you want?" Meath asked bitterly.

"I know you don't know it yet but we are helping you and a lot of other people too." The girl replied.

Meath didn't understand and he didn't think it had anything to do with the drugs either. "What do you mean? Where is Nicolette? And where am I?" He barked.

"She is safe, we did not harm her." The girl said again honestly.

"Enough questions now let's get moving, they might have sent people out looking for us by now, and we were told not to tell him anything." The man grumbled to her as he walked over and helped Meath to his horse.

"I know I was just…" The girl said before he cut her off.

"Yes I know you were just trying to ease his mind, but you know our orders." He said after Meath was back on his horse and they were moving again.

Even though things were beginning to clear up, Meath still wasn't sure on what was going on. His mind still raced, but he couldn't keep his thoughts together enough form a plan.

~   ~   ~

"Nicolette, child calm down, we are doing everything we can to find him." Lady Jewel said trying to calm her.

Nicolette was pacing her room holding back tears still trying to get her mind around what had just happened.

"I still don't understand why you two were out there that early in the morning alone anyways." Rift grumbled, but was sure he knew the reason. That little whelp had stolen the princess' heart many years ago and now that they were older it had only intensified.

"I told you I just wanted to talk to him and spend time with him like we could when we were kids." Nicolette barked back frustrated, she was in no mood for anyone's disapproval or accusations.

"Are you sure you have no idea who they were? They could have been savages just dressed differently?" One of the generals asked, wanting to be sure he had all the details and the best idea on who the kidnappers were.

"They were not savages for the last time, there was a man and a girl the man had black hair, clean shaven, buck skinned pants and vest. The girl was wearing the same, and was blond, blue eyed and they spoke our language perfectly without a barbarian accent, and they have Meath, and… they have the gift." Nicolette roared at the poor general who backed up as she walked towards him.

"Yes your highness I was just making sure I had all the details, we will get Meath back I assure you." He said trying to hide the fact that he was scared of her wrath. No one had ever seen the princess this angry before and no one knew how to deal with it.

"Leave us, both of you." Jewel told Rift and the general. Neither hesitated in the least on getting out the door as fast as they could. "My child you must calm yourself, I've never seen you like this before." Jewel told Nicolette in shock herself.

"Yes well I have never had the man I…" Nicolette cut herself short before remembering she couldn't let anyone know. "I have never had my best friend get kidnapped before either." She corrected herself, but from the look on her aunt's face, she knew she hadn't done a very good job.

"We will get him back. Now tell me the truth, why were you two down there?" Jewel asked, sitting on the edge of the bed gesturing for the princess to sit next to her.

Nicolette dropped her head as she walked over to the bed and sat next to her aunt and was silent for a few moments. "I just wanted to talk to him about everything that's happened the last week, and thank him for helping me." She lied, hoping her aunt would believe her.

"I know child, you've been through a lot, and I thank the Creator your alive, and I thank that boy and his friends to no end for helping you get here safely." Jewel replied, deciding not to press the matter anymore. "But I will leave you alone for awhile, you need your rest, if I hear any news about it I will let you know right away." She said as she stood and went to the door looking back at her.

"Thank you, Aunt." Was all Nicolette said while she stared down at the floor holding back her tears.

~ ~ ~

Nicolette sat on her bed as tears streamed down her face, she hoped he was all right and that they would find him and the bastard that had taken him. She cursed herself for not being able to help him, if only she would have been stronger and faster, she might have been able to stop them or if she had any idea how to fight Meath might still be here with her safe.

Just then there was a light knock at the door, she got up and answered it. When the door was open there stood Zehava, Dahak and Shania.

"We just heard what happened and came as fast as we could." Zehava said as he hugged her, she let silent tears fall on to his shoulder.

"We will get him back don't worry we've been through worse." Dahak lied not sure of what else to say.

"I know I just can't believe he's gone." Nicolette whimpered as they all came in and she shut the door.

"Does he always get into trouble like this?" Shania asked trying to change the mood a little.

"As much as I hate to say it, yes he does." Zehava chuckled.

"I thought as much, I've only known you guys for a short while and already he's got himself into more trouble then the rest of you put together." She said hoping to make Nicolette smile. Even though Nicolette and her hadn't seen eye to eye on much so far, she felt sorry for her to have the man she surely loved be taken from her.

Nicolette didn't even hear them, she was standing by the doors of her balcony staring out at the sea.

"It will be ok, he'll be back, he'd do anything to get back to you." Dahak said looking around the room for the others to back him on this.

Nicolette sighed as she turned to face them with a serious look on her face. "He wouldn't have been taken if I knew how to fight!"

"You can't blame yourself for that, Meath is a good fighter and a wizard at that, and even he couldn't stop them." Zehava said.

"Ya and the people who took him were wizards too." Dahak added.

"That's not the point, it was because he didn't want them to hurt me that he didn't stand a chance, if I could fight then we might have had a chance." Nicolette cried and Zehava was afraid of where this was going. "I want you all to show me how to fight and use a sword and to be quick and all that, the ways of a warrior."

The room was silent for a time no one was sure how to answer her, then Shania piped in. "Well since no one else in this room will answer you I will. I will teach you everything I know."

Zehava looked to Dahak and he nodded his head in agreement. "And so will we." Zehava said getting up off the bed.

"Thank you." Nicolette said looking back out to the sea while saying a prayer to the Creator to watch over Meath until they could find him.

"But I warn you its not going to be easy, its takes dedication and time." Zehava told her.

"I understand I will do whatever it takes so this never happens again." Was all Nicolette said, they could all see that she meant every word.

"Well when do you want to start?" Dahak asked.

"Right now!" Nicolette said turning to them.

"What, no not today, you must rest and clear your mind." Zehava begged her.

Nicolette stared at him angrily. "What am I going to do? Sit in my room all day crying? When I could be out there learning how to make sure something like this never happens again?"

"Well I don't care what they say, let's go, I will teach you right now." Shania said, ignoring the look Zehava was giving her.

~ ~ ~

Meath woke again from the rocking of the horse, he didn't know when he had passed out again, and he only remembered vague parts of when he was awake last. His vision had cleared totally and his mind was no longer scattered. He looked around and could tell it would be getting dark soon, he looked up and saw the two people riding in front of him. He summoned his gift to burn the roped, pain shot through his body like before when he was being held prisoner at the barbarian camp. He tried to fight back the moan but they had heard him.

"Alright we will stop again." The man in front of him said to the girl in the lead.

"Is he awake again?" She asked looking back.

"Yes, and he just tried to use his gift." The man laughed as he climbed down from his horse and walked over to Meath.

"Where are you taking me? Why are you doing this to me? Where is Nicolette?" Meath ordered trying to sound threatening, but his voice wouldn't let him with the pain he was feeling.

"Calm down, the only thing I can tell you right now is the princess is safe, back at Dragon's Cove, we did nothing to her, it was you we came for." The man said unhooking Meath from the horse so he could get down and stretch his legs.

Meath climbed down from his mount and as soon as his legs hit the ground he dove forward, knocking the man to the ground and began to run in to the lightly wooded forest to escape his captors. Meath had no idea where he was running to or where he was, but at that moment anywhere was better then with these wizards.

He was only a few hundred steps into the woods and the ground began to shake under both his feet causing him to fall hard to the ground. With his hands bound, he crashed into a log with his shoulder.

"What the hell was that?" Meath moaned to himself trying to get to his feet again.

"That my friend was I." Kara said, who now was only a few feet away from him.

"That's impossible!" Meath said looking at her dumbfounded.

"Oh is it now?" She laughed, touching the ground with a finely crafted walking pole in her hands as it began to rumble and shake again, not quite as bad as the first time.

Meath stared at her in amazement, never in his life had he ever seen such a thing as this.

"You bastard if you ever do that again I will..." The men yelled as he caught up to them rubbing the back of his head from where it had hit the ground.

"It's ok, I got it under control now, he's not going anywhere." The girl called back. "Are you?" She smirked looking back at Meath.

"What's going on? Who the hell are you people?" Meath moaned in frustration, not sure whether he should move.

"We can't tell you that, the only thing we can tell you is your coming with us one way or another. Now you can fight us the whole way and make our job a lot harder then it has to be or you can come along peacefully and make things a lot easier for all of us, but either way you will come." The girl assured him sternly.

"Please do things the hard way." The man grumbled, glaring down at Meath and rubbing one of his fists in his hand.

"Daden, help him up, we will make camp now and get an early start in the morning." The girl replied as she started off to the horses.

"Ya ya fine, come here you." Daden said as he grabbed Meath's bound hands and pulled him upright hard and began pushing him forward back to the horses.

"As you have already found out your powers are useless to you as long as that rope binds your arms, and to save you the trouble of finding out later, don't try and cut through them, it will only cause you greater pain. The only way to get out of them is if one of us takes them off." The girl said looking back at him to make sure he understood.

Meath didn't say anything just kept walking to the horses with an angry glare on his face. He hated this feeling of helplessness.

"And even if you did get out of them, your powers are no match for even one of ours." The man said, giving Meath another push and almost knocking him to the ground.

"Daden stop it. He is not to be harmed." The girl reminded him.

"Yes I know Kara, but I owe him one." Daden said, wanting to push Meath again but holding back the urge as Kara glared.

"Now I promise you, if you don't try anything stupid you will not be hurt. But if you do, I can't promise that Daden will control himself again." Kara told Meath after they had gotten back to the horses and started unpacking the things they would need to make camp.

Meath still didn't say anything, he knew if he did it wouldn't be nice and wouldn't help his case any. He just wished he knew what the hell was going on and what these people wanted with him.

~   ~   ~

The sun went down and the three sat around a small fire cooking some rabbits Daden had caught. The smell made Meath's stomach rumble madly, the last thing he remembered eating was the fruit in his room back at Dragon's Cove before he had left to meet Nicolette, before all this had happened. He wondered if they were going to share with him or just let him starve.

He still hadn't said anything to either of them, he didn't know what to say and wanted to see what kind of people they were and what their weaknesses might be before attempting escape again.

Kara took the two rabbits from the spit laid them on a clean board and began cutting chunks off. Daden grabbed a piece and plopped it into his mouth, shaking his head and spitting it back into his hand because it was too hot.

"Well of course its hot, it just came off the fire." Kara laughed at him.

Once the rabbits were all chopped up and nothing was left but the bones Daden asked. "Should we feed him too?"

"Of course we feed him too, don't be an idiot." Kara snapped at him while grabbing a few pieces and put them in a bowl. She walked over to where Meath sat bound to a tree.

"I know you don't understand but you will soon enough, I promise." She said as she handed the food to him and looked at him with a look that told Meath she sympathized with him.

Meath ate the meat slowly, not wanting them to think he was as hungry as he was, he ate and he watched them eat and listened to their small talk.

"We have to make better time then this, tomorrow we only make one stop to rest." Daden said as he ate greedily.

"The horses will hate us, but yes I agree we still have a long way ahead of us." Kara replied wiping the juices from her mouth.

"In a few days travel is going to get slow, especially if he tries anything funny again." Daden complained looking at Meath who made sure not to let them know he was listening.

"I don't think we will have any problems from him, he knows he can't escape now." Kara said grabbing another chunk of rabbit.

Meath didn't know where they were heading, but tomorrow he would make sure he was paying attention to see what direction they were headed.

After he had finished eating, he rolled over and laid down on the wool blanket Kara had put out for him, he faced away from them and off into the trees.

"I will take first watch." Daden said as he got up and stretched.

"Are you sure? You haven't been sleeping well this whole trip, I could take first watch?" Kara replied putting the fire out.

"No that's ok, I will watch him first." Daden said, looking Meath's way as he said it.

Meath didn't care, he wasn't going to try to escape yet anyways. He didn't sleep at all the night before, aside from what he'd gotten while he had been drugged, which wasn't very restful. Tonight he would get as much rest as he could, for who knew what might happen tomorrow.

"Ok, well wake me when it's my time, good night Daden, night Meath." Kara said as she crawled into her bedroll and dozed off.

Meath wondered how they knew his name and so much about him, they could have heard his name and that Nicolette was a princess while they were at the Cove, but for some reason he was sure they had known before then. There was no way they should have been able to know where they were, but yet they did. Meath wondered if it had something to do with the strange and strong powers they seemed to possess. So many thoughts and question went through his head that he had a hard time falling asleep, but weariness finally over powered his thoughts and he drifted off.

~ ~ ~

"Wake up its time to go!" Kara said as she shook Meath awake.

Meath eye's opened as he rolled over expecting an attack, then his eyes met Kara's and he knew she had no intent on hurting him.

"Sorry if I startled you but its time to go." She said and then walked over to Daden to wake him.

Meath rode silently the whole morning, they had eaten on their horses as they traveled Meath had discovered they were traveling to the east, back towards the jungle. There was still a few days of travel before they would reach the Sheeva River, but he was sure they would be crossing it a lot further north then most people ever did. It looked to Meath that they were traveling behind Sheeva Lake, but that didn't make sense to him. Then again, none of this did.

He thought about Nicolette most of the morning and how she was doing with him being taken like this, he hoped she would be ok without him. He knew by now there would be people out looking for him but these strangers seemed to know how to cover their tracks well. They had even seen the small markings in the ground Meath had put there during the night in hopes someone would find them and be able to follow. He should have known he would have to do better then that to fool these two.

~ ~ ~

Nicolette woke late the next morning, every muscle in her body hurt from the training she had done the day before.

"Well they told me this would happen." She groaned as she pulled herself out of bed slowly.

"I wonder where they are." She said to herself.

They had told her they would come and get her as soon as the sun came up to continue her training, but from the looks of the sun it was almost noon.

Nicolette got dressed into her training clothes and slowly made her way through the hallways, trying not to look as sore as she was to people who she passed by. No one talked to her long, they all knew she was in a bad mood about Meath being taken and no one wanted to have her rage put upon them.

She had a small smile on her face at knowing they were scared of her, no one in her whole life had ever been afraid of her before, but now everyone seemed wary.

She stopped one of the kitchen servants in the hallways and asked the young girl where Zehava and the others were.

"They are out in the garden your highness." The girl said as her eyes darted this way and that trying to find a reason to have to leave.

"Thank you." Nicolette said to her before walking away.

By the time Nicolette had made it to the garden her blood was already boiling and her sore muscles seemed a thing of the past, when she saw them all sitting on the grass talking she couldn't hold it anymore.

"Why didn't you wake me this morning!" She commanded.

Everyone stopped talking and looked over to see the very unimpressed princess.

"Well we all figured you needed your rest." Dahak said, wishing someone else had said it.

"Don't say that, I told you we should wake her up." Shania put in, not wanting to take the blame for them.

"You said you would get me as soon as the sun was up!" Nicolette barked back angrily.

"Well you can't over do it, you won't become a fighter in a few days." Zehava said getting up and walking over to her.

"And I won't become any kind of fighter if you keep treating me like a weak little princess either!" She screamed at him. "Did they let you take days off when you were a little sore from the day before in the army?"

Zehava looked back at Dahak who hadn't gotten off the ground and showed no intention of doing so. "Well no but…" he tried to say.

"Well then why do you think that I must have a day off? Is it because I am a girl? Because I am a princess? Or just because you don't think I have what it takes?" Nicolette raged out.

Everyone stood there staring at her, even the gardeners had stopped what they were doing and just looked at her.

"I am sorry, I just thought you might enjoy a good sleep before you trained more, but now that I see you are serious about this. We will not treat you any less then how we were treated in the army from now on." Zehava said, nodding his head.

Nicolette stared at him long in the eyes to show she was dead serious, and didn't want to be treated any different and truly wanted to learn to fight.

"I told you she would be mad if you didn't wake her." Shania said as she finally came over and apologized for not making them wake her up.

"That's ok as long as it doesn't happen again." Nicolette said firmly.

"It won't, I promise." Zehava said, glad he wasn't getting yelled at anymore.

"So what is it today that we do?" Nicolette asked, still with adrenaline pumping through her veins.

"Well we go for a five mile jog fully equipped with sword, dagger, spear, shield and a ten pound pack of water and food." Zehava said with a small smile as Dahak finally walked over to stand with the group, groaning about hearing the days plan.

"That's fine by me." Nicolette said with a nod of her head as she turned to go get ready.

"What's all the commotion down here about?" Lady Jewel bellowed as she ran across the garden to where the group stood and Rift followed not far from her side.

"There's nothing the matter now." Nicolette assured her.

"What's this I hear about you training to be a fighter?" Rift asked looking sternly at Nicolette unimpressed.

Zehava and Dahak took a step back not wanting to be in his way if he decided to get angry about the idea.

"Yes, I am training and they're helping me." Nicolette told him bluntly.

"What? Are you mad child? Why would you do such a thing to yourself? Fighting and being a warrior is for men, not women." Jewel cried out in disbelief.

"I am a women and I am a warrior!" Shania cut in, taking offence to what was said and crossing her arms, not backing down from Rifts stares.

"I will not let you continue this nonsense." Rift ordered.

"How dare you tell me what I can and can not do! Who do you think you are? I will do as I please, Rift, and don't think you can stop me." Nicolette barked to him as she put her hands on her hips and glared at him.

Rift was taken back by this and his eyes widened, he had never heard the princess talk to anyone this way before, let alone him.

"Yes your highness, I am sorry, I was just trying to look out for your well being." Rift said, sinking his head. Never before had he felt so beaten as he did at that moment in those short words she had taken his whole fight out of him.

"My child, are you sure about this? You have been through a lot lately I think you just need sometime to think about everything that's happened and come to your senses. Then you'll see this isn't what you truly want." Lady Jewel tried to reason with her.

"Aunt, I need to do this." Nicolette told her and their eyes connected. "For me, it helps me not feel so weak and powerless."

Jewel bowed her head with Nicolette wishes. "As you wish my child, just please be careful."

"I will I promise." Nicolette said, as she looked back at the still shocked Zehava and Dahak.

"We have five miles to run don't we?" Nicolette said as she began walking.

"Yes… yes we do." Zehava said slowly walking past Rift, making sure not to look into the man's eyes.

Chapter 13

Meath had been traveling with his captors for six days and now they were deep in the heart of the jungle. They had crossed the Sheeva River three days ago by means Meath had never imagined possible until he had witnessed it. Daden and Kara had summoned their gifts and somehow combined their powers and made the very earth and rock come together on either side to form a sturdy dirt bridge right across. Meath could tell it had drained both of them a lot to do so and began to wonder just what these two could do with their powers together if they tried. Meath wondered if Ursa had any idea that there were wizards out there that could do such things with their powers. Meath at first had been not sure whether or not he wanted to cross, but after seeing Kara cross he felt a little safer. Once they had all crossed and were safe on the other side, it crumbled away into the fast flowing river leaving no trace of it ever happening.

Neither one of them had tried to talk to Meath since the first night, they had given up and Daden looked to be happy with Meath's silence, while Kara seem to be bothered by it, but had decided not to say anything.

They had made good time traveling as far as Meath knew, only because Daden kept saying so, still Meath hadn't learned anything useful to where they were taking him or why or how much longer until they got there.

Soon night had fallen upon them once more and again the two sat talking while Meath listened and ate quietly, until Kara could no longer take Meath's silence.

"You know as much as you like to think we are your enemies, we're not. Once we get to where we're going you will see we are actually helping you." She said as she brought him over the last piece of fish and handful of jungle berries and a mango that she had already peeled for him.

Daden had left to go get fresh water, now Kara thought she might be able to get Meath to open up.

"It's not healthy for a person to be so quiet." She said sitting down beside him, hoping to get him talking a little.

A few minutes passed and still Meath said nothing. "Come on Meath ,don't be like this, tell me what's on your mind, what your thinking, anything! I'm not like Daden, I do feel sorry for what is happening to you, really I do. But that I cannot change, but what I can do is try and make this experience a lot more pleasant 'til you see the purpose of it." Kara said to him, seeming truly concerned for him.

Meath just stared into her eyes blankly as he had been trained to do as a soldier when being interrogated by an enemy. But inside his mind he was trying to find a way to use this compassion to his advantage, a way to manipulate his present situation to help him escape.

"Well I won't press you, but know I am here if you want to talk. I am the closest thing to a friend you have right now Meath, just remember that." Kara whispered to him as she got up and went back to the horses just as Daden got back with water, he looked annoyed seeing Kara talking to Meath but didn't say anything.

Again Meath watched and learned, he was beginning to see by the way Daden talked to Kara and looked at her that he liked her as more then just a traveling and work companion, but he also noticed that she didn't seem to have those feelings for him. That's the only reason she was out here with him, because she was ordered to be by whoever had sent them out to collect him.

Before long they were traveling hard again, Meath could see smoke from in the distance it looked as if they were nearing a small town. Though he was not too familiar with all the small towns and villages out this far north, he did know that most likely there was a road that would take him back to Draco and then back to Dragon's Cove.

By now they were already thick into the jungle and traveling was becoming hard for the horses. The hidden jungle path they were using was becoming uneven and dangerous to the safety of the horses and riders.

"Tomorrow we will sell the horses back to the man we bought them from in Tigris." Daden said to Kara as they set up camp a few miles from the town.

"I thought we would make it before it got dark." Kara moaned wanting to sleep in an inn or even a barn.

"I know, me too. Normally I would say lets keep going 'til we're there, but the path is too dangerous and I don't want risk breaking one of the horse's legs. And with all the barbarian attacks of late, I don't want to draw any attention to ourselves by coming in the night, especially with him." Daden replied eyeing Meath.

"I sure am going to miss the horses, it is so much easier traveling with them." Kara replied, starting a small cooking fire just big enough to cook with and not something the town's folk would see.

Daden chuckled. "Oh come on, you love it out here, back home that's all you do is complain on how you wish you were out here on adventures running the land. Now that you are all you do is complain and wish you were home."

"I'm not complaining, I'm just saying we have been gone a long time and been doing nothing but traveling hard for almost eight weeks." She said, trying to redeem herself a little, knowing he was right.

They all sat around a small fire eating what was left of their supplies, which consisted of a handful of berries, some dried meat and a small loaf of hard, stale bread. They had moved Meath closer to the fire this night as Kara had used her gift to deracinate a large root to tie his restraints to.

"We will pick up supplies tomorrow in town so we don't have to hunt along the way anymore, it will only slow us down." Daden told Kara wanting to be through with this mission already and back home.

"What are we going to do with him tomorrow?" Kara asked referring to Meath. "You know as well as I do we can't just march in there with him tied up without drawing curious stares and causing trouble. If they found out who we were they wouldn't be so kind to let us stay, I'm sure."

Daden nodded his agreement having not thought of that yet. "Yes I am sure our friend here won't exactly play it cool in there either. Isn't that right?" He teased towards Meath.

Meath just sat there staring hard at him, wondering what they were going to do with him after all. If they left him alone that might be his chance to run, but he doubted they would.

"Well we can't just leave him alone, he is crafty like we were told he would be." Daden mumbled to himself, annoyed.

"Well you go into the town and I will stay with him, you trade the horses back for what money you can get for them and buy the supplies and I'll watch over Meath." Kara replied, even though she had wanted to go into the town and have a warm bath and maybe buy something to bring back with her to remember this trip.

"Are you sure Kara? Maybe I should watch over him." Daden asked not liking the fact that she had taken such an interest in Meath.

Kara sighed and shook her head. "You know as well as I Daden that you will be far better off selling the horses and buying supplies and not getting ripped off or finding trouble, a lone girl walking around in town may attract trouble."

"True enough I guess. I will go first thing in the morning, as soon as the shops are open. I will be as fast as possible." Daden told her, looking over at Meath to see if he would give himself away at all as to if he were planning an escape. H couldn't tell with Meath's blank stare. "You know him being so damn silent all the time is really starting to piss me off."

"Oh Daden, calm down, let him be, he will talk again when he is ready." Kara scowled at him.

Meath couldn't help but wonder where Kara had picked up her accent, it was so soft and sweet sounding and her words just seemed to flow off her tongue. Meath bet if she sang the birds in the trees and animals near by would all stop to listen in awe.

"You take first watch tonight." Daden grumbled while he unrolled his bedroll and crawled into it.

Kara just shook her head and turned back to Meath and winked as if she could tell he was chuckling inside like she was.

Meath began to wonder how he could escape being alone with Kara in the morning, how he might use the fact that she had taken an interest in him to his advantage. But he was sure she would not be easily fooled, she was not one to be taken lightly. Before he knew it he had fallen asleep and his dreams brought him back to the cove where he had last been with Nicolette.

~ ~ ~

Meath woke to a sharp sting in his shoulder and his eyes opened wide to see Daden standing in front of him with a dart and a cocky smile.

"There, now I'll know for sure you won't be causing any trouble." He winked to Meath.

"Damn it, Daden I told you that wouldn't be necessary." Kara barked angrily rolling out of bed.

Daden turn around and walked passed her towards the town. "I'll be back in an hour." He said as he walked to the road that lead into the town with the horses.

Meath fought hard against the drug that was attacking his senses and making him want to sleep, he could see Kara standing in front of him and her mouth was moving but he couldn't hear anything. It didn't take long before the drug won and Meath fell into a deep sleep.

Kara found the potion in her pack and rushed over to Meath and poured it down his throat, knowing that its effects would take time to work but at least in a few hours the drugs Daden had given him would be worn off instead of taking the better part of the day.

"I'm sorry Meath." Kara whispered, knowing full well Meath couldn't hear her. "Damn that Daden really is hard headed." She slumped down beside Meath and rested up against the giant tree she had tied him to the night before.

~ ~ ~

Meath woke to the feeling of cold water hitting his face hard. He jumped forward not sure of where he was or why water was hitting him.

"There, see? He's awake, now lets get going, we still have a long trip ahead of us." Daden said, sounding more like an order.

Kara helped Meath stand though the drugs effects had been diluted by Kara's potion, Meath was still feeling dizzy and nauseous. Kara didn't say anything to Meath, just gave him a helpless smile and pointed in the direction they were heading.

Meath didn't have it in him to fight or run at the moment so he started off behind Daden, he tried hard to remember the landmarks and direction they were going but it all just blurred in the end.

They traveled for hours without a word, Kara walked behind Meath and Daden lead the way. By now the drug had worn off thanks to Kara's potion and Meath was fully aware of everything.

"We will stop and rest here for a while." Daden told them when he walked into a small clearing. "We should be able to make it to that cave we camped in on the way to get him by dark."

"Good, it looks like it's going to rain tonight." Kara replied bitterly as she took a gulp of water from her skin and handed it to Meath.

Daden looked back at her and shook his head in frustration. "You know Kara, I don't understand what your problem seems to be, you should have thanked me for drugging him when I went into the town. He might have tried something you know, you could have gotten hurt or worse even killed." He told her through gritted teeth trying to justify his actions.

Meath could sense the tension growing between the two and smiled to himself, and knew he could use this. With Daden and Kara frustrated with one another they wouldn't be watching him as well as they should, tonight would be his chance.

"Let's go, I am done my rest!" Kara called back to them as she stormed off to the east taking the lead.

Meath stood and began to follow her and as soon as he was passed Daden he cracked a smile, he could hear Daden mumbling angrily.

They traveled straight through the rest of the day and just into the dusk without any conversation or stopping. Once in awhile Kara would yell back that there was a sink hole or poisonous snake off to one side, but Meath was sure she was only doing so out of obligation then anything.

They made it to the cave just as the last few rays of sun dropped behind the mountains. They ate in silence near a warm fire a dozen feet into the cave. Meath could tell the cave was manmade; the sides were rough and jagged from pick axes and hammers. The cave entrance wasn't very high or wide but as you made your way inside it expanded into a fairly large chamber. He guessed it must have been made by bandits as a hide out and a place to stash the goods that they stole.

"Look Kara, I'm sorry about what I did back there, I...I just thought it was best." Daden pleaded trying to end this feud growing between them before it got worse.

Kara stared hard at him for awhile before replying. "It's not me you should be saying you're sorry to, now is it?"

"You've got to be joking? You can't be serious?" Daden moaned knowing full well she meant it. "You know what, fine, Meath I am sorry I drugged you because I figured you would try to escape! There, are you happy?"

Kara started laughing lightly. "Ok fine, I forgive you, but I'm not a little girl anymore. I can take care of myself you know."

"I know... I just worry is all. I don't want to see you get hurt again." Daden remarked.

"Well it's late and we all need our sleep, we should be safe enough in here tonight." Kara said making sure to stop the direction of Daden's topic not wanting to think about it.

Kara tied one end of the rope they were using to lead Meath around with to her leg. "This is so you stay put." She told him with a smirk and a wink.

"I think your right, this is a pretty deserted area. I'll go set up a warning signal, just in case someone happens by this way." Daden said while pulling out a long thin length of rope and a few bells.

Soon Daden and Kara were fast asleep, and Meath watched the embers of the fire glow in the other wise pitch-black cave. He knew he couldn't escape this night, not being tied to Kara's leg. She would never have tied it there if she knew she wouldn't wake up if he tried to move. Frustration began welling inside him, he was beginning to wonder if he was ever going to be able to get free. He still didn't know what these people wanted him for and where they were taking him. He wondered what was going on back in Dragon's Cove, and what his friends were doing, if they were looking for him or assumed him dead after so long. Ursa would be back soon and have a plan to stop the evil wizard in Draco. Maybe he had made it back early and they had already done that he wondered. That would mean they would soon be looking for another suitor for the princess. That thought tore at his heart horribly and tears began streaming down his cheeks silently. He shook the thought from his head but those thoughts played in his mind till sleep took him in its embrace.

~ ~ ~

"Wake up Kara, now!" Daden screamed as he rushed back into the cave and went straight for his things. Dawn was just breaking over the mountains and the air was still chilly for this late in the morning.

Kara and Meath both bolted up right and were on their feet in a flash. "What is it Daden?" Kara asked in a rush, her blood was already pumping hard now.

"Barbarians are all around out there they've seen me and are on their way here, we have to get out of here fast." He bellowed as he threw his pack on and drew out a long dagger. Meath knew that being a trained wizard that Daden most likely wouldn't even use the dagger, that it was merely there for comfort.

"Oh great, just what we needed!" Kara cried with fear gripping her words. "How many are there?" She asked grabbing her things

"I could only see thirty five but that's not what worries me." He paused for a moment and drew a deep breath. "They have ten high priests and priestess' with them."

The blood from both Kara's and Meath's face drained, barbarian shamans were minor tricksters and illusionists, but high priests and priestesses were deadly with their art of black magic. It was a whole different kind of gift, not like that of a wizards, it was something dark and evil.

"Untie me, I can help, I am a wizard too and a soldier. I know how to fight!" Meath begged, knowing the trouble they were now in.

"Like we could trust you! Now let's get out of here and fast." Daden said, running for the entrance and Meath lead by Kara followed in fast pursuit.

They ran out of the cave just in time to see four barbarian warriors and three priestesses come into view.

"So much for a clean get away!" Kara groaned while wasting no time summoning her gift, three large trees fell crashing in the barbarian's path and into one of the warriors, crushing him and blocking the rest momentarily.

Just as she had finished that, Daden set the tree's she had fallen ablaze, killing another two that were wildly climbing over in fast pursuit.

All three started to run the other way hoping to lose the barbarians in the dense jungle. Just as they reached the first set of trees, vines lashed out smashing Meath and Kara to the ground several feet away. Daden had seen the attack moments before and rolled off to one side avoiding the hit, as he stood a barbarian club crashed into his side cracking ribs and dropping him to the ground, gasping for air and coughing up blood.

Kara watched in horror as Daden was hit again in the back, without thought she let loose a bolt of energy that ripped through Daden's attackers chest sending him sprawling backwards to the ground dieing.

"Cut me free, I can help damn it!" Meath pleaded to her knowing their chances of escape were fading fast.

Kara pulled her boot knife out and in a blink Meath's bounds were cut.

Meath bolted to action running straight towards two enemies that had just made their way around the burning trees, he called forth his gift as flames poured forth from his outstretched arms, engulfing the two. Meath snatched up one of their crude rusted swords, the weight of the blade almost made Meath want to leave it, he knew he'd never be able to fight well enough with it, but instinct wouldn't let him drop the weapon. He needed to know he had something other then his gift to rely on. Three more barbarians emerged from behind the burning trees. Knowing full well he couldn't fend them off, Meath ran back to where Kara was now standing.

"We can't win this, we've got to run!" Meath screamed trying to find a gap in the enemy that now had them almost completely surrounded.

"We can't leave without Daden." Kara cried watching her friend summon spell after spell killing or wounding enemies left and right, but he was growing weaker each time.

Meath heard chanting just in time to push Kara to the ground with him as a boulder from the ridge above crashed right where they had been standing. They jumped to their feet and turned to see three priestesses standing a dozen feet away, the fighting had stopped and everyone was eerily still. Barbarians were bowing to their spiritual leaders and chanting in their native tongue.

Daden's powers were almost exhausted as he sat crumbled to the ground waiting for whatever fate had planned for him.

"This might be our only chance." Meath whispered to Kara.

"What are you talking about, we're as good as dead, we can't win now." She whispered back with a scared and shaky tone.

Meath turned to her with a look of sheer desperation. "I know, but what have we got to lose, right? Get ready." As he finished the words he bolted into a dead run towards the priestesses with sword held high.

One of the priestesses howled in laughter at Meath's charge to death, she swung her arm out releasing an ark of black power that nailed Meath in his shoulder sending him back and to the ground shuddering, but not before he had released his own gift, sending a blast of wind at the priestesses along with the sword he had been holding. The rusty blade impaled through the belly of one, sending her to the ground screaming madly and gurgling. Another was caught off guard and blown back into a tree, winding her momentarily. The third had countered his attack with a spell of her own dissipating it around her and was now summoning an attack of her own.

Kara watched in horror and amazement at Meath's daring move but now understood what he meant; she dropped to her knees and slammed her hands flat on the ground causing tremors and quakes to rattle the earth around them. Before the priestess could cast her spell the quake tripped her up and shook her to the ground along with many other barbarians that had gotten back on their feet, enraged and ready to attack the three for the death of one of their spiritual leaders.

By now Daden had made it to his feet and slashed his dagger across the throat of the barbarian closest to him, spinning back the other way driving it into the chest of another that had just noticed what was going on.

Seeing an escape, Meath staggered to his feet and sprang into a run, making sure to grab Kara's hand to help pull her along as he went. As they reached Daden, a vine shot up from the ground catching Meath's leg pulling him hard to the ground as it curled up his thigh, the thorns of the vine tore and ripped his flesh as it climbed. Daden stopped and slashed the vine with his dagger freeing Meath to continue their escape. Seeing they would need more time, Kara stomped her foot hard against the ground and dragged it back a few inches. The earth split a few dozen feet long and two full-grown men's width, separating them from the enemy for a few more moments, but it had cost her a great deal of strength and energy. She almost fell, but Meath grabbed her and pulled her on.

They ran for a few miles, covering their trail everywhere they could, adrenalin alone had kept them going this long. The barbarians had given up the pursuit for the time being, so they stopped at a small pond to rest and clean their wounds.

"I thought we were gonna die back there." Daden coughed holding his side with the broken ribs, which burned painfully.

"We would have, if I hadn't freed Meath!" Kara said while trying to catch her breath.

Then it clicked to everyone and Meath knew this was his only chance to escape. Before anyone could say another word or even react Meath took off running into the jungle.

"Damn it, stop!" Daden yelled trying to run after him but falling to the ground from the pain in his side and back.

"Meath come back, you can't do this, not now!" Kara cried and started off after him but stopped, seeing Daden fall to the ground.

"Go after him!" Daden cried in pain and frustration.

"But what about you? I can't just leave you here, what if the barbarians find you? They'll kill you!" She said helping him back into a sitting position near the pond.

"We need him, now go!" He ordered. "I'll be fine, I promise." He assured her.

Kara took one last look at him before running off into the jungle after Meath, she was still weak of mind after using her gift to escape the barbarians but adrenaline kept her going.

~ ~ ~

Meath knew he was leaving an easy trail to follow, but he had to get far enough away before he could tend to his wounds and cover his tracks.

His left shoulder and arm that had been hit by the priestess blast burned horribly, and his leg had gone numb from the loss of blood. He knew he'd have to stop soon or he would risk bleeding to death.

Finally exhaustion and blood loss dropped him near a small stream that he was sure lead to the pond he had left Daden and Kara at. He didn't even cup the water in his hands but plunged his face into the cold water and drank till he was full.

He then ripped away his leather riding pants up to his knee on his tattered leg, and soaked his leg in the water, washing away the dried blood and dirt, but soon noticed that his wounds were turning a charcoal black and the black skin seemed to be slowly spreading throughout his leg. He quickly tied it off to stop the oozing blood and hoped it would slow or prevent the blackness from going any further up his leg. He took off his shirt and looked at his charred, torn shoulder. The wound was having the same affect as the one on his shoulder.

"What I wouldn't give to have my potions with me." Meath moaned knowing full well that his potions wouldn't help other then to numb the pain and slow the infection. He didn't even know what it was he seemed to have, or any idea how to heal it.

He stood up and was glad to find his leg was still fairly numb and that he could still put weight on it. He found a walking stick, then used the sun to find west hoping to find a road or path soon, if he didn't he would have to find shelter before nightfall. Other then his gift, which he didn't think he could concentrate enough to use, he was weaponless, which made him easy prey to anything that could be about.

He walked until it got dark and had to hide twice from barbarians that were out searching for him and the others. The only shelter he found before total darkness was a small overhang in a rock wall, which he took without complaint. It was just high enough for him to sit up in and a little longer then the length of his body.

The night seemed colder then normal, he didn't know if that was from loss of blood or the fact he hadn't eaten all day. He wanted to light a fire but knew with the barbarians searching for him that he had better suffer through the chill of the night.

Hunger began to grip his thoughts and Meath started searching under rocks and rotten logs around his shelter, eating the bugs and insects that hid under them. He thought back to when he was training in Drandor with Zehava and Dahak and the first time they had to eat bugs to pass the survival test. Dahak had vomited before he had even swallowed Meath never understood why he had stayed in the army, he always hated it and everything they did.

After eating a few handfuls his stomach stopped hurting and he drifted off to sleep wondering if he would ever see Nicolette or his friends again, or if he would even wake up.

~ ~ ~

Kara sat in a large dead stump she had found an hour before nightfall and decided she would stay for the night, not wanting to get stuck out in the jungle with no shelter. She gathered some large leafs and built a temporary roof incase of rain and to help keep her hidden, she had almost been sighted several times by barbarians and didn't want to get caught while she slept.

Not knowing how much longer she might be out here looking for Meath and then getting back to Daden, she rationed her food wisely only having a small chunk of dried meat and some cheese.

She had followed Meath's trail and was sure he couldn't be too far ahead of her, his wounds were bad and that would mean he was traveling slow. She hope she could get to him in time, she knew his wounds were worse then he might think. Priestess's magic was an evil thing indeed, his wounds would already have started rotting and decaying and if it spread long enough it would kill him. If she didn't find him within the next day, she wasn't sure if she would be able to help him.

She wondered if Daden was all right and had found a place for the night, she laughed to herself, of course he was all right. Daden was too stubborn to be otherwise. Kara knew once she found Meath she was going to have to subdue him somehow, she knew he wouldn't come willing. Kara wished she could just tell him the truth of the matter, but it was not her place to, she had her orders. She didn't want to have to drug him again and bind him with enchanted rope, Kara hated that thought, but knew that would likely the only possible solution. She curled up in her stump and drifted off to sleep, and dreamed of being back home in her own room, safe and warm.

Chapter 14

Ursa slowly got off his horse as he neared his destination, he walked his horse the rest of the way as thoughts flooded back into his mind of his time spent here long ago as a young man. He took an apple from a nearby tree and gave it to his horse who ate it greedily. He scratched behind the beast's ear letting it know it had done a great job getting him here swiftly.

Ursa could feel the energy in the air it made the hairs on his arms and neck tingle, it had been so long since he had last been to Solmis' Haven, but he still remembered it down to the last blade of grass. He had spent the better part of his youth here, learning, training and practicing in the arts of his gift. It felt just like yesterday since he had been in the same spot he walked now casting his first spell, a bolt of energy that didn't release in time and left the young Ursa very sore and hair standing on end. He chuckled at the memory and it reminded him of Meath's first spell that had left the boy with no eyebrows. Ursa smiled widely and shook his head, how he in his youth reminded him so much of Meath. The questions, the eagerness, the stubbornness and even the attitude, yes how they all seemed to fit.

He came to a well-worn path that led to a wooded area, beyond those trees was the man he had come all this way to see. The man who in so many ways was the closest thing to a father he had ever truly known and respected.

Ursa took the saddle and reins off his horse so it could graze freely on the sweet, grasses and cloves of Solmis' Haven.

He began down the path into the woods towards the large log cabin that waited at the end of the path. It was not a long walk but each step brought back so many memories and thoughts, everything was the exact same as it had been when he had left all those years ago, not a single tree had aged or been blown down by a winter storm, not a single rock had been moved or dislodged from its resting place.

Before he knew it, he was standing in front of the same log cabin that he had lived in for many years. A place he would always call his home. Excitement welled up inside of him like a child about to get a present, he could not wait to see Solmis again, though he knew he could not stay long to reminisce with his old Master, he would be sure to come and visit again as soon as he possibly could after everything was righted again.

Ursa knocked firmly on the door, and after several moments opened it and let himself in. Familiar smells assaulted his nose, from the mint leafs Solmis uses for his tea and potions, to the smell of oak and cedar that the cabin was built from, it all smelt the same.

Ursa looked over to the hearth that was burning slowly emanating just enough light in the dark corner to show Solmis sitting in his chair, where he spent many hours in meditation or just relaxing and watching the flames of the fire. It had been over forty years since Ursa had seen his mentor, and from what Ursa could see, he had barely aged at all. Solmis had been somewhere in his sixties when Ursa had first arrived more then a half-century ago. But Ursa wasn't surprised that the man was still alive. As a boy he had heard stories about Solmis' Haven being enchanted and those who stayed there would live long past their expected years.

Ursa just stood there, not sure how to approach his old mentor and friend, he was beginning to wonder if the old hermit even realized anyone was in the house with him. The man in the chair didn't say anything or move. Maybe time had finally gotten to the old wizard, the thought almost brought a tear to Ursa's eyes. No it was a test, he was sure of it.

"After all these years you still feel the need to test me, Master?" Ursa asked about to take a step towards him when he was assaulted with the feeling that something was amiss.

"Don't move or else!" A voice from behind Ursa commanded. "Who are you and what do you want?" The voice barked coldly.

"My name is Ursa and I came here to see my old friend and mentor about some urgent matters." Ursa replied calmly even thought he was unsure of what was going on.

"Turn around slowly, any sudden movements and I'll blast a hole right through you!" The voice snapped, a little less intimidating then before.

Ursa put his hands out to the side and slowly turned to face a young woman with a finely crafted wooden staff pointed straight at his chest, he could tell she meant what she said, for the staff's head was fitted with a perfectly round smoky black gem that swirled and sparked with power ready to be expelled.

"If you are who you say you are then you won't mind answering a few questions." She said licking her lips, not easing up on the staff at all.

"As you wish my child, I will answer to the best of my ability." Ursa replied politely, not wanting to set her off in any way, believing she truly would kill him if he tried anything.

"First don't ever call me 'child' again. Now what was master Solmis' favourite food?" She asked, not taking her gaze from his.

"Well that's easy my ch…." Ursa stopped himself. "Then what might I call you?" He asked. "You know my name but I do not know yours."

"Don't play me for a fool, old man. Now answer the question or else!" She ordered tightening her grip on the staff causing the orb on the end to swirl even faster.

"His favourite food is duck roasted in onions and wild black mushrooms with a nice warm cup of spiced apple cider rum." Ursa replied, realizing if he were to get himself out of this mess he would have to play along.

"What was his favourite spell?" She asked seeming to accept his first answer.

"He always favoured communicating with the animals." Ursa answered wondering how long this was going to go on.

"My name is Talena." She said lowering her staff. "Sorry about that, but I had to be sure it was really you, I could take no chances."

"I understand, I would have done the same if I were you." Ursa said relaxing his posture. "Now it is imperative that I speak with Solmis!"

Talena flinched at the name. "I'm afraid that is impossible."

"What do you mean?" Ursa questioned, looking back to where he had seen Solmis in his chair but now there was nothing, then it dawned on him that Talena had question him in past tense, he sighed knowing the truth now, no one could live that long, not even Solmis.

"He passed last winter." Talena said knowing that's what he was wondering.

"And you?" Ursa asked. "Who are you and where do you fit in?"

"I was his apprentice for the last five years." Talena replied, placing the staff in its holder on the wall and walking over to the hearth.

"Why are you still here then? Why didn't you go off and continue your training with a new Master?" Ursa asked joining her near the fire.

"I was told to wait for you." She said looking up from the flames into his eyes, seeing his confusion she continued. "Several years before Solmis died he had a vision, a very dark, disturbing vision. He knew he was going to die soon and that he would not be able to help, for his time would end before the vision would ever start to take place."

"Did he tell you what his vision was?" Ursa asked eagerly hoping for something that might help him in his cause.

Talena shook her head. "No, he said that if he told me certain aspects that had to happen wouldn't, and the out come would be worse then his vision." She replied.

Ursa sighed out loud. "And is this what you were supposed to wait for me for? Was to tell me this?" Ursa asked a little frustrated and annoyed.

"Yes but there's more." She stopped and took a deep breath. "You have to take me with you."

"I will take you to the first city and from there you will have to find a new mentor or life, that is up to you." Ursa grumbled wondering what to do next. He had hoped that Solmis would have been able to shed some light on his problem.

"No I must stay with you." Talena insisted taking a step towards him.

"I already have an apprentice and a very big problem on my hands. I cannot help you my dear, I am sorry." Ursa told her kindly but firmly. "Maybe one day I can finish your training, but right now I cannot."

"You don't understand..." She tried to get out before she was cut off.

"No, you don't seem to understand. I cannot take you with me, I cannot teach you. My friends and home are being threatened by a great evil and army and I need to find away to stop it, and to do that I need to find out who this great evil wizard is." Ursa barked. "And I came here hoping that Solmis could help me, and use his foresight to help find these answers I seek." Ursa finished his tone more of a whisper now.

"I have Solmis' foresight now!" Talena cried trying to get a word in.

Ursa stopped and turned to her somewhat unnerved. "What did you say?"

"After Solmis' vision, he knew you would come to seek his guidance. He also knew he would be long dead before you ever got here. He also knew he couldn't find you and disrupt the flow of events that would lead up to now. But he knew you would need his help, that's why he found me and made me his new apprentice. Since his vision he dedicated his time and studying to see if the rumours were true, that one could take another's gift or pass on ones gift to another." She said take a deep breath making sure she had Ursa full attention. "He discovered it to be true, that one could take another's gift, with the proper spells and ceremony. He took me in and trained me to be the one whom he gave them too." She said as tears began to stream down her face.

"So what you're telling me is that Solmis gave you all his great knowledge and powers of his gift?" Ursa asked, hardly believing what he was hearing.

"In a sense yes, he died before the end of the ceremony so I only received some of his gifts, but I did get his gift of foresight, which is what he wanted, and what you need." She explained.

Ursa didn't know what to think, in all his years he had learned that stealing or giving of ones gift was impossible, yet everyone knew the rumours. Could they be true? "How did the ceremony work?" Ursa asked.

"I was told never to tell you." Talena whimpered not wanting to anger Ursa but not willing to break her promise either.

"I just need to know a few things, to know if I can believe you. Do not tell me all of it just answer me this; did it require a dark ceremony of pain and brutality?" He asked.

Tears flowed freely now down her face as vivid memories flowed through her mind. "Yes, the only way is an evil way, one that only the Keeper himself could ever have conceived." She answered him almost afraid of his reaction. "But it was the only way."

"So it is true then…" Ursa muttered. "Well what do you see? Use his foresight and tell me what I need to know."

"I… I can't." She cried.

"Why not?" Ursa asked confused.

"Solmis had decades of training to use his gifts and the gift of foresight is one that takes great training and resolve of the mind. I do not know how to use it on my command, it just comes to me in flashes." She replied, feeling weak and wishing she could do as he asked.

As frustrated as Ursa was by her answer, he understood and could not blame her. "I need you to try, I need to know who it is that is pretending to be Prince Berrit, I need a name, a place, something."

"I'll try." Talena replied sitting on the floor going into a meditated trance trying to tap into Solmis's gift that he had given her.

~ ~ ~

For hours Ursa sat watching her on the floor concentrating on his questions. Trying to connect with the gift she now had, but could not control. Ursa knew even Solmis sometimes took hours, if not days to summon a forced vision, so he sat and waited. He did not want to risk missing anything if it came.

The light from dawn slowly began to pour into the windows and bringing life outside, Ursa wondered how long they would have to wait. He knew he had to be patient, even though time was not on his side. He stood and stretched his old bones and went to the large table in the cooking area where he grabbed a bunch of grapes and began eating them. He looked around the house, and now that he knew the truth the place almost seemed to lose that heart-warming joy.

He was jolted out of his thoughts when he heard a crash on the floor over where Talena had been sitting, she now was shuttering violently, Ursa ran to her side and she stopped, her eyes opened wide and she jolted up into a sitting position.

"Are you alright?" Ursa asked her.

"Your friends are in great danger you must get to them." Talena blurred as she came out of her trance.

"What is it? How are they in danger?" Ursa bellowed.

"The castle is going to be attacked, everyone will die." She said as she stood. "We must hurry!"

Ursa didn't need to be told twice. "Grab what you can and whatever food and water you can." Ursa barked, grabbing his own things and stuffing his pack with whatever he could see that he could make useful. "Do you have a horse?" Ursa asked her.

"Yes I do, in the back in the sable." She replied still dizzy and disoriented.

"Grab what you can and meet me outside in the front." Ursa said as he went out the door, he stopped just outside and turned to her. "Do you know how to use that staff?" He asked.

Talena turned to him and chuckled. "You better believe it."

~   ~   ~

They rode all day and long into the night trying to make the best time they could, but finally had to stop for the night, the horses were exhausted and were in need of rest and water while Ursa and Talena were not much better.

Neither one had said much the whole time they had traveled. "So what did you see exactly? To the last detail." Ursa asked her after they had eaten and settled down.

She was silent for awhile recalling what she had seen. "Well I saw a castle by the ocean being over run by thousands of barbarians. There was a woman and some soldiers in a room talking, they were saying if only Ursa was here and if only Meath had not been taken and killed that they might stand a chance."

"Do you know when this is going to happen or if it has happened already?" Ursa asked hoping there was more to it.

"No I don't... I'm sorry." She replied wishing she could tell him more.

"Ursa leaned back on the tree he was using for a back rest and sighed. "It is ok, hopefully it has not already happened and we will be in time to help prevent it."

They sat watching the fire in silences for many minutes until Talena broke the silence. "I am sorry."

"I told you it was alright, it's not your fault. You saw what you saw." Ursa replied.

"No not about that, about Solmis, I am sorry about... well about everything." She said looking straight into his eyes.

"I know, and so am I, but Solmis believed this needed to be done, he was a great wizard and man and wouldn't have jumped into anything he was not sure of, so we have faith he was right and do as we must." Ursa assured her. It seemed to help put her at ease. "Let us not talk of these things, we still have a long journey ahead of us and we will need as much sleep as we can get. I will take first watch, you get some sleep." Ursa said.

Talena chuckled softly. "I almost forgot, we both can sleep well tonight." Ursa cocked an eyebrow at her, not following what she was getting at.

"Solmis knew he would be deep in his studies most of the time and would not be granted the time to training me properly, so he cheated a little and made this staff for me, it will only work for me and can do things those with just the gift cannot."

"How does it work?" Ursa asked, intrigue by this magical item. He had known wizards, sorcerers and sorceresses that had staffs that were enchanted with the ability of fire, or energy or even healing and such. But each staff could only hold one or two spells and even those spells were limited.

"Well it taps into my gift when I want to use it." As she said the words the gem at the top glowed dark red, as if a flame danced at the top of it. "Or even ice." The flame died and the gem went a light blue and Ursa could see ice forming around the top.

"That is amazing!" Ursa blurted out.

"It magnifies my gift, without the staff I could cast maybe four or five fire balls before I was weak, but with my staff I can switch between fire, ice, energy, wind at a thought and cast ten times that many." She said with a smile.

"That doesn't explain how we can both sleep tonight without have someone stay watch." Ursa said, still in awe.

"I was getting to that." Talena stood up and slammed the end of her staff into the ground several inches and muttered some words, and for a moment there was a flash from the gem. "There we're safe, as long as we stay within ten or so feet in every direction of the staff."

Before Ursa could ask Talena piped in. "We are hidden in a magical veil to anyone that happens by. All they see is grass, trees and ground. But we can still see and hear them."

"What happens if they stumble in?" Ursa asked, having heard of such spells as this but never witnessing one before.

"Well the intruder will get a nasty shock and the spell will dissipate, but by then we should be well on our guard." She said with a smile.

"Well, well, Solmis always did know how to do things." Ursa laughed getting into his bedroll. Both of them were fast asleep in moments.

~   ~   ~

They traveled long and hard the next day and into the night again, using Talena's staff at night so they both could get well rested without stopping long. Ursa was beginning to like the young girl now that the awkward part had passed and she had opened up and was more herself. Ursa could see why Solmis had chosen her, she was smart, witty, and had a way about her.

It was mid morning of their third day of traveling they came across a large pond that Ursa had passed on his way to Solmis' Haven, they stopped and let the horses drink while Ursa rooted around in his saddlebag.

"What are you doing?" Talena asked.

"We are making great time with both of us being to be able to rest at night, we are over half a day ahead of what I was getting here. On my way through I stopped here for a night and discovered this pond has some of the best tasting trout I have ever had. And seeing as how I am hungry, and I am sure you are too, I thought while we are here we might as well take advantage of it." Ursa finished as he found his fishing line, bobber and hook he was looking for.

He baited the hook with a large worm he found under a rock he had flipped over. Ursa and Talena sat on a fallen tree near the pond just talking about things of no matter while they waited for their lunch to bite. It wasn't long before they had a large trout cooking over a fire.

"Believe me, once you eat this you won't ever forget this pond." Ursa told her as he flipped the fish over making sure it cooked all the way through.

Talena was just about to say something when a dozen men exploded through the jungle around them shields up and weapons ready.

"It's him!" One man cried over his shoulder to the others.

"We have you now, Ursa!" Another barked angrily.

Within seconds Draco and Zandorian soldiers surrounded Ursa and Talena.

"What's going on?" Talena asked Ursa, gripping her staff hard.

Ursa sighed, he had almost forgotten about the soldiers that would still be looking for him, Meath and the princess. These men had probably been out here searching since the first day.

"Where's the Princess you traitorous pig?" Demanded the commander of the group while pointing his sword at Ursa's chest.

Ursa shut his eyes for a moment knowing more innocent people had to die, but he hoped not to kill all of them. "Run!" Ursa cried releasing a ball of energy into two men in front of them, blowing them to the ground hurt but not dead. He grabbed Talena's staff and pulled her along sending a wall of flames up behind them to cover their escape for a few moments.

Ursa ran for a long while, not looking back, just holding onto Talena's staff and pulling her along. He no longer heard the sound of men following them as he stopped, only then did he realize Talena wasn't at the other end of the staff, no one was.

"Talena!" Ursa yelled, hoping she was not far behind. "Ursa you fool how could you be so stupid not to notice that you lost her." Ursa barked to himself, he slowly made his way back the way he had come, hoping and praying that she was not far behind and that she was safe and had found a place to hide.

Ursa made it back to where he and Talena had been stopped. No one was there, the horses and supplies were all gone, there was no sign of Talena anywhere.

Ursa was sure they would have left someone to watch for his return so he decided to play right into their hands. He walked out into the opening looking for the direction they would have gone so that he could follow, all the while keeping his eyes and senses on his surroundings. It was not long before he saw two men hiding behind some trees, waiting for the right moment to spring their attack.

"If you're looking for the girl, she is still alive... at least for now." A Zandorian soldier said coming from a place that was nowhere near where the other two were hiding.

Ursa knew the ruse for what it was, one man would keep him distracted while the other two attacked from behind.

"Where is she?" Ursa ordered the man.

The man laughed. "I will be the one giving the orders, you old coward." His tone became deadly and showed he was no longer amused. "Where is the princess? What have you done with her?"

"Where is the girl? Tell me that and I may tell you what you ask." Ursa shot back, not giving an inch.

"You do not get to make the demands you minion of the Keeper." The soldier barked back getting very worked up.

Ursa chuckled slyly. "Oh I believe I do, seeing as how I have a princess and you merely have a peasant girl that I keep around for my entertainment." Ursa reminded him and that seemed to put the man in his place. "That and I am a minion of the Keeper, I can do terrible things to you." Ursa said giving the soldier a crazy stare.

Ursa heard the pull back on the bowstring and stepped to the side, turning just as the arrow sizzled past him and embedded itself into the Zandorian soldier's chest, which was meant to distract him.

Before the man could load his bow and pull off another shot the bowstrings snapped as flames engulfed it, his companion charged wildly towards Ursa with sword ready to strike.

Ursa didn't want to kill them if he didn't have too, he summoned his gift and a blast of wind hit the charging man square in the chest, knocking him to the ground, Ursa could already hear the sound of the other bowman running for all he was worth through the jungle to get away.

Ursa walked over to the Zandorian soldier with the arrow imbedded into his chest, who was trying to hold on to life. There was nothing Ursa could do for the man, the arrow had hit his lung, he was as good as dead.

He turned to the man he had blown down who was just now coming to after the air from his lungs had been knocked out, dazing him.

Ursa slammed his foot down hard on the man's guts, causing him to cry out and vomit. "Where did they take the girl?" Ursa commanded in a voice that seemed to silence everything around them.

"I'm not going to tell you anything you traitor!" The man cried in defiance.

"Maybe you didn't hear me, I said where did they take her?" Ursa ordered again putting his foot hard on his throat.

He coughed and struggled under Ursa's foot. "Go ahead and kill me, I don't fear death." He yelled up at Ursa. "The Creator will take me into his arms knowing I defied a child of the Keeper." The Zandorian screamed.

Ursa smiled widely. "Oh you have nothing to fear about death my boy." As he said the words he waved his hand over the soldiers head showing him the ball of energy forming in his hand. "It's what I'm going to do to you before you die that you need to fear."

~ ~ ~

After a few hours Ursa had gotten the information he wanted and was on his way to find Talena. He did feel bad for what he had done to the soldier, he had not killed him but he did have to torture him a great deal to get what he wanted. He had wanted to heal the man but had no time to and didn't want to waste any energy he didn't have to. He knew he would need to be as strong as he could to get Talena out safely, if she was even still alive.

~ ~ ~

"I told you I don't know what you're talking about." Talena cried and a soldier punched her hard in the guts.

"Wrong answer little girl, just tell me what I want to know and it will all stop." A big Zandorian brute said to her as he paced the large tent.

"Now let's try again, where is the princess? Where did Ursa put her?" He screamed in her face, showering her with his sweat and spit as he did it.

"I don't know what you're talking about!" Talena tried to say firmly, even though the three men in the room could tell she was terrified.

"She's not going to talk captain, let the boys have some fun with her." One of the big brutes in the tent said. "Maybe after that she'll feel like talking." He said with a wicked grin.

"Not yet, I believe she will talk, just give her some time." The captain said. "Let's give her some time to think about her options." He chuckled as they all left the tent.

Talena had never felt as alone and helpless in her whole life as she did right now. She couldn't believe Ursa had just kept going after she had tripped and fell behind. No, she couldn't blame him. She knew he didn't know that she had tripped, she knew if he had known he would have stopped for her, even if it meant dying.

How she wished she had her staff, these men wouldn't be so tough if she only had her magical staff. She wondered if she could free her hands with her gift. She hadn't used her gift in a while and even when she did use it, it was hardly well or efficient. She concentrated hard trying to block out all the noises outside the tent, all the soldiers laughing and cursing. She focused all her attention on burning the ropes that bound her hands to the pole in the middle of the tent. Her eyes opened wide and she tried not to scream as her gift burnt her hands and not the rope. She whimpered and fought back the tears and the scream as best she could. She had no idea how badly she had burnt herself, but she was sure by the pain that it was bad enough. Talena sat there knowing she had better not try it again, she knew it was hopeless, she was no good without her staff. She had become too reliant on it when she should have tried to learn what she could of her gift without the staff. Though these thoughts did her no good now, she promised herself if she made it out of here she would practice more without the staff.

~ ~ ~

"Well are you ready to talk yet?" The large Zandorian captain asked after throwing a bucket of cold water on her to wake her.

Talena hadn't even noticed that she had fallen asleep, but now that she was awake again with cold water dripping on her burnt hands she remembered the pain and what had happened. From what she could tell it was the next morning already.

"What's a matter with you?" The captain asked, seeing that she was in pain. "What happened to your hands?" The man barked to her when he walked around her and seen her hands. "Who did this to you?"

Talena didn't know what to say at first. She didn't want to give away that she had the gift, she knew what Zandorians did to those with the gift.

"I said who did this to you?" He yelled again looking hard into her eyes.

"What difference does it make? I am a prisoner and you will probably kill me anyways after doing far worse then this." She whimpered, wondering if she could actually get away with him believing one of his men did this to her.

He smiled a sinister smile at her and began pacing the room. "Maybe so, I do not know what I shall do with you yet, but what I do know is I gave an order that you were not to be harmed... yet." He turned to face her again. "Now who did this to you?"

Talena smiled to herself in her mind. "It was the man who said to let the men have their way with me." She whispered out trying hard to play it out like it actually happened.

"Markect, why that little slimy bastard, he has disobeyed for the last time!" The Captain grumbled as he stood up straight with a fierce look on his face. "Delmont!" The captain barked.

"Yes sir" Said a younger man who was just outside of the tent standing guard.

"Bring me Markect, now!" He yelled clearly becoming more enraged by the moment.

Talena wondered what was about to happen, if Markect said she was lying, would he believe him and then punish her? It was all out of her hands now, there was nothing more she could do, whatever was about to happen was going to happen.

"What the hell is going on? Get your hands off me, I out rank you soldier, I will have your head in a rope you whelp!" Markect bellowed while two large men brought him forcefully into the tent.

"Do you care to explain?" The captain snarled angrily at him.

"Explain? Explain what? What is this about?" Markect stammered.

The captain walked over to him and punched him hard sending Markect staggering back with a broken nose.

"What the hell was that for, you son of a bitch?" Markect cried looking up at him, blood dripping form his nose.

The big Zandorian took a deep breath before replying. "Don't play dumb with me, I gave you an order that she was not to be harmed yet! And once again you have disobeyed an order."

Markect stood straight and glared at him. "I did nothing, I have not harmed her, why would I have?"

"You dare lie to my face you bastard?" The captain yelled while he slammed his fist into his face again cracking his jaw this time.

Before Markect could even recover from the blow, the captain drew his dagger and buried it deep into his chest and wretched it out just to slam it in again.

"Let this be a lesson for everyone!" He yelled out to all those that now stood in the tent and outside. "No one is to disobey an order again, or you shall see the same fate." He finished and he stormed out of the tent. "And someone see to the wounds on her hands!"

~ ~ ~

Ursa had found their camp late in the evening on the second night Talena had been captured, it had been almost two whole days now, he truly wondered if she would even be alive. He knew soldiers and what they did to prisoners, especially female ones. He shuddered at the thought. He had scouted out the camp, it was a small one. He only counted fourteen soldiers, but he wasn't about to risk everything until he knew where she was being held.

Finally he saw a large Zandorian exit from one of the bigger tents and he heard the man yell back into it "You will talk sooner or later, of course now its too late, my men grow hungry for the feel of a woman. I have given you plenty of time to comply with my questions. Tonight you are their play thing." He barked as he went through the camp rousing his men and informing them of their new rights for the night, which many of them ran off eagerly to enjoy those rights.

Ursa drew in a deep breath, he could not let this happen to her, he had to act now. He bolted into the camp trying to get as close to the group of soldiers as he could before giving himself away. He was but a stone throw away before someone saw him and charged. He was the first to die, a mighty blast of light shot right through the left side of his chest and sent him twitching to the ground.

"We are under attack!" A cry from somewhere in the camp came.

Ursa was sure everyone knew he was there now, while five men rushed towards him with shields high and spears at the ready.

"Shields are only good against novices." He grunted, as if insulted while he summoned a gust of wind that slowly blew harder and harder against their shields. The men fought hard to keep their ground and leaned hard into the oncoming wind, fighting to stay upright and gain ground. But as fast as the wind came it stopped in an instant and all five toppled forward, getting tripped up and crashed to the ground. Seconds later fire engulfed them all. Ursa didn't even hear their screams, he just kept walking towards the tent. The twang of bowstrings sounded, Ursa sidestepped in time to see two arrows strike the ground where he had been standing. He turned to the bowmen who were fast to reload but not as fast at hiding. Several arcs' of energy erupted from Ursa's fingertips and ripped through the three bowmen in the far corner of the camp.

Ursa turned to keep walking as he lifted his leg he felt the sting of an arrow in the back of his thigh. "Blasted you're getting slow Ursa my boy!" He scowled to himself pulling the arrow out and healing it only enough to slow the bleeding until later when he could finish the job.

Two more men charged forth from the tent with weapons drawn, looking around at their fallen comrades and saw the wizard walking towards them. As if they had planned it, both dropped their weapons and ran for all they were worth the other way.

Ursa reached the tent with no further resistance, he was sure the rest had fled into the jungle to escape certain death. Not many men wanted to do battle with a trained wizard. There he saw Talena, tied to a pole with her clothes still on.

"Thank the heavens." He prayed, moving to untie her.

"I knew you would not leave me." She beamed, glad she was right at what kind of man he was, though she had no idea that he would come to her rescue.

"We have no time for talk, we must get out of here and find somewhere safe." Ursa insisted.

They ran out of the tent and headed for the way Ursa had come in, they were just about to clear the last tent when the huge Zandorian soldier Ursa had seen exit the tent and gave his men the order to rape Talena stepped out in front of them, his blade leading the way. Ursa pushed Talena to the side, she crashed into the ground several feet away but he himself had not avoided taking a hit across his shoulder and back. The mere force of the blow, though it was not life threatening, still sent Ursa to the ground hard.

"You're not so tough wizard!" The man cried lifting his sword high in the air, ready to bring it down on Ursa's head.

Ursa quickly rolled to the side and avoided being cut in half and was back on his feet. The Zandorian turned back to him more enraged than ever just in time to see a ball of fire leave Ursa's palm.

Ursa went to Talena's side and helped her up. They ran into the jungle long before his screams had stopped.

Chapter 15

"Come on, faster! You're going to have to be faster then that!" Zehava urged as he and Nicolette sparred on the grass with wooden swords that almost weighed the same as the real things.

Nicolette parried Zehava's low thrust and swung it up high, but wasn't fast enough to get her own blade down to block his slash across her mid section. He let her know it by tapping her lightly on the stomach with his wooden sword.

"Every move has a counter move to either better your advantage over your enemy or to put you both back on even terms." Zehava told her again.

They had spent the last few days teaching her how to use a sword, and though she was improving, it was slow going, Zehava could not blame her, in the army you had years of training and fighting, and so far she had only had a few days.

"I know I know, its just this sword is too heavy. I can't move it fast enough and control it because the weight throws me off balance." Nicolette complained again, growing a little frustrated.

"I have to say, you are getting a lot better then before." Dahak replied hoping to encourage her a little.

"Well that's enough sword play for the day I think, now we jog five miles with loaded pack and then we'll see how well you can shoot a bow." Zehava said packing up their equipment.

"Where is Shania today, Zehava?" Nicolette asked, packing her things up.

"Ya where's your girlfriend buddy, I haven't seen her all day?" Dahak teased.

"I don't know she told me she had something to do in the city today and that she would be back later on." Zehava replied, ignoring Dahak's comment. "No matter she can take care of herself, now let's get a move on."

"Man, and I thought once we finished training in the army that would be the end of all the darn running." Dahak complained throwing his pack over his shoulders.

~ ~ ~

"Ursa should have been back by now your highness, we must act now before it's too late." Uvael, Dragon's Cove's advisor told her.

Jewel paced the room where her sick husband lay, too weak to speak now. "Maybe we should give him one more day, I am sure he just fell a little behind, he might have the answers we seek." Jewel replied, trying to convince herself more then her advisor. They had had this conversation the day before when Ursa's deadline of a week had ended, she had already given him an extra day.

"Your highness, with all due respect, you have a duty to your people, and that this evil wizard that has found a way to fool so many is not only a threat to Draco but Dragon's Cove and the whole kingdom. We may have a plan of action that might solve the whole ordeal without war or having the whole kingdom in an uproar." Uvael pleaded. "You must think of the big picture here, my Lady, a lot is at risk."

Jewel went to her husband's side and looked down to him, how weak and defeated he looked. "What I wouldn't give for you to be well my love." She looked hard into his eyes, knowing he could hear her, for his eyes had tears in them. "I do not know the best course of action my husband, I was never trained in the arts of war and battle and how to rule in such a manner, but I shall do the best that I can my love." She whispered to him. "Send the assassins to Draco Castle, their payment of fifty thousand gold coins will be waiting here for the one that brings me this demons head." Jewel ordered to Uvael, her voice again stern.

Uvael bowed his head and backed out of the room. "Yes my lady, I believe you have made the right choice."

"I pray that I have..." Jewel whispered to herself.

~ ~ ~

"You are all clear on what needs to be done?" Uvael asked one more time to the five assassins Dragon's Cove had hired four days ago, in case Ursa didn't make it back on time with a plan.

"Of course's we do, you nag worse then a woman." One of the assassins laughed in a deep, thick accent. He was the only one of the group from the desert kingdom far to the east.

"I am just trying to make sure there are no mishaps, no one may know who you are and what you are doing there. This has got to be clean and flawless." Uvael told them firmly.

"We heard ya the first time." Another one barked back. "We are assassins. We've trained our entire lives to do this very thing, we understand the stakes."

"Yes well I guess you are right." Uvael muttered. "Well then you are all clear on payment then? Which ever one or ones make it back here with the target's head gets fifty thousand gold coins. If you work together then you will have to split the reward any way you like, that is not Dragon Cove's problem." The mention of the large reward had the men's eyes glistening with anticipation.

"Alright men, go do your job and may the creator grant you much luck." Uvael ordered, giving them a bow of his head.

"Ahh, luck is for sissies." One of them muttered on his way out.

"Wait Pavilion, I need to speak with you." Uvael called to the last assassin that was about to exit the room, who stopped to regard him.

"What is it now, old man?" Pavilion asked with more then a hint of annoyance.

Uvael looked around and out the door to make sure that the others had left before answering. "You know you have a great advantage over these men in this, being a sorcerer and a stealthy assassin. You know your part in this, Pavilion. You are the only one that stands a chance, you let the other four do their thing and when this evil wizard is distracted, you finish him."

"I know what I am to do, I fully understand the plan my lord." Pavilion replied.

"Good, we can not afford any mistakes, if you have to kill the others, then so be it. They are nothing but criminals anyways." Uvael whispered to him. "This false Prince Berrit must be killed at all costs. If the only chance you get will blow your cover, do it and get out of there as fast as you can. If you are captured, make sure you give them this ring." Uvael told him, handing him a small crafted ring with Uvael's own personal symbol. "This ring should buy your freedom."

"And what if it doesn't?" Pavilion asked not really caring either way.

"Then know you died for a great cause and I will be sure your name goes down in history as a hero, not a villain." Uvael assured him.

"Like it matters now anyways, I have nothing left but death." The assassin replied walking out the door.

"You will have fifty thousand gold coins, more then enough to start a new life Pavilion." Uvael called to him but he was already gone.

~   ~   ~

"Come on Dahak, hurry up!" Zehava called back to his friend, who was still trying to catch up.

"I'm… coming. I hate running." Dahak huffed back to them.

"Well Nicolette, time to see how good you are with a bow." Zehava panted and handed her a hunting bow and a quiver full of arrows.

"Last time I shot a bow was a few years ago when I went hunting with Rift." Nicolette said taking the bow and strapping the arrows on her back.

"Well good, so you have the general idea already." Zehava said pointing to the three targets he had set up earlier. One was at twenty yards the second was at thirty-five yards and the last was fifty yards. "Now I'll let you take a few practice shots to get use to the bow and to see how well you are from there."

Nicolette loaded an arrow into her bow, pulled back and took aim, she let fly just as Dahak finally caught up to them and crumbled to the ground exhausted and covered in sweat.

"Nice shot!" Zehava gasped as he looked to see Nicolette's shot was only a finger span away from the center of the closest target.

Nicolette smiled and reloaded and took aim again and let fly. Zehava watched as the arrow left her bow and drove into the second target an inch away from the center

"Holy crap Zehava!" Dahak coughed out. "She's better then you!"

"Well… I think you might be right, Dahak." Zehava said shaking his head in disbelief. "Why didn't you tell us you could shoot?" He asked.

Nicolette turned to them both with a big smile. "Well I didn't think I was that good compared to everyone else who has training. Rift just gave me a crash course one day, so he could have someone to hunt with."

"That must have been one hell of a crash course!" Dahak said, finally getting off the ground.

"You're a natural, Princess." Zehava told her in amazement.

Nicolette took a small bow in play and loaded again for the last target. "And please don't call me princess." She said, then let fly her arrow.

Everyone watched her arrow clip the top corner of the target and then crash to the ground.

"You can't get them all, all the time." Zehava said not at all discouraged by the miss.

Nicolette quickly reloaded her bow and let fly another arrow that slammed hard into the last target, but this time it hit dead on the center.

"Wow!" Zehava and Dahak both said in astonishment.

They all spent the last hours of the afternoon out practicing their shots, and by the end of the day Nicolette's shots had improved even more. Her moral and confidence were higher then ever, and she was truly beginning to feel like she had made the right choice.

When they got back to the castle they went straight to the kitchen and rounded up some food for them all to eat out in the garden. The whole way to the garden they chatted about Nicolette's great shots and how she could out shoot most of the boys in the army.

"There you guys are!" Shania yelled as the group walked into the garden to their regular spot.

"Shania, there you are, where have you been?" Zehava asked putting his tray of food down on the bench.

"Ya Shania, you missed Nicolette make a fool out of Zehava and me in archery!" Dahak boasted, not feeling bad for being the worst shot out of the group.

"That don't surprise me, woman naturally shoot better then men." Shania teased. "I told you Zehava, I had to go to city to get something." Shania said pointing to the other bench where a large box sat on top. "That is for you, Nicolette. It should help in your sword practice from now on."

"You didn't need to get me anything Shania." Nicolette said, walking over to the box and opening the lid. She gasped at what she saw.

"What is it?" Dahak asked, not waiting for her to answer and just walking over to see for himself.

"Oh my!" Nicolette exclaimed, pulling out a thin, slender scimitar from the wooden box.

"Hope you like it." Shania said well curling her arm around Zehava's, which no one seemed to notice, not even Zehava.

Nicolette held the blade in one hand and swung it left and right a few times to get the feel for the magnificent blade. The sword was light enough to use single handed with ease, but it could also be used two handed for stronger attacks and defensives.

"I love it, I can't even begin to tell you how much I love it." Nicolette beamed, running her hand down the smooth, smoky, straight, grey blade. "Thank you Shania, so much."

"Let big men use their big knives." Shania said with a laugh, looking up at Zehava with a joking smile. "It is just as strong and sturdy as a man's big knife too!" She promised.

Dahak got closer looking at the sword in awe. "That must have cost a fortune, how did you pay for it?" Dahak asked, admiring the finely crafted silver handle, which was the perfect thickness for a woman's hand, the guard was curved downward to deflect the enemy's blade rather then stop it.

"Just cause I am savage doesn't mean I ain't got coins!" Shania boasted proudly.

"Well I bet tomorrow's sword practice is going to be a lot different." Zehava chuckled, looking into the box and pulling out a wooden duplicate of Nicolette's new sword to practice with.

~ ~ ~

Nicolette placed her new sword in its sheath by her bed next to Meath's sword that he had been given by Saktas. The two swords seemed perfect beside one another, like they were meant to find each other. Both were equal in beauty and strength and yet, like their owners, they had two different beginnings from two different places and would surely have two different ends. But yet when they were together like they were now, all that seemed irrelevant. All one could see was two great swords that balanced each other perfectly.

A tear rolled down her cheek at the thought of Meath, how she missed him. She prayed he was alright and safe. She could hardly believe it had been nine days since he was taken, and none of the trackers that had been sent out had found him. The trail went cold several miles from the Sheeva River in the northeast.

As soon as Ursa returned and explained his plan, they would all leave and go find Meath. She knew her aunt and Rift would try and stop her, but she was determined to go along for the search no matter what. The tears began to roll freely down her cheeks at knowing that even after they found Meath and returned and defeated the false Prince Berrit, who was in her castle and ruling her country, nothing more could come of her and

Meath. Friends were all they could ever be once everything was corrected. She shook the thoughts out of her head. She would not allow herself to think of that now, so much still had to be done and if she was ever going to find Meath, she had to be strong. Ursa would be back tomorrow she prayed, he was already two days late and that was not like the great wizard at all. She hoped he faired well and had not befallen trouble. He was their only hope in finding Meath and saving her kingdom. Although she knew it was wrong of her, she feared more for Meath then her kingdom and her people. She knew Ursa wouldn't stop until he found him, not like everyone else who had given up the search and presumed him long gone or dead. No, she would not believe any of it, he was still alive, she could feel it.

"You are out there and still alive." She told herself.

She climbed into bed and blew out the candles on the night table. "Please come back to me Meath, I need you." She whispered and fell asleep.

~ ~ ~

"Get her, Zehava! Look out! Nice block." Dahak screamed while watching Nicolette and Zehava spar again, this time Nicolette was holding her own ground much better then before.

"Will you shut up, Dahak!" Zehava barked over his shoulder, dodging a well placed slash for his right calf.

"She giving you that much trouble?" Shania teased, knowing full well the new sword evened the odds a lot more, though Zehava was still the better swordsman. She could already see the vast improvement in Nicolette's attacks and blocks. Over the days that she had watched them, Shania had known the whole time that Nicolette would never be able to fight with a man's sword. Shania also knew Nicolette wasn't one that would be able to use two small swords like she did, not many people could. Shania was sure she had found what Nicolette had needed.

Zehava smashed down an overhead attack but Nicolette's sword was up and deflected it to the side in a flash. Zehava used the momentum from her block to slice down low for her knees but she easily dodged the attack, taking a step backwards.

"Very good, you're getting better." Zehava remarked lunging his sword forward for her chest.

"Thank you." She replied, parrying the attack almost too late, but then used the opening to launch her own sword straight forward for his guts.

Zehava anticipated the move and side stepped while spinning a full circle around to land a light blow to her back to let her know she over stepped and dropped her guard and would be dead.

"Ya, you got her man, I knew you would!" Dahak cheered annoyingly.

"Damn, I thought I had you." Nicolette groaned through long hard breaths.

"You almost did a few times." Zehava encouraged through some laboured breaths himself.

"See? It wasn't you, t'was your sword that wasn't working right for ya." Shania remarked, handing them both cups of cool water and sitting next to Zehava on the grass.

"I wanna spar with her next." Dahak said, picking up one of the wooden swords and giving it a swing.

"Why? So you can say you lost to a girl?" Zehava joked and everyone but Dahak shared in the laugh.

"Hey have you forgotten who helped save your ass back there in the barbarian camp?" Dahak grumbled to everyone.

"Of course not, Dahak. How could I forget your brave efforts?" Zehava said, nodding his head to his friend as a show of defeat.

"Well are you ready?" Nicolette asked Dahak as she got up and into stance.

"What, you mean right now? I thought you were gonna rest a little longer." Dahak sputtered. "Ok I guess, I'll try and go easy on ya."

Nicolette dove into action feeding Dahak right and left slashes, driving him back until he was almost backed up against a wall of bushes. Dahak parried and blocked madly trying to sort out the wild attacks. Nicolette change her swings to up high then down low making him change his stance and blocking pattern, not allowing him gather his wits.

Dahak blocked high and before Nicolette could get her blade down for another low strike, he stepped forward and pushed her back with the handle of his wooden sword, off balancing her so he could take the offensive. He swung up diagonally, forcing her to step back again, then he changed direction and went for her mid section.

Nicolette got her sword there just in time to stop it and pushed his blade out wide, forcing him to back step once, but she did not let him gain the ground. She double stepped with him and gave his stomach a light tap with her sword.

"Princess you have gotten very good with that thing." Rift said before anyone else could say anything. No one had noticed him walk into the garden, they all had their eyes to focused on the two sparring.

"Thank you, Rift." Nicolette replied, a little unnerved to see him there, knowing full well he hadn't approved of her learning the ways of a warrior.

"So what is it you plan to do with your new skills?" Rift asked her in an aggravated tone. "You are a princess, and one day soon you will be a queen. What need of soldierly skill will you have? You'll have thousand of soldiers at your command."

Everyone stood there watching Rift and Nicolette in anticipation of what would come next.

Nicolette turned to face Rift eye to eye and fire burned wildly in her eyes of an unspoken passion, of a will all their own that now urged her to unleash all her suppressed feelings.

"What I plan to do with my new skills is try to never be a victim, or at least if I am that I stand more of a fighting chance. In the last month, I have be in several dangerous, even life threatening situations that I or someone that is dear to me could have been killed. All because I couldn't help. And you can't always be there, seeing as how during all of those times you haven't been." She raged on him, stepping towards him with every word, forcing him back the way he came. Never in her whole life had she unleashed like this upon anyone, let alone Rift. Never before had she seen Rift back away and back down before.

"Ye… yes your highness, forgive me for questioning you, and forgive me for not always being there when you needed me." Rift stuttered through a great bow.

"You are forgiven, Captain Rift. Your services and skills are greatly appreciated, do not forget that. And a princess or queen could ask for no better champion. But that does not mean one shouldn't be ready for the unexpected." Nicolette finished, her head held higher then ever before and her authority ringing out clearly.

Rift nodded his head in understanding and took his leave, walking back into the castle preferring his own company for the moment after having been freshly scolded by the young Princess.

Nicolette turned back to everyone with a look of pride on her face. Everyone just stood silent, eyes wide and jaws slack with disbelief.

"What is it?" Nicolette asked walking back over to them.

"Wow, you really let him have it there. I've never seen Rift tuck tail and run from a fight before, whether it be weapons or words." Dahak responded in astonishment.

"I'm not a princess for nothing, you know." Nicolette joked, getting a laugh from everyone.

"That's for sure, you definitely showed him." Zehava chuckled nodding his full agreement.

"Nicolette, dear I must have a word with you." Lady Jewel called down to her from one of the balconies overlooking the garden.

~ ~ ~

"My goodness, child you are filthy." Jewel gasped. "I don't know why you feel you need to do this my dear, but as I have said before I will not stop you."

"What is it that you wanted aunt? Is Uncle alright?' Nicolette asked fearing the worst, for her aunt was clearly a mess.

Lady jewel sighed. "No, it is not your uncle. He has gotten worse, but he has not passed over. That is not why I have called you here. I believed since you are soon to be the queen of Draco kingdom, that I should inform you that due to Ursa being overdue, we had to take action before all was too late. We have sent five assassins to Draco castle to remove this false prince." Lady Jewel said well pacing the room, looking up at Nicolette every once in a while to gage her reaction.

"But what about Ursa, what about when he does get here if he has a plan and sending these assassins ruins it?" Nicolette questioned, though she had to ask herself why. She really didn't care at this moment.

"Well dear, then we will have to figure something out when the time comes, but we could not stand by and do nothing any longer. Even Ursa himself said if he wasn't back that we should do what we deemed best." Jewel answered, stopping to stand right in front of her niece.

"And how do you know this is best?" Nicolette asked bluntly.

"I don't." Jewel sighed deeply with doubt. "But I have to believe it is. With your uncle on the verge of death, and Mathu still too young to rule Dragon's Cove, I must make these choices." Jewel finished and Nicolette could tell her aunt was having a hard time with all of this, as anyone in her shoes would.

"I am sorry for arguing with you aunty, I too am at a loss about all this." Nicolette replied giving her aunt a reassuring hug. "I am sure your plan will work and all will be restored as it should be."

"All we can do is pray, my child." Jewel said. "And I am deeply sorry about your friend, Meath." Jewel added.

"Then why is there no one out there looking for him?" Nicolette questioned, her anger flaring a little again at the topic.

"I told you, the trail died and they could not pick it up again, I am sorry there is nothing we can do, we all miss Meath, he was a great man. And he is in all our prayers, I am sure he will find his way back to us." Jewel said sympathetically, wishing there was something more she could say to help ease her nieces mind.

"Yes aunt." Was all Nicolette said before walking away.

~ ~ ~

Dahak woke to someone knocking on his door lightly, he climbed out of his bed and stumbled to the door.

"Who is it and what do you want?" He grumbled, opening the door to see Zehava standing there fully dressed.

Zehava pushed through his friend and closed the door behind him, checking to see that no one had seen or followed him.

"What are you doing?' Zehava whispered.

"I was sleeping, like most people do at night." Dahak replied sarcastically through a yawn. "What are you doing here this late? Go away I was having a good dream."

"Did you not find the note?" Zehava asked.

"What note? What are you talking about?" Dahak replied, waking up a bit by the urgency in his friend's voice and then noticing the note in plain sight on his bedside table.

"No matter, we're leaving. Get dressed and packed for the road." Zehava told him quickly searching Dahak's room for things to take with them.

"What!? Leaving? Why are we leaving? And where the hell are we going now?" Dahak complained totally awake now.

"They have stopped searching for Meath and will not send more people out to find him. So we are going to find him ourselves." Zehava told him while throwing Dahak's clothes on the bed and gesturing for him to hurry.

"Can't we leave in the morning?" Dahak moaned while getting dressed, already knowing the answer.

"Meath wouldn't just stand by and wait if it was one of us out there!" Zehava snapped back.

"I know, I know, sorry." Dahak apologized, grabbing the last of his things.

~ ~ ~

Zehava and Dahak scaled down the castle wall quietly after making sure no guards were around. They had to be careful to stay in the shadows so the guards in the towers would not spot them. Once they were far enough from view they ran to where the others were waiting.

"Finally, what took you so long?" Shania whispered when Zehava and Dahak were close enough.

"Dahak didn't find his note by his bed." Zehava explained, while checking to make sure his horse was ready to ride.

"How could you not find the note? It was right there in plain view." Shania said with a laugh ,not really surprised at all.

"I was tired when I got to my room and went straight to bed." Dahak said, trying to redeem himself a little.

"No matter, let's go before anyone notices us missing." Nicolette whispered, spurring her horse into a light gallop.

Once the group was far enough away, they kicked their horses into a hard run on the northern road that would lead them too the small city of Lacus by Sheeva lake. From there they hoped to pick up Meath's trail and start their search. Shania was sure she would be able to pick up Meath's trail where it had ended for the other trackers.

~ ~ ~

"Tomorrow we will be in Dragon's Cove, and I believe we will make it before your vision has happened, or so I hope." Ursa said as he stirred the rabbit stew he was cooking over their small fire.

"How do you know it has not already happened?" Talena asked.

"We are not more then half a day from the Castle now and I did not see any smoke, nor did I smell any. If the barbarians had already attacked we would have seen some sign of it already. We wouldn't have made it this far without seeing a lot more savages then we have." Ursa explained to her, his mind going back to the day before when they had encountered a small band of barbarian warriors. "But I do believe your vision may be true, my bones feel the energy in the air, something big is going to happen, and soon I am afraid."

"What are you going to do about this evil wizard in your home?" Talena asked, giving Ursa her bowl to be filled with stew.

"I do not know yet, but something must be done, I just wish I knew his name. If I had a name I might be able to figure out who he is and why he's here and what his weaknesses are so that I might use them against him." Ursa said filling her bowl.

"Tomorrow I will try and have another vision, one that will help you, I promise. I will keep trying 'til I do." Talena said to him with complete genuineness and solid conviction.

Ursa smiled across to her. "I do thank you my dear, Talena. And so does every soul in this Kingdom, even if they don't know it yet." He told her with a smile.

They were up early the next morning and on their way to Dragon's Cove, which they would reach by midday. They traveled a little slower then normal knowing they were so close, Ursa wanted to be able to scan the area to be sure trouble wasn't about.

~ ~ ~

"Lady Jewel, lady Jewel! Ursa is back!" A soldier shouted as he ran into the room where Lord Marcus rested and lady Jewel spent most of her days.

"Thank the Creator." She whispered to herself as she hurried down to the front doors where Ursa and another now waited.

"Ursa, thank the heavens you are alright, we were getting worried about you." Jewel proclaimed, glad to see her friend alive and well. "And who is this you have with you?" She asked regarding Talena.

"She is, I guess, the reason I left in the first place." Ursa replied.

"Did you find the answer you went seeking for?" Lady Jewel asked, eager to hear what he had found.

"I am afraid I have not, at least not yet." Ursa informed her sadly.

"Well, since you were late and we did not know when or if you would return, we have a plan that we sent into action." Jewel announced, almost afraid to see what Ursa's reaction would be. "But let us talk of these matters privately." She said while gesturing him to follow her. "You two show Ursa's friend to a guest room and have a hot bath and whatever she wants brought to her." Jewel ordered two servants that were coming down the stairs.

"I will come find you shortly, Talena. Do not worry, you are in good hands." Ursa assured her, knowing she had to feel uncomfortable being left alone like this with strangers. He turned and followed lady Jewel to the meeting room.

~ ~ ~

"We have sent five expert assassins to Draco Castle to dispose of this evil wizard, one of the assassins is Pavilion, the wizard assassin." Jewel told him.

"When did you send them?" Ursa asked, becoming a little concerned.

"Yesterday morning, we are confident in their ability to get this job done." Jewel said, looking for some hint of Ursa's mind on this matter.

"I pray they are." Ursa told her, recalling the only time he had ever met Pavilion.

"So who is the girl you have brought back with you?" Jewel asked, pouring herself some water from a pitcher on the table.

"She is the last apprentice of my master, Solmis." Ursa started, filling his own cup with water. "I went to see Solmis because he had spent many years expanding his gift of foresight."

"So he could see the future?" Jewel questioned before Ursa could continue.

"In a sense yes, he could see things that were happening or were going to happen, but it was almost impossible to put a time frame on his visions." Ursa continued after a long swallow from his cup. "Sometimes if he thought about certain questions or people long and hard enough, he could force a vision about them. Now of course, not being able to put a time on them, it was hard to know if the visions were now or twenty years from now." Ursa continued.

"So what happened? Was he not able to help you?" Jewel asked eagerly.

"Unfortunately he was not. He passed away long before I arrived." Ursa began, then filled lady jewel in on what had happened when he arrived there and the vision that Solmis had had several years before about Ursa arriving, and then about how he had passed some of his gifts on to Talena.

"So you are telling me that girl you brought with you has the gift of foresight?" Lady Jewel asked, almost in disbelief. "Well let's get her to answer our questions."

Ursa sighed knowing this was going to happen. "I have been trying, but you see, Talena never studied the ability of foresight. Unlike Solmis who spent half his life or more learning to use it, and still was no where near perfecting it. But visions do come to her, ones that may be able to help and I do believe if she tries, sooner or later she will be able to help us with the answers we seek." Ursa told her.

"Well then what do we need to do to get her to have one of these visions?" Jewel asked.

"You leave that up to me I will do what I can to help her answer our questions." Ursa said, praying that it would work.

"How do you even know that she can have these visions?" Jewel asked, confused a little about the whole matter.

"Well, I have already seen her have one. I believe Dragon's Cove is to be attacked by a large army of Barbarians." Ursa told her, straightening in his chair to look at her and show her he was not kidding in the least.

Jewel almost laughed out loud. "Ursa, do you know what kind of army the savages would have to come up with for us to have to worry?"

Before Ursa could answer, a guard ran into the room. "I am sorry for the intrusion my lady, but we've just received several reports from incoming scouts that there are several large bands of savages grouping together on all three roads to Dragon's Cove."

"What?" Jewel cried, jumping to her feet. "Well send word to the armies and dispatch them."

"My lady, I don't think it will be as easy as that this time." The man replied nervously.

"Why not, how many are there?" Jewel asked, almost afraid to hear.

The man took a deep breath before answering. "The count on the northern side was around about six hundred, to the east twelve hundred and to the south just under eight hundred, my lady. They are getting larger by the hour."

"Ready the men. We prepare for war and get the people of the city behind the castle walls. Tell the generals to meet me in the library." Jewel commanded, trying to keep her voice calm, though both the guard and Ursa could tell she wanted to break down.

"And send someone to get Antiel and Lepha to the library." Ursa shouted before the man had gotten to far away.

"Where is Meath and the others? I need to talk to them." Ursa asked Jewel.

"Oh my, I had almost forgotten about them. No one has seen them all day, they're most likely out training the poor princess again." Jewel told him.

"Training her for what?" Ursa asked confused.

"She wants to know how to fight, every since you left and Meath was kidnapped," She started but was cut off.

"Kidnapped!?" Ursa bellowed jumping from his chair. "What do you mean kidnapped? Why didn't you tell me this before?"

"Yes, I am sorry Ursa, the day after you left apparently two young wizards came while the princess and Meath were out and they took him for some reason." Jewel told, him kicking herself for not telling him earlier but it had truly escaped her mind with the other pressing matters at hand.

"And no one went after them?" Ursa yelled in frustration, but knew if anyone were to stand a chance it would have had to have been the two castle wizards.

"We did everything we could Ursa, you must believe me. The trail went dead, they could not track them. I am sorry." She answered him. "If you want to know more, you'd have to ask Princess Nicolette and the others."

"Find her and the others and have them come to the library. I must go talk to Talena." Ursa said through long irritated breaths.

~ ~ ~

"How come we did not know of this earlier?" Jewel barked to everyone in the room. "How did three large armies just sneak into our land with out us knowing?"

"We do not know, my lady." One of the generals replied nervously.

"Isn't that your job? To know these things?" Jewel screamed, irritated.

"Well we have known that there has been a large amount of barbarian activity lately, but that's normal for this time of year, nothing seemed out of the norm. A few small towns sacked and robbed, a few dozen caravans and supply wagons, but nothing unusual." Another general put in.

"And why hasn't anything been done about all this? I wasn't aware that we just let things like this happen." Jewel asked, trying to calm herself a little.

"With all due respect, my lady, it's not like we let things like this happen. And when it does, it's not like we don't try and help and find the bands that do this." The first general said, wishing that Lord Marcus were well and dealing with this.

"What the generals are trying to say, my lady, is that the land of Dragon's Cove is large and we do not have the men to patrol it all. The barbarians are very skilled in remaining hidden, even in less wooded areas. And from what it looks like, they moved in small groups so they were not as noticeable, then once there were enough of them they all began grouping together." Uvael, Dragon Cove's advisor, explained to her.

Jewel took a deep breath to help relax her nerves. "Fine, it's too late for any of that anyways, but what can we do now?" Jewel asked hoping for an easy solution.

"Well it looks like they plan to take the city and then the castle. I would think the best way would be to gather our armies from where ever we can get word to them, and get all the people of the city that are able, armed and trained as best we can under such short notice." One of the generals replied, standing up so everyone could hear him.

"Lady Jewel, lady Jewel!" A guard cried as he ran into the library, with a long rope and a folded up piece of paper. "We searched for the princess and the others but this is all we found. This rope was found hanging over the wall on the northern end of the grounds. We found this note in Dahak's room." The man bellowed out almost to fast for anyone to understand, and handed lady Jewel the note.

Chapter 16

Pavilion watched as the other four assassins made their way through the city towards the castle. Pavilion had to admire them, they were by far the best assassins he had ever met, they had all made it to Draco Castle late in the evening of the third night. They all had made great time, though men fuelled by the promise of riches normally did. The four assassins had all traveled together to Draco, Pavilion wondered if they did so for the company or to brag about how many men they had each killed and who they have killed, to try and intimidate the others. Pavilion doubted any of them would be so easily intimidated; they were the finest at their trade. Once they had reached Draco Castle, they all went their separate ways, for that was the way of assassins and of greed. Pavilion had not traveled with them but at a distance. He could have easily passed by them and made it to Draco hours before them, but instead he stayed behind watching them from a distance, learning from them, who they were by their movements and their skills. Pavilion was a loner now, and preferred the company of silence rather then men at the best of times.

As Pavilion watched the four men swiftly manoeuvre through the streets and back allies, he finally lost sight if them. He knew he could easily find any one of them again, but decided he too had better get to work. For if what he had been told was true, this would be his greatest target. For most men, that thought alone was enough to bring some form of emotion, be it happiness, excitement or even scared it did nothing to Pavilion.

~ ~ ~

"We all want to go to Mandrake's aid, but we can not divide our forces anymore then we have. With all the barbarian activity lately we don't know what they are planning, they could easily march on us next and we must not be caught off guard." Prince Berrit argued.

"Damn it you little piss ant, Mandrake is in the hands of those bastards we can not just sit by and let them keep it. You heard Dagon's messenger, he still has a formidable army he just needs as many as we can spare to help take it back." Tundal roared with anger and frustration.

"Lord Tundal, do calm down, you know as well as I that I am making the right choice. If Lord Dagon had any chance of taking back his castle, he would never have lost it in the beginning. Mandrake is lost to us for the time being, but I do promise you that we will take it back when we have a better idea of what is going on, and we are not at threat here." Prince Berrit calmly replied. "Now tell Lord Dagon to retreat and to make his way back to Draco, where we can better know our enemy." Berrit finished.

"Retreat!?" Tundal and the messenger said in union.

"That's his home, and you're telling him to run? He'll never do it." Tundal shouted.

"Go and tell him my orders, messenger!" Berrit commanded sternly, sending the man away with a wave of his hand.

"You son of a bitch, you are not the king of this kingdom, what makes you think you have the right to make such orders?" Tundal screamed, getting up from his seat to stand in front of Prince Berrit, his blood pumping.

"That's right, my dear Lord Tundal, I am not king. At least not yet that is. But soon I shall be, once my wife to be is found and returned. So if you would like to stay on my good side, you would do well to mind your tongue!" Berrit threatened.

"Are you threatening me?" Tundal asked bluntly. "Do you dare threaten me? I will see to it you never become king, you brainless pig. I shall personally see to it that you are escorted back to your country and never allowed to return, you half wit. Once the princess returns we will see how long your welcome lasts. King Borrack may have wanted this union, but I strongly believe if he was still alive he would never let you marry his daughter, and neither shall I." Tundal raged, turning to leave.

"I think not." Berrit hissed angrily, pulling his dagger.

"Why you son of a whore!" Tundal growled, turning back to him, his own dagger now in hand and at the ready.

"There's just one thing I forgot to tell you, my good Lord Tundal." Berrit hissed again. "I'm not Prince Berrit." As he finished the words his features transformed into his true self.

"I knew something smelled fishy, you heathen devil." Tundal barked slashing his blade forward.

Astaroth side stepped the assault and drove his dagger home through Tundal's rib cage into his beating heart, and give the dagger a good twist.

"Foolish old man, you should have just listened, though I was growing tired of you anyways, and this saves me the trouble of killing you later." Astaroth muttered bitterly yanking the dagger out.

"My love, your anger is making you sloppy." The alluring voice of a woman said behind him.

Astaroth turned to see Vashina, his partner and lover, standing a dozen feet away with a dangerous looking man at knifepoint.

"Who is this?" Astaroth muttered clearly frustrated.

"I am assuming he was working for Lord Tundal and was going to try and kill you, I saw him sneak into the library from the back, like only a highly skilled assassin can, so I followed and low and behold, once you killed poor Lord Tundal, he went to make his move while your back was turned. You may thank me later, my dearest." Vashina cooed seductively with a wink.

"Well, well looks like we have our cover up." Astaroth snarled, thrusting his dagger into the man's chest several times.

"And I wanted to play!" Vashina moaned disappointedly letting the dead assassin fall to the ground.

"Later my love, now make yourself scarce, then meet me in my room in a few hours. This is going to take some time to straighten out." Astaroth told her, then turned and screamed for help, falling to the floor to stab the fallen assassin a few more times for show, well transforming his features back to Berrit's.

"What is it? What happened here?" Three soldiers shouted rushing into the room viewing the bloody scene.

~   ~   ~

"Well my love, there's one problem out of the way." Astaroth laughed well taking a large sip of wine and sinking back into the huge tub.

"I can't believe that old man would act so boldly as to hire an assassin." Vashina said, watching him from the bed.

"No matter, I am just glad he's gone, and it was so convenient that our good friend Tundal would pick such a well known assassin too. The guards all recognized him, which made it all the easier to convince them that the assassin tried to kill us both. Lord Tundal's a hero; he jumped in front of us to help Prince Berrit, but unfortunately took a fatal blow." Astaroth laughed evilly, recounting the story he told everyone. "Come, join me my pet." He beckoned Vashina.

His smile grew as she walked over to the tub, swaying her perfect hips seductively, her right leg all the way up to her silky thigh peeking out of the large slit up her black skirt. Once she was by the tub she began to pull off her tight, dark red leather shirt. Slowly she lifted it above her firm and slender stomach inch by inch, knowing each second intensified his lust. Finally she pulled her shirt over her head, releasing her large, full, firm breasts. She shook her head making her long blond hair look wild and untamed. His excitement grew and was evident by his laboured breathing. She ran her finger down between her breasts and continued down her smooth stomach to the spiky, silver, belt that kept her long black skirt up. She unfastened her belt and let it fall to the floor with her skirt, leaving her completely naked except for her enchanted knife sheath, which held eight small throwing knives and was strapped to her right thigh. She almost never removed it. The enchanted sheath had an endless supply of throwing knives, no matter how many knives she threw, she knew there would always be eight more at the ready, as fast as she could throw them they would replenish. It was an extremely rare item she had acquired many years ago, at an extremely high price.

"Things aren't going as smoothly as we had first expected they would." Vashina reminded him with a smirk, as she slid into the steaming tub.

Astaroth frowned at her. "Yes my love, I am well aware of that. That Ursa getting away with the princess is defiantly causing a few minor problems, but other then that, everything is going accordingly. Our barbarian friends have taken out Mandrake and are preparing as we speak to take Dragon's Cove. And now they believe enough in our cause that the high priests and priestesses are joining in the war." Astaroth cooed wickedly as a grin spread widely across his face.

"I would so have loved to get a taste of that Ursa's gift, and his young apprentice too." Vashina commented while pouring more rose scented oils into the steaming bath.

"We will have them soon enough my love, but for now we will have to settle for those wizards that shall be here in a few days." Astaroth replied, turning his attention to the other side of the room.

"You're just now realized, my darling?" Vashina teased, having sensed someone in the room long ago.

An arrow shot out towards Astaroth's heart from the far side of the room, he summoned his gift and the arrow ignited in flames, incinerating long before it reached him.

"Come out and you may be spared fool!" Astaroth commanded stepping out of the bath just as another arrow sizzled out from behind the grand book shelve. Again the arrow ignited in flames, but as soon as it did the arrow exploded sending sparks and flames into Astaroth's face. He threw his arms up in defence of the flaming shards.

Another assassin took his cue and leaped out from behind the large drapes with both short sword and dagger in hand and charged at full speed towards Astaroth's unguarded back.

Vashina saw the attacker and let fly two throwing knifes. The assassin deflected both blades with his in a split second without slowly his charge. His skills were impressive and his experience and abilities quickly apparent. He reached his target, his sword down and to the side and swung upwards, hoping to get a quick finish without his enemy ever seeing it.

Astaroth did see it, and now his anger was enraged, his arm came from across his face towards the attacker and with it, several small icicles formed in an instant and shot from Astaroth's palm to embed deep into the assassins chest, sending him staggering backwards.

Another arrow sliced through the air towards Astaroth's unprotected back, but his senses alerted him and he spun around and grabbed the arrow in mid air, stopping it before it pierced his flesh.

Astaroth's anger raged uncontrollably and wizard's fire flared to life across his shoulders and down his arms as he walked towards the hidden attacker.

The assassin, knowing the plan had failed and his chances of survival were limited, came out from behind the book shelf, dropped his bow and went to his knee's, begging for his life.

Vashina was out of the tub and was alert and on guard, scanning the room for any other unknown invaders that might show themselves. She turned her attention to the assassin on the ground that was now holding a small hand held crossbow aimed directly at her. A wicked smile crossed her lips as a tiny flame licked the bowstring and snapped it before he could take his shot.

"Please do not kill me!" The assassin cried to Astaroth who now was standing before him.

The flames dissipated and Astaroth's eyes bore into the man's soul. "Tell me why I should spare your life after you tried to kill me and my lover, assassin." Astaroth questioned ruthlessly.

"I… I have four children your greatness, they need me. I only do this to feed them!" The assassin stuttered pathetically.

"Well I guess their going to be orphans now!" Astaroth hissed, kicking the man hard in the stomach and knocking him over. "Now enough of your games and lies. Tell me who sent you and I might spare your life… for your children's sake." Astaroth said growing impatient.

"I do not know, your greatness. He sent an urchin with a letter to me and it said that if I killed you, I would be richer then my wildest dreams." The assassin bellowed.

Astaroth turned his head to regard Vashina and what she thought. The assassin saw the opening and took his chance, lunging at him with a poison tipped dagger. Astaroth was no fool and was well aware of the assassin and his tricks. He grabbed the assassin's attacking arm and twisted it to the side, causing the man enough pain to drop the dagger. With a look of sheer evil, Astaroth grabbed the man's face with his free hand and began to summon his gift. Fire wavered in his hand, slowly burning and blistering the assassin's face, head and neck. His screams could have woken the dead, but Astaroth didn't relent. The assassin's flesh began to melt and peel away from his bones, he kicked and thrashed but it was too late and soon death consumed him. Finally Astaroth released him and let him fall limp to the floor. All that remained of his face was a charred, blackened skull.

He turned his attention back to Vashina and the other badly wounded assassin, who had both watched his display of power. Vashina was grinning widely while the assassin had pure dread glistening in his wide open eyes.

"Now, maybe you will be of more use to me." Astaroth said, calmly walking over to the man. "Who sent you?"

"It… it was Lady Jewel of Dragon's Cove." The assassin whimpered, truly afraid knowing his wounds wouldn't kill him, but these two surely would.

"What, why? How do they know?" Astaroth barked.

"The great wizard Ursa and Princess Nicolette made it to Dragon's Cove and told them the truth about you." The man cried.

"So it wasn't old Tundal after all." Vashina chuckled, looking down and seeing her enchanted throwing knife sheath was full again as it always was.

"How many assassins were sent?" Astaroth ordered.

"Just us two, I promise." He bellowed pathetically.

"Just the two of you, why do I get the feeling you're lying!" Astaroth hissed. "One already tried to kill me today, before you two showed up." He screamed smacking the man hard in the face, leaving four burns where his fingers hit.

"Maybe Tundal did hire one on his own." Vashina said as if it really didn't matter, putting on her clothes and throwing Astaroth a robe.

"No I don't believe so, Ursa doesn't seem to be stupid, nor one to take chances." Astaroth said still glaring at the assassin. "Last chance assassin, tell me the truth or suffer a fate far worse then your friend."

The assassin held his ground and didn't reply until flames ignited in Astaroth's hands. "Ok, they sent five of us to kill you. They wanted to be sure it got done." He cried out, backing his head away as the flames got closer.

"Let me have some fun with him." Vashina pouted, with a sexy and seductive smile.

Astaroth stopped the flames and backed away, giving her what she wanted.

"Please don't kill me! I will help you! I know who the other assassins are, I can kill them for you." The assassin begged, while trying to sit up. The pain from his wounds kept him down.

"What makes you think we need your help? We already stopped three of you." Astaroth mused. "Besides, your wounded. You'd hardly be of much help to us."

"No, no I am not hurt badly, please I will help you, no charge." He pleaded desperately.

"Funny thing about assassins, their loyalties always lay with the better offer." Vashina remarked with a smirk.

"I would rather work for you, yes. You are far more powerful then everyone else, it would be an honour." He said, forcing himself to sit up this time and doing his best to wince away the pain from the melted icicle wounds.

Astaroth paced in front of him, knowing he wouldn't be as bold as the other to try and attack him. "Yes, we could use your help I am sure." Astaroth said looking at the man who was now smiling a black tooth grin. "But then again, how do we know we can trust you? That you won't betray us like you did those in Dragon's Cove?" Astaroth questioned, raising his eyebrow.

"You have my word, your greatness!" The assassins replied, bobbing his head up and down.

Astaroth turned to Vashina and gave her a nod, before his head had even stopped moving, three knifes were embedded in the assassin's chest.

"What are you doing?" He gurgled, slumping to the floor.

"I never trust an assassin." Astaroth snapped well his lover continued to pump knife after knife into the man. Her aim was so precise that she had twelve blades in him before he finally died.

"And I was beginning to wonder what happened to my darling wife to be and her wizard guardian." Astaroth said after Vashina had ceased her attack on the long dead assassin.

"Well they won't be alive for long then." Vashina said, searching the assassin's bodies for anything she might want.

"I want you to go to Dragon's Cove and see to its downfall. If Ursa and his apprentice are there, that means Dragon's Cove has four wizards to defend it." Astaroth told her.

"Dragon's Cove will fall my love, they don't need me. Besides, I would be of more use to our cause here, by finding the last two assassins and making sure no one else tries to stand against you now that Tundal is gone." Vashina argued. "And it's not as if the wizards at Dragon's Cove will be that large of a threat, they don't know half of what they can do with their gift like we do."

"No matter, I want you there to be sure nothing goes wrong. I have a feeling that Ursa could be more trouble then we know. He is wise and powerful, I will not take anymore chances." Astaroth said out loud, though it was more to himself as a reminder. "Once we have total control over Draco Kingdom with the help of our barbarian "friends", we will be unstoppable, Vashina, and nothing will stand in our way. We will smoke out all those with the gift and consume it, and once we are strong enough we will live forever as gods." Astaroth roared with great enthusiasm.

"Fine, I'll go help the savages." Vashina mumbled. "Though I do hope you have fun here. With Tundal dead, no lords of Draco kingdom are left here to help see to the ruling until you are made king, if they still make you king that is." Vashina added and began to walk away.

"Vashina!" Astaroth said loudly and with great authority. She stopped to regard him.

"Yes? What is it?" She asked callously.

"If we are to make this work my love, we need to work together and not have any doubt in one another." He said, not looking back to her.

"Of course, I have no doubt we will succeed." She replied coolly.

"Good, you know we need each other in this, we can't do it alone." He told her, still not meeting her eyes with his.

"I want what you want, Astaroth. I will stand by your side 'til the bitter end, we will rule this whole country soon enough my love." Vashina answered back.

"Go now Vashina, to the meeting place. Stay hidden until I get there." Astaroth ordered as he turned around to face her. "And Vashina, if you can, keep the wizards alive and bring them back with you." He finished.

"Of course, my love." She said as she turned and seemed to disappear into the shadows as she could do so well.

Astaroth walked over to the large full body mirror that was in his room. "Oh mother, how you should have believed in me." Astaroth growled to himself while transforming back into Prince Berrit. "How I do grow tired of being this sad, pathetic Berrit." He hissed. He left his room knowing later that night he would have to dispose of the two bodies elsewhere.

~ ~ ~

He watched Astaroth features change back into those of Prince Berrit's and walk out of his room. Pavilion wondered if he had missed his chance to attack, he also wondered if he had attacked if his fate would have been the same as the other two. It didn't matter to him if he died, true life as he knew it was long over, he was just an empty shell of a mortal now.

He wondered if the names of these two and what he discovered about them would benefit Dragon's Cove more then him trying to kill them. If he failed, the information would be lost. He truly doubt that anyone else would be able to get it. Then again, he wondered if Dragon's Cove would still be there when he went back, if he ever made it back.

Pavilion followed Astaroth with such stealth and grace, there were times he would have been able to deal him a lethal blow. He hesitated, wondering if Vashina was watching him, ready to strike if he made such an attempt. She too seemed to posses the same stealth as he. He knew his mission was to kill this man, this wizard, but something told him not yet. Something told him to watch, wait and learn. He followed Prince Berrit outside the castle and watched him change forms again into a patrol guard to get passed the soldiers watching the gates.

Pavilion followed him off the road to the city and into the jungle, he had to give his enemy credit; he moved silently and swiftly and did well to leave no trace. But Pavilion could follow the trail of a leaf blowing in the wind. Pavilion knew Astaroth was doubling back and trying to give anyone who might be following him the slip. Soon he knew they were close to their destination because he passed several savages lying in wait and watching in case they were needed.

~   ~   ~

"Vashina you can come out now." Astaroth said, stopping in front of the four savages and changing his form back to himself.

Within a blink, Vashina was at his side as if she had come out of no here and the barbarians were taken aback by her sudden appearance.

Pavilion wondered where she had learned how to move like that, how to be as stealthy as he was.

"Were you followed?" One of the barbarians asked. His stature and confidence gave the impression that he was a leader in this small group of savages.

"I wouldn't be standing here if I was." Astaroth snapped.

"Things are going perfectly, Mandrake fell with less effort then expected." The barbarian leader said with almost perfect English, and only a small hint of his ancestral accent.

"Would you expect anything different?" Astaroth replied with a smile. "How soon will Dragon's Cove fall?" Astaroth asked.

"We will attack in three days." Another barbarian of the group said.

"What? Three days? They will be fortified in three days." Astaroth barked angrily.

"Not enough men to attack yet, must wait for more." Another savage put in with a thick accent.

"Well start the attack now and as more tribes come, you can send them into the fight. The longer you wait, the more time the enemy has to set up defences." Astaroth argued.

"Too many men would die that way, must wait for larger army before attacking. Winning back our land do us no good if we all dead." The thick accented barbarian replied.

"We are also waiting for a few of the high priests and priestesses to arrive to help in the battle. With them there, it will inspire our warriors and encourage them to fight harder." The leader replied, sensing Astaroth's rage. "Dragon's Cove will fall, no doubt. You leave that to us."

Astaroth did well to compose himself, he hated acting inferior to these savages, but if he was to get what he wanted he had to play his part. "I hear you have been having problems with Mandrake's refugee's and Lord

Dagon's small army. You were supposed to have the south east contained by now, you said you could handle it." Astaroth said, making a concerted effort to keep the bitterness out of his words.

"Yes, they are ambushing many of the groups of warriors that are trying to that leave the castle to go Dagon's Cove. They are also doing well to keep our brethren tribes in the east from joining the army in Mandrake. Lord Dagon and his men know the country side better then we do, which is making it hard for us to find them and finish them off." The leader said, frustrated. "But we will deal with them, we are slowly crushing their forces, it won't be long before they are destroyed." He finished, calming himself a little. "Besides, weren't you supposed to be king by now, making things easier for us to take over this country?"

Astaroth took a deep breath so he would not kill the man where he stood. "Yes well, it seems we are both having a few minor set backs, but all is well. Tomorrow I shall send word to Drandor and tell them to send aid to Dragon's Cove. By the time they arrive, you should have Dragon's Cove and you should easily be able to defend against the reinforcements. Once Drandor's army arrives to aid Dragon's Cove, your army will march from Mandrake to overtake Drandor. If of course, Lord Dagon and his boys aren't still causing too much trouble for you." Astaroth said, reminding himself of the big picture. "And once you have those three castles secure, I shall order the surrender of Draco Kingdom to your leader. You will have you land back and I get Draco Castle as my home." Astaroth said, while in his mind he envisioned the looks on all the barbarian faces when he betrayed them after they completed what was needed.

"Fine, I shall tell our leader that everything is going as planned. And so it had better, Astaroth." The barbarian barked while walking back into the jungle.

Several minutes passed before Astaroth spoke. "Once I no longer need him, I am going to enjoy killing him, slowly." He hissed to Vashina.

"Now, now my love, play nice with the pawns. We need them, remember." Vashina reminded him with a sarcastically sweet voice.

"Go now, to Dragon's Cove. See to it that it is ours within the week." Astaroth told her. Before he could turn to face her, she was gone.

~   ~   ~

Pavilion couldn't believe what he had witnessed and had heard, this was so much more then Dragon's Cove believed it was. This wasn't just one man causing problems. This was what everyone had always feared; the barbarians finally had the edge they needed to take over Draco Kingdom, and they were succeeding.

Pavilion knew what he was sent here to do, but now he knew killing Astaroth wouldn't be enough, things were already set in motion. The information he knew was far more valuable. He had to get back to Dragon's Cove, he had to warn them of what was transpiring; he just prayed he could get there before it was too late.

~ ~ ~

He watched from afar the activity around his castle and city. There was so many more now then there had been when they had first arrived. As his scouts had guessed, there must have been three times the number and there would be many more if he and his men weren't doing their part in weaning the enemy numbers as best they could. It seemed for every man they killed, two more took his place. But that would not stop him, he would fight until he won back what was his. Or until an enemy blow took the life from within him.

Lord Dagon turned his horse around and headed back to one of the small camps he and his men had set up around the land. From his original thirteen hundred soldiers, only eight hundred remained. But more and more refugees from all of the town's and small cities that had been sacked or threatened by the barbarian invasion were joining his army everyday, in hopes to help rid the land of these monsters. He had close to two thousand men now, most simple farmers or shopkeepers, but they all had one thing in common; they had lost their family, friends and homes to the same enemy, and a man that has lost everything fights harder then five men who have everything.

Dagon had several small camps of a hundred men set up all along the eastern river flowing out from Mandrake's lake. They kept the smaller bands of tribes of barbarians from coming out of the wastelands and joining with the large army already residing in Mandrake castle. But many of the tribes were sending their warriors across the lake in boats from Mandrakes harbour, avoiding Dagon's men. Dagon had already run his lines thinner then he would have preferred, so there was no way they could guard the whole lake and stop the boats. The rest of his soldiers were in three larger groups of three hundred. They were doing their best in stopping all the barbarian warriors from leaving Mandrake that were heading west.

Lord Dagon knew the barbarians were up to something. Every day more and more bands left the castle and traveled to the North West.

Dagon and his men did their best to see too it most of them never made it far. In the beginning, the barbarians came out in small packs of a hundred or so, so it was easy for Dagon's men to overwhelm them. Now they were growing smarter and sending out several larger bands at a time of four or five hundred so Dagon would have to join his three groups into one instead just to take on one of the enemy armies. Too many were getting through to wreak havoc on Draco kingdom.

Dagon prayed that the messenger he had sent to Draco castle to Tundal and Berrit asking for the aid of a few hundred more men would soon arrive with another army. He had also sent messengers into Zandor to Besha were he also asked Lord Andras for the aid of his armies. He had strong doubts that any aid would come form Zandor.

Dagon arrived back to his camp and watched his men prepare for the battle that would soon take place. The barbarians had sent out the largest army thus far the day before, twenty five hundred warriors fully armed and armoured. Along with them were three-dozen heavily loaded wagons. He knew weapons and food supplies would be found in those wagons, but he had no idea where they were heading with them. They were up to no good and he wasn't about to let them get away with it if he could.

He had called in a hundred men from both of his other groups patrolling the North West. Along with his three hundred he had an army of five hundred and they were about to break camp and begin the chase. They were out numbered at least five to one, but not a single man complained or showed fear. Dagon knew a straight out attack would only get his men killed. He had something different in mind, something that he hoped would work without the loss of a lot of men.

"What are you thinking my lord?" Jarroth asked, riding his horse up to Dagon's.

Dagon looked over to Mandrakes Champion. Jarroth was more then that, he was Dagon's best friend. They had grown up together, trained together, fought wars together and talked of things you would only talk about with someone you completely trusted.

"I'm thinking tonight is going to be a bad night to be our enemy." Dagon said with a smile.

Jarroth patted Dagon's back. "That it will be, my friend. Tonight we will all get our fill of enemy blood."

"It is almost dusk, tell the men to eat a light meal. Once it's a dark, we ride out." Dagon told him, staring off into the distance.

~ ~ ~

Five hundred men marched through the night as silently as they could, using the moon as their only source of light. Traveling was easy the whole way, this part of the country was only lightly wooded. They stopped a mile away from the enemy camp to prepare and sent out their most experienced scouts to spot out and eliminate the barbarian sentries.

Dagon split his men into three groups, two were for the main assault, and one was for the surprise distraction. He sent a hundred men with bows and a full quiver of arrows to the north on one side of the enemy, they were to be the diversion. Once they were in place, they would start to launch their attack of flaming arrows down on the enemy from the north. Their orders were to fire at will until their quivers were spent, then to retreat and circle back south east a few miles behind where Dagon and his men now waited.

Once the bombardment starts, the bulk of Dagon's force would charge in from the south, catching their enemy off guard and from behind. Dagon's men were to fight fast and hard until the enemy got organized, then they were to retreat to where a hundred more archers waited to cover them, but their arrows would not be seen by the enemy. No fire would be added to these ones. Once their arrows were depleted or the enemy forces that followed were killed, they too were to draw back to the south and join with the whole force again, where they would regroup.

"Fight well this night Jarroth, and may the creator guide your blade." Dagon said to his friend, clasping his hand firmly as a gesture of luck.

"You as well my friend, I shall watch your back." Jarroth replied.

~   ~   ~

The sky flared to life from the north as it began to rain down flaming arrows. Dagon drew his sword and spurred his horse forward, leading his three hundred riders into a charge. They met the barbarian encampment in a frenzy, taking full advantage of the confused, half asleep warriors that were scrambling to put out fires on their tents and on themselves.

Dagon's men cut in hard and with force leaving dead or dieing savages everywhere. For several long moments it was a slaughter, most of the barbarians didn't even notice they were being attacked from behind. But soon they were organized enough to put up a resistance and Dagon's men were forced to sound the retreat. Back to the south they rode, but not nearly as hard as they could have. They were making sure that barbarians were following. Not nearly as many of the enemy followed as Dagon had hoped, but those that had were soon showered from the night sky by silent death.

"Congratulate yourselves men, you all fought gloriously, but that was only the beginning. We have a lot of work to do this night if we are to win this battle. We attack at dawn boys, now lets get to work." Dagon cheered to his men and they cheered back.

"We only lost twenty four soldiers and eleven are wounded to the point that they can no longer fight." Jarroth told Dagon after his speech.

"I was hoping for less, but that is still a low number." Dagon replied, his thoughts elsewhere.

"What is it?" Jarroth asked, knowing full well something was playing on his friends mind.

"I feel something is amiss and not right." Dagon responded, looking his friend in the eyes.

"I think I understand, we have had our homes taken from us and don't have the resources regain them, that can do a lot to a man." Jarroth said to him.

Dagon sighed gravely. "I don't think that's it… but maybe you are right." Dagon gave in. "Well my friend, let us get to work, there is much to be done if we are to even the odds in the morning."

Dawn came quickly and once again, Dagon's men prepared to march on their enemies' camp. But this time the strategy was different, Dagon knew his men were still tremendously outnumbered and would be over run if they fought head to head. He was hoping to fool the enemy one last time to even the odds, and if all went as planned, they could end this battle this very morning.

Arrows were running thin, so out of the two hundred archers, only a hundred were given arrows. The remaining men were to use their sword in this battle. The rest of Dagon's men, almost four hundred strong had made wooden spears and were to ride hard into the enemy camp and take their best shot with their spear, then fight as hard as they could until the enemy organized against them and they had to run. Dagon knew the barbarians would chase in full this time. That's why he and his men had shaped the battlefield in their favour.

A half-mile away from the enemy camp, his men had prepared for a stand off, the woods in this area were thicker and a little harder to manoeuvre in. Dagon's men had several dozen large tree's ready to fall by a single axe swing to the few ropes that held them up.

They had gathered all the bark, logs, dry wood and leafs they could find in the area and piled it almost as high as a man in a semi circle about a four hundred and fifty feet long, leaving a twenty foot gap in the middle where Dagon's men could run through when they retreated. The wall was soaked with all the lamp oil and touch oil and rags they had, which Dagon knew would be enough to get the dry timber wall burning hot and fast.

Behind the wall were the hundred archers with what arrows they had left. When Dagon and his men came running back, the archers were to light the wall a blaze and then slow the enemy down as much as they could with the arrows they had. Once Dagon and his men made it behind the wall, the last ones through would have to guard the opening, fending off the barbarians from getting through while the rest of Dagon's army would begin to launched the hundreds of wooden spears they had piled up. Several well placed men would sever the ropes holding the huge trees, crushing many barbarians in their wake.

After the tree's fell, there would be no more tricks. They would have to fight the hordes of barbarians that were left, which everyone hoped wouldn't be many.

Dagon could see that many of his men were tired and weary from the long day and night that they were having. He knew most of them by name and had fought beside most of these men many times before. He knew they would last and make it through this battle.

"We are ready my lord." A young dark haired soldier said.

Dagon nodded to him to let him know he was glad to hear that. "Sharpen your blade my boy, and keep your senses sharp out there." He told the young man who was just a year or two older then his eldest son Ethan.

"I will my lord." The boy said then started to walk away but stopped. "It is an honour to fight with you my lord; we will get our home back." The boy finished then walked away. That brought a smile to Dagon's face as he rallied his men into a charge.

~ ~ ~

A tall muscular barbarian barked out orders to a group of warriors that had been piling the bodies of their comrades all night so they could be burned. Many of the barbarians had gotten no sleep that night, they had been busy moving the dead, tending the many wounded and putting out the fires from the attack in the night. The last of the bodies were thrown onto the massive pile, just as Dagon's men came into sight of the camp in a full charge.

~ ~ ~

Once again they had caught the barbarians off guard, the enemy ran this way and that trying to get out of the way of the trampling horses and swinging swords, while others ran to warn the rest of their army.

Dagon crashed hard into a group of confused savages with his horse and trampled over many of them, crushing bones and life out of them as he went. He worked his sword left and right, taking down handful after handful of the enemy as they scrambled to get organized and find a weapon. A tingling sensation over came him and his eyes shot right to left trying to see what the trouble could be. Then he heard the long dull sound of horns from the distance. His eyes spotted the trouble from the far end of the enemy camp, as hundreds upon hundreds of barbarians poured out of the forest to join their brethren in battle.

Dagon and his men held strong for several more moments killing enemies left and right, but soon for every one they killed, ten more were there to replace them. The retreat was sounded and Dagon and his men rode hard out of the camp, being pursued by more then they were prepared to handle.

Dagon's mind raced as he kicked his horse's flanks, urging it to go faster. He could see the wall of timber flare to life as the archers set it a blaze. He raced through the opening his horse hadn't even fully stopped before he was on the ground yelling orders and getting ready for the battle that was about to take place. He fought the urge to tell his men to retreat now, he knew the enemy was far larger now then he and his men could handle. But yet he couldn't bring himself to give the order. He knew they could hold the enemy for a while and kill their fair share before they needed to run.

The archers took aim and let fly, taking down the first line of barbarians that charged towards them, while the rest of Dagon's men got through the opening and prepared themselves for the battle.

"It was a trap, I can't believe it." Dagon cursed to Jarroth who was now by his side.

"There was no way to know." Jarroth yelled over to him, picking up one of the make shift spears.

"We can't beat them, there is too many of them now." Dagon cried, launching a spear into the throng of enemy soldiers and striking one in the chest.

"Maybe not, but we can hold them for now and wear down their ranks." Jarroth shouted, impaling a savage on the other side of the fire.

Dagon watched in horror as the hordes of enemies rolled towards them and the archers fired their last arrows and started on the wooden spears. "We can not win this one, my friend." Dagon cried, firing another spear into the mass of enemies. "Sound the retreat as soon as I give the order!" Dagon shouted, and Jarroth nodded his understanding.

Bodies piled high all around the ten foot opening, for every one of Dagon's men that fell, they took with them five or more savages. The ropes were cut and the dozens of large fur tree's fell into the cluster of enemies, crushing and killing a dozen or more under each one.

Confusion sprang out through the ranks of barbarians as the trees crashed down upon them. They pushed each other down and trampled one another to death trying to avoid the falling trees. It bought Dagon and his men some precious time and they used it as best they could as the men holding the gap and many more charged into the crowd of barbarians, cutting them down and hacking them apart while they searched the sky for more falling trees. The spears were running low, so each man picked his shot carefully, making sure each shot counted.

As soon as the last trees fell, the confusion stopped and the barbarians pressed their attack furiously, trying to over take the Dagon's men before any more surprises happened. But Dagon was out of surprises now, he had been counting the odds to be in their favour by now, but that was far from the case. More and more savages kept swarming in and he could tell they were out numbered more then five to one and the odds were growing against them with each passing minute. The men were back holding the opening now, but were tiring fast, even with the constant swapping of men so others could rest a little. The only thing that was saving them from being completely overrun was the constant problem the enemy was having climbing and tripping over the dead and wounded that littered twenty or more feet in the front and to the sides of the opening. In some places the bodies were three or four deep now.

"They're breaching the ends of the wall!" Several men screamed and men rushed to both ends of the flaming wall to stop the enemy from getting through their only defence.

The spears were depleted and the burning wall was dying down. Savages were beginning to brave diving through the flames to the other side.

"Its over, we have to run!" Dagon shouted to Jarroth who was by his side, helping him kill all the savages that dared to come through the wall.

Jarroth looked at him gravely, knowing that that time had come indeed and ran off to give the order.

"We will stay here and buy the rest of you some time to run!" Several men cried together that were holding the opening. They all knew it was suicide, but not a man argued, they just held their ground and battled the enemy. When one fell dead, the others spread out a little more to make up for it.

Dagon and what was left of his men rode hard back to the east, most of the horses had run off, so every horse now carried two riders, some three. Forty men had stayed behind to help cover their retreat, while less then two hundred fled with their lives. Dagon rode with his head hung in shame the whole way back, kicking himself for not pulling his soldiers out of there sooner.

~ ~ ~

"My lord Andras, there is a messenger here to see you sir. He says he is one of Lord Dagon's men from Mandrake." A servant cried, running into the grand garden where Lord Andras and his wife soaked in a large, naturally heated pool, one of the many found in this region.

"What did you say?" Andras shouted, giving the man his full attention and pushing his wife to the side.

"Yes my lord, a messenger from Mandrake." The servant said again.

"Well bring him here, damn you." Andras barked, climbing out of the hot pool and putting on his silk robe.

Moments later the servant returned with a haggard, half dead man who was being held up by two other servants.

"My god, get this man some food and water!" Andras snapped and the first servant ran off to do so. "Why are you here, messenger?" Andras asked the man.

"Lord Dagon... begs... for help... Mandrake..." The messenger started to say between deep breaths and violent coughs. Finally the servant rushed back with a large skin full of cool water followed by was another servant with a large tray of fresh fruit, berries, meat and cheese. The messenger took the water skin and downed several large gulps which helped clear his rough, scratchy voice and seemed to revitalize him a little.

"Mandrake was over taken… by savages… and the land is swarming with them… more and more each day, Lord Dagon asks… for your help." The messenger started.

"Yes I know Mandrake was taken over by those monsters, but why aren't Prince Berrit and the lords of Draco doing anything about it?" Andras asked, cutting the man off.

"We don't know… sent messengers there… no word back." The messenger coughed.

"Take this man to a guest room and let him rest, bring him to me once he is rested and revived again." Andras order.

~ ~ ~

"You can not seriously be thinking about this my lord!" Meresin bellowed franticly.

"Meresin, I know you are my advisor, that is why I asked for your opinion on the matter. But you don't seem to be looking at the big picture here." Andras snapped at the scrawny man.

"I am my lord, I see it as such; the barbarians are strong enough to take a stronghold like Mandrake and that means they're strong enough to take Besha Castle too." Meresin explained in one long breath.

Andras stormed around the room running his hands through his thick brown hair. "What do you think, Velkain?" Andras asked his champion.

"I will stand by you no matter what your choice is my lord." Velkain replied in a deep voice that had come to be expected with his massive frame of nearly seven feet and three hundred pounds. It was rumoured that he had barbarian in his blood, which gave him his size and strength, but no one dared to ask him.

"That is not what I asked." Andras shot back.

"I care not for those of Draco kingdom my lord, but I would be lying if I said I would rather see it in the hands of filthy savages." Velkain replied.

"Someone bring me the messenger and fetch my two sons." Andras commanded.

~ ~ ~

"Kain, we are to ride to battle, get your things ready my son." Andras said with a smile to his oldest boy, who smiled back at him excited to finally hear those words leave his fathers lips.

"Yes father." Kain replied, running off to fetch his armour and sword.

"What about I father, am I to ride with you?" Andras youngest son Jamus asked.

"No my son, I need you to stay here to take care of your mother and our land, and to see to it that no savages step foot in Besha's boarders." Andras said, knowing his boy was hurt that he could not come along.

"But father, I can fight. I want to come." Jamus whined.

"Jamus, you have your place here. Do not disobey or argue with me." Andras said firmly and Jamus finally nodded his head in agreement.

"My lord, this is madness, you truly should rethink this." Meresin pleaded.

"I have already made up my mind Meresin; Lord Dagon I know would help us if we were asking for this of him. We are allies now, if you don't remember." Andras said.

"But sir, the treaty was never properly signed and the princess hasn't even been found yet. She is likely already dead, which means Prince Berrit will not be marrying her and will not be king, which means we are not allies." Meresin cried running after Andras who was already on his way to his general's quarters.

"That's enough, Meresin! I will not have you second guess me anymore! I am the lord of Besha, not you, and if I hear one more discouraging word from you, I will cut out your tongue!" Andras raged on the tiny man who shrank against the wall.

"I... I am sorry my lord, I meant do disrespect." Meresin whimpered.

Andras stormed away to inform his generals of the news and see to it that his men were ready.

~   ~   ~

Early the next morning Lord Andras, his son Kain, the messenger who was almost fully recovered and six hundred hardened soldier's road north to Lord Dagon's aid.

~   ~   ~

Astaroth, in the form of Prince Berrit stood by Lord Tundal's wife, Lady Tora and their children Thoron, Salvira, Calmela and Drandor's champion Raven while watching the smoke rise into the sky from Tundal's pyre. Dagon's family, Lady Angelina and their two boys Ethan and Leonard were also present. The courtyard was packed full of those who had known, loved and respected Lord Tundal.

Astaroth did well to pretend to grieve, but inside was a wide smile. How he couldn't wait until all of these people were delivered the bloody truth, when they would all fall to their knees and beg for their pathetic lives.

~ ~ ~

Several hours later Prince Berrit, Dagon's wife and children, Tundal's wife and children, along with Raven and Mathu, Tami, Avril and the chil dren of Dragon's Cove along with their champion Barkel and several of King Borracks dearest friends were all summoned to the library to discuss who was to rule Draco Kingdom in its time of great need.

"I am to be king as soon as the princess is returned to us safely, so I should be Draco Kingdom's Steward until Princess Nicolette returns." Prince Berrit, said knowing no one was going to buy that.

"Like hell that's going to happen, Zandorian!" Raven shouted angrily, still not sure whether he believed Berrit about the death of his dear friend, Tundal.

"Well we need someone who knows how to rule a kingdom, and I don't see anyone else." Berrit barked. "I am sorry I snapped there, I am just as frustrated as the rest of you. I too wish Lord Tundal was still here to help see to the ruling. Yes, we disagreed on things, but that happens. I am simply trying to look out of the best interest of Draco Kingdom, and yes I am somewhat new to ruling alone, but given our present problems, I don't know anyone who would know how to better deal with them. Things like this have never happened before." Berrit explained and had all of their attention for once. "I just want what's best for my kingdom." As soon as the words came out he realized he should have stopped short. Everyone was in an uproar again.

"Your kingdom? You wish, you slimy dog." Thoron barked with rage.

Barkel stood up and everyone quieted down a little so he could be heard. "We don't even know if the Princess is still alive. If she is dead, then I hardly think the treaty still stands, which means you ain't king of horse shit."

"Why you…" Berrit started to say but was cut short.

"Everyone stop!" Lady Tora cried, halting everyone in mid sentence. "This is not going to get us anywhere, this fighting is not what we need, right now. We need to be strong and help each other. King Borrack is dead and his daughter, the only true heir, is missing and could be dead. Our beautiful country is being overrun with barbarians. Sitting here cursing and yelling at each other because of where we're from and who we are isn't going to solve any of that." She said staring each man, woman and child in the room deep in their eyes as she spoke.

Thoron dropped his head and sighed. "Your right mother, I am sorry."

"Aye my lady, your words are wise beyond your years." Raven added.

"You are right my dear lady Tora." Berrit replied. "So what is it you propose we do?" He asked with only a hint of smugness.

Tora took a deep breath before answering. "I suggest we send riders out to find Lord Dagon and tell him he is needed here. Only he knows the land and how it should be run. It would only seem right for him to take place as ruler until the princess is returned to us and all of this is straightened out." Tora said.

Everyone could tell that her words hit Berrit like a brick, but he held his tongue and did well to smile and agree.

"And what shall we do until Lord Dagon gets here?" Berrit asked.

"We make decisions as a council and a group. We will all do our part in the ruling." Lady Angelina replied.

Astaroth did not like the way this was going, and fought his urge to transform into his true self and torch every soul in the room. He withheld the desire, he had come to far in this, he had to remain calm and with his wits about. So what if wasn't in complete control right now, the plan was already in motion and could not be stopped, not by these fools.

"That makes perfect sense." Raven said, agreeing whole heartedly. "We all know a little about everything, between us all we should be able to help straighten this mess out, at least 'til Lord Dagon returns." Everyone but Berrit cheered their agreement.

"Prince Berrit, do you not agree?" Tora asked.

"Yes. I do agree. I believe you are right in using a council, I truly think that is the wisest course of all right now." He replied with a wide smile.

"Good, now as a council I believe we should ask our neighbours from Zandor if they could send some assistance to help take back our land." Tora stated, and again everyone agreed. "And who better to do that then you, Prince Berrit? Do you think you could help with that, for the good of what may be your future kingdom?"

"I shall send word to my father right away, Lady Tora. I am sure he will send a large army to aid us." Berrit replied, rising up from his seat and taking his leave to go do as he was asked.

Chapter 17

Meath woke to the sound of running water and a soft, soothing voice singing an old song that he hadn't heard since he was a boy. Meath's head began spinning wildly when he tried to open his eyes. He fought to stay conscious. For a few minutes while he lay there, with his world spinning, he forgot who he himself was, where he was and what had happened to him over the last month. He wondered if he was dead and the voice that was singing this alluring melody was an angel that had come to take him back to the creator. Anyone with a voice so sweet sounding must be an angel, he thought. He wanted to know what she looked like. He rolled over and pain coursed through every part of his body like he was on fire. He cried out in pain and the singing stopped.

"Are you ok Meath? You shouldn't be trying to move." The voice told him.

Meath looked up and opened his eyes to see whose voice had delivered the sound of the angels. There, kneeling in front of him was a beautiful young woman that Meath was sure he had met before. She was staring back at him with a very concerned looked on her face. She dampened a cloth in a cup of water that was on the floor and placed it on his head. Meath flinched when the cool water touched his skin.

"Its ok Meath, I'm not going to hurt you." She whispered.

That's when it all started flooding back into his mind. The escape from Draco Castle with Ursa and the Princess, running across Zehava and Dahak and getting their help, being captured by barbarians and tortured, getting to Dragon's Cove, and being taken away from Nicolette. That's where he had first seen this face and heard the voice; it was the face and voice of one of his captors. The memories flooded back so fast it disorientated him even more. He tried to speak but no words escaped his lips before everything went dim and he blacked out yet again.

"Oh Meath, I promise it will all stop soon, the poison is almost out of your system." Kara whispered to him, rolling him over and remoistening the cloth on his head.

Kara had found Meath the next morning after he had escaped her and Daden following the fight with the barbarians. Meath had been badly wounded by the barbarian's vile magic which made his wounds fester and rot at a much faster rate then normal. She had found him under a low overhang by a rocky hill that he had used for shelter. He was already unconscious when she had found him, and the poison in his wounds had spread further then she had expected. She didn't know if she could save him. The last two days and night she had been using every cure, potion and ointment she could possibly think of and find to help heal him. She had used her gift to heal the physical wounds, now it was just the poison working through his system that he had to beat. The battle seemed to be going nowhere, for over the last two days he didn't seem to be getting better, but neither did he seem worse.

Kara wondered how Daden was and hoped he found shelter and safety. She knew Daden could take care of himself, but he too had been wounded in the fight and if barbarians had discovered, him he might not be able to fend them off. She sighed deeply, she could not let all these questions assault her mind, it was driving her to her minds limits. Daden was well and waiting for her and as soon as Meath was able, they would go find him and continue on their way.

~ ~ ~

Meath woke again this time to the sound of birds singing. His head and body didn't hurt nearly as much as it had the last time he was conscious, and this time he remembered everything. He opened his eyes and saw Kara, asleep inches away from him with her back against the inside of the giant stump they were in. Meath looked out the leaf covered opening and saw it was just becoming light out. He slowly rolled himself over onto his arms and knees so he could crawl out. He had to fight hard not to groan and gasp, his body was still weak and stiff and moving still hurt immensely. He was just about to exit when he heard Kara shuffle behind him. All he could think of was that this could be his last chance to escape, so he bolted out of the opening as fast as he could. He was ten steps ahead before his legs gave out underneath him and he hit the ground hard.

"Leaving without even saying thanks for saving my life, or good bye?" A very sarcastic Kara said as she walked over to him.

Meath looked up at her like a kid caught with his hands in the cookie jar, but he didn't say a thing.

"Please Meath, don't make me restrain you. Just co-operate with me, you are still weak and exhausted from your wounds and the poison in your system." Kara explained to him, putting her hands out to offer her help off the ground.

Meath knew he couldn't escape yet, he was far too weak and sore to make it very far. He noticed he wasn't bound by the enchanted rope they had used before to constrict access to his gift, the thought of attacking her with his gift crossed his mind only for a second. He knew she didn't deserve that. She had been nothing but kind to him even if she was kidnapping him, and after seeing what she could do with her gift, he expected she was on guard and he would only lose. He decided to play along until the right moment came to make a run for it, and this time he would not be caught again. He grabbed her hands and used her for support to get to his feet and leaned on her so his legs would hold him up.

"Here, let's sit outside and get some fresh air. I'll start a small fire and cook the crayfish I caught in the creek." Kara said, easing him down so he could sit against a tree in their small camp.

"Thank you." Meath finally said after he was settled and she had put a small fire together.

"You're welcome. I almost didn't think you were going to make it." She said looking up at him. He could tell she had been truly concerned.

"What happened to me? The last thing I remember was finding shelter under an overhang. The rest is blank." Meath asked.

"The barbarians have a way of putting a dark poison into their gift, so even if their attack doesn't kill you right away, the wounds will fester and rot at a fast rate, killing the victim shortly after. Unless it is treated with the right potions and salves." Kara explained.

Meath had heard rumours of dark barbarian magic and what happens to people who were wounded, but he had never witnessed it and had never met anyone who had lived through it. From what he had been told, not many ever escaped barbarian priests and priestesses.

"I will give you one more night to rest, but tomorrow we must get traveling again. We have to find Daden and get back to Salvas as soon as possible, this trip has already taken too long." Kara told him, and then realized she had told him information she shouldn't have.

Meath stared at the ground, his mind racing with questions that he so desperately wanted the answers to. "Why are you taking me to this Salvas' place?" He asked bluntly, hoping now that it was just he and Kara, he might get some answers.

Kara looked at him and was biting her bottom lip. He could tell she wanted to tell him. "I can't tell you, you just have to trust me that this is what has to be done Meath."

"How am I supposed to trust you? You kidnapped me and are dragging me against my will across the country to a place I know nothing about and for reasons I don't know. So you tell me why should I trust you?" Meath barked back to her.

"I know it's a hard thing, Meath, but you need to believe me. This is for the best. For you, for the princess and everyone." Kara said, wishing she could say more to ease his mind.

"I could have left you two to die back there." Meath mumbled, loud enough for her to hear.

"Then why didn't you, Meath? Why didn't you take your chance and run when I cut you free and let the barbarians kill us? Why Meath? Do you know? Cause I know why." Kara snapped back at him.

"Because I'm not a heartless monster that just lets people die." Meath shouted angrily at her.

Kara smiled, liking his answer. "And that's why we came to get you, because you're not a heartless monster, Meath. Not like him, you are different." She replied, again realizing she said more then she should have. "I guess we're even, you saved my life and I saved yours." She quickly added, hoping to curve the conversation.

"So how long was I out for?" Meath asked, submitting to the small talk, knowing there was nothing he could do at the moment except try to earn her trust put the pieces together of why she had taken him.

"Today is day two. I didn't think I was going to be able to save you." Kara told him, using a stick to stir the fire she had made so it would boil the small pot of water she had the crayfish in.

"Why did you save me? Why am I so important?" Meath asked hoping to get some more information.

Kara stared silently at the flames for several moments before answering him, wondering how much she could tell him. "You are needed Meath, for something far greater then you or I could ever know." She said while looking into his eyes with an unknown awe.

"What!? What are you talking about? I think you've got the wrong guy." Meath cried, frustrated with the whole situation.

"No, you are the right one, I can tell by your eyes. They're the same as his." Kara said.

"Who? Who do you keep referring me too?" Meath begged, hoping for an answer.

Kara stopped herself before it slipped out. "I cannot tell you, all your questions will be answered as soon as we get to Salvas."

"What is this place, Salvas? I've never heard of it before." Meath asked, trying to keep the conversation going.

When she didn't answer, he pressed it a little more. "Telling me where we are going and what kind of place it is isn't going to change anything. It might ease my mind a little more." He told her.

Kara finally nodded, accepting his reasoning. "Salvas is a place that only those who have been there know about; it's not on any map." Kara said, her eyes lighting up with excitement as she spoke.

"Well I am sure people have stumbled upon it by mistake, or have seen smoke from the town or something." Meath said.

"No one can see the town, it's hidden by magic. The only way in and out is if you have a key." Kara said, staring down at a finely crafted ring on her right hand. It was a solid band from what Meath could see, but it was not of any metal Meath had ever seen. It appeared to be some sort of smooth black stone, crafted into a ring. "It's such a wonderful place Meath, you will like it there." She finished with a smile.

"How long do I have to stay there?" Meath asked, wondering if it would just be easier to go there for a day or two do what he was apparently supposed to and then leave.

"I do not know, 'til you are ready, I guess." Kara replied. "Could be a year, could be five years. That all depends on you I guess."

"Ready for what?" Meath questioned and Kara went silent again. "So you can't tell me that either." Meath sighed, growing more frustrated with the situation and knowing full well he would have to escape before they trapped him in this place for a year or more.

"I truly am sorry Meath, I wish I could tell you everything you want to know, but I can't." Kara said sympathetically.

"So where do you and Daden fit in?" Meath asked, changing the subject a bit.

"We were chosen to come find you and bring you back." Kara answered, stirring the fire more and adding a few more sticks to it. She reached over and took the small pot off so it could cool before she took the crayfish out to eat.

"Why you two, is it because you have the gift?" Meath asked.

"You are a lot more talkative now that Daden's not around." Kara smirked.

"Well the company's a lot better now, and not as hostile." Meath laughed, taking the hint that he had gotten all he was going to get from her for now.

"How are you feeling?" She asked, handing him a small wooden plate with two steaming crayfish on it.

Meath took the plate after he stretched his limbs a little, testing to see how stiff and sore he still was. "Still pretty sore, not about to win any battles against a group of barbarians like last time." He replied with a chuckle.

"Are you going to come willingly now?" Kara asked bluntly and very seriously.

"It doesn't seem like I have a choice either way, now does it." Meath remarked a little bitterly.

"No you don't, but I would rather not have to drag you there the whole way and make this any worse then it has already been." She said honestly.

"I guess the sooner we get there, the sooner I can leave and find my friends again. Though I am hoping that this can be done and over with a lot sooner then a year or more." Meath lied, hoping she would believe that was how he felt.

"I am glad to hear that, I don't want you to think I am the bad guy here Meath, cause I'm not, and you will see that I am telling you the truth soon enough. As for how long you are there that will all depend on when they believe you are ready." Kara said in good spirits.

By the time they finished eating it was already the afternoon and Kara made Meath get up and walk around to help stretch his muscles. She took him down to the creek not far from their camp and let him wash and clean himself up a little.

Meath was surprised Kara was giving him so much space and freedom. He thought about running while he was down at the creek, but decided it was better if he waited, she could be testing him. He decided to earn her trust a little more, besides, he truly was still sore and stiff and wasn't so sure he could get away from her if he ran. Tonight he would make his escape and he would let nothing stop him this time.

They sat together later and ate their dinner, a small trout they had trapped in a side pool of the creek and the last few dry pieces of cheese. The sky was full of bright pinks and purples as the sun set.

Kara took the few wooden dishes down to the creek to wash and left Meath poking in the fire. As soon as Kara was out of sight, he grabbed her pack and began searching through it for things he could use. Near the bottom he found a long length of the enchanted rope they had used on him. He smiled widely as he stashed it in his blanket. He quickly put everything back the way he had seen it and put her pack back where she had left it. Yes, he would get away, but he would wait until morning. He would be well rested and travel during the day was much easier. He watched the last few colours in the sky fade to night and thought of his friends and how he couldn't wait to see them again. He thought of Nicolette and how he couldn't wait to look into her eyes again and tell her he loved her and that they would find a way to be together.

"What are you thinking about?" Kara asked, catching him by surprise as she walked back into the camp without making a sound.

"Oh, nothing of importance." Meath stammered.

"Anything that makes someone look as happy as you just were would be of importance, I would think." Kara said, sitting down next to him.

"I was just thinking about my friends and how much I miss them and can't wait to see them again once this is all done." Meath said a little bitterly and Kara caught it.

"I know you miss them Meath, and I know you miss her most of all. You will be with them again, I promise. Just trust me and come with me to Salvas, you will see what this is all about and hopefully you can be done with it quickly and be on your way again." Kara said.

"Well let's get some sleep so we can be on our way early to this Salvas place. So I can do whatever it is I have to do, so I can get home and get on with my life." Meath muttered crawling into their small shelter.

~ ~ ~

Meath laid awake, knowing the sun would soon rise and he would finally be free again. His hands played with the length of enchanted rope underneath his blanket. He would do it before she woke up, it would give him that extra moment of surprise so he could bind her hands, rendering her gift useless to stop him. He rolled over and faced Kara, who was only a foot away from him. She was fast asleep on her side. He knew she wasn't a sound sleeper and he had to be fast and accurate. He made a loop in the rope at one end and gave it a good pull to make sure it would close fast and hold strong. Slowly he inched his way over to her and began sliding the loop under her hand and to her wrist. She began to wake up and Meath pounced on her, rolling her on her stomach and holding her firmly to the ground, grappling her hands behind her back as fast as he could before she realized what was happening.

"What the hell are you doing?" Kara screamed, trying to buck him off.

"Changing the plans just a little, I'm not going with you Kara." Meath said after making sure the enchanted rope wasn't coming off. "Don't bother trying to escape; it's the same rope you used on me." Meath said, getting off of her and backing away.

"Meath, please don't do this, you don't know what your doing!" Kara cried, rolling onto her back to face him.

"Oh yes I do, I am going back to my life, and if you or anyone else comes for me again, I will kill them." Meath barked angrily.

Meath grabbed her pack and took out some of the food to leave for her so she would not starve and removed a few other things he wouldn't need. He backed out of the shelter to the sight of a few rays of sun gracing the sky, making the beginning of a new day. He smiled wide, he was finally free again.

"You can't just leave me here Meath! I will die without my gift and my hands bound behind my back, I will be a sitting target, I can't defend myself." Kara yelled out to him.

Meath's smile faded slightly, he hadn't thought about that, he had only thought of escaping. He knew she was right, if he left her like this, she would surely get caught and killed by savages or a jungle cat. But if he released her, or left means for her to free herself, she would follow him and try to catch him again.

Meath threw the large half dried leafs Kara had used for a roof off the hollow stump. Kara sat in the middle staring at him with tears forming in her eyes, but with a hint of relief at seeing that he was still there.

"I'm not a monster, I'm not going to leave you to die. But I can't let you go, now can I? So that leaves one option, you're coming with me until I can figure out what to do with you to be free of you and know I left you safe." Meath said firmly. "Now get up, were leaving."

"Meath please, you don't know what you are doing. We have to go to Salvas." Kara pleaded.

"I'm going home, now either you come with me or you stay here and accept whatever fate becomes you here." Meath said bitterly as he turned and began walking west.

Kara got to her feet and followed, knowing death would surely find her if she stayed and knowing she couldn't go back to Salvas without him. She had to find a way to convince him to go with her, or at least escape her bounds and drag him there against his will.

They traveled in silence for the first couple of hours. On several occasions, Meath had to stop and help her over fallen trees and slippery rocks. Still, nothing was said between the two. Meath knew what she was thinking, he had been in her shoes only a day before.

"Its a lot different point of view being the captive and not the captor, isn't it." Meath said, looking at her with a smug look.

"I know very well what being held captive is like, Meath!" Kara snapped at him in a tone that Meath would never have thought possible from her.

"Well believe me, I would rather not have you captive right now, I would much rather never have met you. All that's happened since you kidnapped me is your doing, so I think your pointing the blame at the wrong person." Meath hissed right back.

Kara followed behind him dumbfounded, not sure of what to say. He was right, in a sense, none of this would have happened if not for her and Daden. But it all had to happen and she still had to get him to Salvas somehow. She pondered telling him everything she knew of why he had to go, but she knew he wouldn't believe her now even if she did. He was doing what anyone in his situation would; he was trying to get back to his life that she had taken him from. No, he was better then most, Kara reasoned. She was sure anyone else would have left her to die, or even worse killed her themselves to get away. That's why she knew he was the one they needed.

"Where did you get that scar on your chest?" Kara asked plainly, not wanting them to lose whatever connection they did have.

Meath stopped where he was for a moment and one of his hands touched his chest where the scar was. "I know what cruelty savages can do and what pain and torment they can inflict." Meath muttered and kept walking.

They walked until dusk and made camp under the thick canopy of a large tree's branches that were bent downward almost to the ground, making for a good, dry, fairly hidden place to sleep.

~　~　~

"Finally, we made it." Dahak moaned as they rode around the last bend of the road leading them towards Caligo city, which was right on Sheeva Lake and their last stop before their search for Meath really started. The city lights emanated a soft welcoming glow in the night sky as they road closer.

It was the forth day that Nicolette and the others had been traveling, they had passed through a few small towns and heard nothing but rumours of the barbarian activity heading towards Dragon's Cove. A lot of the people were fleeing to walled-in cities and places they figured to be safe. Many of those people had fled to Caligo city because it was the closest.

They rode up to the guards at the gates and were halted.

"What business do you have in Caligo city this night?" A big burly, unshaved man asked.

"We are looking for a place to rest and fill our bellies for the night, we will be on our way in the morning." Zehava replied to the man.

The other guard walked through the group, taking a look at their faces. He stopped when he arrived at Shania. "Lift your hood." He told her.

Very hesitantly, she pulled her hood back, revealing her heritage.

"What in the nine hells?!" The guard burst out, taking a step back and drawing his sword.

"What is this then?" The first guard barked, drawing his own sword and looking at Zehava.

"It is ok, she is with us and will cause no harm to anyone." Zehava said, hoping not to draw anymore attention to the group. As far as the country knew, the princess was still kidnapped and the reward was only growing bigger. Though Nicolette hardly looked like a princess anymore, with her dirty riding gear, her sword at her hip and bow on her back. She looked more like a warrior then a princess.

"Like hell, we do not allow any kind of savage within our walls! Have you not heard and seen all the attacks of late? If she comes in here she will be able to tell all her filthy savage friends our weaknesses, and then we will stand no chance." The man bellowed.

"She is our slave, for our comfort and…" Nicolette paused for a moment to make sure she had the guard's attention. "… Our pleasure." She finished with, as evil a look she could summon. "Now, we have had a hard long day." She said, fishing around in her coin pouch and grabbing two silvers, tossing them to the guards. "Let us in." She commanded.

Both guards cracked huge grins and nodded their heads. "Alright then, you can enter. But we had better not hear about you's causing any trouble."

"And maybe a little later, when we're off watch, you might let us get a little pleasure out of that little savage whore." The other guard said, opening the gate for them with a stupid grin on his face.

Zehava fought hard the urge to cut the man's tongue out as he rode passed, but he just smiled and gave a slight nod as he rode by.

"Maybe you can for a price." Dahak said, trying to fit into the ruse.

"I am sorry for that, Shania." Both Nicolette and Zehava said once they were far enough away.

Shania pulled her hood back up. "I am getting use to being the savage slave." She said, almost laughing.

"We will get supplies in the morning, then leave to find where Meath's trail ended by the river. I hope we can pick it up again." Zehava said while riding off the main rode in search for a quieter part of town to find an inn.

"That is if we can find it." Dahak said to himself, but everyone heard him.

"You have to have faith." Shania told him.

"What makes you think if some of the best trackers in Draco can't find him, that we can?" Dahak muttered.

"We will find him, I know we will." Nicolette said, feeling the handle of Meath's sword which was strapped to her saddle.

They found an inn that looked fairly secluded from the main part of town. Nicolette tossed the night stable boy a copper coin and told him to take good care of their horses and he might see silver. The boy smiled wide and assured her the beasts would be treated as kings. Shortly after, they were all in a small room that smelled musky and reeked of cheap ale.

"Well it ain't the castle, but it's a roof over our heads." Dahak said, removing his pack and gear.

"Its better then the castle, a lot better." Nicolette stated with an ample smile.

"What do you mean?" Zehava asked, truly bewildered.

"No rules, no politics, no high stature to uphold… it's freedom." Nicolette told them with complete honesty in her eyes.

A feather could have knocked everyone in the room down at that moment, and soon Zehava and Shania, and even Dahak had to agree.

"I'd still rather be at a castle." Dahak finally muttered sitting down to rub his feet.

"I wouldn't, nothing better then this right here. Friends and adventure." Shania piped in with a smile.

"I agree, were only missing one thing." Zehava said.

"What's that Zehava?" Dahak asked, missing the tone in his friend's voice.

"Meath…" Nicolette whispered, loud enough for everyone to hear.

"We will find him." Shania said, trying to comfort her. "He's not hard to find, just go to where the trouble is." Shania added with a laugh and got a chuckle out of everyone.

"Ain't that the truth." Zehava said. "Well what do you all say about going to the tavern across the street and getting a hot meal and a cold drink?" Zehava asked, trying to change the subject before everyone's morel dropped.

"Ya that sounds good, I am starving now that I think about it." Nicolette replied, looking up from the floor.

"What about Shania? Do you think we can get her in without a problem?" Dahak asked Zehava.

"I packed an extra set of traveling clothes; she can change into those, which should help a little." Nicolette said, handing her some clothes.

"Taverns are dark and smokey, just keep your hood up and I am sure we will be fine." Zehava told her with a smile. He felt bad for her always having to hide her identity, but right now that was the way it had to be. Once everything was the way it should be again, he would make sure she started getting the respect she deserved.

~ ~ ~

The group sat in a corner of the bar where the lights were dimmer and the crowd thinner. The bar was normally never this busy on a normal evening, but since a lot of refugees and other town folk were moving within the walls of the city, the bar was almost full. Everyone was too busy drinking away their sorrows and telling their sob stories to notice them. Zehava had gone off to find a bar maid and ordered four specials, then went back to the table where everyone waited.

"Our food will be here soon." He told them, sitting down next to Shania.

"A nice hot meal, I can't wait! I am wasting away." Dahak moaned licking his lips.

"From what I heard back at Dragon's Cove, we are about a day's ride from where they lost Meath's trail." Nicolette said.

"Tomorrow we will follow the riverside 'til we find something." Zehava said, moving back against his seat so the bar maid could give them their food.

"Four specials and a pitcher of ale for y'all." A busty, blond haired women said, putting their food down in front of them. "That will be two coppers from the each of ya." She said, holding out her hand and waiting for money.

"Here, keep the rest as a tip." Nicolette said, reaching into her pouch and pulling out a gold coin, tossing it her way.

The bar maids eyes widened. "Aye thank you kindly, strangers." She said walking back to the bar.

You guys have to try this stew." Dahak mumbled between each spoonful of his already half empty bowl.

"It would be wise not to flash gold coins around in a place like this, a silver coin would have paid our bill and then some." Zehava whispered to Nicolette while watching the barmaid, who was now talking to the bartender eagerly and looking their way.

"Why, what's wrong?" Nicolette asked as she scanned the room, stopping on the bar and seeing the bar maid.

"I am sure it's nothing guys, you worry too much. Now try this food, its great." Dahak said, soaking up the remains of his stew with a large chunk of fresh bread.

Zehava sighed, picked up his spoon and began to eat his stew while being sure to keep an eye on the room. "I hope you are right, Dahak." He muttered, though no one heard him.

"Wow Dahak you're right." Shania said, amazed after she took a bite of her stew and tasted the heavy flavours of savoury meat and spices. She quickly matched Dahak's pace at gobbling up the meal.

"Lets eat and get out of here; I'm getting a bad feeling." Zehava whispered to everyone, noticing the bartender was now talking to a table where four large brutes sat downing mug after mug of ale.

"Can I getcha all something else?" The barmaid asked when she came to collect their dishes.

"No thanks, about time we call it a night, got a long road a head of us.' Zehava told her, pretending to stretch and yawn.

"Alright then, you all have a great night, hope to see ya again." She said as she left with their dishes.

The group got up and walked to the doors and out, the four brutes at the table watching their every step.

"Let's not go straight to our room." Shania said once they were on the road.

"What, why not? The sooner we are there the safer we are, and the sooner we can sleep." Dahak complained.

"No, no Shania's right." Nicolette replied, catching on to what Shania was saying and both Zehava and Dahak were confused.

"Would you run straight back to your hide out if you thought you were being followed?" Shania enlightened to them.

"Or would you make sure you weren't." Nicolette finished for her.

Zehava smiled and chuckled. "Ok you're right, let's go for a little walk then, keep your eyes sharp and be ready for anything."

They walked through the city, taking lefts and rights through alleyways and on main roads, blending with the small crowds of refugees that were homeless. After half an hour, they reasoned that they were safe to head back to their room. They were a few blocks away from their inn when a group of five men come up from behind them.

"Hey, there you are." A man said from behind them with a husky deep voice. They turned to regard them with hands on hilts, but saw that it was the two guards from the gates and a few of their buddies.

"What do you want?" Zehava asked calmly, hoping to be rid of them.

"What do you think we want?" The shorter guard from the gates said, licking his lips and running his hand through his uncombed hair. "We want a taste of that savage whore like you said we could." He finished with a smile, showing all his broken and rotten teeth.

"Aye, and we brought a few friends along that wouldn't mind a little piece either." The first one said with a chuckle, looking back to his three large friends who all wore stupid grins.

"No one is touching her, she is our toy and only our toy." Zehava said, putting his hand on the hilt of his sword again.

"Oh come on now mate, I got me friends all worked up for some fun. Don't make me disappoint them. Besides, she's a savage, she's not worth protecting." The short one said.

"Sorry to disappoint you, but you will have to look elsewhere you pigs." Nicolette burst out angrily.

"Looky looky, that ones got some spice to her too, maybe we should take her for a while too, what do you say boys?" One of the dirty guards from behind said, looking to his comrades to see their wide grins and nods of agreement.

"Ya, I think your right Clyde, that's a good idea." Another of the brutes laughed, taking a step forward with his arm stretched out towards Nicolette.

In a blink of an eye Zehava's sword was out and he slashed downward, severing the man's hand off at his wrist. "You'll lose a lot more then that if you don't walk away now." Zehava barked while the man howled in pain and backed away, cradling his bloody stump.

"You're going to pay for that you runt!" Clyde hissed as he drew his sword, his comrades following suit.

Dahak and Shania both had their blades out long before that and Nicolette held her small crossbow that she had received from Saktas pointed at one man's throat, while her other hand rested nervously on the hilt of her sword.

"We don't want any trouble!" Nicolette stammered, trying to hold her hand still and not show them she was afraid.

"You should have thought about that before ya cut my friends hand off, wench." The short man yelled, some what jittery.

"You are out matched, we don't want to have to kill you, but we will." Zehava told them with complete calm.

"Out matched?" One man laughed. "How do you figure that one lad?"

"My friend here is an excellent shot and will have one sticking out of your throat before you even move, and I guarantee you she won't miss. One of your friends is missing his sword hand, so he isn't going to be of much help and will die quickly. And I assure you our barbarian friend here is very deadly with her twin blades, and you have offended her. You will all die and for nothing but the sake of your pride. Walk away with your lives, this is your only warning." Zehava told them, not taking his eyes from the threat.

All five men stood there pondering his words and slowly they realized he was right.

"You win this time, but if I see you again, your luck will change. I want you out of the city by the time the sun is out from behind the mountains, if you are still here I will rally every man in the city to hunt you down." The man hissed, backing away with the others.

"Can we please go back to our inn now?" Dahak asked nervously after the men were out of sight.

"Yes, let's go back and get what rest we can. I don't think our friends will be back." Zehava replied, watching the shadows for anything that might be a threat.

~   ~   ~

Dawn came quickly and shortly after, the group was out of the city and on their way down the bank of the Sheeva River. They followed a poorly traveled animal path, but they soon realized their horses would be no good and wouldn't last on the rocky, jagged trail. They took their things and released the beasts, continuing on foot.

They traveled all morning and into the afternoon without stopping for a break when finally Dahak couldn't take it anymore. "Can we please stop for awhile?" He groaned from behind, dragging his feet.

"What's a matter Dahak, can't keep up with us girls?" Shania teased, though she was in need of a break as well.

"This looks like as good a spot as any I guess." Zehava said, dropping his pack and stretching his sore limbs.

Nicolette stumbled over to the rivers edge and dunked her head in, taking a long drink. She was so tired and her feet and legs burned with pain. She had wanted to stop for a break hours before, but her thoughts of finding Meath fuelled her to keep going.

"Try soaking your feet in the cool water, it will help." Zehava said, coming up behind her with his empty water skin.

"What?" Nicolette asked.

"Your feet, I noticed you were stumbling and limping a lot the last few hours. Soak your feet in the water it will help sooth them a little." Zehava told her.

"I was hoping no one noticed, I don't want to be the weakest link of the group anymore." Nicolette sighed, dropping her head.

"Hey, I didn't just come down here to get more water, I came down here to soak my feet too.' Zehava lied. "That was a hard hike, don't feel ashamed. And besides, there's no weak link in our group, we all watch each others backs and do what we can." Zehava encouraged her while taking off his boots and submerging his feet into the river. It brought a smile to her face.

"You guys read my mind." Dahak said, waddling down to where they sat and put his feet into the refreshing water.

They all spent a good half hour with their feet in the water, chatting about summers when they were young and all the foolish things they did.

After they had a quick lunch, they were back following the rivers edge. Several times they spotted signs that indicated barbarian activity but Shania knew that the tracks and campsites were several days old.

They traveled almost until dark, but stopped when they got to a large flat opening right by the river. It was smooth and almost perfectly flat and looked to be man made. They made camp and set up a fairly large cowhide tent that they had bought in the city earlier that day.

Dahak took first watch for two hours then it was Nicolette's turn for the next two hours then Zehava's then Shania's. With four people everyone would get plenty of sleep.

Nicolette sat up in a nearby tree where she was well hidden and could see the campsite in full. Since they didn't have a fire going, all the light she had was from the moon and the stars shining off the water and through the canopy of trees.

Normally she would have been terrified, being alone in the dark like this, but now there was a certain calm about it. She almost felt at peace, like the darkness understood her feelings.

"I know you're out there Meath, somewhere close." She whispered to the night.

She sat there in her thoughts for her two hours and was just about to climb down to wake Zehava when she noticed shadows creeping up from the north. Her heart raced as she grabbed her bow and notched an arrow, pulling back slightly to take aim. She didn't know how many there were, but she aimed on the closest one. She waited to see what they would do, she knew if they were savages, they were here to kill. But what if they were travelers like them. No, she shook that thought away; they wouldn't be traveling in the night if they were travelers. Finally she made her choice when she saw the closest one drew a sword and motion for the others to follow. She let loose her arrow and it struck its target hard in the leg, he howled in pain as he crashed to the ground.

Within moments the campsite was alive, Zehava and Shania were out in a heartbeat, weapons drawn and at the ready just in time. Three large, dark figures ran towards them, one stopped to check on the wounded man on the ground but the other two charged in hard. One wielded a single bladed battleaxe and the other a short sword.

Zehava met the axe wielder half way, knowing the best defence against an axe was not to let the opponent have the time or the room to swing it. Zehava had hoped for a quick kill, but the axe man was a lot faster then he could have ever expected. He shot his sword up high to defect a head chop that would have surely cut him in two. His arm tingled from the block, but he wasted no time. He kicked the axe wielder hard in the knee, bringing him down a little, then smashed the hilt of his sword and fist into the man's face, knocking him back a few steps. It hardly slowed the massive man and seconds later his axe hissed by Zehava's head from the side, and only the slight reflection of the moon off the blade saved him or he would never have seen it coming.

Shania danced her blades off the big mans sword, trying to keep him at bay until she could land a blow. The man swung furiously and from all angles and directions with such force that most of the time it took both of her blades and all of her strength to block the blows. Her shoulders and wrists ached from the repeated blows and vibrations from her attacker.

Nicolette aimed her bow, trying to find a solid hit and help her friends, not wanting to hit one of them by mistake. Finally she let loose again and nailed the man that had stopped to help her first target in the back of the shoulder, dropping him to his knees as he tried to grab at the arrow shaft.

After several seconds, Dahak dove out of the tent, his sword leading the way. He opened his eyes to see that his sword was embedded into the belly of a short stubby man, whose eyes were now wide with pain. Dahak tore his sword out and slashed the man across the chest before running to his friend's aid as a few more men ran into their camp.

Nicolette took aim again at one of the men running into their camp to join the fray. She was sure she wasn't delivering mortal blows, but she knew if she injured them it would help. She fired and missed and went to reload when she saw someone underneath her, she looked down just in time to dodge a spear as it whistled passed her, grazing her thigh and sending her off balance. She hit the ground with a crack and everything went fuzzy as she tried to push herself back up. She knew she was in trouble with the spear thrower not far away.

An axe came down hard and again, Zehava's sword was there to block it. He was tired now and saw more trouble running towards them, weapons drawn. He pushed his attacker back, slashed hard and was blocked. He knew his opponent was a seasoned fighter and had more years of experience, but desperation kicked in. He pulled his sword back and attacked high again, swinging in for an over head chop and giving his opponent plenty of time to see the attack, what he didn't see was one of Zehava's hands pulling his dagger. Once his sword hit the handle of the axe, he shot his arm forward, driving his dagger into his attacker's chest and dropping him where he stood.

Shania heard Nicolette's scream and then a crashing sound by the bushes, fury enraged her as she took the offensive, slashing her blades wildly this way and that, driving the man back a few steps. She spotted Dahak at the side coming to help her, her smile widened when her attacker turned his head to regard Dahak. That's all the opening she needed, she brought her one blade ripping to the side, knowing it would be blocked, her other blade came in from the other side, her opponent had forgotten about her other blade as he defended against Dahak's on-coming thrust. Her sword caught the side of his neck and went up into his jaw, splitting the side of his head in two. Shania turned to see two figures stalking towards the area where she had heard Nicolette. She bolted into a dead run towards them, side stepping an attack from another man as she went, she got her blade down low as she passed by and it bit into the man's thigh.

Nicolette forced herself to stand, knowing on the ground she was a sitting duck. She drew her sword and tried hard to stop the world from spinning. A meaty hand grabbed her from behind and over her mouth, she could smell nothing but booze. Her free hand swung down and connected with the man's groin, causing him to let go of her. She turned to face him just in time to see his fist as it slammed into the side of her face, making the world spin all the more as she was knocked to the ground.

Shania was there in a flash with a quick under sweep of her deadly blades catching Nicolette's attacker across the knees, and her other blade as she passed slicing into his lower back. The man stumbled a little and turned to meet her eyes, but she had disappeared into the jungle, only to appear again seconds later from the side. She buried both blades deep in the fat man's side, his eyes went wide and he tried to yell out, but death had already taken him. Shania ran to Nicolette and helped pull her to her feet and steady her.

"We can't win this, we have to run." Shania cried out, half dragging, half carrying her back to the others.

Zehava and Dahak fought furiously trying to push their attackers back while Shania and Nicolette got behind them. They had landed a few minor hits that had slowed their enemy's attacks, but they could see more coming form behind and they had also taken many minor hits and were losing momentum and tiring out fast.

"We can't hold them for much longer!" Zehava screamed.

"We have to run, but where!" Shania yelled back to him, looking for an exit, but by now there were several men stalking in from all directions.

"You're not going to get away from us, we will have that reward for the princess's return." One of the large men that had yet to join in the battle yelled.

"The river, it's our only hope." Zehava cried well taking another minor hit across his arm.

"The river?" Dahak screamed as his sword rang off his attacker's blade. "That's suicide."

"So is staying here." Zehava yelled.

Zehava and Dahak exploded into a fast attack, driving their attackers back a few steps to buy them some time well Shania grabbed Nicolette again and ran into the river, clutching onto a large floating log that was passing by.

"Its now or never my friend." Zehava cried to Dahak and they both bolted for the river.

"You can't get away that easy, we will find you!" Another man on shore yelled after Zehava and Dahak were too far out to chase.

~ ~ ~

Morning came and the group found themselves across the river, several miles down stream, washed up on shore. Zehava pushed himself up and looked around see that everyone was there, still passed out. He knew they had to get moving or they would be found again, and from the looks of everyone and how he felt, they wouldn't survive another encounter anytime soon.

"Come on, wake up, we've got to keep moving." Zehava urged, waking everyone up.

"What, where are we?" Dahak moaned.

"Down stream a few miles, we must have passed out in the river and the current pushed us ashore." Zehava said, looking around trying to find the best route to take.

"Are you ok?" Shania asked, helping Nicolette to her feet.

"Ya, I think so." Nicolette groaned standing up. She was a little shaky. "My face hurts." She said, bringing her hand up to where she had taken the punch, her cheek and right eye were swollen.

"We can tend to our injuries later, we have to get out of here before they find us." Zehava said, limping into the jungle. They all slowly picked themselves up and followed him.

They trudged along until the afternoon and hadn't made very good time at all, for they weren't following any sort of trail and they were all sore and tired. Finally when they couldn't take it any longer, they stopped to rest and tend to their wounds.

Shania had made it out of the fray with the least injuries, she had a minor nick in her left forearm and a small gash by her ribs, neither needed any attention. Zehava and Dahak had taken the brunt of the damage, both suffered a few fairly serious cuts and a handful or more minor scrapes and bruises. Many of there lacerations needed stitching and dressings. They bit down hard on a piece of wood while Shania cleaned and tended the wounds that needed the most attention. Nicolette too had escaped the attack fairly well, with only a few bruises and scrapes from her fall and a swollen face from being punched.

The group sat there in a rough circle all leaning up against a tree truck or stump, and Dahak rested against one of the two packs they had grabbed in their mad rush to the river.

"Who the hell were those guys, anyway? They weren't barbarians like I had first thought." Dahak asked, stretching the arm that had taken the worst of the beating.

"Could they have been those guys from the city? Out for one last attempt to fix their pride?" Nicolette said.

"They knew you were the princess, I think they might have been bounty hunters or something." Zehava muttered, playing everything in his head again form the city to the fight.

"How could they have known it was me?" Nicolette asked confused.

"Remember the guys in the bar that the bar tender was talking too after you paid with the gold coin? I think they figured it out, and if not, would have been happy with our coins either way." Zehava replied.

"Hey, what's that over there?" Shania said, interrupting the group's brainstorm and getting up. She walked a few dozen feet away and stopped.

"What is it?" Dahak groaned, hoping it was good news and not bad.

"It looks like an old camp site." Shania called back. "And it looks like three people stayed here, and one was a prisoner from the looks of it. Come take a look." She yelled.

That had everyone up and on their way over in a hurry to see what Shania had found.

"How can you tell one of them was a prisoner?" Nicolette asked, praying to herself that Meath had been here.

"Because they tied him to this tree, you can see where the bark is missing and smooth from the rope rubbing against it." Zehava answered before Shania had a chance.

"He was here." Nicolette gasped with a smile and tears in her eyes. "How long ago was it?"

"A week, maybe a little more from what it looks like." Shania said after a brief inspection.

"That means we're on the right track." Zehava said with a big smile.

"Their trail continues to the east." Shania told them after she scouted ahead a hundred feet or more.

"Well what are we waiting for? Let's go find Meath." Dahak cheered and everyone seemed to forget their injuries for the time being as they grabbed what was left of their supplies and headed off.

Chapter 18

"How are we looking out there, Ursa?" Lady Jewel asked as Ursa entered her meeting room. She could see he was exhausted and weak from the constant use of his gift.

"We have stopped them again for the time being, but they will be back at it by night fall." Ursa informed her as he sat down on one of the soft chesterfields in the room to rest his weary legs.

For the last two days and nights, they had been at a constant war with the savages. The barbarians outnumbered them greatly and it seemed more showed up everyday to join in their ranks. Though Ursa was sure the enemy couldn't overrun them in a full on attack, and it seemed the enemy thought that as well, they had only been sending in a few thousand at a time. Once battle was engaged in full, they would retreat and another wave would be sent in a few hours, giving Dragon Cove's defenders very little time to prepare and rest.

"Of course they will, they don't want us to get organized and rested. They're wearing us down and sooner or later they will just send in their whole army in and infest us." Jewel sighed, the last few days she too had gotten little sleep and stress had beaten her down. Her hair seemed a lot whiter then before and her face seemed to have lost that magnificent glow about it, it was becoming weary and dark.

"I fear the worst part is that I saw a priestess among their ranks this time." Ursa said to her, he could see the worry flood through her even more. "She did not cast any spells or wards as far as I could tell, but I believe she was just there to spot out our weak points and how many wizards we have and where they were located when battle commenced." He explained to her, his words further filling the room with dread. "I believe we will see more of them in the battles to come. If the enemies gifted have joined in their cause, then we will be hard pressed indeed."

Jewel sat there staring at the floor for several minutes, deep in thought. "It has been many years since the barbarian gifted have been part of any battles. It means this may be more then what it seems. Their gifted wouldn't have come out of their holes unless it was something big that they believe they can win." She said, staring hard at Ursa. "Tell me honestly Ursa… Do we stand a chance of surviving this?"

Ursa met her eyes with conviction as he spoke. "There's always a chance my lady." He said and stood up to leave, but once he reached the doorway he stopped and turned to her again. "Besides, we have no choice but to win."

Ursa went to his room to get what little rest he could before all hell broke loose again and he was needed. He and the other wizards at the castle, and even Talena, had been using their gifts almost non-stop. If it wasn't against the enemy it was healing the many wounded, and if the enemies gifted were joining in the fight now, things were going to get a lot worse for everyone.

Ursa tossed and turned, his mind racing with so many thoughts all at once that he couldn't get to sleep. He racked his brain trying to figure out how he and the other wizards could be of more use in this battle, how they could use their gift to a greater extent to turn the tides. His thoughts brought him to Meath and what had happened to him and why someone would come and kidnapped him. That worried Ursa all the more in not knowing. He also thought about the Princess and the others that had gone out looking for him. He only hoped they were still alive out there.

"I didn't want to have to do this again, at least not this soon." Ursa groaned, knowing full well he wasn't going to find any sleep. He had been taught how to make a rare potion by Master Saktas, which helped rejuvenate the body and gift without sleep. It was a very uncommon elixir called Manus, that almost no one knew about, and for good reasons too. It was highly addictive and if used continuously it would do the body and mind great damage. Ursa had been addicted to the substance before, in his younger years, when he was a little older then Meath was. Master Saktas had shown Ursa how to formulate the potent elixir and had informed him of its dependence if used often. Saktas had only shown a few people how to create the elixir, and he had hoped Ursa was one of the wiser that would only use it when it was needed. But Ursa had become addicted to it and it had almost destroyed him once, he promised himself it would never happen again.

This was the third time he had used the substance in the last two days, he hated using it, but under the circumstances he knew it might be their only hope. He had even slipped a little into the other wizard's food and drinks the night before to help them stay strong. He knew if they were to stay alive through this, they had to use whatever advantage they could.

Ursa sat back in his chair; he could already feel the elixir coursing through his body, making him feel lighter and less sluggish, his mind more alert. He had made a stronger mixture this time, knowing that if the enemies gifted were to join the battle, he and the others would need to be as strong as they could be.

"Why are you not resting?" A familiar voice said from behind him.

Ursa turned his head to see who it was while he carefully hid his secret making no sudden movements. "Talena, what are you dong here? Shouldn't you be resting?" Ursa questioned, hoping to turn it around.

"I couldn't sleep, so I thought I would come see you, but I had hoped you would be sleeping." She said to him. "I am worried about you Ursa."

"Worried about me? What the heavens for?" Ursa asked, getting up and walking over to her.

"I've noticed you haven't slept more then a few minutes since this has all started. You're going to wear yourself ragged and that's not going to do you or anyone else any good." Talena told him earnestly. "So I made this for you." She finished, handing him a cup with a dark brown liquid in it.

"What is this?" Ursa asked, taking the tin cup.

"A special elixir I learned to make, it helps put you to sleep." She told him.

"Ah I know this one, I could have made it myself you know." Ursa said with a smile.

"I know, but you haven't yet, so I thought I would. Please drink it Ursa. Everyone needs you to be strong and ready out there, not even you can last forever." She reasoned with him.

Ursa took a deep breath and chuckled. Sleep would be good for him, which is why he came to his room to begin with. "Alright you win." He smiled and drank the liquid. "That tasted good." Ursa said surprised.

Talena smiled. "Thank you, I added mint leaves for flavour, it makes people less reluctant to take it."

"You will have to show me one day when this is all over." Ursa said. "But I guess I should let this kick in and get what sleep I can. I suggest you do the same."

~ ~ ~

Ursa woke a few hours later to the sound of armoured men yelling and rushing passed his room. He jumped to his feet, ran into the hallway and grabbed the first soldier he saw.

"What is happening?" Ursa asked impatiently.

"The savages are attacking again, they came out of nowhere." The man cried.

Ursa let the man go and ran to the battlements to join fight. Why hadn't anyone come rouse him when this all started? Ursa cursed himself for taking Talena's elixir, though he had to admit he was feeling a lot better. He made it up the stairs to the battlements and heard the sound of full battle at large on this rainy, foggy night. Captain Rift could be heard in the distance, shouting words of encouragement to men and barking orders to others. Already the enemy was throwing grappling hooks and make shift ladders trying to breach the walls.

Ursa heard an explosion to his right and turned to see Antiel unleashing numerous blasts of energy down upon the enemy. Not far away he could see Talena cursing and yelling with her magical staff as she too rained down attack after attack at the mass of enemies.

"Are you just going to stand there or are you going to join in?" A sarcastic voice said from behind him.

Ursa turned to see Lepha behind him. "Why didn't anyone come wake me?" Ursa bellowed.

"I don't know, I was just about to ask you the same thing. I was just woken by soldiers rushing by my room." Lepha told him, a little frustrated.

"We will have to find out later; we are needed now, let's get to work." Ursa said rushing off to the edge of the wall to find the best place to start his assault.

Ursa was just about to wreak havoc on a large group of archers when he spotted a priestess slowly moving towards the walls. He turned his attention to her and summoned a bolt of energy, it would have hit her square in the chest killing her for sure, but instead it hit some sort of barrier around her. The bolt exploded on impact into several smaller bolts killing and injuring many around her. The priestess glared up at him and began casting her own spell, before Ursa could cast another, a powerful burst of wind erupted from her hands, collecting dozens of arrows, spears and whatever else was in its wake.

"Get down!" Ursa yelled, but few heard him before the attack reached them and laid more then a few dead or wounded.

Ursa was up as soon as he knew it was safe, but the priestess was long gone. He cursed under his breath and began taking his anger out on the abundant enemy below, but his eyes kept scanning the area for any more gifted enemies. Ursa knew if there was one, there was a lot more. Several times Ursa was almost skewered by an enemy spear or arrow, he finally gave up his searching and put all his focus to driving the enemy back.

Ursa heard a scream to his side and saw Talena crumple to the floor. He launched the fire ball he was summoning into a large barbarian that made it up his ladder and onto the wall just in time to be blown off by Ursa. Ursa ran to Talena's side, she was unconscious. He quickly looked her over and found a small wooden dart in her side.

"You there!" Ursa yelled to the nearest soldier. "Take her to safety."

Ursa ran to the wall's edge launching several small attacks down upon the enemy while his eyes darted every which way, looking for the enemy gifted. The soldier beside him toppled into him and fell limp. Ursa went down to help the man thinking he had been struck with an enemy arrow. Ursa's eyes went straight to the little wooden dart in the man's shoulder, the shoulder that was closest to where Ursa had been standing.

Ursa was up in a flash just in time for another dart to skip off the stone wall in front of him, only inches away. But this time he saw where the attack had come from. Two priests stood together, glaring up at him and pulling out another poisoned dart. They were using their gift to launch the darts the great distance with that much accuracy. Ursa wondered if they too were being protected by a magical barrier. He summoned a pillar of fire underneath their feet, engulfing the two priests in a flaming inferno before they could discharge another dart.

"Guess not." Ursa chuckled to himself.

He ran over to where Lepha was making her stand. "Their gifted are targeting us!" Ursa yelled to her over the deafening sound of battle.

"What? How can you be so sure?" She cried back, stopping her attack.

"They hit Talena with this!" Ursa showed her. "I just took out the two priests that took Talena out and then tried for me. They know they are losing too many warriors to us." Ursa yelled to her, pulling her out of the way of an oncoming spear.

Lepha looked at him in frustration. "What should we do?" She cried.

Before Ursa could answer her, numerous flashes of black light erupted just off to the side of them, exploding into the stone wall and blowing a large hole in their defences.

"Get Antiel now, I've got a plan." Ursa urged her cupping his hand out so the fat rain drops pooled in his hand.

Minutes later, all three wizards, Rift and Barkel, Dragon's Coves champion, were all standing off to the back of the wall where they could talk and not be targeted by the enemy.

"What's your plan?" Lepha asked, turning her head to see another streak of energy crashing in the wall, sending bits and pieces of stone everywhere.

"Rift, Barkel on my order I want all the men on the wall to stop their attacks and put their shields up like they would under a volley of arrows. If they don't have a shield, they should find cover fast." Ursa told them.

Both Rift and Barkel looked at each other with confused looks. "I don't know what you're up to wizard, but I do know better then to doubt ya." Rift replied with a wink and he and Barkel ran off to inform the men.

"What's going on Ursa? What is your plan?" Antiel bellowed, wanting to be back defending the wall.

"I hope you've got some strength left, you two, we're going to need everything we've got for this one." Ursa said, covering his eyes from the dust and chunks of stone flying their way from another enemy spell attack.

~ ~ ~

Antiel ran to the side of the wall and scanned the swarms of enemy seeing more then a few priests and priestesses. "We need to be countering their attacks and trying to target them with our own attacks." Antiel yelled back to Ursa.

"Trust me on this, Antiel, we need to do something to turn the tides fast or we are all doomed." Ursa yelled back to him.

"This had better work Ursa, or you have killed us all." Antiel cried back, joining them again.

Ursa knew his words to be right. If his plan didn't work, Dragon's Cove would be without any magical aid, which would mean certain doom indeed. Rift gave Ursa the signal that all was ready.

"Will you please tell us what we are to be doing?" Antiel yelled.

Ursa took a deep breath before answering, how he hoped this would work. "On my signal, we will each summon a downward ice wind from the edge of the wall, as cold and as hard as our gifts will allow us. Keep doing it until we can no longer, we want to freeze the rain." Ursa told them, not believing the words coming out of his mouth.

Lepha and Antiel looked at Ursa confused at first, but then their eyes lit up with the realization of what he was hoping to accomplish.

"You think it will really work?" Antiel asked, getting himself in position. "Nothing like this has never been tried before, or thought of for that matter."

"I guess we will find out, it's the only chance we've got." Ursa replied back to him.

"It had better work or we are all dead." Lepha said with a weak smile.

The three wizards walked to the edge of the wall and as they did, all the soldiers put their shields up high, covering their heads. Those who had no shields found safety behind the wizards or under the roofs of the stairwells.

As if on queue, all three wizards began summoning their artic winds, at first the cold wind just blew the enemy arrows and projectiles back at them killing a fair amount and slowing them down. But soon the fat drops of rain that fell into the wake of sub-zero wind began freezing solid into razor sharp icicles, blowing down into the enemy hordes at such speeds, they penetrated through those with no armour or weak armour, ripping and tearing flesh and bone. Those with shields held them high, blocking the rain of death while backing up, trying to retreat from the massacre. It did not take long for the enemy to realize their doom, a retreat wasn't even sounded. Those who were still alive just ran terrified, trampling those who were too slow or dying.

Ursa opened his eyes just in time to see the enemy fleeing and that he was the only wizard still standing. Lepha and Antiel had blacked out from overuse of their gifts already. Ursa smiled, glad his plan had worked, then nausea and dizziness rushed through him.

~   ~   ~

"What do you mean you had to retreat?" Vashina screamed at the barbarian who had informed her of the failure.

"We had to run. Wizards too great, rain death down on us from sky." The barbarian told her, wondering if she would kill him.

"What do you mean 'rained death upon you'?" Vashina fumed.

"It means we under estimated our enemy and the ability of their wizards." A female voice said behind them. They both turned to see Valka, the high priestess. "And we shall not do it again."

Vashina rolled her eyes at the statement. "Well why weren't you and your priestesses out there helping?"

Valka walked over to her and nodded her head to the warrior, giving him leave, which he wasted no time in using. Once he was gone, Valka's cold silver eyes shot back to Vashina. "Some of my priestesses were out there and many priests as well, and now they're dead! Out of the ten I sent to help on this attack, only four came back alive and one is so badly injured I doubt she will live."

Vashina stared hard at Valka, who seemed to glow with power and awe. Valka hardly looked like most priestesses, who normally looked haggard or possessed. Valka was tall, slender and well shaped. Her silver eyes were captivating and beautiful and her long straight silver hair reached passed her buttocks. Valka was beautiful, Vashina wanted to burn her pretty little face off and run blades over that perfect body. The thought brought an inward smile to Vashina.

"Besides, weren't you sent here to help?" I have yet to see you raise a finger in this." Valka jeered.

"And I shall, as soon as I decide too." Vashina shot back, trying to hide her rising anger. "I have yet to see you out there in all your glory, either."

"I have other responsibilities, Vashina, like keeping this army together, like making battle plans with the chiefs, like finding the enemy's weaknesses." Valka calmly stated.

"I guess a few thousand dead warriors means nothing to you then." Vashina said coldly.

Valka smiled wide. "You guessed correctly my dear; I have thousands more at my disposal and more join everyday in our great cause of conquest for our Goddess, Zepna."

"So Valka, where is your ever faithful lover Meshia at? It seems a little odd she is not at your heels like always." Vashina cooed, wondering if Meshia had been one of the priestesses killed, or at least hoping.

Valka did well to hide the snarl and twist of her face at the mention of Meshia. "I sent her with the others to help see to it that the wizards were taken out, but she failed me and our Goddess Zepna." Valka said, glaring coldly at Vashina with her silver eyes. "But that's of little matter, I have many more lovers. I expect you out there, Vashina, helping in our next attack; he would not be pleased to find you are not doing your part." She hissed, walking away.

Vashina stood there in the night glaring off at nothing. She hated that woman, she had always hated that woman. Ever since the beginning, Valka had been a thorn in her side, a thorn she couldn't wait to remove.

~ ~ ~

Pavilion stood a few dozen yards away, he had heard the whole conversation between the priestess and Vashina and now he watched Vashina standing there alone, grumbling to herself.

He had followed Vashina almost the whole way from Draco Castle, neither had stopped the entire way. Vashina had used some sort of spell or potion on her horse to make it last the entire journey at full speed. Pavilion didn't have the heart to run an animal to death if he could avoid it, he had stopped at every town or village that still had people and traded his horse for a fresh one. Of course the owner wouldn't know about the trade until morning, when they found their horse missing and another in its place.

He had hoped the siege wouldn't be to the extent that it was now; the enemy was dug in solid. It would take more then the forces behind Dragon Cove's walls to dispatch this army. Pavilion had to wonder how long they could even hold off an enemy this large. Somehow he had to get in those walls and tell them what he knew. He wondered if what he knew would even matter at the moment.

"Who's out there?" Show yourself now or be killed!" Vashina ordered, staring hard in the direction Pavilion stood, hidden behind a group of tree's and shrubs.

"Shit!" Pavilion cursed to himself, he had become so carried away in his thoughts that he had forgotten what he was doing and that a very worthy opponent was not far away.

He slowly backed away, staying in the darkest shadows, making not a sound and hoping she would think it was just the wind she heard. But it was too late, Vashina charged in his direction, throwing knives in hand and at the ready.

He sprang into a dead run, knowing he had to get far enough away from the barbarian camp and sentries so if things did come to blows, no one would hear them. He weaved in and out of trees and fallen logs hoping to lose her with his speed and agility, making sure not to give her a clear shot with her deadly daggers. He made sure to not fall into a routine while he swerved this way and that, he knew that was what she was waiting for. Every now and then he could hear the thud of a dagger embedding into a tree not far from where he just was or might have been.

After many minutes she was still hard on his trail and was getting obviously frustrated, throwing more often and more random, knowing he would not commit to a pattern that she could exploit. He knew he would not get away from her without a fight; she was too fast and stealthy for him to just slip away.

Pavilion slowed his pace a little, hoping they were far enough not to be heard and let Vashina gain some ground on him. He could hear her not far behind, gaining two steps for his one. He had to admire her ability to keep up with him, not many ever could and even after their long run, her footsteps still fell almost silently. He knew she was waiting for a clear shot, now that the trees were thinning out which is what he wanted. He faked right, hearing the predictable thud of a dagger where he would have been if he had gone that way. He dove over a large fallen tree to the left, hit the ground in a roll and was back on his feet. He had gone left because the trees grew even thinner here, which would provide her with the clear shot he wanted her to have.

Pavilion had to rely purely on his keen senses and instincts now if he was to make this work. He heard the soft grunt from behind and knew a deadly knife was now loose in the air coming hastily towards him. With speed faster then man was meant to achieve, Pavilion jerked slightly to the left just as the dagger hit his cloak where his heart would have been. The movement was so precise and flawless that it would be impossible for anyone to know he had not really been hit. Pavilion hit the ground hard letting his body go limp and crumple so it looked perfect. He listened as his enemy approached cautiously, wondering if she would embed another dagger into him just in case. No, she was too proud to believe her shot didn't kill him, and she had every right to think that, she was good. She would believe her throw had slipped through his rib cage and entered his heart, killing him almost instantly.

She was only a few yards away from where his crumpled body lay, he could just see her boots from the corner of his eyes. He wondered if she was going to get closer to look at his face. As if satisfied, she turned and walked away without a second look. Pavilion's hand snatched his dagger on his belt behind his back from his enchanted sheath that replaced the dagger within moments and sprang onto his feet, in the same motion sent his blade spinning towards Vashina's head.

Vashina spun a full circle and a half catching his blade mere moments before it would have struck home, now was looking back at him holding his blade as if it were a toy.

"How did you?" Pavilion mumbled dumbfounded, feeling the weight of the sheath being full again within moments.

"You under estimated me; you would have run right, into the more wooded terrain had you not been setting me up. But I must say, that was a very tricky stunt you did, anyone else would have fallen for it." Vashina cooed, cleaning under her nails with his blade.

Still Pavilion stood off guard and uneasy, not sure of what his next move would be, never in his whole life had he underestimated an opponent. Then again, never in his life had he met someone with the same skills as him.

"I must ask, where did you learn those skills? That kind of agility and awareness doesn't just happen." Vashina asked plainly, starting to walk a circle around him. He followed in suit, keeping his eyes on hers and matching her step for step.

"I was about to ask you the same thing." Pavilion replied, still unnerved about the whole situation.

"You know it's rude not to answer a lady when she asks a question. And it is a question I do ever so want to know." She mocked with a smile.

"Well I apologize; my up bringing was hardly high class." Pavilion mocked back, his adrenaline pumping hard and his unnerving feeling turning into excitement.

"So why were you spying on me, stranger? Who are you and where do you fit in all of this?" Vashina asked, stabbing his dagger into a tree as she passed and pulling two of her own.

"What makes you so sure I was spying, maybe I was just passing by and you attacked me?" Pavilion replied back, knowing she would hardly believe that.

Vashina stopped and let out a laugh. "Tell me your name at least; I do hate to kill strangers."

"So what, if I don't tell you my name you won't kill me?" Pavilion teased.

"I am afraid not, stranger, I have to kill you either way. But I would like to know your name so I can put it on your grave." Vashina told, him starting to stalk in a circular motion again.

"I under estimated you again then, I wouldn't think you were the type to dig an enemy's grave, let alone mark it." Pavilion said to her with a hint of respect in his voice.

"Don't get me wrong, normally I wouldn't." Vashina responded. "But you are a worthy opponent, and that is something I respect."

Pavilion smiled and nodded. "Well Vashina." He said with a wink. "My name is Pavilion." He told her, letting his gift flow through his body at the ready.

"Well Pavilion, I shall tell anyone I meet that knew you where they will find you." She said with a nod of her head and then launched the two blades in her hands at him.

He easily avoided the blades with a quick side step. He drew both his finely crafted, well-used scimitars and charged towards her, deflecting several more of her knives. He cleared the distance within a heartbeat and slashed his blades in a scissor motion. Vashina jumped back, the tips of the blades missing her only by a thread. Before Pavilion could bring his blades in again, Vashina was in the opening of his arms, her knee found his groin and her elbow found his nose. He stumbled back a step, stunned, and again caught off guard by the attack and the pain. He had no time to react when he saw her foot kick up under his chin, lifting him off the ground and onto his back.

"Come on Pavilion, I know you can do better then that." She teased. "Stop underestimating me!"

Pavilion got to his feet, pushing aside the pain from his groin and face and never letting his eyes stray from hers. Never in his life had something like this happened. He had underestimated her twice now, he would not do it again.

He was back in his stance now and spit the blood from his mouth, putting one of his swords back in its sheath, thinking it might be wise to have a free hand with this one. He stared hard into her eyes; they were beautiful, full of energy and life. He stepped forward in a rush, his sword down low, ready to sweep upwards, his other hand shot behind his back at the last moment, freeing one of his many hidden daggers. She stepped to the side and spun in a circle, dodging his sword and coming around hard with her own dagger. She had taken her eyes off him for a second, and in that time he had pulled his dagger. He ducked down low as her knife swung in high for a fatal blow to his neck. His dagger cut in deep on her right thigh, and the hilt of his sword slammed in hard in her kidney, sending her off balance. Soon he was behind her and he kicked his leg out, catching her in the back of the knees sending her hard to the ground.

"Well, well Pavilion, that's what I want to see." She moaned, rolling over on her back staring at him, holding her side.

Before she could make another move, he had his sword to her neck. "Do not move or I will kill you." He told her sternly.

"Come now Pavilion, do you really think you have the upper hand?' Vashina laughed, throwing her hand out and releasing her gift, blowing Pavilion back hard into a tree with a strong gust of wind. "Did I forget to mention I had the gift?" She laughed, getting to her feet and limping over to him, healing her leg as she went. By the time she was in front of him, the gash he left on her thigh was gone.

"I knew you had the gift." Pavilion coughed, trying to recover his breath.

"If you knew then you should have know better then to play with me." She teased.

"Why?" Pavilion remarked.

Before Vashina could even form the words she was about to speak Pavilions hands shot up, throwing dirt and rocks into her face and his gift made it all the worse, blowing her back half a dozen steps, giving her no time to recover. He focused his gift underneath her, the ground around her turned soft and muddy and she sank down to her shoulders as if she was standing on water. The ground turned solid again before she could move.

Pavilions victory was short lived, before he could finish her off, a handful of arrows streamed down around him from a band of barbarians coming to investigate the noise.

"Tell we meet again." Pavilion yelled back to her as he ran off into the darkness of night, vanishing like a ghost.

~　~　~

"I said we attack in two hours!" Valka screamed at the massive warrior that stood before her.

"But need supplies, need more arrows and spears and better weapons to fight." The warrior replied hoping his life would be spared.

Valka glared into the man's eyes, anger flaring through her. She wanted nothing more then to kill this pathetic mass of muscle. But she knew it was not his fault, he was only telling her what she knew but didn't want to hear. It was true, their supplies hadn't been coming in lately and what they did have was fast depleting. Their main source of strong, crafted weapons and food were from Mandrake, but the refugee's and the lord of the castle had formed an army that kept hindering the supply trains. She had not expected Dragon's Cove to hold out this long, and now it seemed like it would take another week or more to wear them down. But they did not have a week's worth of supplies, not for an army this large.

"Their wizards must be exhausted after that vast display of their powers. Now is the time to attack, when their weak and cannot help." Valka cried out.

"We have other problems, too many warriors die before they get to fighting. Have to climb over dead comrades to make it to walls before we can fight." The brute added, seeing that he would live another day.

Valka paced her tent for a while deep in thought, considering the brute's words. Yes he was right, she knew better then to doubt this one, he had fought in many battles and in some he had even been the one to tip the scales to victory.

"Yes, I understand. How many wounded are there that can't fight or won't be around for much longer?' Valka asked, a plan forming in her evil mind.

The warrior cocked an eye at her. "What you thinking?" He said.

"Well we need time to replenish our supplies, and we need to clear the field of the dead." She cooed. "And how do we dispose of the dead?" She asked.

"We burn them." The man said, his face beaming with understanding.

~ ~ ~

"Hey Dan, you think we can hold the wall and win this war now that the enemy has their gifted involved?" A young burly soldier asked his friend while they patrolled a part the southern side.

"I don't know Mick, I sure as hell hope so," Dan started to reply but stopped short, staring off into the night.

"What the hell is going on out there?" Mick muttered. "Are we under attack?"

"I don't know, but we had better sound the alarm, cause this can't be good." Dan replied, running off to ring one of the large warning bells.

"How many are coming?" Another soldier asked, running to the edge of the wall to see.

"I can only see a couple hundred at most, and they don't seem to be armed." Mick replied, squinting into the night.

"It's got to be some kind of trick or something." The soldier said.

"What are they doing?" Mick muttered. "They're throwing something every few steps."

Soon Dragon Cove's walls were alive with soldiers ready to fight, but battle had yet to break out.

"What the hell's going on out here?" Rift and Barkel both barked together.

"We don't know sir." Someone shouted in the crowd.

"They're dumping something on all the bodies out there." Another replied.

"Maybe their bringing their dead to life, to attack us." Someone cried out and that got whispers and cries from all over.

"Don't be stupid, ya babies." Barkel yelled out. "And even if they were bringing back the dead, we killed them once we can do it again!" He cheered, raising a shout of appreciation from everyone, trying to keep their moral high.

"What do you make of this, wizard?" Rift asked Antiel, whom two soldiers were holding up.

"I don't know, but they're using their wounded and dying to do it. Once they're in range of our arrows, kill them." Antiel said weakly, and the two soldiers holding him up turned to bring him back to his bed. He was the only wizard that was awake yet, but he was hardly able to help. If Dragon's Cove fell under an attack now, they would have no wizards to help defend it.

Before Antiel had made it a few steps, the sky behind him lit up and all he could hear was the gasps and curses from everyone on the wall.

"Everyone inside, shut and lock all doors and windows that lead outside." Rift ordered.

~ ~ ~

"Rift, what's happening out there?" Lady Jewel asked, watching people left and right stuff all the cracks and holes in the doors and windows with rags or wax.

"They had lit their dead ablaze with the aid of some sort of fuel that has made it ignite a lot faster then normal. I think they intend to smoke us out." He told her.

"Will it work? We will be safe in here, right?" Jewel asked, getting a little frightened.

"As long as we can keep most of the smoke out we should be fine." Rift replied.

"How long will it burn for?" Uvael asked.

Rift stopped yelling orders for a moment and thought about it. "I don't know if you've seen the field of dead outside the castle walls, but I would say there's more then a few thousand dead out there. Most not far

from the castle walls, which also means things are gonna get hot in here."
Rift said.

"How long Rift?" Jewel asked.

"Well from our last reports, before the smell and smoke got to thick,
they were adding to the blaze, throwing tree's and anything that would
burn to the pile. I would say it will burn hard and hot for two or three
days, then smoulder for another day or two before we could safely go out
there." Rift answered, frustrated.

Jewel was now pacing the hallway, biting her lower lip. "But we will
be safe in here right?'

"If we can keep the smoke out and stand the heat, then yes, I think so."
Rift said, already smelling the gut turning smell of burning flesh. "They
have put us at a stand still for the time, we can't leave and they can't come
at us."

~   ~   ~

Talena's eyes slowly opened, and even though they were blurry she
knew the person she saw standing before her was Ursa.

"What happened to me?' She asked roughly, her throat was sore and
dry.

"You almost died, that's what happened." Ursa told her. "You were hit
with a dart tipped with a rare and extremely deadly poison that barbarians
like to use." He said, handing her a cup of water.

Ursa had only been awake for an hour and he still felt drained and
weak, but he had taken some of his secret herbs once he had heard about
what was happening outside. He wanted to be able to help if he was
needed.

"All I remember is standing up there fighting, then a wave of pain came
over me so fast and then…" She stopped and her cup of water slipped form
her hands, soaking her bed. She didn't seem to notice.

"What is it, Talena?" Ursa asked, getting closer to her.

"Then… then I had a vision, yes I remember now. There was a young
man, long brown hair and well built."

"Meath! That's Meath." Ursa gasped, cutting her off.

"He was with a young woman, he had her prisoner, and they were deep
in the jungle hiking somewhere. They were talking and she was trying to
convince him of something but he hardly seemed to care. Then they saw
a group of people under attack by rogues or savages, I don't remember,

but they were losing and needed help. He recognized them and ran off to help…" Talena said.

Ursa almost jumped out of his chair. "Then what happened?" He cried.

"I don't know, everything goes blank again." She replied. "I'm sorry, that's all I saw."

"It's ok." Ursa assured her. "Is there anything else you remember? Any land marks, which direction they were traveling, anything at all?"

"They were traveling west, I know because of the way the sun was sitting in the sky. And they weren't far away from a small mountain, I remember seeing it on their right side, which I guess would be north." Talena said, trying to remember every little detail that might help.

"I think I know the place." Ursa stated. "Do you know if that has already happened or is happening or will happen?" Ursa asked, though he doubted she would know, most times there was no way of knowing.

Talena just shrugged, giving him all the answer he could expect from her.

"I need to get out of here and over there somehow." Ursa muttered to himself.

"We can't leave, we are needed here and there is no way we could possibly make it past the hordes of enemies." Talena reminded him.

Ursa leaned back in his chair and began scratching his long white beard, deep in thought.

"What are you thinking, Ursa?' Talena asked, wondering what was going to happen next.

~ ~ ~

Pavilion stood perfectly still, camouflaged in a group of trees as four barbarian scouts passed by him, no more then an arms reach away. As silently as death and as swiftly as the wind, Pavilion stepped out behind them grabbing one that was lagging behind the others. Pavilion held his hand hard over the savage's mouth so he could not make a sound. In the same motion he ran his dagger across his victim's throat. Before the dead barbarian hit the ground, Pavilion was gone again. The other three turned to investigate the noise of their comrade gurgling on the ground. Before they could react, Pavilion's hand appeared out of nowhere, snatching another scout by the head and with a quick twisting motion, snapped his neck. The other two turned to see another one of their brethren fall lifelessly to the ground. They both looked up just in time to see their stalker upon them.

This was the fourth scouting party he had eliminated this night. He dragged the bodies off into the woods and did his best to hide the corpses. Day was fast approaching and Pavilion still had much he wanted to accomplish.

He looked over to the clouds of smoke rolling to the west, though the wind was blowing east. The enemy gifted were fuelling the flames and blowing the smoke straight at the castle.

Yes, he had lots to do before the sun came up. He was sure the priests and priestesses would be taking turns fuelling the smoke and flames, which meant the ones that were resting would be vulnerable.

Chapter 19

Astaroth sat in the library again listening to the ladies of Draco kingdom and their eldest son's and the castle's only wizard, Keithen, ponder about what they should do concerning the siege happening at Dragon's Cove. They had just recently received word about it and now they had to come up with a solution everyone would be satisfied with, which meant picking apart any and every suggestion any of them made. They had been in the library ever since they'd heard the news about their allies' trouble, which was several hours ago. Astaroth wanted nothing more then to unleash on this room full of simple-minded fools, to show them the truth that he was behind everything. But no, he had to play things safe still, he could not throw it all away, not while things were still going somewhat as planned.

"What do you think about all of this, Prince Berrit?" Lady Tore asked.

Berrit lifted his head to look at everyone. He had been off in his own world and had forgotten all about everyone else around him.

"Yes, you haven't made a single suggestion or comment this whole time Berrit, and we really could use your opinion." Lady Angelina said.

Astaroth kicked himself for not paying attention. "Well…" He started. "Well, I believe we should send aid to them, they are in need and we have the resources to help. Let us send half our army and we will send messengers to Drandor and get them to do likewise. The savages will have no place to run, and between the three armies, we will crush them." Berrit said with rising enthusiasm, hoping they would agree so the take over of Draco would be a lot easier with fewer men to defend it.

Everyone just stared at him oddly for a while, before finally Tora spoke. "Well it is obvious you have not been paying attention, Prince Berrit, or else you would remember that we have already thought of that possibility.

And you would also remember why we don't think that would work." Tora said in a belittling voice.

He did well to hide his glare, but inside he was picturing how much he would enjoy disposing of her very slowly. He didn't know how he would do it, but he knew when the time came it would be ever so sweet.

"I agree with Prince Berrit, I think we need to send aid, and fast!" Ethan piped in.

"Yes… I second that, send help." Keithen chimed in, though he doubted anyone was listening, no one ever listened to him.

"And what, leave us defenceless?" Thoron argued.

"They would come to our aid and you know it!" Ethan shouted across the table to Thoron.

"Not if they expected they were next to be attacked, they wouldn't." Thoron yelled back, his anger rising.

"Enough you two!" Tora screamed, her voice cracking like a snapped whip with anger. She quickly composed herself again. "If they take Dragon's Cove, it could be Drandor or Draco castle that they take next. We cannot be sure, there has been very little barbarian activity around here of late." Tore reminded them.

"They took Mandrake, it's just a matter of time before they take Dragon's Cove if they don't get help, whether its Drandor or us next, we are in trouble." Prince Berrit replied.

"I just don't get how this is all happening? How could they possibly be doing this? How did they know we were weak and unprepared? How did they know?" Thoron asked frustrated, everyone just looked back and forth from one another, knowing there was no answer but desperately wanting one.

"Turn of luck maybe, or maybe Ursa and his whelp Meath were working with them, informing them every step of the way." Berrit said.

"That's a filthy lie!" Lady Angelina screamed. "Ursa would never work with them."

"Is it?" Berrit replied, raising an eyebrow. "Doesn't it strike you as odd that ever since Ursa kidnapped the princess and escaped from the castle, the barbarians seem to have the upper hand? Master Ursa knows every castle's weakness and strengths, he also knows how many wizards are in each and what they are capable of doing." Berrit roared. "And do you really think those mindless savages are capable of doing what they've done without the aid of someone like that?"

Everyone in the room stared at him in shock, but after several seconds his words seemed to ring a fair bit of truth to them.

"Ursa would never help those bastards, you lie you Zandorian heathen." Ethan raged, not believing a word of it.

"Son! Calm yourself at once." Lady Angelina sternly told him, though not disagreeing with him. "None of us want to believe it, but we have to take into consideration that it might be true."

"Well from what our trackers and search parties have said, after they were chased out of Darran they went north-east." Berrit said. "And the man that was helping them hide is a well known merchant, which was known to deal with the barbarians from time to time for certain items." Berrit finished, knowing full well it was all a lie, but doubted anyone would think to look into it. "I know I am a Zandorian, and we have been enemies for a long time, but in coming here to marry the beautiful princess and make peace between our kingdoms, we set those differences aside. Foul times have befallen Draco kingdom, worse then anything we could ever have imagined, and I am only trying to help. I know what I saw the night king Borrack was killed, it was Ursa, believe it or not. You hold your country's fate in your hands."

Everyone was silent for several minutes, pondering his words, hearing the truth of his speech whether they wanted to or not. It did seem like he was right. Even Ethan was caught in Berrit's words for a moment.

"We greatly appreciate your insight, Prince Berrit, and I know it will help later on. But we have strayed from the real issue; we need a plan of action." Tora finally reminded them all.

"Well first we need to put Draco Castle on full alert and begin readying out defences and offences so we are not caught off guard like Mandrake and Dragon's Cove." Berrit said, hoping to end this long boring conversation. It didn't matter how well prepared they were, Draco Castle would fall.

"Yes, that is a good start. There still has been no word on whether Lord Dagon has been found. Let us send another four messengers out to find him, and another five to Zandor to request aid." Lady Angelina said. "We need everyone involved and working together in this if we are to survive."

"Another matter at hand is the need to make more room for all of the refugee's that are coming into our city everyday. All of the Inn's are full, all the barns and stables packed and the streets and alleys are littered with families." Tora said, knowing this was something none of them had a clue how to solve. No one could have guessed or known about the eight thousand or more people that had moved into their city for protection.

"Well let us send out the word that if the men join our army, they will be accommodated and fed in one of our army camps outside the city, which will free up some space for others. And those who do join, their families will be given rations and we will provide them with a place to stay. With most of the men out in the army we can get the women to help make the many blankets and other things that the women can do to help." Ethan told them, remembering from his training in Drandor that in times of need, they would have to use everyone they could.

"Yes that is a good idea, when war finally does reach us we will need all the help we can get. Better to have everyone ready and trained and prepared now." Tora said.

"But that doesn't fix the problem of how we are going to feed them all." Angelina stated. "With all the towns and farmers coming to the city for protection, there is no one manning all the fields and livestock."

Astaroth could hardly take it anymore, he just wanted to scream at them all and obliterate them. "Send soldiers to gather all the livestock still around the towns and villages, then bring them all here to the castle to be taken care of until needed. Send large groups of soldiers and farmers to the crops in the fields to take what is ready and bring it back, whatever isn't ready they can stay and continue to farm. The soldiers will keep careful watch around the towns to ensure no savage armies come. At any sign that it might happen, they can retreat back to the castle." Berrit announced, his frustration showing. "That will also help in the growing population; many of the families will go back to their homes with the soldiers because they will feel safe."

"Well Prince Berrit, I agree with your course of action and I am sure everyone else does too. That seems the smartest thing we can do for the time being." Tora said. "And I thank you again for showing us all that we have been at this for far too long this day, and we could all use a break so our minds can refresh."

~ ~ ~

Astaroth sat in a steaming bath in his private quarters, irritation bursting from him because he was not yet king as he had planned. He cursed himself for not being able to make everything fall into place. He focused hard on the large metal tub he was in, using his gift to heat the water until it was unbearable, and then he cooled it down again.

He had his senses on full alert, knowing there was still another assassin out there waiting to strike. How he wanted that assassin to show himself now, so he could take his frustrations out on someone. He hoped the assassin would follow him outside this night, when he went to make sure none of the messengers made it far. He hoped these ones would put up more of a fight then the last, he did love it when people tried so hard, only to fail. He sank down into the tub, submerging his whole body. Either way, he would get some satisfaction out of this night.

~ ~ ~

Astaroth watched the riders leave the city walls and tread down the eastern road towards Mandrake. He smiled wide, they were traveling together for the first part of the trip, until the road forked and then those going to Drandor would part. Of course it was wise to do so; there was safety in numbers, but not tonight.

It took him little effort to get ahead of them and now he waited in plain view in the middle of the road, in the form of Prince Berrit. It would give him the element of surprise once the fun started, and since he wasn't going to let any of them live, it didn't matter if they knew the truth. He loved to see that glisten of terror and confusion in his victim's eyes.

"Prince Berrit! Is that you?" The lead rider asked, slowing his steed to a stop a few yards away. The other riders formed a semi circle around him, their hands cautiously on their hilts.

"Yes, it is I." Berrit barked, in an annoyed voice looking down at the ground.

"What are you doing out this late, my Lord, and this far from the castle? 'Tis dangerous out here!" The same man asked in a weary tone.

"Well you see, there's a problem with your mission." Berrit answered, still staring down at the ground.

"And what might that be?" Another rider asked.

Berrit lifted his head, his eyes glowing in the torchlight as he stared at them. "Well the problem is, I can't let you accomplish it!" He hissed, revealing his true form.

"What in the nine hells!" The lead rider yelled.

"It's a shape shifting demon!" Another cried, drawing his sword.

"The rumours are true!" Screamed another.

A sadistic smile grew on Astaroth's face when the first rider charged in swinging his sword. Astaroth stood perfectly still and calm as the rider closed the gap. Once he was steps away, a rock spike shot up from the earth right through the belly and back of the horse, stopping just in front of the rider and throwing him from his dead mount face first into the ground in front of Astaroth.

Astaroth didn't want any of them escaping now that they knew the truth, so with a mere thought and little effort, a great circle of flames erupted from the ground all around them, ten feet high and blistering hot to everyone but him, trapping them all inside. The soldier on the ground lifted his head just in time to see Astaroth's dagger leave his hand. The blade was buried to the hilt between his eyes before he could react.

Three soldiers dismounted and rushed him, blades leading the way, while two fumbled with their crossbows trying to load them and watch the action at the same time. The other three messengers were not so courageous and searched the flaming wall for a way out.

Astaroth cockily stepped into the array of swinging blades, easily dodging and side stepping the terrified men's attacks. He danced though the swings and thrusts, lining them up until finally one man rushed in and thrust for Astaroth's chest. He was expecting the attack and he easily evaded it just as one of the other men rushed in with a wild swing. Neither men realized the trap in time to stop their momentum; two bodies hit the ground in a bloody mess as they ran through each other's blade.

Astaroth turned to see his plan had worked perfectly, that evil smile crossed his lips. His keen ears heard two clicks and he knew two bolts were heading his way. The third man swung his sword, hoping to catch Astaroth off guard well he mussed over the two dead messengers. Astaroth caught the man's wrist in a flash and yanked him in front, using him as a shield, catching the first bolt, the second arrow pierced through Astaroth's side.

Astaroth raged, his anger flaring, not because of the pain, but because he had let them get a hit on him. He grabbed his human shield's head and broke the man's neck, nearly tearing it off with unknown strength. He marched towards the two bowmen, who dropped their bows, knowing they could never reload in time. They kicked their mounts into a charge towards Astaroth, hoping not to share the same fate as their comrades. Before either man had closed half the gap, Astaroth had both men and beasts ablaze.

The last man standing, who still searched for an escape, turned to see no one left but the enemy. He un-strapped his battleaxe from his side, knowing it wouldn't help him; he was no fighter.

"How pathetic." Astaroth teased drawing his own sword.

Before either could make a move, Astaroth's blazing wall fizzled out.

"What the?" Astaroth growled, turning to see two figures riding hard towards them and knowing one of them was gifted.

The messenger didn't take any time bolting into the jungle now that the wall of fire was gone. Astaroth saw the messenger take off from the corner of his eye. He released his gift, sending a streak of energy, that burst into a large tree blocking his target. Astaroth was about to do it again when his senses told him to move, he dove forward into a roll just as two blasts of fire crashed into the ground where he had been standing.

He was on his feet and had a fireball of his own soaring towards the two newcomers, who he now knew were both gifted. The two wizards had plenty of time to react. Astaroth cursed, knowing he would have a hard time defeating these two so easily and he still had to find the other messenger. He darted away into the dense jungle after the man, and hoping to evade the two wizards until later.

~ ~ ~

Astaroth sat in his room, frustrated and angry with himself. He hadn't found the other messenger, nor did he find the two wizards again. His powers were weak now; he had used a lot of strength to keep the firewall up and burning as long as he had. He had healed his wound and knew he had better not use anymore of his gift incase he had to turn into Prince Berrit for any length of time.

"Bastard rogue wizards had to interrupt my fun and mess everything up." He snarled. "Now someone else knows the truth of me."

He paced his room, racking his brain for anything that might help in his plan and how he could track down that messenger. He knew there was no way he could get to him now, he was long gone for now. Astaroth would have been questioning himself all night but was interrupted by a knock at his door.

"Of course!" He muttered, shifting back into Berrit's form and opening the door. "What do you want?" Berrit grumbled.

"Sorry your highness, but I was sent to come tell you your presence in requested in the meeting room." Keithen stuttered sheepishly.

"Why? What now? I'm sure it can wait until morning." Berrit barked, hoping to end the conversation as soon as he could.

"I know it is late my lord, but the ladies sent me to tell you that two wizards have arrived and they have interesting news." Keithen replied.

Berrit's eyes lit up. "Alright, I will be right there." He grumbled.

"Yes your highness, I will tell them." Keithen said and ran off.

~ ~ ~

"I am glad you came, Prince Berrit. I am sorry it is such a late hour." Lady Tora said once Berrit was in his seat.

"Yes well, I wanted to see them for myself, so I know who to watch out for." Berrit muttered, playing his Zandorian part.

"Their names are Master Samul and Master Mervyn." Lady Angelina snapped angrily at him.

"Yes, and they have some very interesting, and possibly important information." Tora cut in, not wanting those two to cause a scene.

"And what's that?" Berrit barked in an uncaring tone.

"Well my good Prince Berrit, on our way here to help, only a few hours ago and a few miles back, we ran across a sorcerer massacring your messengers." One of the wizards said.

Berrit glared over at the very tall man as if annoyed that he spoke. He knew these two were going to hinder his plans a lot more then what they already had. "I see, well did you kill this sorcerer and save our messengers?" Berrit asked.

"He got away unfortunately, and as far as we know, he killed all of the messengers. We didn't get there until the end and had no idea what was going on 'til it was to late." The other wizard, who was a lot shorter and who was a little plumper added.

"Of course, and if the two of you couldn't even save a few simple messengers, how do you plan on helping a whole kingdom in this war?" Berrit mocked, knowing he had to get back to his room soon before his powers diminished.

"Why you arrogant, foolish moron, I ought to…!" The shorter wizard burst out.

"Calm yourself, my old friend." Mervyn said.

"You ought to what? Are you muttering threats to a Prince?" Berrit teased, trying to provoke another verbal assault.

"Prince Berrit doesn't understand the gift, we can't expect him too. And I promise you, my good Prince Berrit, we will do everything in our powers to help you in this war." Mervyn said, staring coldly at him.

"Yes, I am sure you will." Berrit hissed sarcastically, quickly using that to take his leave. He was already beginning to feel weak and dizzy.

"I am so sorry for the way Prince Berrit acted." Tora told them sympathetically and somewhat embarrassed.

"Do not apologize for the words of that man, my lady." Master Mervyn said with a wink of understanding.

"Well we do appreciate you coming to our aid." Lady Angelina said earnestly.

"No need for thanks my lady, the land is festering with enemies, our homes to be in danger. The only way any of us can prevent this is to stand together." Samul said.

"What can you tell us of this sorcerer? Do you think he is still around and a threat to us? Is he a rogue, just acting on his own? Or is he working with the barbarians?" Lady Tora asked, getting back to the many issues at hand.

"That is a good question my lady." Mervyn replied. "I believe this sorcerer may be a threat to us. He was indeed powerful and didn't have the demeanour of a rogue. This one was different from any gifted I have ever encountered, and I am not sure if he is working with the enemy or not."

"Well it is late, Master Mervyn and Master Samul, your room's have been made ready for you. Rest well and we will further discus this tomorrow when we are all rested and focused." Lady Tora said with a bow of her head.

~ ~ ~

Astaroth laid upon his master bed, his eyes closed trying to rest, but his mind racing a mile a minute at this new problem that had come to his castle. These two wizards were going to make things very difficult if he could not dispose of them somehow. His greed and lust for power told him to kill them and steal their gift, for they both were very powerful and would swell his own powers. But he knew they we're both smart and cunning and would not be so easily fooled or over powered. Together they would be a large problem. He would have to get them separated and alone, he believe he could easily over power one at a time and then he could take their gift without hindrance.

But once they were gone, what would he tell everyone? They wouldn't just leave, or decide not to help. Then again, why would he have to tell anyone anything? He could act just as clueless as everyone else. Though there was no way he would be able to take one's power and take the other's right away. The process did take a lot out of the body and mind. He would need a day in between and a foolproof plan to trap them both. It might be easier to send them with an army to Dragon's Cove and just get them out of the way. Dragon's Cove should have been overtaken already, but the defenders were doing well to hold strong. The barbarians and Vashina didn't need any more problems. This new problem would be for Astaroth to deal with; besides, he wanted their powers for himself. With those two, his powers would grow exponentially. Yes, he would deal with these two. They wouldn't be much of a match for him once his powers were recharged.

He slept in late the next morning to give himself plenty of time to re-energize his gift. He wanted to be at full strength, or close to it incase he needed it. He stayed in his true form most of the day, only turning into Berrit twice when he left his room to send a servant for food, and to be seen by others so they would not worry about him. That and he wanted to see what the new guests were up to and if the right opportunity arose, he would strike.

He spent almost the whole day and evening in his room, resting and thinking of a plan. Astaroth was smart enough to know that just because he had stolen the essence of eight wizards, that these two wizards couldn't defeat him. These two were over twice his age and that meant they had more battle experience then him. With age comes wisdom and these two things were never to be taken lightly.

Again a knock at his door stirred him from his thoughts. He had been expecting this knock, since he had hardly been out of his room all day, they had sent someone to check on him.

Berrit opened the door to see the young wizard Keithen standing there again. "Yes, what do you want now?" Berrit snarled.

"Sorry to bother you again, I just wanted to make sure you were alright and didn't need anything" Keithen replied nervously.

"What did you say?' Berrit asked off guard. "You wanted to know if I was ok?"

Keithen looked at him sheepishly. "Yes my lord, I know it sounds odd, but I believe you. About Ursa and Meath and all that, and I know you're the only one that can save us in this time of need." He told him with growing enthusiasm. "I know you are Zandorian, and I am a wizard, but I want you to know I am with you. Anything you need, just ask. If it is within my powers, it shall be done." Keithen finished with a smile, hoping his sucking up would get him somewhere.

A smile slithered across Berrits face. "Yes, well thank you. I think you might have helped curve my opinion of those with the gift." He replied as his mind raced with new possibilities.

Keithen was about to run off but Berrit stopped him in his tracks. "You know, there is something you could do for me." He said.

"Anything my lord." Keithen replied with a boyish grin.

"Well I am feeling terrible about last night and how I treated those two wizards who are only trying to help." Berrit said, trying to sound truthful. "I want you to find out what kind of wine or ale they like most. I would like to sit down with them and have a drink, apologize like a man." He finished.

"Yes sir!" Keithen saluted.

"But don't let them know that it is me that wants to know. I want them to be surprised." Berrit told him as he ran off. Keithen waived back to him to let him know he understood.

Astaroth shut his door chuckling evilly, the perfect plan played through his mind. He walked over to his desk and pulled out a pouch of rare enchanted white sand. He had only acquired a few handfuls in his time and that was better then most he'd seen. Most would pay a king's ransom just for this amount. No one knew where the sand came from, or who or what might have enchanted it. He had been saving it for when he might need it most. Now seemed as good a time as any. Once he had these two wizards' gifts, he would be that much more unstoppable.

Early the next morning, Keithen was back at his door with the information he requested.

"Well my lord, I have good and bad news." Keithen said. "Master Samul enjoys Blackberry wine the most, but Master Mervyn says he never drinks, for it clouds one's judgments."

This didn't come to much as a surprise to him, he had known a lot of wizards that didn't drink or only drank a little.

"Excellent Keithen." Berrit replied. "Now find me some Blackberry wine." He told him.

"Right away your highness." Keithen replied gleefully.

He had expected it wouldn't be so easy to dispose of Master Mervyn, he had a rare aura about him, a lot like Ursa had, which Astaroth knew to be dangerous. But Samul on the other hand would be easy to take care of if he could play it out properly. He wondered how much of the sand he would need to put into the wine for the affects he wanted, he had to be sure it would work, failure could mean death. He would use it all, just to be sure; he needed all of Samul's powers to be useless. Then he would have to find away to deal with Master Mervyn.

Astaroth now stood alone in the farthest corner of the castle's royal garden, where no one could see anything. He had sent Keithen to fetch Master Samul.

Now Astaroth waited in the form of Prince Berrit for Samul to arrive. He had to play the part perfectly if was to fool the wizard into believing his apology and have a drink with him. Astaroth had no idea how much of the wine Samul would have to drink to defuse his gift.

"Prince Berrit, I would never have guessed it was you that wanted an audience with me." Samul said, walking over to the small pond and bench where Berrit stood waiting.

Berrit turned to face Samul with a shy and honest smile. "Yes well I…" Berrit coughed, playing his part flawlessly. "I wanted to… apologize for the way I acted when you first arrived." He declared. At that moment a feather could have knocked Samul over.

"Well Prince Berrit, this does come as a surprise, but you really don't need to…" Samul began but was cut off.

"No, I do. I know this must come as a shock to you, a Zandorian apologizing to a wizard, but it is true. I have been under a lot of stress with the death of King Borrack and the kidnapping of my bride to be. And now with this war breaking out all over Draco Kingdom, I almost forgot what this was all about. I agreed to marry the princess and set our old ways aside and begin a new union of trust and friendship. It's just with everything that's happening, my mind clouded and my judgment was off and I'm sorry." Berrit told him.

Samul listened to Berrit's words carefully and truly felt the emotion coming from the Zandorian. "Well I can say I do understand your position, the past month has been rather hellish for everyone, and has everyone on edge." Samul replied. "You know Prince Berrit, I almost misjudged you, but now I see I was wrong. I accept your apology." He said with a smile.

"Do sit and have a glass of Blackberry wine with me, Master Samul, it would mean a lot." Berrit asked, knowing if he refused he would have to act fast.

"Blackberry wine you say?" Samul asked, licking his lips. "Well my good Prince Berrit, you have twisted my arm. How could I say no to my favourite drink."

Samul sat down on the bench beside Berrit and took the cup of sweet smelling and even sweeter tasting liquor. He held it in his hands for a moment savouring the aroma and waiting for Berrit to pour his own cup.

"To saving this country, however we have too!" Berrit toasted, bringing his cup to lips and pretending to drink from it. He didn't know how the wine tasted and hoped Samul wouldn't notice anything was amiss.

"I'll toast to that." Samul said, drinking from his cup and finishing it off in two greedy gulps. "That is good wine, might I have another?" Samul asked, holding his cup to Berrit who filled it again.

"To new friends and new beginnings." Samul toasted, and again Berrit faked a sip while Samul downed his cup.

Berrit didn't know how long it would take when consumed to dispel the gift, and he didn't want to try anything until he was sure. Samul didn't seem to have a problem drinking more, anyway. After another two glasses, Samul tipped his goblet upside down showing Berrit he had had enough.

"I do thank you, Prince Berrit, for the words and the wine. I am glad you called me out here and we have resolved things, but I must depart, there is still much Master Mervyn and I need to learn before we will be able to help in planning." Samul said with a hint of a slur from the wine.

"Before you go, do you think you could do me a small favour?" Berrit asked, preparing to do what he must if his plan didn't work.

"Of course I could, what do you need of me?" Samul said with a jolly smile.

"Could you light this torch for me, I think I am going to stay out here for a while and enjoy the fresh night air." Berrit said, holding up a torch.

"Indeed I can." Samul said, waving his hand in front of the torch. Nothing happened.

Berrit smiled wide knowing his plan had worked. "Well, well seems your gift isn't working."

"I don't know what's happening? This is impossible, I don't know why...?" Samul cried, his tone growing more and more alarmed each time he waived his hand at the torch with no result.

"Really?" Berrit teased. "I know why."

"What? What are you talking about? What do you know about this?" Samul demanded sternly, turning his attention from the unlit torch to Berrit who was no longer in the form of Berrit, but his true self. "By all that is unholy, who are you?" Samul ordered, taking a step back.

"Everything!" Astaroth whispered, punching him hard in the stomach, knocking the wind form his lungs.

"Why are you..." Samul started but was silenced when the empty bottle of wine connected hard across his head. He fell limp to the ground.

"Well that was easy." Astaroth mused.

~ ~ ~

Keithen sat behind a large rose bush many feet away, wide eyed at the treachery he had just witnessed. He watched in awe and terror as the man who was once Prince Berrit bound Master Samul's hands behind his back and carried him down a grown in path leading towards one of the lesser used meat cellars in the castle.

Fear coursed through every part of Keithen, he had been so close to this man so many times and hadn't even had the slightest clue about any of this. But now he knew the truth and everything started to fall into place from the death of King Borrack to the lies around Ursa, Meath and the Princess fleeing from the castle. They too must have stumbled across the truth somehow. Instinct told him to run and tell everybody, but something else told him not to. It wasn't fear, but something different. Something told Keithen to somehow use this to his advantage. Ursa had never believed in him and had spent all his time and efforts in Meath. But now this man, this shape shifting sorcerer, who obviously knew how to use the gift better then most, could teach him everything in exchange for Keithen to keep his secret. Yes it would work, he just needed play his cards right, he knew if he just strolled up to him and told him he was as good as dead. He needed to find something to gain the man's trust, or even some edge over him so he couldn't kill Keithen without getting caught.

Keithen followed Astaroth from a distance, making sure he wasn't seen or heard. Since he had spent most his life behind these walls, it wasn't difficult. Keithen hugged the stone circler stairwell that lead down into one of the coldest cellars, which they only used in the winter to keep wild meat frozen. He watched from around a corner as Astaroth chained Master Samul to one of the walls.

"What's he doing?" Keithen whispered to himself.

~ ~ ~

Astaroth splashed a bucket of water onto Samul, waking him up. He always liked it when his subjects were awake for the process.

"Who are you?" Master Samul yelled. "And what are you doing to me you bastard?"

"What do I want with you? Well that's easy." Astaroth hissed. "I want your gift."

"You're a mad man!" Samul cried. "That's impossible."

"Is it? Astaroth mused. "I beg to differ, considering I have done it several times already."

Samul's eyes went wide in terror as he watched Astaroth pull several items from a pack. "Why are you doing this?" Samul cried, trying to use his gift, finding it still ineffective.

"Because I can, because I want to be a god, because it's my destiny." Astaroth told him with his sadistic smile and an arrogant chuckle. "Now let's begin... Oh yes, I hate to be the bearer of bad news, but once this is over you'll be dead."

~ ~ ~

Keithen watched in horror and amazement for hours while Astaroth tortured and mutilated Samul. Burning him with strange symbols and cutting other symbols into his flesh, collecting his blood and drinking it, and finally cutting out his eyes and heart and consuming them both. By the end of the ritual, the room was alive with energy and power. Even someone without the gift would feel the raw power in the air.

Once Astaroth had eaten Samul's heart and eyes, both their bodies began to convulse violently and Keithen could see Samul's raw essence, his gift flow from his body and into Astaroth's. As fast as it had began, it was over and the bluish, grey light that was torn out of Samul faded and Astaroth lay silent on the cold cellar floor. The air shifted uncomfortably back to cold and damp, almost like the feeling of death. Keithen had to wonder if that was because of the withered, broken Samul that hung from the wall.

Keithen watched as Astaroth began to get up slowly, but yet seemed stronger, firmer and more defined. He could see that Astaroth had truly taken Samul's essence. This was something he wanted; this was the man he wanted as his mentor.

"Teach me to be like you, I'll do anything!" Keithen blurted out as he stepped around the corner where he had been hiding. He caught Astaroth completely off guard.

~ ~ ~

Dagon stood on a hillside not far from where he and his men were camped; he watched the sun rise from the east. It had been almost a week since the battle he and less then half his men had escaped from, and still he thought about how he could have done things differently and how they might have won that fight or escaped with more lives. Dagon knew how he could have saved more, he should have retreated as soon as he had seen the ruse for what it was, but he hadn't, he couldn't. His pride had got the best of him, he just wanted to make those murdering bastards pay for taking his home.

"I knew I would find you out here." Jarroth said, walking up behind him. "Stop beating yourself up over the past, what happened has happened. I don't blame you, the men don't blame you." Jarroth told him, knowing exactly what was on his friends mind.

Dagon didn't say anything, he couldn't. He kept staring off at the sunrise.

"Our scouts have spotted a small band of enemy moving towards Mandrake castle from the northern shore. We plan on attacking them long before they can make it." Jarroth explained to him. "You should come with us my lord, it would do your blade good to taste enemy blood again." He called back as he made his way to the camp.

Dagon signed once Jarroth was gone. He knew his friend's words were true. He had lost battles before, lost many good men to war; friends and family. It wasn't that, it was because of why he lost that was haunting him. His pride had gotten in the way, his pride had killed those men. Too much had happened in the last month for anyone to handle it lawlessly.

"My lord!" A soldier called to him.

"Yes, what is it?" Dagon replied, not even turning to face the man.

"There is a Zandorian messenger here with news from the south." The soldier told him.

"Take me to him, now!" Dagon gasped.

~   ~   ~

"What news do you have from the south?" Dagon questioned, not even waiting for his horse to slow before he jumped off and was running towards the messenger.

"Well my lord, one of your messengers made it to Besha and told Lord Andras of your problem. There is an army of six hundred hardened warriors and many supplies two or three days march away." The messenger said.

"Thank the heavens." Dagon said. "When you return to Besha, please tell your Lord I send many thanks."

"Well my lord, you will be able to bestow your thanks to him personally. He and his eldest son are the ones leading the army." The Zandorian informed him.

Dagon's eyes lit up with possibility, finally they would have an army to do the damage needed and possible take back his castle and free his land.

"Get this man anything he needs!" Dagon ordered, marching off with hope growing in each step, something he hadn't had in days. The weight of failing was lifting.

That evening, Lord Dagon and his men feasted on what they could in celebration of their re-supply to come. There was no ale or wine at the small feast, for alcohol was something none of them had seen in weeks, but even if there had been, not a man would have indulged; they all needed their senses and reflexes at best.

"It's good to see you yourself again." Jarroth told Dagon as the evening began to tone down.

"I am sorry my friend, for my foolishness. Your words did help, even if it didn't look like it. Thank you for not giving up on me." Dagon replied.

"I never have." Jarroth laughed, clasping Dagon's hand firmly.

"We will get our home back and force those bastards back to the wastelands where they belong." Dagon shouted, rousing a cheer from everyone around.

"An army of six hundred strong might not be enough to take our home back, my lord." Jarroth said solemnly.

"I know, but it's a start." Dagon told him, not letting anything damper his good mood.

"Sir, sir." A young soldier yelled, running up to him.

"What is it?" Dagon asked, giving the man his full attention.

"There is another messenger here." He gasped.

"Ah, well give him food and water and a place to sleep tonight, but we have already heard the good news." Dagon said.

"No my lord, this man isn't from the south, he says he is from Draco Castle." The soldier told him, trying to keep his voice low. "He was found wondering the woods, almost dead with exhaustion."

~   ~   ~

Dagon entered the small tent where the ragged man had been given quarters. Dagon could tell this man had important news to tell him, he could feel it in the air, it made his skin tingle with anticipation.

"What news do you bring from Draco? Do they send as army to aid us?" Dagon asked.

The messenger's eye's slowly opened to see Dagon. "No my lord, Draco Castle is in need of you." He whispered not able to speak much louder.

"In need of me? What for?" Dagon bellowed, getting down closer to hear the man.

"Prince Berrit is not who he appears to be." He wheezed out. "He is a shape shifter."

"What? This doesn't make sense, this can't be true." Dagon muttered in disbelief. "You are tired and weak, you are talking tails, not truths, come speak with me when you are well." Dagon said, ready to leave, but the man grabbed him and gripped him with intensity.

"I know what I saw my lord! Heed my words; Draco Castle needs you." He whispered.

"Why isn't Lord Tundal doing anything about this? Why didn't you tell him all this? He would be able to handle this." Dagon argued, beginning to think the man mad.

"Tundal is dead!" The messenger barked.

"What?" Dagon said sternly, his attention completely with the man again.

"He was murdered by an assassin, but I now believe he found out the truth of Berrit and then was killed by him to prevent him from telling everyone." He said slowly. "Now the ladies are trying to run the kingdom but things are just getting worse. This country is falling apart at the seams; you are the only one that can fix it."

"Rest now my good man, we will talk more tomorrow when you can tell me everything." Dagon told him. The man released his grip on Dagon as he rose from his position over the messenger letting him leave the tent.

It was almost too much for Dagon to bear, yet he knew the man wasn't lying. Dagon's family was at Draco Castle and so was the family of his late friend, and if all this was true, they were in trouble. Everyone was in trouble. Dagon knew he had to get there and try his best to straighten this out before it was too late. The kingdom was falling apart, war was everywhere, and Draco was the only stronghold left. He knew what he had to do...

Chapter 20

Nicolette and the others traveled hard for several days, finding more signs as they went that only proved they were on the right trail of finding Meath. They had also found several larger camp sites that were only a few days old that seemed to be traveling west. Shania informed them that they were traveling heavily armed. They had yet to come across any such armies or any barbarians.

Since their desperate swim across the Sheeva River, things had gone rather well for Nicolette and the others. They had found plenty of food and fresh water and their wounds were healing faster than normal thanks to Shania and her salves.

"Look, there's smoke coming from over there." Dahak said pointing northeast.

"Must be a town" Zehava said. "Not many of those up this way."

"Let's head that way and see if they know anything." Nicolette replied. "They came this way on horses, but travel gets a lot harder, maybe they went to the town to find an easier way or at least stopped for supplies." Nicolette said to everyone excitedly.

Zehava changed the group's direction a little so they would head towards the town and not go past it. "We won't make the town this day, but we can get close enough so they'll see our fire and know we're coming."

"Maybe Meath's there." Dahak said, making conversation.

"I doubt it, I find it hard to think Meath's kidnappers would take him to a little farming town. But there's a good chance they passed through the town." Zehava finished, not wanting to disrupt their good spirits.

"We'll find him soon." Nicolette said, more to herself then the others.

"I wonder why they would take Meath." Shania said baffled. "I mean, he's just a guy with the gift. It's not like he's a prince or a king or anything."

"Ya, why would someone take Meath?" Dahak replied.

"I guess we'll find out soon enough." Zehava answered back.

They stopped and made camp about an hour away from the small town. This time, instead of Shania and Dahak going out to collect food, Nicolette went, leaving Dahak and Zehava to set up camp.

Nicolette and Shania came across a small pond crawling with crayfish. They quickly got to work flipping rocks and collecting the small, fast crustaceans.

"So you and Dahak seem to have taken a liking to one another." Nicolette said, knowing it was obvious.

Shania blushed and swiftly turned her head hoping Nicolette hadn't seen. "He is funny and cute and, and I really enjoy being around him." Shania blurted out trying hard to keep her voice unrevealing.

Nicolette was smiling and shaking her head, finding it amusing that Shania was so embarrassed by something like this. Nicolette had noticed that Shania and Dahak had slowly been spending more and more time together in the last several days. Not only when they went hunting, but also when they traveled. Shania was always right there in front of Dahak and in the evenings, their bedrolls seemed to get closer and closer as the night progressed. Nicolette knew it was growing to be more then just a friendship between the two, and she really couldn't blame her; Dahak had taken a bigger interest in Shania then Zehava ever had.

"He is sweet and has a good heart." Shania finally said, after seeing Nicolette was deep in thought. "Zehava doesn't need me." Shania murmured and took a deep breath. "Zehava is strong and brave and can do everything on his own. I just get in his way." Shania confessed. "Dahak is different, he has those qualities but in a different way. I like being needed, I like knowing I am helping and am valued, and Dahak makes me feel that way."

Nicolette could see what Shania was saying and understood fully. "You should tell Zehava, he will understand."

Shania went silent for awhile before answering. "I know… but I still have feelings for Zehava." She confessed. "I'm so confused; I don't know what to do… I… I don't want to hurt anyone."

"Its ok Shania, it will all work out and Zehava will understand." Nicolette assured her, knowing that Zehava had likely already come to the same conclusion as she had.

"Thank you." Shania said to Nicolette, glad to have been able to talk to someone about it and get it off her back. "But right now we need to find Meath, this can wait 'til after." Shania said.

"Well hopefully that won't be long now, we are getting closer everyday." Nicolette replied cheerfully.

"Meath's lucky you know." Shania said. "To have such good friends I mean, friends that would go out a search for him, risking their lives just to find him."

"That's what friends do; he would do it for any one of us." Nicolette replied. "We would try and find you too if this happened, you are our friend." Nicolette finished, knowing Shania still didn't feel like part of the group.

"Thank you." Shania whispered to Nicolette.

"For what?" Nicolette asked. She knew Shania was happy to have been acknowledged as a friend, but the tone of her voice too her by surprise.

Shania took a deep breath and looked up at her, wiping away some stray tears. "For everything, for this talk, for letting me come with you guys, for accepting me, for being my… friends."

Nicolette didn't know what to say, but she doubted she needed to say anything more. They shared a long silent moment just looking into each other's eyes. What needed to be said was communicated in that moment.

"Well we should get back." Shania finally said, washing her face in the cool water to hide the tears.

"Ya, we've collected enough food for the night." Nicolette replied, looking into her bag that was almost full with the small creatures.

"Let's see if we can sneak up on Zehava and Dahak." Shania said with a playful gleam in her eyes.

"I'm not so quite in the woods, I think I'll give us away." Nicolette answered with disappointment.

"Its easy, I will show you." Shania boasted, happily getting out of the water and showing her how to place her feet.

~ ~ ~

"I wonder what's taking Shania and Nicolette so long." Dahak said with more then a hint of worry in his tone. "You think they're ok?"

Zehava smirked, noticing that every time Shania's name crossed his lips, it had a completely different tone then normal. "I am sure they're fine, we would know if there was trouble." He assured his friend. "Besides, they are both fairly capable of defending themselves."

Dahak sat uncomfortably for a moment before he spoke. "Do you really think we'll find him?" He asked with more then a hint of doubt in his voice.

Zehava knew this was something that was playing on everyone's mind, even his own. "I sure hope so." Was all he could say.

"What if he's… you know?" Dahak choked out.

"Naw, Meath ain't dead, that ones got a horse shoe up his ass." Zehava said and they both shared in a good heartfelt laugh. "He's still alive, I can feel it."

"I hope you're right, man." Dahak replied. "No, I know your right." He finished confidently.

"Who's right?" Nicolette asked coming out from the tree's and into their camp with Shania right behind her.

"Holy crap!" Dahak stammered, falling off his log he was using as a seat. "I didn't even hear you guys coming."

"I am training her to move silently through the woods." Shania declared proudly.

"Well you're training is going well then." Zehava said, a little shocked himself; he had only heard them seconds before they got to the camp.

"So who's right?" Nicolette asked again, walking over to the fire and dropping her bag of crayfish.

Zehava and Dahak looked at each other quickly, trying to think of something to say other then the truth to preserve the mood.

"I am!" Zehava piped in. "Dahak didn't believe I could hit that tree over there with my dagger from here, but I did as you can see." He said pointing to the tree twenty feet away with his dagger protruding from it.

"You did that?" Shania asked, somewhat impressed, but not so sure it was true.

"Of course I did, I've been practicing." Zehava lied. He had lodged it into the tree earlier so he would remember to sharpen it later that night.

"Ya, he's good. I couldn't believe it." Dahak said, playing to the lie.

"Let's see you do it again." Shania said cockily, retrieving his blade and handing it to him.

"I don't know if I could do it again, to be honest. It was kind of a fluke." Zehava said, hoping to get out of it.

"Come on Zehava, you did it once you can do it again." Dahak said, helping to dig his friend deeper.

Zehava looked to Dahak and chuckled, wishing he could reach out and give his friend a cuff upside the head. "Fine, I'll try again, but don't be surprised if I miss."

"You can do it Zehava." Nicolette encouraged him as she stood up from the fire and boiling water and went off to the side to watch.

Zehava took aim and readied himself, the whole time wondering if this could have gone any different, he laughed to himself and realized it didn't matter. The blade whistled through the air, blade over handle and hit its target with a twang as it bounced off and to the side.

"Need more practice." Shania teased, turning to help Nicolette with dinner.

"I told you it was all a fluke to begin with." Zehava said, collecting his dagger so he could sharpen it.

Soon they were eating and everyone talked about past adventures and experiences. Their childhood memories comforted them long into the evening before they each took turns taking watch while the others slept. Every night they spent without Meath was another day he was lost to the hands of his captors, and falling asleep became more and more difficult as his absence grew longer. Before the sun had even fully touched the sky they were up and heading towards the town.

When they entered the town, they had no problems from the sentries who had seen their fire from the night and didn't pay that much attention to Shania, who was doing her best to hide her heritage under her cloak. Most of the town's folk were just getting up to tend to their livestock and begin their daily chores, so no one paid them much mind other then a quick glance and sometimes a good morning.

As the four made their way through the town looking for the general store, they passed a small stable house when something caught Nicolette's eyes, something that made her heart beat faster.

"Wait!" She said, turning off course and walking over to the rough old-timer who was feeding a fine, strong black and white stallion.

"What? Where are you going?" Zehava called to her, looking to the others for an explanation.

Nicolette walked right up to the man and horse and instantly the beast recognized her and nuzzled its nose under her hand for a good scratch. "A fine horse you have here." She said to the man, who hesitantly looked up to her.

"Why thank you my lady." He replied. "You and your friends looking to purchase some horses maybe?' He asked.

By this time the others were standing behind her, still confused as to why they were talking to this old horse farmer.

"Maybe this one, what's its history?" She asked, knowing full well she knew this horse's history better.

"Well, I wish I could tell you, but I only know so much about this one. Had a young man sell me this one a few days ago. All I can tell you is it's a fine animal; smart, strong and very friendly, as you can see." The old man told them.

"Can you tell me what the man who traded you this horse looked like?" Nicolette asked.

"The man thought about it for a moment before answering. "Why do you want to know? What's all this about?"

Before Nicolette could say anything Zehava cut in. "We believe the man who sold you this horse is the horse thief we are looking for. This horse use to belong to our lord from Draco Castle." Zehava said, stepping beside Nicolette and standing tall, but smiled to prevent intimidating the horse dealer.

"I knew something was up with that man, he just didn't seem right and all. Well he was well built I guess, dark, short hair and dark eyes and he had an odd accent." The old stable master told them.

"That's him!" Nicolette blurted out excitedly.

"I guess your gonna want to take this horse too?" The old man muttered.

Zehava looked to Nicolette and shrugged his shoulders, knowing they didn't need a horse right now.

"For your help in this, you can keep this fine animal." Nicolette said with a smile.

That seemed to cheer up the old stableman. "Really? Thank you, I do hope you catch that horse thief."

"You wouldn't happen to know which way he was traveling, would you?" Zehava asked.

"Well he left to the west, but we had some hunters out and they saw him meet up with two others and then they head south east, towards the wastelands." The man replied. "Don't know why they would head that way, not much out there but trouble, but I reckon maybe they deserve what they get."

"Thank you for your help good sir." Zehava said, shaking the man's hand firmly.

"Good luck to you!" The man called to them.

"Well let's grab some things so we don't have to hunt and search for food as much along the way. We are close, only a few days behind, we can catch them." Zehava said, his enthusiasm soaring.

"If I'm right, Drake River isn't far from here." Dahak said. "We might be able to make it there be night fall."

Within half an hour, the four were well on their way southeast towards Drake River and Meath. Only once did they stop for something to eat and to refill their water skins in a small creek, then quickly on their way again.

Not a lot of conversation happened that day; everyone seemed to be in their own world, which was fuelling their steps.

"What are we gonna do when we find them?" Dahak asked, the thought popping into his head.

"Save him." Shania replied, as if it should have been obvious.

"Ya I know that, but Nicolette said they were both gifted, and skilled." Dahak reminded them.

"He's right." Zehava said, catching on to what his friend was saying. "It's going to be hard getting past two wizards, and getting Meath away from them safely."

"The gifted die just the same as you or me." Nicolette muttered in the bitterest tone any of them had ever heard from her. She ran her hand down the shaft of an arrow, almost tasting the excitement of the vengeance coursing through her veins.

No one could believe what she had just said, for some reason they all had it in their minds it would be a snatch and grab, but in truth, the chances of a peaceful exchange were slim to none. It would come to blows.

"Well hopefully it won't escalate to a level forcing us to prove that statement, but if it does we will do what we must." Zehava said, a lot less cruelly then Nicolette.

The rest of the afternoon and evening went by quickly and it was only a few hours before night was upon them. They had made great time and were at Drake River, which was a swift, but more stable compared to the mighty Sheeva.

They ate fast and went straight to bed so they could be well rested and on their way early once again. Dahak was first to go on watch and he noticed everyone seemed restless. He knew why though; they were all wondering what was going to happen once they found Meath.

~ ~ ~

Dawn crept around the mountains and trouble crept not far away, hoping to make an easy strike. Revenge stricken, the group of ruffians who had started problems in the town several days before, and who had forced them into the rough waters of the Sheeva River, were still following at their heels. They now stalked in for another attack, this time with more then a handful of brutes to help. In the last couple of towns they had picked up a few mercenaries and street rogues, promising them the group they were hunting had grand rewards to be offered.

"Let's move in before they wake." One man whispered; everyone nodded their agreement.

"Just remember, the one that took my hand is mine!" The big burly one handed man grumbled.

Slowly, the fourteen brutes stalked into the camp, doing their best to keep silent, but most of them were hardly jungle savvy. They had no intentions of playing around this time, at least not until they knew they had the upper hand.

~ ~ ~

Shania sat in a nearby tree. She was the last to stand watch and it was almost time for her to wake everyone. She had caught a viper that had been investigating the intruder that was in its home. She was about to release the deadly serpent to another tree when she noticed the dark shadows below her and all around the camp. Her heart skipped a beat when she counted how many there were. She knew they were badly outnumbered and the enemy was coming in at all angles, making escape impossible.

Shania knew she had to do something and fast to try and even the odds while she had the advantage of surprise. She jumped down from her perch and landed in front of two unsuspecting attackers. One of her blades shot out and cut deep into one of the men's chest, severing one of his lungs and many vital veins and arteries, silencing him instantly. Before the other could react, Shania threw the deadly viper in his face. The irritated creature sank its poisonous fangs deep into the man's face, releasing its venom and causing its victim a searing pain. He cried out wildly, alerting Nicolette and the others and ending his life shortly after.

Within a heartbeat of his anguished cry, Nicolette, Zehava and Dahak were up weapons in hand and at the ready. The cry had also caught the attacker's attention and when they turned to see what had happened, they lost their element of surprise, although they still out numbered their defenders.

Zehava was first into the throng of enemies, swinging and stabbing his blade with calculated movements, doing his best to weaken and kill as many as he could while the enemies were caught off guard, but it wasn't long before Zehava realized just how many had ambushed them.

Before Dahak could even pick a target, a dagger flashed out of nowhere and embedded itself into his stomach. Dahak didn't understand what had happened, all of the sudden he was on his knees. He heard Nicolette cry out a few feet away and turned to see her rushing to him, bow in hand and arrow at the ready. He finally looked down and saw the hilt of the dagger that was protruding from his mid section. Reality crashed into his mind with stark understanding. He heard a thud and a deep cry, only feet away from him as a man fell dead with arrow in his chest. Dahak turned back to Nicolette, who was now right by his side, tears in her eyes and worry across her face. He tried to tell her it was ok, that he couldn't feel anything, but no words came out.

Shania and Zehava both heard Nicolette's cry and turned to see what had happened. Both their hearts almost stopped when they saw what had happened caused Nicolette's cry. Rage fuelled both Shania and Zehava's blades now as they fought their way to their wounded friend.

A sinking feeling over came Zehava as he realized they were doomed. Still outnumber and out matched and the battle had only just begun. He had recognized a handful of the attackers as the men they had run into before at the river, but now there were more trained soldiers and hired mercenaries, he was sure. He could tell by the way they fought and moved.

"How is he?" Zehava called back, he was only a few feet away but he couldn't take his eyes from battle or he too would be joining Dahak on the ground.

"Not good!" Was all Nicolette could say. She too had joined in the fight again, but was losing ground fast.

"Stop!" A loud husky voice commanded and the enemy backed off and moved out of the way. A big brute that the defenders all recognized made his way through his comrades. "You took my hand!" He barked, pointing his large sword towards Zehava. All Zehava did was nod.

"You and me fight, if you win, you get to kill me before you and your friends die. If you lose, you will watch as we kill your friends and then you."

Zehava was surprised the brute had been so honest. He figured he would lie, and tell him if he won they would leave. "Well I guess I had better win." Was all Zehava could think of saying, his mind raced trying to find a way that he and his friends might make it out of this alive. There were few options, none of which seemed likely to save them. They were surrounded now and death was certain, the only thing they could do was try to kill as many as they could before they went down. It was an honourable death for a soldier and a warrior. Zehava supposed he couldn't ask for more and mentally began to prepare himself for the fate he had come too. He would not go easily.

The enemy cheered their large, one-handed friend while they formed an even tighter circle around the defenders, making sure escape was impossible.

Zehava ducked several wild swings that forced him back closer to his friends, which wasn't where he wanted to be. He sidestepped a few slashes to turn his opponent away from the group. Finally Zehava had to connect steel to steel to block a deadly blow. The impact of the block almost made Zehava drop his sword and shook his arm numb. He wouldn't be able to block many more swings like that one. And yet he couldn't end the fight until he knew his friends could make it to safety, even if that meant he couldn't.

"How's Dahak?" Zehava called back to Nicolette and Shania while he dodged a wild swing form the massive, but surprisingly quick man.

"He's still alive." Nicolette yelled to him.

"We have to think of something." Shania whispered to Nicolette. "Even if Zehava wins, we're still dead."

"I know, I know." Nicolette stammered trying her best to slow the blood coming out of Dahak's wound.

"We might be able to make a run for it." Shania told her, after she had eyed the circle of men and found the weakest group.

"What about Dahak and Zehava!?" Nicolette gasped.

"We can't win, our only hope is to run." Shania said. "And yes we would have to leave Dahak, and Zehava if he goes down." She finished, fighting the tears that now flowed freely down her reddened cheeks.

Nicolette starred at Shania, not believing what she had just heard. She knew what Shania was saying was the truth. "I will not leave our friends behind."

"What about Meath?" Shania asked.

"He'd understand I think." Nicolette said after only a moment.

A small smile crossed Shania's face. "You should have been a warrior, not a princess." Shania said. "We will die side by side." They both shared a deep moment of courage and understanding.

The one handed man swung hard and Zehava had no choice but to block again. The hit rang out loud and pain coursed through his hands and arms like fire, causing him to lose his grip and his sword flew harmlessly to the side. Before he could act, a meaty fist full of hilt slammed hard into his face, sending him to the ground in a bloody heap.

~ ~ ~

"Wake up Kara, its time to get moving." Meath said while he packed up his things. He had already been up for an hour, just starring up at the night sky and wishing on the fading stars that he would make it back to his friends soon. He knew dawn wouldn't come for a while, but it didn't matter, he wanted to get an early start. It was just light enough for him to see and they could travel slow until it was brighter.

"You've got to be kidding me." Kara yawned. "There's still another hour or more before the sun comes up."

"We've got to be close to a town or something by now." Meath told her. "And I want to get to one today."

"I really wish you'd reconsider this Meath." Kara sighed, getting up and doing her best to roll up her bedroll with her hands bound tightly.

"And I really wish you and Daden had never come into my life, but you did." Meath replied cockily.

"But you don't understand Meath…" Kara began, but Meath cut her off.

"You're right I don't understand, because you won't tell me. Why should I trust you, I don't even know you. You kidnapped me and dragged me half way across the country against my will. But that's ok, because now I am in control and I am going back to my friends and my life" Meath barked angrily, shutting her up.

Kara really couldn't argue with him, he was right, why should he trust her? He was only doing what one would expect someone to do in this situation, but she still had to do what she must to get him to Salvas, one way or another. "So what are you going to do with me?" She asked.

"I already told you, next town we find I am leaving you there, and if you follow, me I will not be so kind. Now let's get moving, I want to make that happen today." Meath said hard heartedly.

They began traveling west once again at a slow pace due to the dim light. The whole time Kara fought with her better judgment about telling Meath the truth of why she needed him to come to Salvas.

"You can't just leave me tied and gagged in a town." Kara insisted.

"That's the beauty of it, I can." Meath said, not even looking back to see her reaction.

"But think about what might happen to me!" Kara cried to him, shocked that he didn't seem to care.

"I'm sure I will think of something between now and then." Meath replied, drawing his sword to clear their path and make it easier. "But if not…" He finished, knowing it would bother her.

Kara knew she had to think of something fast, they weren't that far from the town they had sold their horse's in. "Have you thought about how we're going to get across the river coming up?" Kara reminded him. "Without my powers I can't do much to help."

Meath almost burst out laughing. "There are many ways to get across a river without the help of magic, but nice try." Meath said back to her.

Kara could take it no more. "There's a lot more at steak here then you just being taken from your friends, Meath." She yelled to him, knowing the only way she was going to get him to Salvas was to tell him the truth.

"Don't care." Was all Meath said.

Kara could hardly contain herself any longer, she knew if Meath knew the truth, he would change his mind, but she had been told not to tell him anything. Then again, she had been told to get him there by any means necessary.

"Look, there's the river." Meath said pointing straight ahead.

"Meath I will tell you everything if you promise to…" Kara started but Meath cut her off.

"Shhh!" Meath whispered, cupping his ears to hear better. "It sounds like there's fighting going on across the river." He told her.

"We should go another way then, it's probably savages." Kara pleaded.

"Someone may need help." Meath replied, running ahead to get a better look.

"Meath wait, I really think I should tell you everything before we go any further." Kara cried to him but was ignored.

Meath stopped behind some bushes not far from the bank of the river, not more then a few hundred feet away was the fighting. He could tell it wasn't savages; it looked more like rogues robbing travelers. But he wasn't sure if he should help, he truly didn't know what was happening. Maybe it was bounty hunters after thieves or murderers. He had no idea which side was good or bad. Perhaps both groups just didn't like one another and were both in the wrong.

Kara caught up to him moments later and hid beside him. "How are you going to help?" Kara asked.

"I don't know if I should, I can't tell what's going on." Meath whispered to her.

"It looks like those two are going to do single combat." Kara whispered.

They both watched as the two men talked for a moment and started in what Meath knew to be a fight to the death.

"It looks like one of them is hurt pretty bad." Kara pointed out to the two people huddled over another lying down.

Meath's attention turned to the two figures that looked to be women huddled over a limp body. Finally Meath could take it no longer. "I have to help them." He blurted out, not really understanding why he felt the intense urge to do something.

"How are you going to do that?" Kara asked again.

"Maybe I can take a few of them out with my gift." He thought out loud.

"It's too far, you'll never make it and even if you do, you might hit someone else." Kara reminded him.

Meath was already getting closer to see from a better angle. The closer he got, the more he thought he recognized the defenders. Once he was in place and was about to summon his gift, he heard the name Dahak from someone across the river. Meath's face went white and his legs almost gave out. How had he missed it before? Two girls, two guys and they fit his friends perfectly from hair to size, even the way they fought.

By the time Kara made it to Meath, she too recognized one of the defenders across the river, it was the princess.

"Free me, Meath, and I'll help." Kara pleaded to him.

But Meath wasn't listening; he didn't even realize she was behind him. Panic flashed through him when he saw Zehava lose his sword and get taken to the ground. Before Meath even knew what he was doing, two massive bolts of energy created from pure desperation exploded from his now outstretched hands, soaring across the river and tearing through the chest of the huge man towering over Zehava. The bolt didn't stop there, it blow a hole right through the large man and struck the man standing behind him.

"You are the one." Kara whispered to herself, knowing full well that was a distance that most experienced wizards would be hard pressed to make with that strength and accuracy.

Meath was just about to unleash another deadly assault on the scattering band when he noticed two thin darts in his arm. He looked up just in time to see Daden swing a thick branch that connected with the side of his head. Before Meath lost consciousness, his eyes went back to the scene across the river as he got a glimpse of his friends making a final stand against their enemy.

Characters List

19-Meath- Main Character/Wizard/Warrior/From Draco

17-Nicolette- Main Character/Princess of Draco

70-Ursa- Main Character/Great War Wizard/ Draco Castle

18-Dahak- Main Character/Soldier/Meath's good friend/ From Drandor

19-Zehava-Main Character/Warrior/Soldier/ Meath's best friend

16-Shania- Main Character/Savage/Warrior

16-Talena- Main Character/Sorceresses

29-Pavilion- Main Character/Assassin/Wizard/Warrior

26-Astaroth- Evil Sorcerer/Wizard/False Prince Berrit

22-Vashina- Evil Sorceresses/Assassin

36-Kinor- Evil Shaman/\Barbarian Leader

36-Rift-Captain/Nicolette's Champion/Warrior

22-Prince Berrit-Prince of Zandor

46-King Borrack-King of Draco/Nicolette's father

42-Lavira-(dead) Queen of Draco/Nicolette's mother

48-King Danta-King of Zandor/father of Berrit and Kayreil

41-Queen Glenelle-Queen of Zandor/ mother of Berrit and Kayreil

15-Prince Kayreil- Younger brother of Berrit/ from Zandor

50-Maxwell-Draco Castle's head chef

42-Halpas-Borracks Champion

39-Lady Jewel-Lady of Dragon's Cove/Nicolette's aunt/mother of Avril,
    Tami and Mathu

44-Lord Marcus-Lord of Dragon's Cove/father of Avril, Tami, Mathu/
Nicolette's Uncle

17-Tami-Lady/daughter of Marcus/Jewel

12-Avril-Lady/daughter of Marcus/Jewel

16-Mathu-Lord/son of Marcus/Jewel

38-Lord Dagon-Lord of Mandrake/father of Eathan, Leonard

34-Lady Angelina-Lady of Mandrake/mother of Eathan,Leonard

15-Eathan-Lord/eldest son of Dagon/Angelina

13-Leonard-Lord/youngest son of Dagon/Angelina

41-Lord Tundal-Lord of Drandor/father of Salvira, Calmela, Thoron

39-Lady Tora-Lady of Drandor/ mother of Salvira, Calmela, Thoron

16-Thoron-Lord/son of Tundal and Tora

18-Salvira-Lady/daughter of Tundal/Tora

15-Calmela-Lady/daughter of Tundal and Tora

44-Lord Andras-Lord of Besha, father of Jamus and Kain/from Zandor/
father of Sheanna

39-Lady Seera-Lady of Besha/mother of Jamus, Kain, Sheanna/
Zandorian

18-Jamus-Lord/son of Seera/Andras

20-Kain-Lord/son of Seera/Andras

15-Sheanna-Lady/daughter of Seera/Andras/from Zandor

48-Lord Zefer-Lord of Samel/father of Zora, Zeke, Kayron, Sonya
/Zandor

41-Lady Zacoha-Lady of Samel/mother of Zora/Zeke/Kayron, Sonya

17-Zora-Lady/Daughter of Zacoha and Zefer

12-Zeke-Lord/son of Zacoha/Zefer/Zandor

18-Kayron-Lord/son of Zefer/Zacoha/Zandor

15-Sonya-Lady/Daughter of Zacoha/Zefer/Zandor

51-Lord Bartan-Lord of Laquaco Cove/father of Edroth/Aranna/Zandor

46-Lady Nisheena-Lady of Laquaco Cove/ mother of Edroth/Aranna/
Zandor

22-Edroth-Lord/son of Nisheena/Bartan

18-Aranna-Lady/daughter of Nisheena/Bartan

42-Azazel-Old dead barbarian leader that king Borrack killed

36-Barkel-Champion of Dragons Cove

37 Raven-Champion of Drandor

36-Jarroth-Champion of Mandrake

39-Nazroth-Champion of Zandor

31-Kazon-Champion of Prince Berrit

24-Curson-Champion of Prince Kayrel

33-Zorkain-Champion of Samul

36-Velcain-Champion of Besha

34-Duncan-Champion of Laquaco

53-Kabriel-King Danta's advisor

41-Furlac-Mandrake's advisor

46-Rashin-Drandor's advisor

52-Uveal-Dragon Cove's advisor

48-Meresin-Besha's advisor

50-Gediel-Samel's advisor

51-Elmos-Laquaco's advisor

46-Shakti-Draco's new advisor

54-Antiel- Wizard at Dragon's Cove

51-Hunznoth-Wizard at Drandor

34-Lepha-Female Wizard at Dragon's Cove

60-Melech-Wizard at Drandor

52-Lazay-Wizard at Mandrake

18-Keithen-Apprentise Wizard at Draco/Meaths revival

32-Shahariel-Tracker that goes with Rift

29-Adhar-One of Master Saktas's servants

42-Saktas-Ursa's friend/rich merchant in Darnan

16-Padiel-One of master Saktas's servants/stable boy

43-Zomen- Great stone smith

38-Kinor-Barbarian shaman

19-Kara-Female Wizard from Salvas

18-Tabitha-Female Wizard at Salvas

24-Daden-Wizard at Salvas

22-Javan-Wizard at Salvas

47-Zada-Female Wizard in Salvas/Protector of Salvas

56-Master Wizard in Salvas

28-Valka- High Priestess/Vashina's rival

25-Mick-Soldier in Dragon's Cove

24-Dan-Soldier in Dragon's Cove